COUNCIL
ıL SERVICES
d on or before

THE OTHER WOMAN

Ellie and Dan are proof that opposites attract. He follows instructions and she throws the manual away. He loves sport whereas Ellie's allergic to exercise. Ellie doesn't have a mother. And Dan does—a mother who wants to take over . . . EVERYTHING.

At first Ellie is thrilled to be part of the close, loving Cooper family. But when she and Dan decide to get married and wedding plans progress, she starts to wonder: is it normal for Linda and Dan to speak on the phone twice a day? How on earth do they come to be having a large reception when all she wanted was a quiet register office do? In fact, is she marrying Dan . . . OR HIS MOTHER?

And Ellie's problems have only just begun. When she discovers she's pregnant she realizes that Linda's only been rehearsing for the real takeover. Linda seems to want to live her life through Ellie and, in the words of the immortal Princess Diana, there are three of them in the marriage . . .

THE OTHER WOMAN

Jane Green

WINDSOR
PARAGON

First published 2004
by
Michael Joseph
This Large Print edition published 2005
by
BBC Audiobooks Ltd by arrangement with
Penguin Books Ltd

ISBN 1 4056 1069 7   (Windsor Hardcover)
ISBN 1 4056 2057 9   (Paragon Softcover)

British Library Cataloguing in Publication Data available

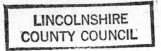
Printed and bound in Great Britain by
Antony Rowe Ltd., Chippenham, Wiltshire

Acknowledgements

For their help, support and kindness:

Heidi Armitage, Maxine Bleiweis, Margie Freilich-Den and all at the Westport Library, Deborah Feingold, Dina Fleischmann, Anthony Goff, Charlie & Karen Green, Stacy & Michael Greenberg, Dr Melanie Mier, Louise Moore, Jean Neubohn, Donna Poppy, Deborah Schneider, Marie Skinner.

THE OTHER WOMAN

1

Pulling a sickie is not something I'm prone to do. And, while I'd like to say I feel sick, I don't. Not unless pre-wedding nerves, last-minute jitters and horrific amounts of stress count.

But nevertheless this morning I decided I deserved a day off—hell, possibly even two—so I phoned in first thing, knowing that as bad a liar as I am, it would be far easier to lie to Penny, the receptionist, than to my boss.

'Oh, poor you.' Penny's voice was full of sympathy. 'But it's not surprising, given the wedding. Must be all the stress. You should just go to bed in a darkened room.'

'I will,' I said huskily, swiftly catching myself in the lie—migraine symptoms not including sore throats or fake sneezes—and getting off the phone as quickly as possible.

I did think vaguely about doing something delicious for myself today, something I'd never normally do. Manicures, pedicures, facials, things like that. But of course guilt has managed to prevail, and even though I live nowhere near my office in trendy Soho, I still know, beyond a shadow of a doubt, that should I venture outside on the one day I'm pretending to be sick, someone from work will just happen to be at the end of my street.

So here I am. Watching dreadful daytime television on a cold January morning (although I did just manage to catch an item on 'updo's for weddings' which may turn out to be incredibly useful), eating my way through a packet of custard

1

creams (my last chance before the wedding diet goes into full acceleration) and wondering whether there would be any chance of finding a masseuse— a proper one—to come to the house last minute to soothe the knots of tension away.

I manage to waste forty-five minutes flicking through the small ads in the local magazines, but somehow I don't think any of those masseuses are what I'm looking for: 'guaranteed discretion', 'sensual and intimate'. And then I reach the personal ads at the back.

I smile to myself reading through. Of course I'm reading through. I may be about to get married but I'm still interested in seeing what's out there, not that, I have to admit, I've ever actually gone down the personal-ad route. But I know a friend who has. Honestly.

And a wave of warmth, and yes, I'll admit it, smugness, comes over me. I don't ever have to tell anyone that I have a good sense of humour, or that I look a bit like Renée Zellwegger, but only if I pout and squint my eyes up very, very small, or that I love the requisite walks in the country and curling up by a log fire.

Not that any of that's not true, but how lovely, how lucky am I, that I don't have to explain myself, or describe myself, or pretend to be someone other than myself ever again.

Thank God for Dan. Thank you, God, for Dan. I slide my feet into huge fluffy slippers, scrape my hair back into a ponytail and wrap Dan's huge, voluminous towelling robe around me as I skate my way down the hallway to the kitchen.

Dan and Ellie. Ellie and Dan. Mrs Dan Cooper. Mrs Ellie Cooper. Ellie Cooper. I trill the words out, thrilling at how unfamiliar they sound, how they will be true in just over a month, how I got to have a fairytale ending after all.

And, despite the cloudy sky, the drizzle that seems to be omnipresent throughout this winter, I feel myself light up, as if the sun suddenly appeared at the living-room window specifically to shine its warmth upon me.

*   *   *

The problem with feeling guilty about pulling sickies, as I now discover, is that you end up too terrified to leave the house, and therefore waste the entire day. And of course the less you do, the less you want to do, so by two o'clock I'm bored, listless and sleepy. Rather than taking the easy option and going back to bed, I decide to wake myself up with a strong coffee, have a shower and finally get dressed.

The cappuccino machine—an early wedding present from my Chief Executive—shouts a shiny hello from its corner on the kitchen worktop, by far the most glamorous and high-tech object in the kitchen, if not the entire flat. Were it not for Dan, I'd never use the bloody thing, and that's despite a passion for strong, milky cappuccinos. Technology and I have never got on particularly well. The only technological area in which I excel is computers, but even then, now that all my junior colleagues are messing around with iPods and MPEGs and God knows what else, I'm beginning to be left behind there too.

My basic problem is not so much technology as paper: instruction manuals to be specific. I just haven't got the patience to read through them, and almost everything in my flat works eventually if I push a few buttons and hope for the best. Admittedly my video recorder has never actually recorded anything, but I only ever bought the machine to play rented videos on, not to record, so as far as I'm concerned it has fulfilled its purpose admirably.

Actually, come to think of it, not quite everything has worked that perfectly . . . The freezer has spent the last year filled with ice and icicles, although I think that somewhere behind the ice may be a year-old carton of Ben & Jerry's. And my hoover still has the same dustbag it's had since I bought it three years ago because I haven't quite figured out how to change it—I cut a hole in it when it was full one time and hand-pulled all the dust out, then sealed it back up with tape and that seems to do the job wonderfully. If anything, just think how much money I've saved myself on hoover bags.

Ah, yes, there is also the super-swish and super-expensive CD player that can take 400 discs at a time, but has in fact only ever held one at a time.

So things may not work the way they're supposed to, or in the way the manufacturers intended, but they work for me, and now I have Dan, Dan who will not lay a finger on any new purchase until he has read the instruction manual cover to cover, until he has ingested even the smallest of the small print, until he can recite the manual from memory alone.

And so Dan—bless him—now reads the manuals, and gives me demonstrations on how things like hoovers, tumble dryers and cappuccino

4

machines work. The only saving grace to this, other than now being able to work the cappuccino machine, is that Dan has learnt to fine-tune his demonstrations so they last no longer than one minute, by which time I'll have completely tuned out and will be thinking either about new presentations at work, or possibly dreaming about floating on a desert island during our honeymoon.

But the cappuccino machine, I have to say, is brilliant, and God, am I happy I actually paid attention when Dan was showing me how it worked. It arrived three days ago, and thus far I've used it nine times. Two cups in the morning before leaving for work, one cup when I get home, and one, or two, in the evening after dinner, although after 8 p.m. we both switch to decaf.

And, as I'm tapping the coffee grains into the spoon to start making the coffee, I find myself thinking about spending the rest of my life with only one person.

I should feel scared. Apprehensive at the very least. But all I feel is pure, unadulterated joy.

Any doubts I may have about this wedding, about getting married, about spending the rest of my life with Dan have nothing whatsoever to do with Dan.

And everything to do with his mother.

2

'There were three of us in this marriage . . .'

I remember watching Princess Diana roll those huge sad eyes as she looked up at the camera and said those now infamous words, and I wondered what on earth she was talking about, wondered just how she managed to be so unbelievably dramatic.

And now, weeks away from my own wedding, I know exactly what she meant, the only difference being that I'm dealing not with a mistress but with a matriarch.

Frankly, I can't decide which is worse.

I met Dan, fell in love with Dan, and agreed to marry Dan thinking I was marrying, well, *Dan*, but as the months of preparation have unfolded, I'm beginning to see that I'm marrying Dan, his mother, and on a slightly less intense level, his father, brother and sister.

Don't get me wrong. For a while I was completely over the moon about this. In the beginning, when we first met and Dan introduced me to his family, I was thrilled. Thrilled to have found the family I'd always dreamt of. A warm, large and loving family, brothers and sisters, parents who were still together and happy.

When Dan confessed on our third date that he went to his parents for lunch every Sunday, I made up my mind there and then that he was going to be the one. A boy who still loves his family, I thought. A family so close they get together every week. What more could a girl ask for?

6

With hindsight, I was bound to think that, given that my own dysfunctional family had fallen to pieces right around the time my mother died.

*　　　*　　　*

Not that it was the happiest of families that was destroyed. My mother was an alcoholic: unpredictable, manipulative, self-obsessed. When sober she had the capacity to be exactly the mother I wanted. She could be kind, warm, loving, fun. I remember how much I adored her when I was very young, how she'd take me to puppet shows, laugh delightedly when I giggled at Punch and Judy, scoop me up into her arms while I wriggled and then cover me with kisses.

But she wasn't often sober. My mother and father were forever hosting cocktail parties, forever finding excuses to drink. I'd hear the music and laughter, and would leave my bedroom and sit on the top step of the stairs, trying to see the glamorous evening dresses without being seen.

Then, in the beginning, she was wonderful when she was drunk. 'I'm not drunk,' she'd laugh, 'just a tiny bit tipsy.' But her personality became huge when she was drunk, her happiness magnified a thousandfold by the alcohol. More affectionate, more vibrant, just *more*.

But as the drinking progressed, things changed. Her happiness turned to disappointment, disgust, disease, and the alcohol continued to increase it. Where once she had been fun, she became sullen; where she had been loving she became distant; where she had once covered me with kisses, she attacked me with insults.

7

In time, my father withdrew from both of us. He'd try to talk to her but it would end in a screaming match, so he'd grab his coat and go out, for hours at a time, sometimes all night.

I learnt to read the signs, know when she had been drinking, know when to stay away. My friends were few and far between, but they were loyal, and understood when I needed to stay the night, several nights a week.

I can't say I was unhappy. Somewhere I was aware that my friends didn't have mothers who were angels one minute then devils the next, and, while I occasionally envied the stability and warmth I found in their homes, I never missed it in my own. It was, after all, the only home I knew.

On 23 March 1983 I was sitting next to my best friend Alison in a history lesson. We were learning about the First World War, and I had drifted away into a reverie involving me, Simon Le Bon and true love. I'd just got to the part where he gazed into my eyes before the magical first kiss, when Alison nudged me sharply.

I looked at her to see her gesturing at the classroom door. Through the glass I could see the headmistress, Mrs Dickinson, approaching, as did the rest of the class. A collective gasp went around the classroom, for Mrs Dickinson was clearly about to come in, and, aside from morning assembly, Mrs Dickinson was a formidable presence who was very definitely seen and not heard.

I'm sure she probably was a lovely woman, but the entire school was terrified of her. Even the sixth-formers. She rarely seemed to smile, and stalked around the school, steely-grey hair in a helmet around her face, head held high, staring into the middle distance with a terrifying gleam in her eye.

The entire class stopped breathing as we watched the door handle turn, and then she was in front of us, asking to have a word with Mrs Packer, the history teacher. The two stepped outside and the class erupted, urgent whispers leaping across the room.

'Do you think someone's in trouble?'

'Is she going to give out a detention?'

'What do you think she wants?'

'Maybe Mrs Packer's done something wrong?'

And then the door opened and the two women came back in, Mrs Packer now looking as serious as Mrs Dickinson, and even without looking at them I knew they were going to call my name, and I knew it was going to be terrible.

'Ellie?' Mrs Packer said gently. 'Mrs Dickinson needs to talk to you.'

I felt all eyes upon me as I gathered up my books and walked to where Mrs Dickinson was standing, and tried to ignore the gentle hand on my shoulder as she guided me out of the room and closed the door.

She didn't say anything walking down the long corridor towards her office, and if I'd been older, or more confident, or less in awe of her, I would have stopped her and asked her to put me out of my misery, to tell me immediately what was going on, but I didn't. I shuffled along next to her, looking at the ground, knowing that my life was about to change, but not quite knowing how.

And in her office she sat me down and said, in quite the most gentle of voices, that there had been a terrible accident, and that my mother had died.

I remember sitting on that hard chair and thinking that I really ought to be crying. I thought of a recent movie I'd seen in which a girl had been told that her horse had been shot, and how she'd dissolved into tears, had jumped up screaming 'No! No!' I thought perhaps I should have done the same thing, but it didn't feel real, and I couldn't think of anything to say, or do, other than look at the floor.

I think my lack of reaction made Mrs Dickinson more uncomfortable than she had ever made me. She waited for me to cry, wanting, I think, to be able to put her arms around me and offer some comfort, and when I didn't, she found herself at a loss.

She filled the silence by telling me that sometimes terrible and tragic things happen, and that my father still loved me very much, and that my mother would always be watching me from heaven.

I often wished she'd never said that last bit. She said many other things, but that was the sentence that remained. *My mother would always be watching me from heaven*. I know she meant it to be a comfort, but for years afterwards I only ever thought about it when I was having sex. I'd be lost in the throes of ecstasy with a lover, when all of a sudden I'd be filled with the horror of my mother watching me from heaven, and I'd hurriedly have to pull up the duvet and cover us both.

Even as I sat in her office, listening to Mrs Dickinson continue her soliloquy on grief, I thought about my mother watching and almost shivered with the creepiness of it.

And then my father arrived to pick me up, and

he put his arms around me and cried, and still I couldn't express anything, still the numbness was too overwhelming.

My father tried very hard to continue a semblance of family life, but since we had never really had it, he didn't quite know what he was supposed to be doing.

He'd attempt to make dinner during those early days, and we'd sit at the table awkwardly. He'd ask me the odd question about school, I'd answer as succinctly as possible, both of us acutely aware of the silence, the lack of shouting, the lack of tantrums and broken dishes.

After a while he gave up. He'd phone and say he was working late, or had a meeting, or had plans. He withdrew from me in much the same way that he had withdrawn from my mother, as unable to relate to me as he had been to my mother.

I can't say I minded. Not then. I discovered boys, and dope, and parties. Not drink, though, never drink. Alison would stay over every weekend, and we'd spend our Friday and Saturday nights hopping on and off buses, looking for parties to crash all over West London, getting home high and happy in the early hours of the morning, with no parents around to tell us what to do.

My father remarried when I was eighteen. I've met her a few times. Mary. Strait-laced. Reserved. Kind. And dull. Everything my mother wasn't. She seemed nice, though, and my father seemed to be happy. By that time I felt much like an orphan anyway, and didn't begrudge his remarrying in the slightest, not that I ever seemed to see him.

People laugh today when I tell them about my wild youth. Not the bit about my mother dying, not that, but when I tell them I was a dopehead, that I would regularly trash our house with parties, that my first two years at university were spent sleeping with pretty much anyone who'd have me.

They'd laugh in disbelief, because looking at me now, with my sleek, chic conservative clothes, my understated make-up, my high, but not too high, elegant shoes, they can't believe I ever did anything rebellious in my entire life. Dan always says that's why he fell in love with me. Because I looked like a librarian, but dig a little deeper and naughty Ellie—as he called her—would come scrambling out.

*   *   *

We met just about the time when I had decided that I wasn't going to get married. Ever. I'd spent too many nights dreaming of a family, of a house filled with children, and laughter, and noise, of a home that was almost precisely the opposite of my own childhood home in every way. I'd spent too many nights dreaming of a future that never materialized, dreaming of men who never turned out to be the men I wanted them to be.

And so I'd decided to concentrate on work. At thirty-three I was the Marketing Director of a small chain of luxury boutique hotels—perhaps you know them, perhaps you've even stayed in them. Calden, they are called. Just Calden, as in, are you staying at Calden? Named after their founder, Robert Calden, they are Schrager-style for about half the price, although don't quote me on that.

I loved my job as Marketing Director. I loved writing the marketing briefs, coming up with our objectives, the tone, the deliverables, and seeing them come to fruition.

I loved the thrill of developing new image campaigns for our brand, of then taking that positioning statement and briefing the creatives at our advertising agency, and seeing them come back, a couple of weeks later, with their presentation on boards, most of which still, even to this day, blow my mind with their creativity and brilliance.

I loved the various promotions I put together to increase, as we say in marketing, Rev Par—revenue per average room. Coming up with direct-mail promotions to entice our top 10 per cent of customers to stay even longer, with the incentive of, say, an evening's private shopping at Selfridges, or stay two nights, get the third night free.

Unsurprisingly the kind of people who stay at Calden—the high-end leisure and business traveller—usually jumped at these promotions, and I swiftly became the golden girl in the marketing department.

I was busy, my career was going well, and I was happy. Despite the fact that I had always thought of friendships as rather transient, I had managed to find myself good friends at work who had become even better friends outside of work, and my social life was a whirlwind.

And one December night I had a meeting in the top-floor conference room of Calden, Marylebone High Street, with a couple of executives from American Express with whom I'd been trying to link up for months. I'd put together a proposal for a promotion with their Platinum cardholders: book a weekend at Calden through American Express, and we'll throw in dinner at a top London restaurant and a chauffeur-driven car.

The meeting went well, and afterwards we all went down to the bar for a drink. Calden might not have been entirely to my taste—I tended to prefer hotels that were more traditional, more luxurious—but I did love the bar, and particularly the fact that it was currently one of the hottest places to see and be seen, and I—thank goodness—despite my boring black business suits, was never turned away by the doormen.

Votive candles were everywhere, dotted on low sleek tables, clustered on thick, modern shelving. Tall-stemmed glass vases held single stems of scarlet amaryllis, shocking splashes of colour against the stark whiteness of the walls.

Instead of chairs there were sofas—huge squashy sofas. And a line of games tables along one wall—backgammon, chess, even *Monopoly* and *Trivial Pursuit*. These were one of the reasons why our bar was so hot: our weekly games night (my idea, if I do say so myself) had been written up in *Time Out*, followed by *Metro* and the *Sunday Times* Style section, and was now almost impossible to get into.

But tonight, a Tuesday, was a quiet night. We took a bank of sofas tucked into a quiet corner, close to one of the giant fireplaces with a gas fire that almost, almost felt real, and settled down with Mojitos for the group, and a cranberry juice and soda with a splash of lime for me.

Small talk was being made, as the business pressures began to ease off our shoulders, when something made me turn around. It was that feeling that someone was staring at me, although I

14

realized that only with hindsight. Behind me on another sofa was a man frowning at me. I looked at him questioningly, but he didn't change his expression, so I looked away.

But even as I tried to join in the conversation, I kept feeling his frown fall upon the back of my head, and it was a struggle not to keep turning round. Eventually they left—wives and children to get home to—and when I got up to leave I saw the man was still there.

He came over and stood over me, very tall, very serious.

'Why are you staring at me?' I said, uncharacteristically boldly.

'I'm sorry. It's just that I'm sure I know you from somewhere.'

I rolled my eyes. 'Aren't I supposed to say I bet you say that to all the girls?' I wasn't trying to be funny, I was almost sneering at the time. I was tired, I'd had a long day, and I was not in the mood for clichéd pick-up lines.

'No, I'm serious. You look very familiar.'

I was about to come out with another line, but he did look serious, and slightly perplexed.

'What's your name?' he said.

'Ellie Black.'

And his face lit up.

'I knew it! We did meet before. About four years ago at a barbeque at Alex and Rob's house. Ellie Black! I remember you. You work in marketing at Emap, and you live in Queen's Park!' He said this triumphantly, proving he wasn't just coming out with a pick-up line. Of course he was right, I had been at that party and did work for Emap at the time, and, despite not remembering him in the

15

slightest, I shifted my features from exasperated to surprise with just a faint hint of pleasure.

'Of course!' I exclaimed. 'And now I remember you. But I'm so sorry, I don't remember your name.'

'That's fine. It's Dan Cooper. I was working for Channel Four, Producing. We said we'd get together for lunch but, well . . .' He shrugged. 'I suppose we never got around to it.'

And then I remembered. I was going out with Hamish, and we were still in the first flush when I was convinced he would be the father of my children, and we'd had a row because he'd decided to go back up to Scotland to see his family and hadn't invited me.

I'd gone on my own to a barbeque at a neighbour's house, friends of friends, and hadn't known anyone there, but had walked in and immediately felt at home.

Dan marched up to me with crinkly eyes and a large smile, and introduced himself, offering to get me a beer, and I remember thinking how nice he was, and what a shame I wasn't single.

I'd flirted harmlessly with him for most of the evening, enjoying the attention, enjoying the sensation of being wanted, and when we left and he mentioned calling me about lunch, I said sure, that he could call me in the office any time.

I had gone to bed with a smile on my face, and had been woken up by an early-morning phone call from Hamish, apologizing profusely and saying he missed me and couldn't stop thinking about me, and of course all thoughts of Dan flew out the window.

By the time Dan called, a couple of weeks later,

I had absolutely no idea who he was. We had an awkward conversation, at the end of which I said I had a really busy schedule at the moment, but that I'd call him when it eased off a bit.

And that was the last time I ever thought about him. But standing in the Calden bar, staring at his open, friendly face, I suddenly did remember him, and these were the things I remembered . . .

That when he smiled he smiled with his eyes.

That he was very tall. The sort of tall that makes you always feel protected and safe.

That he was a man who was at ease with himself and his place in the world.

That he once had a cat called Tetley.

Dan Cooper looked down at me, frowning again. 'You don't remember me,' he said.

'I do,' I replied, a smile starting to form.

'No, you don't. Don't worry. I'm sorry to have bothered you.'

'But I do remember you. Stop!' I reached out and took his arm to stop him turning away. 'I'll prove it. When you were four years old, you had a cat called Tetley.'

And then it was his turn to smile, and soon we were sitting next to one another on a sofa, and by the time we left, three hours later, my face hurt from smiling all evening, from smiling, and talking, and laughing.

We walked out together and he hailed a taxi and put me inside.

'I would suggest lunch but I know what happened last time,' he said, and I did something that is so out of character I sometimes still can't believe I had the temerity to do it.

I leant forward and kissed him. A long, soft kiss

17

on the lips, and delightedly my stomach fluttered in excitement.

And when I pulled away and saw his face I winked. 'You'll never know unless you try,' I laughed, palmed a business card into his hand and sat back as the taxi took off.

He phoned the next morning and met me for lunch that day. Ordinarily I would have been put off, would have thought he was too keen, but I wasn't a fickle twenty-something any longer. I was thirty-three and had been around the block enough times to know a good thing when I saw it.

There were many things I grew to love about Dan very quickly, not least of which was that I could see, beyond a shadow of a doubt, that he couldn't wait for children, would be, in fact, the sort of father that I had always wanted for myself.

But I also loved his smell. How he always smelt of lemons. That he knew everything about Arsenal and would happily while away hours with his friends in the pub, discussing the finer merits of a match in 1984.

I loved that he had a wardrobe full of beautiful clothes that he never wore, spending most of the time in rugby shirts, or huge sloppy sweaters that were soft and cuddly, clothes that always felt wonderful to me.

I took him to meet my father, when things were clearly growing serious. We drove up to Potters Bar and had an awkward pub lunch with Dad and Mary, and I was saddened to see that my father and I had grown so far apart there was no way to bridge the gap. But I was pleased we had done the right thing, and the next step was meeting his family.

I almost felt as if I already knew them from the

many stories, the pictures dotted around Dan's flat, hearing his mother's voice on his answer machine.

I loved hearing him talk about his childhood, about his brother and sister, about coming from what I considered to be such a large family.

'Are you sure they'll like me?' I said from time to time in the days before my first Cooper family lunch.

'Of course!' Dan kissed me and gave me a reassuring squeeze. 'They're going to love you.'

'But your mother didn't like your last girlfriend. How do you *know*?'

'Trust me, I *know*. And anyway, she turned out to be right about my last girlfriend, didn't she?' The last girlfriend had run off with an actor, and apparently Dan's mother had said the minute she met her that she knew she couldn't trust her. But of course she only said this after the fact.

'She's going to love you and you're going to love her. If I didn't know better, I'd say this was a match made in heaven.'

'Ha bloody ha,' I said, but it made me smile, and even as I suffered wardrobe crisis after wardrobe crisis, planning for the big day itself, I found myself looking forward to it. Wasn't this, after all, the family I had always wanted?

3

Dan's parents live in a large Victorian house on a quiet leafy street on the borders of Hampstead and Belsize Park. It is the house Dan grew up in, and he loves that his bedroom is still his bedroom, that the

19

house is filled with memories of his youth.

He drove me past one day, wanted to pop in and say hello to his parents, but I wasn't ready to meet them yet. I needed to spend far more time preparing myself.

Not that I was frightened, I just wanted them to like me. In truth, I wanted them to *love* me. Particularly given Dan's mother's disapproval of previous girlfriends, I wanted her to meet me and think I was perfect for him, to know that I was The One.

Dan and I already knew that we had a future together, and Dan had told his family how serious it was. And although it shouldn't have mattered as much as it did, I yearned for his family's approval, needed so desperately to be welcomed, to be treated as one of their own.

And just looking at the outside of the house made me long to be part of it, part of them. It was the type of house I had always dreamt of. Large but not too large, imposing without being excessively grand, ivy trailed up the red brick, reaching almost as high as the three gables.

The windows were leaded lights, and the driveway a huge sweep of gravel complete with a huge old oak tree in the middle and a few weeds pushing through, weeds that presumably the gardener would be dealing with soon.

Linda and Michael Cooper. He is a barrister, QC actually, and, having Googled him, I know he has a reputation as one of the best. He works in commercial law, has his own chambers somewhere in Middle Temple, and in photographs looks far less imposing and grand than his reputation would lead you to believe.

Handsome in a faded, greyish sort of way, he is, in every photograph I have seen of him in Dan's flat, eclipsed by his wife. The lovely Linda.

Linda Cooper, née Campbell. Born and bred in Hampstead, survivor of South Hampstead High School for Girls, no less, drop-out of Oxford University, where, unusually for girls of her generation, she was studying history.

Dan's version of the story is this: His mother and father met at university where Linda's Biba-inspired clothes and Twiggy-inspired figure made her the talk of the town. That she was bright, and strong, and opinionated didn't hurt either. Not with legs like that.

She was the girl everyone wanted to be seen with, the girl who always had her head thrown back with laughter, who seemed oblivious to the attention she generated everywhere she went.

Michael was the star of the rowing team, and as such had something of a strong following himself. Linda in fact had spotted him at the annual Oxford-Cambridge boat race, and decided there and then that she would get him.

Of course getting him wasn't the problem, but falling pregnant, nearly eleven months later, proved to be somewhat more difficult.

They were young, they were in love, and they were quite certain that they were meant to be together. So what if they had to make a few changes?

They were married, quickly, at Marylebone Register Office, a Mary Quant empire-line mini-dress and a large bouquet of creamy roses covering Linda's growing bump.

Linda gave up her history degree, happy at the

21

time to play at being a wife and mother, and when Dan was born she was quite certain she had done the right thing.

Dan still has pictures of Linda, gorgeous despite giving birth weeks before, cradling her tiny baby, gazing adoringly into his big blue eyes (now brown, just in case you were wondering).

Emma arrived three years later, followed three years after that by Richard. They were all living in the suburbs of London by then, Linda being the ideal housewife, befriending all her neighbours, hosting tea parties for her children.

Dan says she is the perfect mother. He says he adores her and that I will too. He says that while she is still strong, opinionated, outspoken, she is also warm, loving, kind.

In the pictures of Linda with her children, she is always beaming; more reserved in the pictures with her husband. Dan says that the children are all the apple of her eye, but that his parents are still together, and still as happy as can be expected, which is something of a rarity these days.

I've asked Dan if he is the favourite, and he has shrugged. Richard, he says, is the baby, and Emma the rebel. Possibly he is the favourite, but that's only because he's the eldest. His mother calls him every day, sometimes twice, and he claims to tell her everything.

I don't know if this is normal. I have nothing to compare it with, but if I had a mother who loved me and made me the apple of her eye, I am quite sure I would love her calling me every day. She would be my mentor, my best friend. I'm certain I would ask her opinion on everything, and so, in the very beginning, I never thought it strange, never

22

caught even a whiff of anything odd.

I spent many hours quizzing Dan about his family, trying to learn as much about them as possible before meeting them, trying to work out who they were, what they were like, who they wanted me to be.

And eventually the big day arrived. Sunday lunch at his parents'. With Richard and Emma too.

My wardrobe crisis had resolved itself in a pair of classic black trousers and white shirt, a silver chain around my neck and flat black shoes on my feet. The perfect outfit for a warmish day in spring, but even for me, I looked conservative. How could they possibly not love me, I thought. I look like the girl next door.

At the last minute I pulled my hair back into a ponytail and threw a bright green sweater around my shoulders. 'Ready!' I shouted down the stairs to Dan, who was impatiently tapping his foot.

I ran down the stairs and Dan started laughing.

'What? Do I look awful? Why are you laughing? Shit. I'm going back in to change.'

'No, Ellie!' Dan started to apologize. 'It's only that you look just like my mother. You don't normally wear clothes like that, that's all. I'm not used to seeing you look like that.'

I groaned. 'Oh, God. That's awful. I have to change.'

'No!' Firmly now. 'We don't have time. And anyway, you should take it as a compliment. My mother's the most elegant woman I know, and you look gorgeous.'

'Really?' I started to relax.

'Really. You couldn't be more perfect. They're going to love you.'

I shouldn't have been the slightest bit surprised when Linda, or Mrs Cooper as she was to me then, opened the door in black trousers and a white shirt, a chain around her neck and an orange sweater around her shoulders. The only differences between us were that her clothes were clearly designer, her shirt silk, her sweater cashmere and her necklace gold.

I stood back to examine her as she threw her arms around Dan and embraced him with an enormous hug.

Withdrawing, she turned to me, a warm smile on her face. I smiled back and faltered slightly, unsure whether to shake her hand or kiss her on the cheek, not wanting to do the wrong thing.

I'd brought peonies and held them out to her, saying how lovely it was to meet her. She took the flowers and thanked me, putting her arms around me to give me a quick squeeze, and I instantly relaxed.

'Ellie,' she said, taking me by the arm and leading me inside, 'we've heard so much about you. And look at you!' She gestured to her clothes, and then to mine. 'We look like twins!'

I laughed and followed her into the kitchen. 'Dan's here everyone!' said Mrs Cooper, as Dan's father put down a knife on the chopping board and came over to shake my hand.

'How do you do?' he said, rather formally I thought, but then he smiled and I knew I liked him. 'Sorry,' he apologized, wiping his hand on a tea towel. 'They've put me to work with the tomatoes

24

and I'm covered with the juice.'

I laughed as another voice said, 'We're just trying to prove to him that it isn't all women's work. Hi!'

Emma was sitting at the kitchen table, flicking through a copy of *Hello!* And eating handfuls of honey-roasted nuts from a small ceramic bowl in the middle of the table. She glanced up and said hi to her brother, looking me up and down and making me instantly wish I had dressed differently, for I could see immediately she thought I was dull, conservative, middle aged before my time.

And who could blame her, for Emma, a year younger than me, looked much like she had stepped straight from the pages of a trendy magazine: skinny low-slung trousers and high pointed boots, a tight shirt and bright red streaks in her hair.

'I'm Emma,' she said, 'obviously. And you, obviously, are Ellie. How weird,' she said, smiling. 'You're dressed just like Mum.'

Dan's father looked me up and down and then looked over at Linda, and laughed.

'Good Lord!' he said. 'What an amazing coincidence.'

'I know.' I made a face. 'I feel slightly ridiculous, as if I'm trying to be ten years older than I am.'

'No. You look good. Classic. Mum would love it if I dressed more like you. She's always telling me not to spend money on the designer labels because they're only in fashion for a season and it's a waste of money. "Buy a few classic pieces," she says, but that look just isn't me.' I love that Emma is instantly chatty—she makes me feel immediately at home, as if I've known her for ever.

'But you look great,' I said, smiling. 'I wish I could dress more like you, but I'd feel like a fake. Like everyone would look at me and know I'm not really trendy, I'm just pretending to be.'

Emma laughed. 'Part of this is for my job.'

'What do you do?' I asked, although I already knew.

'I'm a stylist,' she said. 'Mostly magazine shoots. So I'm mixing with models and photographers all the time, hence the need to look the part. Dan says you work for Calden.'

I nodded.

'I was there last night! That's a great job, what an amazing bar.'

'If you can get in.'

'I spent the opening week befriending the doormen,' she confided. 'I now count Luke and Sean amongst my closest friends.'

'That would be until they make a pass at you and you reject them.'

'I don't think they'd dare,' Emma laughed. 'I think they just love all the attention from the *laydeez*.'

Dan came up behind me and put his arms around my waist. 'So what do you think of my baby sister?'

'I'm only your baby sister by age,' Emma snorted, throwing another handful of nuts into her mouth. 'In terms of maturity I've got about ten years on you. Didn't anyone ever tell you how much more advanced girls are than boys?'

'I'd argue with you if you weren't wearing such pointed boots,' Dan chuckled. 'I still remember that time you kicked me in the balls with those stilettos.'

Emma shook her head and looked at me. 'Can you believe it? I was fourteen at the time and he still hasn't forgiven me.'

'Children, children,' Mrs Cooper admonished, walking over to the table and sitting down, pulling the magazine over to get a better look at the latest pictures of Jennifer Lopez. 'No rows today, thank you. We haven't been together like this in weeks.'

'You mean two weeks.' Dan smiled as his mother shrugged. 'So where is my errant younger brother anyway?' continued Dan. 'Up to no good as usual?'

'Oh, don't start,' Mrs Cooper said. 'He had to meet . . .'

'. . . a man about a dog?' Emma interjected, and their father suppressed a chuckle from the other side of the kitchen.

'Stop it, you two,' he said. 'He had a meeting about a new internet venture.'

'A meeting? On a Sunday morning? Are you serious?'

'You know Richard. His working hours never fit in with the rest of us.'

'That's because he never does any work.' Emma shook her head. 'Thank God he's got you and Dad to bail him out or I'd be throwing him pound coins on a street corner every morning.'

'Emma!' Mrs Cooper looked annoyed. 'Just because Richard hasn't yet found his niche in life doesn't mean he's not going to. And I won't have any talk about us bailing him out. You know nothing about it, and may I remind you of who bought you that laptop computer recently.'

'Only because you were buying one for Richard and you got a better deal if you bought two.'

The tension was building, and, while it was

interesting to see the family dynamic, I was starting to feel uncomfortable, so I decided to change the subject.

'Mrs Cooper, is there anything I can do? Can I help at all?'

She turned to me, visibly relaxing. 'No, Ellie, we're all set. I've made Dan's favourite, roast beef and Yorkshire pudding.'

'I didn't know that's your favourite.' I looked at Dan. 'Why didn't you tell me? I would have made it for you.'

'Ah,' said Mrs Cooper, standing up. 'But it will never be quite like his mother's, will it?' I sat, trying to digest this statement, wondering whether it was an insult or whether it was just an adoring mother, when she patted me on the arm. 'And you mustn't call me Mrs Cooper. Call me Linda. Mrs Cooper always makes me think of my mother-in-law.' She cast a glance at her husband and dropped her voice. 'And frankly I'd rather not think about her if at all possible.'

'Mum!' Emma said. 'She only died a few months ago. At least let the poor woman turn cold in her grave before you start bitching.'

'You're right. I'm sorry. God rest the old cow's soul,' Linda said in a voice low enough for her husband not to hear, and Emma rolled her eyes and went back to her magazine.

*   *   *

'Aha!' Dan leapt up and gave his brother a big hug. 'The prodigal son returns.'

'Richard!'

Linda bustled over and practically shoved Dan

28

out of the way to hug him, after which he bent down and planted a kiss on Emma's cheek, then shook my hand with a cheeky grin.

And I could see at once that he got away with murder. He was a thinner, younger, cuter version of Dan. I think Dan is charming, but this is mostly because I love him and because he is well mannered and polite. Richard, on the other hand, oozed so much charm that it was quite possible one of us would have to fetch a mop to clean it up off the floor.

'You must be the lovely Ellie,' he said, giving me a kiss, and despite myself I felt a faint flush. 'Thank God, Dan seems to have finally inherited some of my good taste after all.'

'Good taste? Are you being funny? Your last girlfriend looked like she'd just stepped off a street corner in Westbourne Grove.'

'I take it you've met my bitter sibling.' Richard raised an eyebrow.

'I think you meant to say *better* sibling.'

I sat back and enjoyed the show. Michael and Linda were finishing the food, while Dan, Rich, Emma and of course myself, the observer, sat at the kitchen table. I watched them bicker and laugh, with comments that could be construed as insults disappearing under the love that was clearly so strong and so true.

'Tell me, Ellie, do you have brothers and sisters?' Linda called from the kitchen.

I shook my head regretfully and walked over to her. 'I always wanted a big family, but my mother died when I was a teenager, and my father's remarried.'

Linda stopped, her face filled with concern. 'Oh,

29

how awful,' she says. 'How did she die?'

'In a car accident when I was thirteen.' Naturally I omit the part about her being drunk at the time.

Dan's father looked stricken. 'Dreadful,' he murmured. 'What a terrible thing to happen to someone so young.'

'Oh, you poor thing,' echoed Linda. 'So young. Are you still close with your father?'

I shook my head. 'He remarried and lives in Potters Bar, so I don't really see that much of him. He has two children with his new wife, though, so officially I suppose I have two step-siblings, although I've only met them a handful of times.'

'And that's it?' Linda seemed horrified. 'No other family? Uncles? Aunts? Grandparents?'

'Nope, and it's fine. I'm used to it, but I always dreamt of having brothers and sisters and being part of a big family like this.'

'Good,' she said, putting an arm around my shoulders and giving me a squeeze. 'Because you can now be part of our family. How does that sound?'

'It sounds great.' And it did.

*   *   *

Lunch was delicious. And long. And raucous. Dan, Emma and Richard seemed to regress to their teenage years as the meal progressed, and I couldn't help but join in, feeling like a naughty schoolgirl, giggling at private jokes that the parents couldn't hear.

There was no doubt whatsoever that Linda wore the trousers in this household. Michael looked vaguely bemused by what was going on, was jovial

30

and sweet, but said less and less throughout the meal, mostly because he was constantly interrupted by his wife.

Dan and Richard were clearly adored by their mother, who couldn't stop smiling every time she looked at them. She quizzed Richard on every aspect of his life.

'So do you think this internet venture is going to work?' she asked.

Richard nodded, his face now serious. 'I actually think we're on to a big one,' he said. 'The meeting this morning went really well and as soon as we've worked out the financing it's a goer.'

'Um, I hate to be the one to burst your bubble'— Linda rolled her eyes as soon as Emma started to speak—'but has anyone actually told you that the dotcom boom is over?'

'Actually, Emma,' Linda answered before Richard had a chance to speak, 'the good ideas are still surviving. Look at Amazon. Look at Google. What about eBay? It's just settled down. People aren't able to make the ridiculous amounts of money they were making in the early years, but if this is as exciting an idea as Richard thinks, then there's no reason why it shouldn't take off.'

'But that's what you said about the concierge service thing he was doing last year. And what was it before that, some self-help motivational course?'

'There were bloody good reasons why those didn't work out,' Richard said defensively. 'And mostly bad timing. How were we to know competitors with more funding were setting up at the same time?'

'Um . . . research?'

'Emma,' Linda said icily, 'can you just give your

31

brother a rest for a change?'

'Yeah,' agreed Richard. 'When your earnings fall into the six-figure category, then we can talk.'

'Why, so you can fleece me for your next business venture?' Emma grinned and Richard hit her playfully.

'Don't be ridiculous,' he laughed. 'Why would I try to fleece you when Dan is (a) much nicer than you, and (b) has more money than you?'

'And don't forget Dad of course,' Dan said. 'He's the investor you need to really hit up.'

'Dad,' said Emma in a wheedling voice, 'you know that car I've been talking about . . .'

'Forget it,' Linda said. 'Your car is perfectly fine. Can we all stop talking about money now, please? Whatever will Ellie think?'

*   *   *

What I think is how lucky they are to have each other, to have all of this, to be able to fight, and bicker, and laugh, and push and shove, and know that at the end of it they all still have each other.

And of course they don't know this, don't know any different, much as I don't know any different myself.

How lucky they are. And how unaware of how lucky they are. Especially Emma. I watched Emma with her mother, felt the tension between them, and felt saddened that Emma had no idea of how grateful she should be to have a mother, let alone a mother like Linda.

If I were Emma and Linda were my mother, I'd be so proud, and *so* grateful. I'd hang out with her and bring her with me on shopping trips. We'd

32

meet for lunch and swap gossip, and I'd fill her in on man troubles and friendship dilemmas.

She's the sort of woman you could go to a spa with, sit and have a makeover with, be terribly girly with, without feeling the slightest bit guilty.

And when things went badly, when I was dumped, or lonely, or life wasn't going in quite the way I expected it to, I'd run home to be fed chicken soup, and beef stew, and roast beef and Yorkshire pudding by Linda. I'd want her sympathy and her friendship, her acceptance and her understanding.

If I were Emma, my mother would be my best friend, and, as much as I liked Emma, as easy as I found it to talk to her throughout lunch, I could see that the relationship was not an easy one, and I so badly wanted to show her what she had, to tell her about my own life, about having no one. Until I met Dan.

4

'They loved you,' Dan announced the next day. 'Not that I'm surprised.'

'They did?' I couldn't hide the relief and delight in my voice.

'Absolutely.' And he grinned. 'In fact my mother said you were perfect for me.'

'Uh oh.' I pulled away from cuddling up against Dan on the sofa and gave him a sharp look. 'You're not one of those men who only goes out with women your mother disapproves of, and gets bored with everyone she likes?'

Dan started to laugh. 'No, Ellie. I'm not going

anywhere for, oh, I don't know'—he looked at his watch—'at least an hour.'

*   *   *

We'd just started living together at that point. Dan had moved into my flat, bringing hardly anything with him, but, as he pointed out, he still had ample storage in his bedroom at home, so if he felt a sudden and desperate need for, say, the electric guitar he learnt how to play when he was eighteen, he only had to run over to Hampstead to pick it up.

I'd never lived with anyone before Dan, had always prized my independence, worked hard to make my flat exactly as I wanted it.

But once it became serious, once Dan started spending six out of seven nights at my place, it seemed ridiculous for both of us to continue paying a mortgage, and since my flat was fractionally larger but a million times more comfortable, we decided that his should be the one to be rented out.

I'd lived in my flat for five years. The happiest years of my life. It was the first time that I truly understood what it meant to be settled, the first time I knew what it was to have a home.

I trawled through the junk shops, furnishing the rooms on a shoestring, and weekends were spent halfway up a ladder, paintbrush in hand.

I'd bought all the interior magazines— *Architectural Digest, House & Garden, World of Interiors*—ripped out the rooms that I liked and then tried to imitate them on very little budget at all.

I had colleagues, friends, who would move every few years, get bored with their flats, want to move

34

on to something bigger and better, but I never felt like that. I knew that my flat was everything I'd ever wanted, and I couldn't imagine ever needing anything more.

Dan loved my flat from the moment he first came over (fifth date, I cooked: artichoke salad, monkfish with roasted tomatoes and garlic, chocolate mousse and strawberries. Naturally we ended up in bed together, and the next morning I knew that in all probability I'd never sleep with anyone else again). Dan always said that my flat was exactly how he'd want his flat to be, if he had any style.

I thought he was joking, until the following week when I went over to his flat in Kentish Town. On the fifth floor of a huge apartment building, I walked in the door and immediately looked for a comfy sofa on which to collapse to recover from the walk up.

Nothing. No furniture. Just boxes of clothes, a futon that had definitely seen far better days, a huge flat screen TV and hundreds and hundreds of video tapes.

'I'm afraid it's not very cosy,' Dan said, walking into his bedroom to gather up clean clothes for the following week at my house.

'That would be the understatement of the year,' I said, shocked that anyone could live like this. 'When did you move in? Yesterday?'

'I'm hardly ever here,' he said, smiling.

'Clearly. But how come you're hardly ever here when you've managed to spend the best part of last week at my place? If you were never home, how come you found the time to be with me most of last week? Surely I haven't been that much of a boon to your social life?'

Dan grinned, arms full of shirts and t-shirts. 'Social life? What social life? I had no social life before I met you.'

I slapped my forehead. 'Of course! I should have known. You were at Calden that night for, what? A business meeting?'

'Actually I was,' he said, nodding. 'You know us TV types. Why meet in a boardroom when there's a perfectly good bar round the corner?'

'Actually I don't think I know you TV types that well.'

'Oh, no?' He raised an eyebrow and dropped the clothes on the floor as he walked towards me. 'Then perhaps it's time for us to get to know one another a whole lot better.'

*   *   *

Two weeks after Dan moved in, the doorbell rang. It was a Saturday morning and Dan had gone to the gym for his regular weekend workout, leaving me, finally, with some time all alone.

As excited as I'd been about Dan moving in, the apprehension was starting to strike. I'd always envisaged living together as some sort of romantic ideal: waking up in one another's arms, laughing over fresh orange juice and toast on a Sunday morning. Much as I'm ashamed to admit it, I think that my idea of living together was something I'd chopped together from various rather cheesy TV commercials.

But the reality was that this was my flat, paid for by me and decorated for me. I had chosen every piece of furniture in there, and had decided where to place it. If I didn't like something, I moved it.

And all of a sudden I had to find more space for Dan's stuff, including things that I couldn't stand. His collection of framed film posters, for example. *Chinatown. Dirty Harry. Once Upon a Time in America.* I'm sure they would have looked amazing in, say, Dan's room in his university hall of residence, but honestly, at thirty-five you would think he'd have something a bit more, well, grown-up. I'd banished them to the corridor, where they were stacked, face in, waiting for Dan to hang them.

And while I understand that an enormous flat screen plasma TV is what every little boy dreams of having when he grows up, it didn't quite go with my oh-so-feminine decor. I realized pretty quickly, though, that this was one battle I was clearly not going to win, and so I tried very hard to ignore the huge black rectangle lurking like a prophet of doom in the corner of the room.

Selfish? Of course I was. Who wouldn't be selfish after living by themselves for effectively almost twenty years? I was used to doing things a certain way, and had never had to think about anyone else. I understood what the word compromise meant; I'd just never had to live it.

There Dan was, removing the photo frames I'd delicately placed on his stereo in an effort to make it more feminine, more in keeping with the rest of the room, and there I was, watching him while biting my tongue so as not to scream at him that this was my house and I didn't want his stupid bloody stereo there in the first place.

'I know it's difficult,' Dan said after our first tiny row, two days after he moved in. 'You've lived on your own for years and I haven't lived with anyone for a long time. We're both used to having our own space; it's going to take a while for us to adjust to having another person there. But Ellie'—he reached across the table and took my hand—'it's worth it. I love you and I want to spend the rest of my life with you. This is just a tiny glitch and we both need to compromise.'

I nodded, amazed that I had found someone so perfect for me, someone who loved me that much, who was able to be that honest about it.

'You're right,' I said. 'I'm sorry.'

'Does that mean I can continue to leave my underwear on the bathroom floor?'

'Oh, ha ha. Don't push your luck.' But I acquiesced when he leant forward and kissed me hard on the lips.

*   *   *

And that Saturday morning, when the doorbell rang, I was mildly irritated, having just settled down to enjoy my solitary Saturday morning ritual of tea, croissants and the *Telegraph* in bed. The March drizzle outside helped to ease my guilt— there's nothing like lying in bed when it's grey and raining outside. And I had no idea who could be ringing the bell.

I shuffled into my bathrobe—I've been meaning to get a dressing gown for ever but somehow I never get around to it—and, with mussed-up hair and eyes puffy and crusty with sleep, went to answer the front door, only to find Dan's mother beaming on the doorstep.

'Ellie!' she said, planting a kiss on my cheek and

pushing past me into the hallway as I froze, mortified that she was seeing me looking like this. 'I hope you don't mind me dropping in, but I realized if I waited for an invitation from Dan I'd be waiting for ever. Now where can I put these?'

She was carrying an enormous bunch of tulips that she carted into the kitchen, where she began to open cupboards, looking, presumably, for a vase.

Shit. The kitchen looked like a bomb had hit it. We'd made dinner together the night before, and Dan had come up behind me as I was clearing up and run his hand up my inner thigh, and the next thing you know we had abandoned all hope of restoring the kitchen to its former, immaculate self and run to the bedroom, leaving everything to the morning.

I'd once heard that the mark of a true chef is someone who cleans up as they go, and despite being addicted to every food programme on the box, despite watching Gordon, and Jamie and everyone else wiping off their boards and getting rid of garlic skins and parsley stalks before starting on the next bit, I could never quite get the hang of it.

But oh, how I wish I'd tried that bit harder. I looked at the devastation through Linda Cooper's eyes and crumpled.

'I'm so sorry about the mess,' I said weakly, picking up food-encrusted plates from the kitchen table and carrying them over to the sink. 'I can't believe you've seen my flat looking the messiest it's ever been. I'm so embarrassed.' I opened a cupboard door and handed her a square glass vase.

'I have a wonderful cleaning lady who's looking for more work,' she said with a smile. 'I'll give her a call if you like and see if she can come this week. How does that sound?'

'Oh. Great,' I said feebly, never having considered the idea of anyone other than myself cleaning my house. And frankly, with the exception of this morning, I like to think I do a good job, although there was no point in saying this. If I were Linda Cooper, I wouldn't believe me.

'Anyway,' she trilled, snipping the ends off the tulips and arranging them expertly in the vase, 'it'll only take me a second to clean this up. Were you about to jump in the shower? I'll have this place spotless by the time you've finished.'

Now I know I shouldn't have taken this personally, and I know she was only trying to help, but nevertheless I felt that I, or my cleaning capabilities, had been somehow put down, and I wasn't happy.

I also felt horribly vulnerable in my greying, fraying bathrobe and hair all over the place, not a scrap of make-up on. I knew that I'd only be able to cope with the humiliation if I felt strong enough, and I'd only feel strong enough with my body armour, aka make-up and clothes, firmly in place.

And so I slunk off to the bathroom, leaving my boyfriend's mother elbow-deep in Fairy Liquid.

*   *   *

Half an hour later I emerged, hair scraped back in a ponytail, white t-shirt and jeans, feeling like I could take on anyone.

'I made coffee for us,' Linda said brightly, as I walked into a now-gleaming kitchen. 'And I hope you don't mind but I washed all your vases—they were all quite filthy.'

I'm mortified. 'Linda, you didn't have to do that.'

'No, no. I know you young people don't have time to clean properly, and it was the least I could do. Now come and sit down and let's you and I get to know one another better.'

*   *   *

By the time she left I had the whole Cooper family history, including a far better picture of the family dynamic.

It seemed that Linda was not as secure as I had thought at our first meeting, and that there was definitely a touch of resentment about not having been able to pursue a career. I had already guessed that she was one of those women who fulfilled their ambitions vicariously through their children, and everything she said confirmed that to be true.

She was extraordinarily proud of Dan, who is clearly the golden boy thanks to his excellent degree and prolific career as a television producer. His last documentary had won several awards and generated an impressive amount of press coverage, which Linda had cut out and collected into a scrapbook.

Richard, she said, had yet to find his niche. Twenty-nine seemed to be old enough to know what you were going to do with the rest of your life, but Linda said he was a dreamer, and that he'd get there eventually.

'And Emma?' I asked. 'She's so outgoing, she has such a big personality. You must love having a daughter like that.'

'She's like the girl with the curl in the middle of her forehead. When she is good she is very, very good, and when she is bad she is horrid.'

'Horrid? Really? She seems so charming.'

'That's because she's not your daughter.' Linda smiled. 'I know your mother died very young and don't take this the wrong way, but the teenage years between a mother and daughter can be very difficult.'

'No, I know,' I said. 'I may not have had my own mother but I went through it all with my friends.'

'Well, Emma's always been a rebel. Of course I love her, but I don't really understand her. And frankly, at her age she should really have settled down by now. I mean, look at you, Ellie. You're roughly the same age, aren't you?'

I nodded.

'And you have your own flat, a good job, financial independence. Emma just drifts from job to job and party to party, moving in with friends or boyfriends whenever the wind changes. Oh, I don't know,' she sighed. 'Maybe it's part of being creative.'

The key turned in the lock of the front door and I breathed a sigh of relief. Befriending the boyfriend's mother was one thing; listening to her moan about her other children was something else entirely, something I wasn't willing to deal with yet, not with this family I was only just getting to know.

'Mum!' Dan's face lit up as he entered the kitchen. Kissing her first, he then came to kiss me.

'Yeuch. You're all sweaty.' I pulled away. 'I take it you had a good workout today.'

'Yup. I'll shower in a minute. What are you doing here, Mum?'

'I hadn't heard from you, so I thought I'd better come to see your new flat.'

'Nice, isn't it?' Dan grinned.

'It's a definite improvement on the last place.'

'That's not difficult,' I threw in, disappointed that she hadn't described my flat as something other than as an improvement.

'Men!' Linda rolled her eyes at me and again I warmed to her, loved being included in the conspiracy, even if I didn't quite believe it myself.

*   *   *

A couple of months passed, months that were, at times, difficult, at other times more wonderful than I could have imagined. I loved having someone to talk to every night, never having to go to bed and feel lonely.

But at other times I'd look at him and seethe with resentment. I hated having to watch *The Simpsons* when all I wanted to do was curl up quietly with a book; was pissed off that I seemed to be the one who had to think of what to eat for supper every night, not to mention cook it.

On the whole I would say the good times far outweighed the bad, and even though we had arguments, they blew over quickly, and were never bad enough to make either one of us question our relationship.

In late May Dan won an important television industry award for one of his programmes. He phoned me as soon as he heard and told me he'd be taking me out to Zuma for dinner, that I should dress up, that we were going out to celebrate.

I wore a classic black dress that I'd picked up in

43

the sale at Nicole Farhi, my tastes somehow having grown more sophisticated now that I was part of a couple. As a single girl I had mixed and matched, tops from Hennes, trousers from Zara, sweaters from Joseph. Now, even though we rarely went to restaurants like Zuma, we socialized more than I had ever done before. I'm not the competitive type but I often felt slightly frumpy with the girlfriends and wives of his friends, and had decided to take myself in check and start to buy better clothes. Even if they were in the sale.

Dan's friends were, for the most part, from school. Having drifted away from everyone with whom I was at school, I found it extraordinary that he still had 'his boys', as he called them. They meant everything to him. I knew very early on that if Dan and I were ever to get serious, I'd need to woo the boys just as much as I wooed Dan.

There was Simon, his pre-agreed best man, should Dan ever decide to get married. Ahem. Funny, good-looking, charming. I had no idea why Simon was still single, but Dan said he was terrible with women, and that I would discover this for myself eventually.

Tom, Rob and Cheech, whose real name was apparently Nicholas, although he'd been Cheech for so long that when I asked why he was called Cheech, Dan couldn't remember. I gathered eventually that it had something to do with various exploits at university involving a bong.

Tom and Rob were married, their wives being Lily and Anna respectively, and the other two were in desperate need of home-cooked food, so as soon as we moved in together I had the boys over for supper on Friday, which soon became a weekly

44

tradition. Each week I'd do a roast, complete with potatoes, vegetables, gravy and bread sauce, and I always made sure I had a pudding reminiscent of their days at boarding school: spotted dick, apple pie and custard, treacle sponge. I made sure I traversed their stomachs on the way to their hearts, and it worked.

Dan had told me, after the first Friday night, that all four boys agreed I was 'a keeper'. This was apparently the highest praise a girl could get, and I was, in fact, the first girl on whom all four had agreed. I was so happy I hardly slept.

Luckily the two wives were lovely, if not perhaps the friends I would have chosen for myself, but as soon as I'd kitted myself out in suitably fashionable clothes, I felt almost as if I'd been part of the gang for ever.

*   *   *

We'd arranged to meet at Zuma, Dan coming straight from a late editorial meeting at work. I felt perfect in my dress, trendy yet elegant in my new Jimmy Choo heels, as I followed the maître d' to the table, ordering my usual non-alcoholic drink while I waited for Dan to arrive.

'I'm so sorry I'm late.' He swept in a few minutes later, leaning over the table to give me a quick kiss. 'You look lovely,' he said, and I smiled as he took the wine list handed to him by the waiter and read through it, pretending to look as if he knew what he was doing.

'What do you recommend?' he asked the sommelier after we had ordered our food, and nodded sagely when a 1996 Château Beychevelle

45

was suggested, as if that were precisely the wine Dan would have ordered himself.

'Do you think we would have got kicked out if we'd ordered a half of house red?' I whispered.

'Something tells me this isn't the kind of place where you can order a half bottle of plonk.' Dan grinned. 'Not that I'm complaining.'

'Me neither.' I smiled, thinking how lovely it was to be this spoilt. 'So, tell me about your day.'

*   *   *

We talked, and laughed, and filled one another in on the events of the day, spoke about our future, shared our separate dreams of what our future together might hold, and were delighted to find we were in agreement: a house with a big garden, no more than two children, and perhaps, at some point, if we made enough money, a second home in the country, or maybe even France. A dog would be good, we agreed, but nothing too big, not for London living. I wanted a West Highland Terrier, but Dan said those were dogs for girls, and he'd have to have, at the very least, a small Labrador.

Desserts came and went, and then creamy lattes, at which point Dan's face suddenly became serious.

'What's the matter?' I watched as the colour drained out of his face and he turned a paler shade of green. 'Are you okay? Oh, God. Is it something you ate? What is it, Dan? Talk to me.'

Dan cleared his throat and reached over the table for my hand, and I knew. I swear to God that as soon as I heard him clear his throat I knew what was coming, and I'm sure I stopped breathing for a few minutes, and when he started his rehearsed speech about how he had always wanted to get married but didn't think he'd ever find the right girl, my heart was beating so loudly I could hardly hear him.

Of course I said yes.

5

We took a taxi home, kissing and cuddling on the back seat as I held up my hand to examine the engagement ring. It felt so odd, wearing a ring on that finger, a ring so beautiful that I wanted to flash my hand at everyone we passed.

Dan hadn't done anything as obvious as stop at a jewellery shop and ask me which ring I liked, but he'd remembered one time when I was flicking through a magazine and had pointed out a ring that was absolutely stunning.

'I can't believe you remembered!' I kept saying, holding my hand in front of my face and watching the diamond flash in the sparkle of the street lamps. 'I can't believe you did this.'

'I wanted to surprise you,' Dan said, kissing my right ear, 'and I thought that it wouldn't be the same if you didn't have the ring.'

'You're right. It probably wouldn't have felt real. Oh, my God!' I squealed as I flung my arms around him. 'We're getting married!'

*   *   *

As we walked into my flat the phone was ringing. I picked it up to hear Linda on the other end of the line.

'Well?' she trilled happily as I looked suspiciously over at Dan.

'Well?' I threw back at her.

'Well, do I have another daughter in my family?'

I smiled. 'Yes, Linda. You do.'

Linda shrieked and called Michael over to the phone.

'Congratulations, Ellie,' Michael said warmly. 'Wonderful news, and I know the two of you will be very happy together.'

And then Linda was back on the phone. 'I'm so excited!' she said. 'I can't wait to start planning the wedding. Oh, my goodness, when is the big day?'

'I have no idea,' I laughed. 'We haven't even talked about it.' Even as I spoke I was thinking, what are you talking about, *you're* planning the wedding? This is my wedding, and I'm thirty-three years old, and the Marketing Director of Calden. If I can't plan my own wedding, then what the hell would be the point?

'What about winter?' Linda said. 'I know it's only seven months or so until December, but I *adore* winter weddings. *So* smart! You could have beautiful wine-red roses for the flowers, and we'd have more than enough time to get everything done.'

'Dan and I will have to talk about it,' I said. 'But I'm sure you'll be the first to know when we come up with a date.' I didn't bother saying thanks for your offer of help but I'm sure we'll be fine, although I made a mental note to say it at some point in the near future.

'Oh, I know, I know, it's none of my business, it's just that I've waited so many years to make a

48

wedding for Emma, and obviously I haven't been able to, and now I can do this for you.'

'I know.' I suppressed a pang of guilt—she was only trying to be nice after all, and really, shouldn't I be more grateful that she is this excited? 'I understand completely. Dan's right here, talk to him,' and I handed the phone over to Dan and hovered until he said goodbye.

'Dan,' I said slowly when he put the phone down, 'did your parents know you were going to propose?'

He looked sheepish. 'My dad didn't but my mum was in on it.'

'Oh.' I felt strange that I hadn't been the first to know, almost as if Dan had put his mother first, as ridiculous as that sounds. I know that mothers and sons have special relationships, but I was the most important woman in his life now, and in telling his mother first he'd placed her back on top, and that bothered me. No matter how I looked at it, it bothered me, but I knew that if I said my thoughts out loud, Dan would think it ridiculous. It probably was ridiculous, but I couldn't help feeling that my bubble had been somehow deflated.

'I'm sorry,' Dan said, 'I wanted to surprise everyone too, but I needed my mum's jeweller to make the ring, so I had to tell her.'

'Oh, okay. I understand, it was just weird, hearing the phone ring as soon as we walked in and then your mum obviously knowing.'

Dan placed a solemn hand on heart. 'I swear that if we ever get engaged again I promise I will tell no one else before you. How does that sound?'

'Ridiculous,' but his words had the desired effect. I grinned and allowed myself to be swept up

49

in a hug.

'Good. Now let's phone everyone else.'

*   *   *

Dan phoned Richard first, then Emma, and then the boys. He passed the phone to me each time so that they could congratulate me, and then handed the phone over so I could phone my friends. Not that I really had people to phone. I'd become so used to work taking over my life; I never thought it strange that I didn't seem to have friends outside of work. But, in the event, I called Sally, my closest friend from the office, and Fran, the PR for Calden, who I knew would be thrilled.

I hesitated over phoning my father. We had only spoken twice over the last year, and both times had been awkward. He'd invited me to Potters Bar for lunch, but I'd been busy and there really didn't seem to be much to say. Both times the conversation had dwindled down to 'So what else is new?' and neither of us had anything else to talk about. But he is my father, and however awkward things may be between us now, from time to time I think back to my childhood, to how much I adored him, to how he was my knight in shining armour. When my mother was 'ill', as we used to call it, my father would always be there to look after me. He was the one who turned up to watch our gawky, amateur plays in junior school. He was the one who came in to see my teachers whenever there was a problem, and when I was ill he was the one who would spoon me medicine and soothe my brow. I try not to think of those times too much. The loss of my mother was bad enough, but when I think of

50

the father I lost, the father I knew from my childhood, the pain becomes almost too much to bear. I can barely reconcile that father with the father I speak to occasionally today, and so I rarely do. I rarely think about the past, yet that is where our few conversations so often go, because a shared history, after all, is the only thing we now have in common.

I took the coward's way out. I did phone, but not until the next morning, when I knew he'd be at work, and Mary would be ferrying the kids to school. I left a message on his answer machine and said I hoped I'd see him soon, and that he could call me at work, where I could screen my calls or tell an assistant I was in a meeting.

Still. I did the right thing.

*　　　*　　　*

Everyone makes a huge fuss of me at work. Women I hardly know fuss and coo over my engagement ring, everyone wants to hear how he did it, was it on bended knee (no), and when would we actually tie the knot.

At lunchtime Fran and Sally insist on buying me champagne, although, as we all joke, it will be on expenses.

'Just think,' Sally says, looking around the bar, 'this is where you first met.'

'I know.' Fran grins. 'That means there's hope for you yet.'

Sally is the quintessential serial dater, whereas Fran has been married to Marcus for five years. They have two children, Annabel and Sadie, live in a house in Notting Hill that is the envy of all her

51

friends, and Fran has a reputation as one of the hottest PRs in town.

She's also terrifying—at least when you first meet her. Frighteningly trendy, sporting the latest designer clothes; at our first meeting, when she was supposed to be pitching for our business, I felt like the little match-girl in comparison. But the more I get to know her, the more I like her. In truth, she isn't a woman's woman, but when she decides she likes you, she'll do anything for you. She teases me regularly about my lack of social life, my church-mouse tendencies, as she calls them, and even though I don't see her often outside work—her 'real life' seems to revolve primarily around her children—I love our frequent lunches and drinks.

Sally, who usually accompanies us on aforementioned lunches and drinks, has spent many hours asking Fran whether she can find her a man like Marcus, and Fran has on occasion fixed her up, but it never works out. Sally is still waiting for someone to sweep her off her feet. She believes that unless she hears violins playing at the moment that he kisses her, then he is not her soulmate. She has the most spectacular, wonderful, romantic romances, but as soon as she realizes her latest man is in fact human after all, the bubble bursts and she decides it cannot possibly be True Love.

'Still,' Sally says, shaking her head. 'I can't believe you met the man you're going to marry here.'

'Are you kidding me?' I start to laugh. 'You're the one who's always saying that this is your dream job precisely because the most gorgeous men in London are right here, on your doorstep.'

'Well, I know that,' Sally says, 'and gorgeous they

most definitely are.' We all pause and look around the room, noting the significant number of beautiful people scattered around the Calden bar. 'But marrying material? I think not.'

'You think wrong,' Fran says, ordering another bottle of champagne. 'I think what you're trying to say is that the men *you* choose aren't the marrying kind. Clearly it's not *where* you pick 'em, it's the *men* that you pick.'

'I think I do a pretty good job,' Sally sniffs. 'What about Alex? Both of you thought he was lovely.'

'He was,' I agreed. 'You were the one who said you couldn't stand his constant stream of jokes. Frankly I thought he was a bloody good catch. And, let's face it, he adored you.'

'She's right,' Fran says, nodding. 'Alex was great.'

'That's just because you didn't have to listen to him snorting with laughter all the time. God, he drove me mad.'

'They *all* drive you mad,' Fran says. 'You've got to lower your expectations or you'll end up as a mad old spinster.'

'But you didn't lower yours,' Sally says. 'And neither did you, did you, Ellie?'

'Okay, perhaps I didn't lower my expectations,' Fran says, 'but there are things about Marcus that drive me mad, that have always driven me mad, but I wouldn't walk out on him as a result.'

Sally and I are instantly intrigued. 'Things like what?' asks Sally.

'Okay.' Fran orders skim lattes all round. 'Things like he poos with the bathroom door open, and expects me to come in and chat to him while he's doing it.'

'Urgh,' Sally and I chorus in unison, Sally never having reached the stage in a relationship where she could ever envisage such a thing, and me still being vaguely prudish about bathroom habits.

'Exactly. You're right. As I keep saying to Marcus, it's not clever and it's not funny, and sometimes it drives me insane, but I love him so I have to accept it.'

'You would *definitely* dump someone over that,' I say, looking at Sally pointedly.

'Bloody right,' she says in horror. 'Dumping in public deserves to be dumped. So what else does he do?' She leans forward with an evil grin. I do the same.

Fran sighs. 'Sally, you're pathetic, do you know that?'

'How else am I supposed to learn what I should and shouldn't put up with unless an old married woman like you tells me?'

'Okay. He farts in bed.'

'Silent and violent?' I offer.

'Not even. Loud and revolting. I swear to God, my husband's bottom is the deadliest weapon this country possesses.'

Sally starts shaking her head. 'Sorry, but I don't think you should have to put up with that. That's disgusting.'

'Well, I know you wouldn't put up with it,' Fran laughs. 'That's part of your problem. Marcus isn't superman, he's human. He does disgusting things just like everyone else, and marriage isn't the romantic happy ending you seem to think it is.'

Sally turns to me. 'Are you sure you want to get married? Just think, Dan seems like the perfect man now, but a few months down the road and

54

he'll be picking his nose and scraping it on the pillows.'

'But he does that already,' I say innocently, as Sally widens her eyes in horror. 'God, Sally.' I smack her arm playfully. 'You are so bloody gullible. Anyway, I agree with Fran. You do get rid of them the minute they do something you don't like.'

'Just because you've both ended up with smelly dirty men doesn't mean I have to.'

'True.' Fran shrugs. 'You could always become a lesbian.'

'I could, but it would be a shame to let so many men go to waste.'

Fran turns to me. 'So, newly engaged Ellie with that ever-so-sparkly rock on her finger. How does it feel to be engaged, and what kind of a wedding do you think you're going to have?'

I laugh. 'Give me a chance, I've been engaged less than twelve hours. Ask me again next week and I should have a better idea. As for what kind of wedding, my future mother-in-law has already said her preference is a winter wedding—'

'No!' Sally interjects, looking horrified. 'Tell her it's none of her business.'

'I wouldn't do that,' I say with a smile. 'Anyway she's really nice, and I actually think we're going to be good friends.'

And Fran laughs so hard she sprays latte all over the table. 'Oh, God, I'm sorry.' She wipes her eyes, then reaches over to pat my hand. 'You're just such an innocent sometimes.'

'Why? Because I actually like my future mother-in-law?'

'Everyone likes their future mother-in-law,' Fran

states firmly. 'The hatred only sets in once you become married.'

'But you don't hate your mother-in-law,' Sally says. 'I thought you got on really well.'

'I don't hate her now, but I would say we tolerate one another at best. Frankly it's much easier when we don't have much to do with one another.'

'But why?' I'm truly confused. 'I've never understood the whole mother-in-law thing. Why does there have to be animosity? Why can't you get on?'

'Why is the sky blue?' Fran shrugs. 'Why is grass green? Some things just *are*.'

I shake my head. 'I know that you don't get on with yours, but it's different for me.'

Fran raises an eyebrow.

'No, really, it is. Remember I don't have a mother. I haven't had a mother since I was thirteen. I've dreamt of marrying into a family exactly like this for almost twenty years. And you know what, Linda is lovely, and she's welcomed me into her family. I can't imagine ever having a problem with her.'

'And it doesn't bother you that she felt the need to express that she has a preference for *your* wedding?' Fran pushes.

'I think she was just trying to help. And to be honest I wouldn't mind a winter wedding myself.'

'Couldn't agree more,' Sally says. 'Spring weddings are just so *done*. Winter weddings can be lovely, so smart. Log fires, rich reds and purples, candlelight.' She disappears off into a reverie.

'I take it you're going to be using Sally,' Fran laughs, knowing that Sally excels in her role as Events Organizer at Calden, and has already put together two of the most spectacular celebrity weddings of the year.

Sally snaps out of her dream. 'I'd love to do your wedding,' she says eagerly. 'I haven't done a friend's wedding in ages. And we'd have so much fun.'

'No crystal thrones and white doves, then?' I warn, referring to the last wedding she did that featured in every newspaper in the country, not least because of its huge cost and lack of taste.

'How many times do I have to tell you those thrones weren't my idea?' she says. 'I kept telling them it was a bit over the top, but ultimately they were paying my bill.'

'Let me talk to Dan about it,' I say. 'We've only been engaged a minute and I feel overwhelmed already. But thank you for offering. I appreciate it hugely and I know you'd do a wonderful job. I'll let you know, is that okay?'

'Of course,' Sally says. 'I'm sorry, I didn't mean to push, and I know how overwhelming it is. So,' she says, leaning forward eagerly, 'do you know what kind of a dress you're going to have?'

*　　*　　*

'How's your day at work?' Dan says when he rings me later that afternoon.

'I'm completely champagned out,' I laugh, already battling a headache from drinking far too much in the middle of the day. 'Yours?'

'I'm beered out,' he says. 'Taken out for celebratory drinks at lunchtime.'

'Does that mean we can have an early night tonight?'

'Absolutely. My parents said they wanted to pop in quickly just to congratulate us in person, but other than that I think take-away, TV and bed.'

'Great minds think alike. Now I know why I agreed to marry you.'

*   *   *

'Dan!' Linda flings her arms around him as Michael smiles at me warmly and gives me an awkward hug. 'Congratulations,' he says into my ear before pulling away. 'I couldn't be more delighted for you.'

'Ellie!' Linda turns to me, and, as she puts her arms around me, I think how wrong Fran is, how lucky I am to have someone like Linda, and how I could never possibly hate her, no matter what she does.

'We've brought champagne,' Michael says, as Dan and I exchange looks, neither of us saying a word.

'Do you have champagne flutes?' Linda and Michael disappear into the kitchen while I shake my head at Dan.

'We have wine glasses,' he says, looking at me for confirmation. I nod.

'Oh, well, at least we'll be able to tell people what to buy you for an engagement present,' Linda laughs.

Engagement presents? What engagement presents? What on earth is she talking about? Wedding presents I expect, of course, but I'd never heard of engagement presents.

I look at Dan, who shrugs. Clearly he doesn't know either.

Linda and Michael walk back in with four wine glasses and the open champagne bottle. They pour and hand out the glasses, and we all raise them in a toast.

'To Dan and Ellie,' Michael says, as we smile and I pretend to sip, although the very smell of the stuff is turning my stomach ever so slightly.

'Now, there's something your father and I want to discuss with you.' She looks first at Dan, and then at me. 'I know that traditionally the bride's family pays for the wedding . . .' I keep a straight face because we are after all living at the beginning of the twenty-first century, not in the 1960s, and to be honest I'd presumed that, my own family circumstances notwithstanding, Dan and I would pay for the wedding ourselves.

'. . . but your father and I have sat down and talked about it and we would like to pay for the wedding. No, I don't want to hear anything different. We know that you'll want to move out of this tiny flat and get somewhere bigger, so you should be saving your money for that. We won't take no for an answer,' she finishes triumphantly.

Dan looks at me to gauge my reaction. I look back at him to try to gauge his.

'Um, thank you,' he falters nervously before I leap in to save him.

'Thank you!' I go over to each and give them a kiss. 'That's the most wonderful gift you could have given us. You're absolutely right about our wanting to move, and this is the best start for our married life. I can't believe your generosity.'

Linda looks thrilled. 'Wonderful.' She claps her hands together. 'Oh my goodness, so much to do, I hardly know where to start. We did agree on a winter wedding, didn't we, Ellie?'

I swallow while nodding my head. She is paying for my entire wedding—what right do I have to request anything she might disagree with? And anyway, Sally did say spring weddings were *done*, and I'm sure it will be lovely.

'We'll have to start making lists,' she continues. 'There's the venue, the caterers, the flowers, oh I hear wonderful things about Absolute these days. Oh, and the church. Maybe I should call tomorrow. Let's see. Claridges would be lovely if they're free, the Connaught's too small, maybe the Mandarin Oriental. Or we could do Searcy's.' It is as if someone has pressed the play button and off she goes. Linda keeps talking as I watch her in amazement and Dan shrugs.

Nothing that she's talking about makes sense to me. I didn't think Dan and I were Claridges types. I was thinking more about a small wedding at a register office somewhere, then perhaps a reception at Calden, but Linda hasn't stopped muttering to herself, and I figure I'll let her enjoy her dream a little while longer.

Plenty of time to tell her it's not what we want, that our wedding will be small, that, much as we appreciate their paying for the wedding, it is Dan and I, after all, who are getting married, and that they will have to respect our wishes.

Plenty of time for that.

6

Tom told Dan that planning a wedding was like rolling a tiny snowball down a mountain. The further along it went the bigger it got until it was completely out of control, and the very best thing Dan could possibly do was stay well out of its way.

And that's not even taking into account the additional hassle and stress of trying to buy a new flat. I love my flat, but we've decided to start afresh with somewhere new, somewhere that's *ours*. So I've been trying to keep my flat immaculate for viewings—not an easy task, let me tell you—and leafing through pages and pages of estate agents' details, trying to find time on Saturday mornings to fit in all the viewings.

Three months after getting engaged I have to say I understood exactly what Tom meant.

'That's why people use someone like me,' Sally huffed, when I confessed how I was feeling. She had finally forgiven me for not using her, but that was only because Linda seemed to have everything in hand and didn't feel a wedding planner was necessary.

'Darling, if you feel that strongly about it we can always pay for the wedding ourselves, and then you can do exactly what you want,' Dan would say, every time I brought up how little the wedding had to do with us, with me.

'No, I'm not saying that,' I always said, because the costs also seemed to be spiralling out of control, and now that the hotel had been booked, the menus chosen, and the flowers decided, I didn't want to start again from scratch.

And I felt unable to argue with Linda. Her personality was so forceful, that when she'd made a decision, nobody ever seemed to argue with her. Except of course Emma, which was clearly why they didn't get on.

I'd seen Linda and Emma have some terrifying rows—terrifying because I hated confrontation, because I'd always thought that rowing like that would inevitably lead to abandonment. But a day or so later everything always blew over and they were back to being, if not friends, then mother and daughter.

I loved Emma. One of the joys of marrying Dan was having a ready-made brother and sister, and Dan was so close to them, I suppose it was inevitable that I would be too.

In Emma I found the sister I had always wanted, the best friend I never knew I missed until I met her. I loved how nothing scared her, how everything in life was an adventure, how she never seemed to worry about anything and took pleasure in everything.

Initially I'd just see her on Sundays at Dan's parents', but then she'd call to speak to Dan and we'd end up chatting for a bit, and after a while she'd pop in on the weekends, and the more I got to know her the more comfortable I was with her.

We'd meet for lunch at Calden, or one of the neighbouring cafés on Marylebone High Street, and she'd fill me in on her glamorous lifestyle and latest men while I tried my best not to be too envious. It wasn't as if I'd given up a similar lifestyle once I met Dan, more that the possibility was gone: I'd never have the opportunity to go clubbing with the hottest name in pop music, or sleep with the man *Cosmopolitan* had recently called one of the ten most eligible bachelors in the UK.

Not that I'd ever wanted that. Should I have chosen, I could have hung out in Calden every night, mixing with the stars Emma talked about, the stars you read about in the gossip pages every morning, but even when I had the opportunity I was more interested in having early nights so I could be up early, ready for work the next morning.

I was invited to a school reunion a few years ago and for weeks I seriously thought about going. I was curious to see what my classmates were up to, and yet still felt that not enough time had gone by, knew that as soon as we stepped into the Great Hall we'd instantly revert to the bitchiness and cliquishness of all sixteen-year-old girls.

But mostly I thought about how surprised they would be to see me, to see how I'd turned out. I imagine they would expect me to be more like Emma: a party girl, someone unwilling, or unable, to settle down.

I didn't go. The thrill of finding out whether they had changed, what they now looked like, didn't outweigh my fear that they would be disappointed, or surprised, by me.

Sometimes I surprise myself, but I have only ever craved those coke-fuelled nights and one-night-stands since meeting Dan, and even then I know it's just because the grass is always greener, because Emma's life sounds so fantastic, although I'm sure it wouldn't make me happy.

* * *

Emma phones one Thursday morning around eleven thirty. 'Hi, Ellie, it's me. I've just finished gathering clothes in Portland Street and I'm starving. Do you want to have lunch?'

'Definitely.' I look at the Pret A Manger sandwich and Diet Coke sitting on my desk, and decide I could do with a break from the office. 'Do you want to come here?'

'Would you mind if we met out? I've got a craving for sushi.'

'Sure.' This is yet another of the things I love about Emma. She doesn't ever say, 'Oh, I don't mind. Where do you want to go?' Just like her mother, she has an opinion on everything, which would bother me more perhaps if she were taking over my wedding, but as it stands it is just another quality of hers that makes me love her.

We meet at a Japanese café a few doors down, and I arrive to find that Emma has bagged one of the few tables in there, platters of sushi already on the table.

'I couldn't wait,' she says after giving me a hug. 'Is this okay? Do you want to get anything else?'

'No, this is fine. Just tell me there's no eel.'

'Nope, no eel. You're safe. So, how's the wedding of the century coming along?' She grins.

'How would I know?' I shrug. 'It's your mother's wedding.'

Emma starts laughing. 'Now you know why I'm never going to get married.'

'No, you can still get married.' I pick up a California roll. 'Just elope and do it on your own terms.'

'Hmm. Not a bad idea. Maybe we could fly away

64

to a Caribbean island and do it on a beach.'

'Emma Cooper! Don't tell me you've never done it on a beach.' I feign shock at the double entendre.

Emma laughs. 'Of course I've done it on a beach. Sandy and very Overrated. I just haven't done *that* on a beach. But there is something wonderfully romantic about getting married by the water's edge.'

'Just as long as you don't go somewhere where you're the eighth wedding of the day.'

'Like Sandals,' we both say at the same time. And laugh.

'So is she driving you mad?' A slight pause, but we both know who she's talking about.

'Not mad. Just ever so slightly insane.'

'I have to tell you, she's my mother, I never had a choice, but you could get out. Seriously, it's not too late.'

'I know,' I groan. 'But then there is Dan, and I know you may not believe this, given that he's your big brother, but I do actually love him.'

'But are you in love with him?'

'Of course. Why else would I be marrying him?'

'I see.' She nods gravely. 'That is something of a problem, then. I guess you'll just have to learn to live with her like the rest of us.'

'I know, but that's part of the problem. The rest of you are her children: you can stand up to her, or have those huge rows because you know you're still going to love one another when it's all over. You're still family.'

'And you're just too damn nice,' Emma says. 'You're terrified she's going to hate you if you tell her that actually you don't want topiary trees all over the ballroom.'

65

'Exactly! So you heard about the topiary trees?'

'Yup. Ridiculous. Completely over the top. Just like my mother.'

'This so isn't the wedding I want. Can't *you* say something to her?' I plead.

'I've got enough arguments of my own with her. I'm afraid it's up to you. But if you do want my advice, I'd have to say don't be such a people-pleaser. You are, after all, the mother of her future grandchildren. She has to be nice to you, and even if you piss her off, she'll get over it. You'd be far better off if you stood up to her from time to time.'

I don't say anything. There's no need because of course she is absolutely right.

'So what does Dan say about all of it?' Emma asks. 'I don't suppose he sticks up for you?'

'Poor Dan. I think he's in an impossible situation. He *says* he agrees with me, but when push comes to shove he won't actually do anything.'

'Yup, that's my brother,' Emma says.

'I'm serious. He just runs away. He keeps saying he won't be put in the middle, and that if I have a problem I have to resolve it directly with her, but as far as I'm concerned he's my future husband and he should be defending me.'

Emma peers at me through her chopsticks. 'If I were you, I'd want to hit him.'

I laugh. 'I very often do. Not actually hit him, but think about it.'

'You know of course that Dan and my mother have a special relationship.'

'Please don't tell me anything disgusting,' I say slowly.

'Oh, God, nothing like that, but I swear to God there is a serious problem with Dan.'

'You mean she's in love with him?'

'I mean he can do absolutely no wrong in her eyes, and even though I couldn't say the feeling was completely reciprocated, I do know he loves his position, and he probably wouldn't do anything to rock the boat.'

'In other words your family is as fucked up as mine, and I should really be thinking twice before marrying into it?'

'Basically.' Emma shrugs, then laughs when she sees the look of horror on my face. 'Ellie, don't be worried. My family's no more dysfunctional than any other family I know, and actually I think we're all doing pretty well, all things considered. Trust me, you could have done a lot worse. Anyway, we have to find a way of getting rid of the topiary trees.'

I groan. 'Please don't remind me.'

'And can you take a longer lunch break? I'm dying to look at the cashmere in Brora.'

Off we went, up and down Marylebone High Street on this cold, crisp September day. Into Brora. And Agnès b. And Rachel Riley. Emma ended up with three shopping bags, and I ended up with nothing.

'By the way, your mum is insisting on taking me wedding dress shopping,' I say, as we finally pause outside Calden to say goodbye.

'I know. And, much as I love the idea of being your bridesmaid, please don't walk down the aisle in a cream puff.'

'I'll do my best.' I make a face and then brighten with an idea. 'Hey! Why don't you come with? I'm hopeless at sticking up for myself with your mother around, but you could do it for me.'

67

Emma thinks about it. 'When are you going?'

'Saturday. She's got a load of places in the West End and then a couple of places in North London.'

'Okay,' Emma says. 'I'll come and protect you, but in return I want a favour myself.'

'Anything.'

'Put me in peach or lilac and I swear to God I'll never stick up for you again.'

'Sounds like a deal to me.'

*   *   *

Every time Linda winds me up to the point that I'm dreading seeing her, she does something so unexpected, so lovely, that I forgive her completely and always end up hurt and surprised when she manages to upset me again.

On Saturday morning she comes to pick me up, and, climbing into the car, I almost crush a small box sitting in the middle of the passenger seat.

I pick it up and place it on the dashboard, but Linda says, 'Ellie, that's for you.'

'For me? But why? It's not my birthday.'

Linda smiles. 'I know, but you are engaged, and I kept meaning to give these to you but I was . . . oh, I'll tell you when you open them. Open them now and then we'll go to pick up Emma.'

I open the box to find an incredible pair of diamond flower earrings nestling inside, the most beautiful, delicate earrings imaginable, and immediately I start shaking.

'Oh, my God,' I keep repeating. 'Linda, these are beautiful. I can't accept these.'

Linda looks thrilled. 'You can and you will,' she says. 'They belonged to my mother, then I wore them to my own wedding and now I want you to have them and wear them to yours.'

'But I can't accept them. You have to save them for Emma.' I try to hand the box to Linda, but she shakes her head. 'No, Ellie. I always said that they would go to the first one in the family to get married, and Dan is the first, and you're now part of our family.'

'But Emma would be devastated,' I splutter, although I'm not sure it's true, Emma being the kind of girl who is likely to get married on a beach in the Caribbean, doubtless in a bikini with brightly coloured crystal earrings. If, that is, she gets married at all.

Linda smiles. 'First of all, my darling daughter doesn't look as if she's going to be getting married any time in the near future. Second, said darling daughter doesn't know about these earrings—'

'But that doesn't mean I should have them,' I interrupt as Linda holds up a hand to stop me.

'Third,' Linda says triumphantly, 'I have a beautiful diamond necklace that is far more Emma's style, and if, please God, the day ever comes that my daughter gets married, she will have the diamond necklace.'

I open the box and look at the earrings again: small solitaire centres with marquise-shaped petals, forming a perfect daisy. 'Are you sure?' I whisper, never having seen anything this beautiful outside the window of Cartier. 'Are you really sure?'

'I'm really sure,' Linda says, and her delight in giving me this wonderful gift is almost palpable. 'But maybe you shouldn't say anything to Emma just yet.'

'Linda, I don't know what to say.' I give her an

69

awkward hug. 'This is the most incredible present I've ever had in my life.'

* * *

Emma climbs in the back and leans forward to give first her mother, then me, a kiss on the cheek.

'So what's new?' she says to the air, as I shoot a nervous glance at Linda, then flush a bright, hot red.

With memories of Basil Fawlty dancing in my mind, I clench my teeth and think, Don't mention the diamonds. Don't mention the diamonds.

'Not much, darling,' Linda says. 'How about you?'

'Not much,' Emma says. 'But are we going to be anywhere in Knightsbridge? I've got a pair of shoes on hold in Harvey Nichs. It won't take a minute.'

My flush, thankfully, fades, and I turn to Emma. 'Another pair of shoes?' I ask, knowing that she bought a pair of Prada sandals earlier in the week.

'They're in the sale. So it doesn't count. Both pairs combined cost the same as one pair. Honestly, it would have been rude not to buy them.'

'You and Richard,' Linda sighs. 'You're both hopeless with money.'

'Yes, Mummy.' Emma rolls her eyes. 'Where is that necklace from again?'

Linda reaches up and smoothes her fingers over her Bvlgari necklace. 'That's different,' she says. 'I'm a lot older than you and I can afford it.'

'You mean Dad can afford it,' Emma protests.

'I mean *we* can afford it. Since when were you earning enough to buy all these designer clothes?'

70

'Since I started staying with friends and using my money for the important things in life.'

Linda sighs. 'Are you ever going to grow up, Emma?' And Emma just laughs.

'Not if I can possibly help it.'

*   *   *

'Seriously,' I whisper in the changing room of the second bridal gown place, while Emma's helping zip me in and Linda's outside acting like the Queen, sipping cappuccino and chatting away to the sales assistants, 'how do you afford all your designer gear?'

Emma laughs. 'Being a freelance stylist isn't nearly as lowly or low-paid as my mother seems to think. Plus I get huge discounts. And half of the clothes my mum thinks are designer are knock-offs from Portobello for a couple of quid.'

I look suspiciously at her Pucci shirt. 'Not Pucci, then?'

'Fucci, more like,' she laughs. 'If you've got the shoes and the bag, everyone will assume everything else is real.'

'Blimey. I'm impressed.'

'Now you know why I'm such a good stylist.' She winks as she turns to look at the right side of the changing room. 'I thought you said no cream puffs? Why are we even bothering in here?' She gestures at the five dresses adorning the walls in the oversized changing room. All five are huge, white and meringue-like.

'It keeps your mum happy,' I say, obviously not telling her why it's so important to keep Linda happy, how this is the least I can do after she gave

71

me such a generous and thoughtful gift.

Emma winces and says, 'Forgive me for saying this, but they all make you look like a house.'

I turn and put my hands on my hips, looking her sternly in the eye. 'Good job you're going to be family, Emma. If a friend said that to me, I'd chuck them.'

'Well, that explains why you haven't got any friends,' Emma ribs me, not knowing how close to the truth she is. 'Okay, I take it back, but don't you think you'd be far more beautiful in something simple and elegant?'

'Of course.' I shrug. 'But your mum needs to see how disgusting I can look before she appreciates the plain Grecian column.'

'Ah, I see,' Emma nods. 'Clever plan. Now why didn't I think of that?'

*   *   *

Four bridal shops later even Linda is starting to lose her enthusiasm. I don't help matters by putting on each meringue, walking out of the dressing room to show her and deliberately hunching my shoulders and pushing my stomach out so that I look as awful as I can.

'I never realized you had such bad posture,' she said at one point. 'You must learn to put your shoulders back, Ellie.'

Finally I spy the perfect dress. Close-fitting, bell sleeves, silk and chiffon, dreamily simple. I nudge Emma, who goes to have a closer look.

'Mum,' Emma says, bringing the dress over, 'what about this one?'

'It's a bit . . . nothing, isn't it?' Linda looks

disdainfully at the dress, which is, quite honestly, my idea of heaven.

'It's just that she's tried on big dress after big dress. It might be nice to see Ellie in something a bit different. Just for comparison.'

'Ellie?' Linda still looks doubtful. 'Do you want to try this on?'

'Sure,' I say, doing a silent scream of laughter with Emma the minute the curtain is drawn.

'Wow,' Emma says, as she looks at my reflection in the mirror.

'Wow,' I echo, wondering how it is that I never realized I was this beautiful, this thin, this elegant. The dress hides all my worst features and brings out all my best.

I open the curtain and glide, swan-like, shoulders back, into the shop, where Linda puts down her coffee cup open-mouthed.

'Now that's more like it,' she says, smiling for the first time in two and a half hours. 'Ellie, you look like a princess.'

'You're sure you don't want her to try on another fifty cream puffs?' Emma has an evil glint in her eye.

'Oh, do be quiet. How do you feel, Ellie? Do you love it?'

'Love it? It's the most beautiful thing I've ever worn in my whole life.'

'Then that's it,' Linda says. 'That's your dress. I knew we should have gone with something simple in the first place.' Emma and I try not to laugh.

Diamond earrings, I tell myself. Don't piss her off now.

*   *   *

'Well?' Dan rings on the mobile while we're in the car going home.

'Well, we found it,' I say, smiling. 'The most beautiful dress you've ever seen.'

'Don't tell him,' Linda screeches loudly next to me. 'Don't tell him a thing about it.'

As if I was going to. 'Clearly,' I say, 'I'm not allowed to tell you anything about it.'

'But did you have fun?' he says, anxious that Linda and I should be best friends again, that I won't be coming home to bitch or moan, that he won't have to listen to me say anything derogatory about his mother.

'We had a great time,' I say, and it's true. We did. I felt like a normal woman, having a fun shopping day with her mother and sister. Well, almost. But I did feel like I belonged, and that was the greatest feeling in the world.

7

We've finally found the flat of our dreams, and if I thought the pressure was bad before, it's nothing compared to praying for an offer on our flat, having to reduce the price, and then finally accepting an offer and attempting to go for a simultaneous exchange.

Estate agents and lawyers are calling me all day, and I've got such anxiety about something falling through, or being gazumped, that I go into panic mode if my mobile isn't permanently clamped to my hand.

And today we're in the middle of planning the spring campaign. I've just finished giving my presentation when my mobile starts to vibrate.

I don't understand this vibrating feature. I had assumed it would be silent, unobtrusive, but the phone's practically leaping around on the table and buzzing very aggressively as our Chief Executive, Jonathan, who's talking, stops and raises an eyebrow at the phone.

'Sorry,' I mumble as I reach for the phone, expecting it to be the lawyer yet again and knowing I'll have to excuse myself for a few minutes to take his call, but, as I pick up the phone, I see Linda's name flashing on the screen.

Oh, for God's sake. And thank God for caller ID. I hit the divert button to send her straight to voicemail and apologize to everyone. Two minutes later it rings again. I divert it again.

Two minutes and three separate sets of vibrations later, my boss sighs and stops talking to look at me pointedly while I blush a deep red. 'Do you think perhaps you ought to take that call?' he says, the vibrating phone being rather more obtrusive and noisy, given the quiet conference room, than it might otherwise be.

'I'm sorry.' I turn the phone off immediately, inwardly cursing that bloody woman. 'It's not urgent and can certainly wait until this meeting is over.'

Less than five minutes later Sandy, one of the marketing assistants, pops her head round the door.

'I'm sorry to interrupt,' she says timidly, 'but there's an urgent phone call for Ellie.'

Oh, for fuck's sake. I scrape my chair back and

excuse myself, stamping over to my desk to pick up the phone, the irritation clear in my voice.

Of course it's her. The woman who doesn't know the meaning of the word patience. Who, when she wants something, wants it at the latest *now*, if not yesterday.

'Hello?' I'm trying my damnedest to be polite, to try to hide my fury because she is, after all, my future mother-in-law. And, irritating and infuriating though she may be, the last thing I want to do is alienate this woman who is not only the mother of my husband-to-be (I still can't think of the word 'fiancé' without grimacing) but is also paying for my entire wedding.

Plus I'm the quintessential people-pleaser—the result of having an alcoholic mother and having to tiptoe around and be on my best behaviour in the mistaken belief that this was the only way to keep her happy. I'm only happy when you're happy, and I may not like you, but I'm going to do everything in my power to ensure you like me.

And therein lies the madness, and the reason why I am not able to chastise my mother-in-law for embarrassing me at work, or tell her not to call me during the hours of nine to five. Make that twenty-four hours.

'Hello, Ellie,' Linda says brightly. 'How are you?'

'Fine, thank you.' My teeth are gritted and there's a long pause before I spit out, 'You?'

'Fine. Is there something wrong with your mobile? I've been trying you for ages.'

'I was in a meeting.' My voice is cold. 'You could have left a message and I would have called you straight back after the meeting.' Instead of dragging me out for something that I know is going to be ridiculous, I add. Silently of course.

'Oh, silly me,' Linda laughs. 'I thought perhaps the phone was broken, and of course if I'd known you were in a meeting I would never have disturbed you.'

I bet she knew I was in a meeting. I bet Sandy told her. 'So is everything okay?' I say finally, after an awkward silence.

'Absolutely fine. I just wondered whether you and Dan wanted to join Michael and me for supper tonight. We were thinking of trying that new Indian in the village. Around seven thirty?'

I really don't believe this. Did this woman actually pull me out of a meeting to invite us for supper? Is this the hugely important reason that she had to speak to me immediately and couldn't possibly leave a message?

'I'm sorry, Linda.' I fake an apologetic voice. 'But Dan's been shooting in the North and he's exhausted, and I've had a really tough week. I think we're just going to have an early night . . .

'But thank you,' I add quickly as an afterthought, knowing how easily offended my mother-in-law can be.

'Oh,' Linda says, a hint of my previous frostiness in her own voice. 'But I just spoke to Dan—he's on the train home, by the way—and he said it sounded fine. I was just phoning you to let you know.'

'Oh.' Great. So now she's tricking me as well. Why in hell did Dan say yes? 'Oh,' I say again, faltering. 'Okay. I'm sorry. You should have said. I mean, if Dan says it's okay, then it's okay.'

'Wonderful,' Linda says. 'Come to us at around 7.15. See you later!' And she's gone.

'Sandy?' I screech, marching over to Sandy's desk, determined not to take it out on her, but I need to vent my frustration on someone, and Sandy, unfortunately, is the closest and of course the easiest to blame.

'Uh huh?' Sandy looks up nervously from her computer.

'Did you realize that was my future mother-in-law?'

'Yes.'

'So why didn't you tell her I was in a meeting, for God's sake?'

'I did,' Sandy says. 'I told her and she said it was urgent and to get you out of your meeting.'

'Oh, for God's sake.' I shake my head as Sandy looks stricken.

'I'm so sorry,' Sandy says. 'I did try to tell her but she was . . . well, honestly, she was a bit scary.'

And I sigh and back down. What else can I do. 'No, I'm sorry. I'm just taking it out on you, and I know how scary she is. She's just got such a bloody nerve.'

Sandy shrugs and turns back to her computer, as I debate whether I have time to phone Dan and scream at him now, or whether it should wait until after the meeting.

No. I need to cool down before doing anything, and I go back to the meeting, although the first fifteen minutes go completely over my head, as I am far too busy fuming over Linda. But then the launch of Calden, Edinburgh, takes over, and by the time the meeting is over, an hour and a half later, my frustration has abated. I phone Dan as soon as I'm back at my desk, and manage not to shout or scream the way I definitely would have done an hour and a half previously, although Dan knows, the minute he picks up the phone, that something is wrong.

'What's the matter?'

'Your mother. As usual.'

'Oh, come on, Ellie.' Dan does nothing to hide his exasperation, which frankly is also starting to get me down. He's about to become my husband— isn't he supposed to be supporting me?

'Oh, come on, nothing. She dragged me out of a big meeting, saying it was urgent, then tricked me into turning down her dinner invitation tonight before telling me you'd already accepted. Thanks a lot, Dan. I wish you'd ask me before you—'

'Hang on a minute!' Dan interjects. 'I didn't accept anything. She mentioned something about dinner and I said I was exhausted and we'd probably have an early night, but that I'd have to talk to you first.'

'Well, that's just great. So she's been as manipulative as usual.'

'Oh, for God's sake,' Dan snorts, 'can't you just give it a rest? All I've been hearing for weeks now is you bitching about my mother.'

'That's because you never stand up for me. If you were to actually show some balls and defend me, or agree with me when your mother is manipulative or unreasonable, then it wouldn't wind me up as much.'

'If you're so unhappy about it, why are you bloody marrying me?' Dan snaps, no longer bothered that the entire train carriage is eagerly listening in to his row.

79

'That's a bloody good question,' I shout, and then, even though I don't mean to, even though I know it's the worst thing I can possibly do, I slam down the phone, and for a split-second, just a tiny split-second, I feel a whole lot better.

*   *   *

We meet at the flat just before six thirty. I, of course, spent the rest of the afternoon feeling horrible, hating myself for being so mean, knowing that most of it is pre-wedding stress, but this doesn't feel like much of an excuse. I feel even worse when I see how upset Dan clearly is.

I know how he feels, really I do. Weeks before, when we managed to talk about it calmly, Dan explained how he feels pulled between the two most important women in his life, and I understand that. Really I do. And I explained that I need his support, that I am, or at least should be, the most important woman in his life now, and he nodded and said he will try harder, and that it is just an adjustment.

Maybe if things were different in my own family I would understand more, I think sadly from time to time. Maybe if I were a Daddy's girl, Dan would be battling with my father. Maybe this is all par for the course, part of becoming a woman, a wife, a truly emancipated adult.

'I'm sorry,' are the first words out of my mouth as Dan walks in and dumps his duffel bag in the bedroom. 'I'm sorry for the things I said and I'm sorry for putting the phone down on you.'

And I expect Dan to do what he always does after these fiery rows: to put his arms around me,

80

to apologize in turn, but Dan doesn't say anything, just sits down on the sofa opposite me and looks at the floor, and for the first time I feel a horrible unease wash over me. Oh, God. Please don't let him say something awful. Please don't let him be having second thoughts.

'Dan, I said I was sorry,' I whisper, fear constricting my chest, making me unable to speak any louder.

'Dan? Would you just say something?'

A couple of minutes pass, and Dan raises his head and looks at me, his eyes filled with sadness.

'It's just so hard for me,' he says. 'I understand how stressful this is, and I know my mother can be overbearing, but I just can't keep hearing about how awful you think she is. She's my mother, Ellie, and whatever you think about her she's only trying to do the best for us.'

'I know—'

'No, let me finish. The thing is that, as far as I can see, my mother's going out of her way to make you feel part of the family. We're all used to spending a lot of time together, to doing things together, and all my mother wants is for you to feel included, but everything she does seems to be misinterpreted by you, and I'm just getting sick of it.'

I sit in silence. Ashamed.

'Whatever you think of her, she's not a bad woman. She loves me and she wants me to be happy, and she thinks, she *thought*'—he looks at me pointedly—'that welcoming you into our family would be the way to do it. It should be making me happy, but instead I'm just watching you get more and more wound up by this and I don't understand

81

why.'

And he's right. Of course he's right. Could I have been any more heartless? Any more horrible? How could I have jumped to these terrible conclusions when it all now seems so clear? Because Dan's rationale is so rational, and I am so obviously the bad guy in all of this.

Shame fills my body, and when Dan has finally finished speaking, the only words I can say for a while are: I'm sorry.

And then, 'I know it's not an excuse, Dan, but I think that at times I just find it overwhelming. I don't know how to handle it, having never had a family of my own.'

'But you always said that's what you wanted.'

'I know. And it's true. It's just that it's taking me longer to adjust than I'd expected. You need to give me time.' I take a deep breath. 'I haven't ever really had a mother, and I know she's trying to fill that role, but I don't know how to *be* with a mother, and even though I thought that's what I wanted, I think it's just much harder than I'd realized.'

Dan nods. 'I understand all of that,' he says finally. 'I do. And I know she can be difficult, but she's only difficult because she loves us.'

'She loves *you*,' I point out gently.

'But she's trying to love you too,' he says.

'I know.' I sigh as I catch sight of the clock in the hallway. 'Oh, shit, Dan. We're supposed to be at their house in less than five minutes.'

'No, we're not. I cancelled.'

'You did? And you're still alive?'

'Oh, ha ha. Don't push your luck. After our warm exchange on the train, I decided that dinner with them would be over-icing the cake somewhat.'

'Did she mind?'

'No, of course not. And anyway, if I wasn't exhausted before, I really am exhausted now.'

'So does that mean we get to have our early night?' I grin, a twinkle finally back in my eye.

'That would depend on what exactly qualifies as an early night,' Dan replies, beckoning for me to join him on the sofa, where he wraps an arm around me and pulls me close, making me feel safe, and warm, and loved.

'Do I take it you really have forgiven me, then?' I say, reaching up to kiss him.

'I've almost forgiven you,' he says, smiling as he pulls away. 'Why not take me to bed and make me forget all about it . . .'

*   *   *

The next day, as I'm about to leave the office, I start to feel period pains. Just slight cramps, the usual indicator that my period is on its way. And what perfect timing, because a period now would mean no period on my wedding day. I grab a Tampax from my bottom drawer and run to the loo, but there's no blood. Nothing.

So I leave, and, as I'm desperately trying to hail a black cab on Marylebone High Street—yes, I know, something of a joke during rush hour, but I'm exhausted and can't face the tube tonight—it occurs to me that it seems to have been ages since my last period.

When, in fact, *was* my last period?

A cab swings round the corner and stops, and as the person gets out and pays, I dash over and grab the door handle. Once we are on our way, sitting at the lights on Gloucester Place, a vague feeling of unease comes over me, a feeling that is neither comfortable nor familiar. I rummage around in my bag for my diary and flick back furiously to four weeks ago.

I may be completely disorganized, but my diary contains all the information I need to know, and I am pathological about marking my periods. For almost twenty years I have been meticulous in marking when they start, how long they last, and when the next one is due.

But clearly this whole run-up to the wedding and the insanity of my life has thrown me, because four weeks ago I apparently failed to mark down a period. Did I forget? Could I have forgotten? How strange—but then I've never been so busy or so distracted before, and it would be somewhat understandable . . .

I flick back more pages to the period before, which is marked. This means my next period is in two weeks' time.

But hang on. Again, that can't be right. If it's due in two weeks, then I would have had one two weeks ago and I remember exactly what we were doing two weeks ago, and I definitely didn't have my period.

Surely some mistake . . .

Half an hour later I'm in my bathroom at home, sitting on the loo, an empty Boots bag lying on its side on the floor, and I'm staring at a pregnancy test that is showing two very distinct, strong blue lines.

'Shit,' I whisper, over and over, fear and happiness and disbelief all mingling together as a smile starts to spread upon my face. 'What's Dan going to say?'

*   *   *

'Pregnant? You're pregnant?' Dan stops in his tracks and just stares at me, which wasn't quite the reaction I was hoping for.

Dan had a work dinner, so I'd spent the rest of the evening alternately surfing baby sites and dreaming about Dan sweeping me up in his arms and crying tears of happiness.

I'd only known I was pregnant for a few hours and already it had opened up a whole new world for me. I'd spent the rest of the afternoon at babyzone.com and ParentsPlace.

I now know that my due date is 30 August. I know that it's not abnormal to feel cramps in the beginning—hence my vague period pains that weren't—and that it doesn't necessarily mean a miscarriage is on the way. And I also know that it's probably best not to tell people until I'm twelve weeks and in the clear.

Then of course I just had to check out babynames. com. So far my number one choice for a boy is Flynn, and if it's a girl I love the name Tallulah, although knowing Dan he'll want something much more prosaic like Tom or Isabel.

After a while I had read everything I could, so I switched to things like which buggy is best (apparently the trendiest one right now is something called the Bugaboo Frog), whether I ought to be a Huggies or a Pampers girl, and how to decorate the dream nursery for your little prince or princess.

So much to learn! So much I never knew!

By eleven o'clock I'm still online, still surfing baby sites, but the shock finally starts to wear off and in its place is this huge excitement. Dan's been ringing all day but I haven't even been able to pick up the phone because I know I won't be able to keep it in, I'll just end up blurting it out, and I so want to tell him face to face, to see the joy and excitement in his eyes.

Dan's going to be a father! I'm going to be a mother! We're going to be *PARENTS*!

And now, finally, he is home, and I'm standing in the hallway watching my fantasies of Dan sweeping me up in his (strong, manly) arms and covering me with ecstatic kisses sail smoothly out the window.

'Yes, I'm pregnant.' My elation immediately gives way to a burst of fury, followed swiftly by the feeling that I'm about to burst into tears. Clearly the websites weren't lying when they explained what happened to your hormones.

'Aren't you happy?' My voice is starting to break.

There's a pause. 'But weren't you using something?' Dan says finally.

'Oh, Dan, for fuck's sake!' The anger takes over again. Whoops. I can only pray the next nine months aren't going to be this much of a roller coaster. 'Yes, I was using something but clearly it's not one hundred per cent effective, probably because of those bloody antibiotics, but still, that's rather beside the point. I'm pregnant, Dan, and we're getting married in four weeks and I would have thought you'd be thrilled.' By this time I'm on the verge of hysteria, and Dan, clearly realizing his mistake, finally comes out of his daze.

He attempts to put his arms around me in a conciliatory gesture (yes, I'm stiff and unwielding—

86

wouldn't you be?) and places a paternal kiss on the top of my head. 'I'm sorry, darling,' he says. 'I'm just tired and, frankly, in shock. I just hadn't expected this.'

'So you're pleased?'

'Are you?'

'I'm over the moon.' The anger disappears as quickly as it appeared, and a second later I'm hugging him and giggling uncontrollably. 'I mean, at first I was in shock, but now I can't believe it! I'm having a baby, Dan! *We're* having a baby!'

And I squeeze him and don't even mind as he laughs nervously and says, 'Of course I'm pleased. I just didn't expect it to happen quite this soon.'

Oh, bless him. He's in shock. And he's allowed to be, just as I spent the first few hours in shock. And so I lead him over to the sofa and make us both a cup of tea (Caffeine? What's the deal on caffeine? I resolve to get back on the internet just as soon as I've finished with Dan, and anyway, one cup surely won't hurt), and when I bring it in to him I sit down and cuddle up next to him, smiling indulgently at the shock so clearly etched on his face.

'I know you wanted to take glamorous, weekend trips to Europe,' I start gently, 'and I know we talked about waiting a year before trying for children but this is a blessing, and we'll still be able to do all the things we wanted to do, we'll just have someone else to do them with.'

'I know.' Dan nods, as a frown crosses his face. 'But how are we going to tell my mother?'

'Your mother?' I look at Dan in disbelief. Oh, for God's sake. I can't believe what Dan just said. 'What the hell's this got to do with your mother.'

'Oh, come on, Ellie.' Dan rolls his eyes. 'She's only paying for our entire bloody wedding. I think she has a right to know, don't you?'

'No, Dan, actually I don't. Firstly, as you well know, if there were any way possible for us to have paid for this wedding ourselves, we would have done—'

'You didn't say that at the time.'

'No, of course I didn't say that at the time. I thought she was offering to pay out of the goodness of her heart, not because she was going to take over everything.'

'She hasn't taken over everything,' Dan splutters.

'No? Correct me if I'm wrong, Dan, but many moons ago when you first proposed, didn't we talk about a quiet wedding? Something small and intimate are the words that come to mind. Didn't we say we wanted only close friends and family?'

Dan is quiet, and bloody right too. He knows he's not going to win this argument, and more to the point, he knows I know he knows. But the anger is now back and the less he says, the quieter he becomes, the more fired up I become.

'Do you honestly think I wanted three hundred people I hardly know at my wedding?' I shout. 'Do you think I wanted Chilean bloody sea bass or humongous white bloody ribbons tied around the backs of chairs?'

'Well, why didn't you say anything if you didn't like it? God knows you've had enough time.'

'Because I didn't want to seem ungrateful, and because I realized a long time ago that this was not my wedding, this was her wedding, and that the easiest thing I could do would be to give it up and let her get on with it.

'But just because she's involved in every single tiny aspect of our wedding day,' I continue, 'does not mean she has to be involved in every single tiny aspect of our lives, and this has nothing to do with her, so no, in answer to your question, we do not have to worry about how we're going to tell her because we're not going to tell her, at least not until we're back from honeymoon, and the reason we're not going to tell her until then is not because she would freak out at my being—shock horror— pregnant on my wedding day, but because this has nothing to do with her.'

'Of course it has to do with her.' Dan shakes his head. 'This is my child, her first grandchild. She has every right to know.'

'Jesus, Dan.' I shake my head in disgust. 'Do you want me to phone her every time we have sex as well? You know, just in case there's some area of our lives in which she feels left out . . .

'Oh, I'm sorry,' I continue, feeling furious and victorious at the same time, knowing that there's very little Dan can say, 'you probably already do that, don't you?'

Dan's voice turns cold. 'You can be incredibly childish, Ellie. Why don't we carry on talking about this when you remember you're an adult?'

'No, why don't we talk about it when you remember *you're* an adult, and that you don't have to go running back to Mummy for help with everything, and that Mummy doesn't have to know everything about your life.'

'You're always accusing me of having a dysfunctional family,' Dan spits, 'but you're not exactly equipped to talk about normal relationships with your mother, are you?'

89

'You bastard,' I whisper suddenly, tears glinting in my eyes. 'How dare you bring my mother into this?'

'You know what, Ellie? I'm fed up with your being able to say whatever you want about my mother when God forbid anyone says anything to you about yours.'

'I don't have a mother,' I say imperiously, spinning on my heel as I prepare to leave, astounded that Dan would stoop so low, astonished that he knew exactly where to hit so it would hurt the most. 'You may remember that she died when I was a child. I would strongly suggest you stay in the spare room tonight. You'll find the sheets in the bathroom cupboard.' And with that I sweep out of the room, collapse in the loo in floods of tears, and wish I hadn't given up smoking when I met Dan.

*   *   *

By Sunday all is forgiven, and we are both caught up in the excitement of having a baby. But this close to the wedding we have resolved not to tell anyone, and so Sunday lunch at the Cooper house, as much fun as it occasionally is, is something that I just can't handle, given my delicate state.

First and foremost, I know how snappish I've been of late. And second, I have a horrible feeling Linda might guess I will be walking down the aisle pregnant, and I really want to keep it to ourselves until we are back from honeymoon. So I think the safest place for me to be right now is as far away from them all as possible.

Plus of course Linda has been driving me crazy, although at least now I know why I've been so irritable recently. If I thought PMT was bad, it's clearly nothing compared to the early weeks of pregnancy.

The more I've thought about it, the more I've come to see that space is the problem. I know plenty of girls who have problems with their mothers-in-law because they always think no one is good enough for their perfect son, and that the son could have done so much better, and I've realized how lucky I am in that I don't have this to deal with.

My problem falls at the opposite end of the spectrum. Linda wants to be my mother. She's trying much too hard, phoning me every day, three times a day, wanting to meet me for lunch, buying me presents. I know she means well, and I know how ungrateful I seem in resisting her, but it's just too much for me.

I thought, before this, that I would be the luckiest girl in the world if my future mother-in-law, whoever she might be, would take me under her wing and claim me as the daughter she never had. But of course I now see that I'm far too independent for that. That I don't just want any mother, I want my mother, and that that simply isn't going to happen. There isn't anybody who can take her place.

I'm trying so hard to stop Linda from taking over my life. I understand that her intentions are nothing but good, but there is also no denying that Linda believes boundaries are there to be crossed. She seems unable to hear the word 'no'. This weekend I've explained to Dan that I just need some space, need to remember who I was before I became one half of Ellie and Dan.

And if I'm lucky I will find a way to turn Linda into an ally and friend, and she will find a way to accept me as her daughter-in-law and not her daughter. If I'm lucky all it will take is a little space, a little firmness in establishing boundaries, and we will be able to play happy families once again.

So this weekend Dan will, naturally, still go to lunch at his parents'. I certainly don't want to get the blame for both our absences, and besides, Fran has invited me over for lunch, and, much as I now love being part of a couple, there are some traditions I still miss, and the odd Sunday lunch with Fran, Marcus, the kids and various waifs and strays is one of them.

*　　　　*　　　　*

The phone rings just as I'm getting ready to leave the house, having left just enough time to stop and pick up some flowers en route.

'Hello?'

'You're obviously far more devious than you look.' Emma's voice echoes down her mobile. 'I can't believe you managed to get out of lunch today, and now I'm here and I've got no one to talk to.'

I laugh. 'You've got Dan and Richard.'

'But you're the only person who makes this ridiculous Sunday tradition bearable. How did you do it?' Emma groans. 'And, more to the point, why didn't anyone bloody tell me before I arrived? I could have had a lie-in.'

'I'm sorry,' I say, checking my watch and hoping I'm not going to be late. 'But I had a prior arrangement and just for the record, your mum

92

didn't seem to mind at all.'

'No, because she's got her precious Dan all to herself.'

I raise an eyebrow and say archly, 'Please tell me she didn't actually say that.'

'Of course not. But even if she's not missing you, I am.'

'At least that's something. Listen, I've got to go, can we catch up later?'

'Sure, I'll fill you in on the party you've been missing.'

'Just don't tell me anything I won't want to hear.'

'Don't worry. I know my whole family think I don't know the meaning of the word tact, but I'm far more diplomatic than people realize.' I put down the phone, not wanting to think about exactly what Emma meant.

*   *   *

'Ellie!'

'Sally! What are you doing here?'

'Didn't Fran tell you I was coming?'

'Nope, but it was pretty last minute for me too, I think.'

Sally twirls around on the doorstep before ringing the doorbell. 'How do I look?'

'Lovely as ever,' I volunteer, which is true. Sally has a freshness and a sweetness about her. Her hair always seems to be freshly washed and smelling of flowers, although she swears it's her perfume. And I grin as I look at what she's wearing underneath her full-length shearling coat: her sexy Seven jeans that she swears are her lucky charm and always wears when she wants to impress. Or pull. 'So I take it there will be an eligible single man here?'

'However did you guess?' She smiles sweetly.

'But I thought Fran had stopped fixing you up with people. What was that whole discussion about nobody ever being good enough for you?'

'Ah, yes, but that was before Fran mentioned Marcus was friends with Charlie Dutton.'

'Charlie Dutton?'

'You're hopeless, Ellie!' She shakes her head at my lack of knowledge, well aware that I don't pore over *Heat* and *OK!* And *Hello!* in the way that Fran does, that I would never know a celebrity was in the house unless Fran or Sally told me. 'I can't believe you don't know who Charlie Dutton is.'

The door opens and we're swept in on a gust of warmth and noise, hustle and bustle. Fran and Marcus kiss us hello, taking our coats and shoving us down to the kitchen, where we attempt to resume our conversation in hurried whispers while our coats are being put away.

'So who is he, then?'

Sally rolls her eyes. 'Don't tell me you didn't see *Whispers in the Dark.*'

'Well of course I saw *Whispers in the Dark,*' I say. 'Didn't everyone? Why, was he in it?'

'Not in it,' Sally says, as the footsteps of Fran and Marcus clunk down the staircase. 'He produced it.'

'Oh, right,' I say with a shrug. Marcus and Fran are just walking back into the kitchen when I spot a broad-shouldered man with messy hair.

'Are you two okay?' Fran asks, dashing over to the oven to rescue the soup that is bubbling over the edge of the pot. 'We're not being terribly organized today, I'm afraid. Oh, do you know

94

Charlie?'

'Hi, Charlie, I'm Sally.' Sally sashays over with arm extended.

'Nice to meet you.' His smile is warm and friendly, his handshake firm, and Sally is instantly smitten, gazing at him even as he disengages and introduces himself to me. And okay, she does seem to have good taste in this instance. He's very ordinary until he smiles, but when he smiles his entire face changes, and I have to say I am rather taken aback. When he turns away, I wink approval surreptitiously at Sally and give her a discreet thumbs-up, and she grins, and then he looks at us and we both pretend to be busy admiring the kitchen tiles.

'Where are the kids?' I ask, when drinks have been handed round and everyone has been given a role in putting the meal together.

'Outside.' Fran gestures her head towards the garden as I splutter in amazement.

'Outside? Are you nuts? But it's *January*. It's freezing!'

Fran shrugs and rolls her eyes. 'You try telling that to twin four-year-old girls. They insisted.'

I move over to the window to watch two mini Michelin men, bundled up in orange and scarlet puffa jackets, chase each other laughing around the garden.

'I wish my son would insist on going outside in winter,' Charlie volunteers. 'Or any time of year for that matter. He's a TV addict, which would be fine, if slightly antisocial, if he were older, but for a five-year-old it's rather worrying.'

'It would be more worrying if he were watching *Who Wants to be a Millionaire?*' Marcus says, drying

95

up a casserole dish.

'No, far more worrying if he were watching *Tom and Jerry*,' Fran says. 'I cannot believe how violent that show is.'

'But we watched it growing up and we turned out all right,' Marcus says.

'Yes, but still.' Fran shakes her head. 'We know far more about child psychology now than our parents did, and few of us want to make the same mistakes.'

'Is *Tom and Jerry* really that awful?' Up until now I've always felt completely out of my depth in conversations about children, or indeed about any child-related subject, but now that I'm about to get married, now that I'm secretly growing a child of my own, I feel perfectly qualified to join in, to ask questions, hell, to even offer opinions, if it comes to that.

'Who knows?' says Marcus. 'But I was regularly smacked as a child, and I don't know a single person who would smack their child now.'

'I've smacked Finn,' Charlie admits slowly, grimacing as he speaks, knowing he's saying something so politically incorrect this may be the last time he's ever invited here.

'No!' The whole room turns to stare at him, eyes wide, mouths open in shock.

'Yes. I know. It was awful and I swear I felt worse than he did, but he knew he wasn't allowed to draw on the walls, and he watched us, even as we said no, and picked up the felt tips and did it anyway.'

'Do you really feel it warranted smacking?' Fran asks.

'It's the only time I've done it, and yes, I felt that

at that particular time it did warrant it, but I'd like to think it's a last resort, and not something that is ever done out of anger.'

'I can see your point,' Fran says diplomatically. 'It's just that I've never needed to with the girls. Maybe if they did something incredibly disobedient I might.'

'Nah, you wouldn't,' Marcus laughs. 'You'd sooner smack me than smack the girls.'

Fran smacks him.

'Ow! See?' Marcus rubs his arm and gives Fran a fake wounded look.

Sally turns to Charlie Dutton. 'Do you have any more children?' she asks in her politest voice, as I try to suppress a smile, knowing full well that Sally probably knows everything about Charlie Dutton, had doubtless spent Friday afternoon Googling him instead of working on the launch of the new Calden.

'Nope. Just Finn.'

'So where is Finn today?' Sally still fishing.

'It's his mother's weekend this weekend. Shame, because he loves Annabel and Sadie.'

Fran turns from the stove. 'Not to rub it in, Charlie, but when the girls asked who was coming and I told them Finn's daddy, they got so excited because they thought Finn was coming.'

Charlie shrugs, an air of sadness about him that hadn't been there a few minutes before. 'One of the problems of divorce. It's just so awful for the kids, and so difficult to plan anything when their bloody mother announces last-minute changes in plan.'

Fran breaks into the awkward silence that threatens to follow by clapping her hands and

97

ordering everyone to the table, then opening one of the french doors and calling the girls in from the garden.

The girls are immaculately behaved. They sit, side by side, on a bench at one end of the table and pick at their food while giggling together over jokes that none of the adults could even dream of understanding.

Fran and Marcus laugh, and bicker, and contradict one another, and I just sit and bask in all of it, so happy to be back here, so relieved that these lunches haven't changed during my absence, and I realize I haven't laughed this much in what feels like ages. Charlie attempts to join in our discussion, even though he is being monopolized more and more by Sally, but it looks like the fix-up is going well, and by the end of the meal there's a definite chemistry between them, which is lovely, and well deserved.

And then the plates are cleared and a lemon meringue pie ('Don't ask.' Fran rolls her eyes yet again. 'It's the girls' favourite . . .') has been set on the table, and Charlie, whom I've barely spoken to, turns to me.

'So Marcus tells me there'll be wedding bells for you in a few weeks. Are you excited?'

I pause for a second. Excited? It barely seems to encompass what I've been going through for what feels like months now. Nervous? Yes. Apprehensive? Absolutely. Stressed beyond belief? Most definitely.

But excited?

'This is going to sound crazy, but frankly this whole thing has become so immense and so overwhelming, I don't think I've had a chance to become excited.'

'Plus,' Fran interjects on my behalf, 'Ellie has the future mother-in-law from hell who basically thinks it's her wedding. Not that we'd know anything about mothers-in-law from hell,' she says with a sideways glance at her husband, who frowns.

'I thought you and my mother were getting on famously these days,' Marcus says, slicing the pie.

'Famously? Ha! Let's say we can just about bear one another. Anyway, no talking about toxic in-laws. We decided a long time ago that was a taboo subject in this house.'

'Well, you brought it up,' Charlie grins.

'I know. And thanks a lot. Did you want to ever be invited back?'

*   *   *

Sally and I help to clear the table as the men take the twins down to the local park. Sally bombards Fran with questions about Charlie, and when she finally takes a break to go to the bathroom, both of us watch her leave, shaking our heads and smiling.

'She is a lost cause, you know,' I sigh, 'but at least he seems like a nice guy.'

'I know. He's not the problem, she is. It's yet another heartbreak waiting to happen, but what could I do? She practically begged me for an introduction.'

'I've missed this.' I look around the kitchen, at its antiqued yellow cabinets and bright orange Le Creuset pots stacked up on shelves, the perfect heart of the happy family home. 'I can't believe how long it's been since I've been here, and I'm so sorry.'

'Don't be ridiculous. You've got Dan's family to think of now.'

'Oh, God. Don't remind me.'

'You know what? Once you have children, it will all change. You just keep your eyes on the prize. This is what it's all about, creating your own family. Trust me, I learnt the hard way, but none of them matters, parents, in-laws, any of them, not once you have a family of your own. This is what's important, this is what allows you to put up with the rest of the shit.'

'So you're telling me I should get pregnant?' I grin, not sure I can keep it to myself for much longer.

'Just as soon as you've stepped off that aisle. There's nothing you want to tell me, is there?' Fran gives me that narrow-eyed look again, and I falter, about to say no, when she squeals and throws her arms around me. 'I knew it! I knew it!' she says, hugging me, and now it's too late.

'Ssssh,' I warn, delighted that I can finally share it with someone. 'I'm only a few weeks, so we're not telling anyone yet.'

'Don't worry.' She places her hand solemnly on her heart and then throws her arms around me again. 'Your secret's safe with me.'

8

I peer round the living-room doorway at the gang of people amassed to toast us and wish us good luck with our wedding, only two days away now, and I smile at how much I am enjoying seeing my flat filled with people and noise.

I have always been so solitary, such a loner, and never knew just what I was missing in not forming close friendships. I love that I have been able to adopt Dan's friends, and that a whole new world has opened up for me in the process.

Lily sits on the sofa, Tom on the floor between her legs. Anna is on Rob's lap in the oversized armchair. Richard, Dan's brother, is also on the floor, back resting against the sofa, and Dan is on the other chair, beer in hand, bare feet resting on the coffee table.

'Can you believe you're getting married in less than a week?' Lily gets up and comes to join me in the kitchen, elbowing me out of the way as she starts to wash up the discarded pots and pans.

I laugh, because it still feels so unreal, and yet there are times, like today, when I feel that Dan and I are already married, have been married for years. Perhaps this is how you know when you've met your partner, perhaps it is exactly this level of comfort that assures you they must be, after all, the one, because I have never had this with anyone else.

I scrape the last of the food into the dustbin and place the plates gently in the sink. 'It feels very strange. In the beginning I spent so much time focusing on the day itself, the party, that I didn't even think about the commitment, and now that'—I raise my eyebrows—'my mother-in-law has taken over all the arrangements, all I can think about is the commitment.' I look to the doorway and lower my voice. 'And frankly I'm terrified.' Anna walks in to join us, and they both laugh, as do I, to soften the effect of the words.

'Seriously,' I continue, 'I know, beyond a shadow of a doubt that I'm making the right choice, that Dan is absolutely the right man for me, but it still freaks me out that this is it. No more men. No more flings. The same man for, what? Forty, fifty years?'

'Oh, God,' groans Lily. 'Don't put it like that, you make it sound horrific,' and we all laugh.

'Do you think the men think the same thing?' Anna asks. 'Do you think they think about it?'

'Probably,' Lily says. 'My bigger worry was getting rid of the exes.'

'They were still hanging around?' I look at Lily, surprised.

'Tom was still best friends with two of them. I had to put a stop to that!' she laughs, then looks at me. 'What about Dan?'

'It was never an issue,' I say, which it wasn't, but even if he had still been friendly with his exes, I'm not sure it would have been a problem for me, jealousy never having been something I've suffered from.

I know he's in touch with Sophia, his girlfriend from university and the couple of years post, but she is married herself and living in Spain, and when she sends the odd e-mail he reads it aloud to me. Nothing to worry about there.

And there were the obligatory flings through his twenties, and a three-year relationship that ended a couple of years ago because he just couldn't see himself spending the rest of his life with her, and, a few months before meeting me, Lainey, who had run off with the actor.

Everyone, by the time they hit their thirties, has a history, and it never bothered me. I would have been more worried if he'd never had a long relationship.

'He's only in touch with one of his exes,' I say. 'Sophia, but they went out together years ago and she lives abroad. It doesn't bother me at all. Quite honestly I'm happy he's had long relationships. At least it shows he's a person who knows how to commit.'

Anna leans back against the kitchen worktop. 'I never ever thought about the commitment when I married Rob. Past or present. I was so caught up in the wedding I don't think I even realized it was real until we were back from the honeymoon.'

Lily grins. 'So you're one of those girls that I keep reading about who just gets married for the sake of getting married?'

'I suppose,' Anna says. 'Just thank God it all worked out.'

'How long *have* you two been together?' I venture.

'Together six years, married four.'

I'm surprised. Most of the people I know who have been married for longer than two years have at least one child by now. 'I didn't realize it was so long,' I say diplomatically. 'Have you thought about planning a family at all?'

'I think we're probably ready now. There was so much we wanted to do first, but we've pretty much gone to all the places we wanted to go to, stayed in all the hotels we wanted to stay in and we'll probably start trying soon. Lily's my inspiration.' She looks at Lily, who laughs self-deprecatingly. 'What about you, Ellie? Any plans?'

Oh, it's so bloody hard to keep this a secret, and every time someone asks this question—which seems to be averaging out at about nine times a day—I have to fight the urge to tell them, and I can't help wondering whether they've already guessed.

Because, just for the record, I'm huge. Seriously. I can't believe how enormous I feel. I had my final fitting last week for the wedding dress and even the saleswoman was surprised.

'Oh,' she had said, frowning. 'Most of our brides *lose* weight before their wedding,' and I had just glared at her as she made some adjustments to loosen the fit.

And Dan has pointed out that I keep stroking my stomach. Absent-mindedly while queuing for a sandwich, standing in front of the bathroom mirror at work to reapply my lipstick, lounging on the sofa trying to read while Dan watches his beloved football or rugby. Each time I touch my stomach I can't help but make the connection to the growing life inside me.

But I can't tell these girls. Not yet. Not until after the honeymoon.

'We both want a family,' I say, 'but we haven't really sat down and talked about when exactly. In the abstract I'm definitely ready, but I know I don't have any idea quite how your life changes with kids.'

'It does change, and it is a huge adjustment,' says Lily, 'but I can't ever envisage not having the kids now; they're just the centre of our world.'

'Which is why you didn't bring them with you last Saturday when we had lunch?' Anna laughs innocently.

'Trust me, that was for the grandparents. Their one day a week with the kids.'

'Is that your parents or Tom's?' I ask.

'Tom's. Mine still live in Yorkshire, but Tom's are so close that we try to drop them off at some point every weekend. As much as we love them, it's lovely to have a break every now and then.'

'What are Tom's parents like?'

'Great,' Lily says. 'I couldn't have wished for nicer in-laws.'

Anna and I groan simultaneously.

'I know,' Lily laughs. 'That's the reaction I get from everyone, but really, they're incredibly sweet. They love the kids and they love me. Actually, I would count Sandra, my mother-in-law, as one of my friends.'

'Okay,' Anna says, 'so what's the secret?'

'Honestly? I think it's just acceptance. Rather than trying to make each other into something we're not, or wishing each was something, or someone, else, I think we just accept one another as is, and it works.'

'Clearly,' Anna says through gritted teeth, 'you're a much nicer person than I am.'

'I hate to say it,' I add, 'but I have to agree with Anna. I don't think I could be nearly as tolerant as you.'

Lily shrugs. 'All I tried to do was find a way to make it work.'

'Make what work?' Richard walks into the kitchen. 'Any chocolate in this house, Ellie?'

'Of course.' I smile, knowing my future brother-in-law's penchant for sweet things. 'Would I really be the kind of woman your brother would be marrying if I didn't have a constant supply of chocolate?' I walk triumphantly to a cupboard and open it to reveal boxes of Aeros, Kit Kats, Double

Deckers.

Richard puts a hand to his heart. 'Ellie, I never realized this but I think you're a woman after my own heart.'

I smile, warmed by the flattery. 'Take a load into the other room,' I say, as Richard helps himself.

'So what are you women talking about in here?' he asks, before he walks out of the doorway, and Anna, without thinking, says, 'Evil mothers-in-law.'

'Oh?' Richard turns around and raises an eyebrow at me as I stand there feeling the flush rise, completely mortified, but to my surprise Richard isn't taken aback by it, he just says coolly, 'So you've discovered the evilness of my mother, then?'

There is a bit of an awkward silence, broken by Anna swearing and blushing. 'Shit. Oh, God, talk about putting my foot in it. I totally forgot, I mean, I wasn't thinking . . . I'll just shut up, shall I . . .' She tails off miserably.

'Actually,' Lily intervenes, saving the day as I smile at her gratefully, 'I was giving them the secret of getting on with your in-laws, and just for the record, Ellie didn't say anything about your mother.'

'She didn't?' Richard is surprised. 'Well, she obviously hasn't been spending enough time with her.'

I resist the urge to give Richard a hug, and suddenly I know that I have an ally in him. That, as much as Linda bothers me, she seems to bother Richard and Emma even more, and I now know that if the going ever really gets tough, Richard will support me.

I watch Richard walking out the door. Funny

106

that if I didn't know them so well, if I just walked into a room and was faced by Dan and Richard, I would probably choose Richard. In many ways he and I are far more similar, and in some ways perhaps better suited. Except that Dan has a stability I have always craved. I look at Dan and see my future. In his arms I see our children, in his smile I see years of friendship and laughter, and in his voice I hear comfort. Richard is more mercurial, probably more like me, and certainly more like the men I've been out with before, but Dan is my rock, and I know that as long as I anchor myself to Dan I will be safe.

And it's wonderful to know Richard can get as pissed off with his mother as me, particularly because Dan refuses to get involved. Although I don't think it will continue like this; I'm sure it will get better. Fran keeps saying that weddings are one of the most stressful events in your life, on a par with moving house. Incidentally, the flat of our dreams has turned out to be a large garden (estate agentspeak for basement but never mind) maisonette in leafy Primrose Hill. Thanks to Dan's recent award and the surprisingly large valuation of my flat, we've suddenly found that we have far more money than we'd thought, which means Primrose Hill is no longer somewhere I visit on a Saturday afternoon, wishing I could afford to live there. We're expecting to have a simultaneous exchange tomorrow, with completion about two weeks after we get back from honeymoon.

So really, is it any wonder things, or people, are getting on my nerves?

9

'Come on, Ellie, breathe in more.' Linda huffs and puffs as she pulls the corset of my wedding dress tighter, cursing as the two sides will not meet.

'Oh, for heaven's sake.' She gives up eventually and stops, probably terrified her impending sweat will ruin her immaculate make-up. 'This is ridiculous,' she says, sitting down on Dan's old bed in her house. 'I thought you went for a fitting a couple of weeks ago. How is that dress not fitting you?'

I'm tempted to tell Linda about the baby, use it to throw in her face, but even if we had decided to tell her at some point before we actually got married, an hour before walking down the aisle isn't exactly perfect timing, not to mention that Dan would kill me if I told his mother without him present.

'I have had the munchies recently,' I say, nonchalantly trying to explain the rapidly expanding waistline.

'The munchies?' Linda says in horror. 'Most brides are losing weight, Ellie, not putting it on, for Christ's sake. What are we going to do?' Her voice rises in near-hysteria, while I watch in amazement. Because, though everyone talks about the stress of planning a wedding, though I've read practically every article ever written about dealing with the stress of planning a wedding, I haven't really felt it—apart from the arguments with Dan, inevitably over Linda. And during those times when I managed to distance myself from what was going on, I was strangely fascinated to see Linda becoming more and more wound up as the wedding grew nearer.

And now, as the dress shows little sign of closing, Linda looks as if she's going to burst into tears.

'I don't bloody believe it,' she says, her voice wobbling. 'Ellie, do you know how much that dress cost? I might as well have taken my money and thrown it down the toilet.' Her voice actually starts to break. 'How could you do this to me? How could you get fat on your wedding day?' Jesus Christ. Talk about a drama queen. I almost want to laugh.

Emma, who has set up a mobile hairdressing salon in the corner, takes the final pin out of her mouth, pops it in her chignon and turns to her mother. 'Mum, shut up!' she barks, standing up and gliding over in her champagne silk bridesmaid's dress. 'This is Ellie's wedding day. Stop being so insensitive.'

'Don't speak to me like that.' Linda's voice is again on the rise. 'Don't tell me I'm being insensitive when I've spent a fortune on this wedding and the bloody dress doesn't even fit because the bride doesn't give a damn what she looks like.'

Charming.

'Will you all just relax?' Emma picks up the laces of my corset and tugs, drawing the fabric together a centimetre further, but still leaving an inch of tanned skin peeking through the laces. Oh, well, I think to myself, feeling as if I'm watching a farce, at least I had the good sense to book a course of tanning sessions. 'Okay, Ellie,' Emma says, taking control, 'pass me those stockings.'

Emma doubles, triples, then quadruples the

stockings until they are opaque, then lays them gently under the laces against my skin, as Linda sniffs, not wanting to admit how impressed she is with her daughter's skills.

'There.' Emma finishes tying the laces and stands back, admiring her quick-thinking and the finished results, which are, if not perfect, then perfectly fine. As long as I keep my veil on, no one will be any the wiser.

'Okay.' Linda takes a deep breath. 'We should all calm down.'

'You mean you should calm down,' Emma whispers to me.

'Thanks, Emma.' I smile gratefully. 'You're amazing.'

'Ellie, turn around, show us.' Linda has managed to regain her composure. She says happily, 'You look lovely,' and then glances at her watch and jumps. 'Oh, my goodness, it's nearly four. I'll run downstairs and see if the car's here.'

*   *   *

'So.' Emma eyes me up and down. 'The munchies?'

'Yup.' I pretend to be busy straightening my skirt, but of course I'm doing my damnedest to avoid looking Emma in the eye.

'I thought you said you'd been eating hardly anything,' Emma presses, raising an eyebrow.

'When did I say that?'

'Last week when we spoke on the phone.'

'Well, I hadn't, but this week I've been starving. I think it's nerves.'

'But you said you never ate when you were nervous.'

'I lied,' I try lamely, a smile starting to spread, because of course Emma has guessed and I don't care any more about keeping it a secret. I want someone else to know.

'You *are* pregnant, aren't you?' Emma squeals.

'Sssh.' I gesture nervously to the open door. 'Don't tell anyone. We're keeping it a secret until we get back from honeymoon, and I'm only ten weeks.'

'I knew it, I knew it.' Emma flings her arms around me, careful not to muss up my veil. 'Oh, Ellie, I'm going to be an auntie!'

'I know,' I say, grinning. 'But you really mustn't tell anyone, do you promise? Your mother would have a fit if she thought she wasn't the first to know.'

'Oh, God, tell me about it. Don't worry, I won't say a thing.'

'Emma,' I say warningly, knowing that discretion has never been one of her strong points, 'do you absolutely swear?'

'Cross my heart and hope to die.'

*   *   *

The wedding may not have been what I had wanted, or rather it may have had almost nothing to do with me, but it was lovely. The flowers— peonies and calla lilies—spectacular in their simplicity, the food delicious, and the band—Dan and I had preferred a DJ, but Linda and Michael insisted on a band—both loud and lively enough to ensure that people danced most of the evening.

As a bystander, which is frankly how I felt, I had to admit it was spectacular. Quite the most lavish and extravagant wedding I had ever been to. As a bride, once the ceremony was over, I felt completely removed, as if I were both watching a film and walking on air, not the slightest bit present in the moment.

The ceremony was different. It was the one aspect Linda was not able to control, as Dan and I had written our own wedding vows, and I cried when I saw Dan's tears welling, his emotion and love for me shining so clear and true when he spoke his words.

Annabel and Sadie were the flower girls, both unbearably cute in their bridesmaid's dresses, their hair in ponytails, looking ever so serious as they started walking down the aisle, collapsing in giggles halfway down as all the guests grabbed their cameras to take pictures.

And then, almost before I had a chance to take it all in, there we were, husband and wife, and the intimacy and honesty of our ceremony was quickly overwhelmed by the sheer size and scope of the party.

The few people that were there who we could call genuine friends, people like Fran and Marcus, Sally, Lily and Anna, felt like ports in the storm. Whirling around the dance floor, I'd find myself face to face with someone I recognized, smiling at me and spilling over with compliments for me, and I'd again be jolted by the realization that this was my wedding day. My wedding! The fulfilment of all my dreams.

But the biggest shock of all was my father.

I hadn't expected him to come, hadn't even really wanted to invite him, if the truth be known. Dan was the one who had insisted I send an invitation, even as I insisted that he had no interest in me any more, that it would be an invitation wasted, that the only thing that made him my father was blood and that it wasn't enough. I tried to explain how we had nothing in common now, no love, no friendship, nothing.

I knew it would be a wasted invitation, and yet he came.

My father and his wife sat in the fourth row during the ceremony, all dolled up in their Sunday best, looking dull and dowdy only in comparison with Linda and Michael's glamorous friends. Each time I looked at them they seemed uncomfortable, and overwhelmed, and—could I have imagined this?—proud, all at the same time.

Of course I went straight over to him at the reception and gave him an awkward hug, because we both knew that there was little left between us. 'Hello, Dad,' I said, pulling back in astonishment to see tears in his eyes.

I stood in shock as my father choked up, repeating, 'I'm so sorry. I'm so sorry.' He reached for my hand and held on tight as his wife retreated into the background, leaving the two of us together. 'I'm so sorry I haven't been there for you.' And I didn't know what to say, so I didn't say anything at all, just breathed a sigh of relief when someone whisked me away for more photographs.

Later, after the speeches, everyone stopped talking as a middle-aged, balding man in a suit that had clearly seen better days took the microphone and tapped it nervously.

'I know you weren't expecting another speech,' said my father, while I cringed, knowing this wasn't planned, completely embarrassed about what was going on. He cleared his throat nervously, and drew two index cards out of his pocket. 'But Ellie is my daughter and I just wanted to say a few words.

'At 3.27, on the 2nd of September 1970, Eleanor Sarah was welcomed to this world. My wife was in labour for twelve hours and fourteen minutes while I paced up and down the hallway.' He paused. 'In those days we men did the manly thing and waited outside.' He got a laugh, which boosted his confidence, and as he continued the quaver in his voice disappeared. 'A nurse came out and handed me this little bundle, and I looked down at this tiny creature who was screaming, and she stopped crying and looked into my eyes, and at that moment I understood what everyone meant when they said you never loved anything like you love your child.' He stopped and looked through the tables, through the guests who knew what he was talking about, the guests who were younger, who didn't have children and had yet to learn, and he found me and we locked eyes, and all of a sudden I was filled with an unbearable sense of loss and grief. Grief for the father I hadn't known, for these feelings of his that I hadn't known existed, and for the unexpected pleasure and pride in having him speak at my wedding.

'I have not been the best father to Ellie,' he said, as I felt a lump in my throat and a tear slide slowly down my left cheek. 'Her mother died when she was very young.' There was a rustle as people looked at one another, surprised, few of them knowing this, few of them knowing anything about me other than that I was marrying Linda's son. 'And, looking at her today, I'm reminded of my own wedding to her mother. Ellie, you won't remember this, but you look just like her now. You have her beauty, her sparkle, her love of life.' He paused as people cheered, not realizing the impact his words were having on me. 'I didn't know what to do with a thirteen-year-old daughter,' he admitted sadly. 'I loved her so much but I didn't know how to help her. But what I didn't know then, I know now, and Ellie, I want to pass those lessons on to you and Dan, I want you to know all the things I learnt too late. I know that love isn't enough. That you have to cherish the people you love, that saying I love you isn't ever enough, that you have to show that love each and every day, even when life threatens to get in the way.

'If I may quote from someone else far more eloquent than myself, "The greatest weakness of most humans is their hesitancy to tell others how much they love them while they're alive." Ellie, I love you. I may not have told you often enough, but I do. And both of you, Ellie and Dan, love each other, and show one another that love each and every day.'

And with that, he walked away from the stage and started to move towards our table.

'Are you okay?' Dan leaned in and wiped the tears carefully from my face, and I nodded, still too choked up to speak, and then my father was standing next to us, and I stood up and hugged him properly, feeling connected to my father, feeling my father's love for me for the first time in years.

'Thank you, Dad,' I said softly as I pulled away. 'Thank you, and don't keep saying sorry, you don't need to be sorry any more.'

'I do,' he said, smiling sadly, 'but I appreciate you telling me it's not necessary.' He turned to

Dan. 'Maybe when you get back from your honeymoon, you and Ellie will come and stay? Spend some time with us?'

Dan looked at me and I nodded. 'We'd love to.'

Dan grinned and shook his hand. 'Dad.'

Linda came bustling over. 'Hello! We didn't know you were going to speak!' and she pushed me aside to introduce herself to my father. 'I'm Linda, Dan's mother. And this is Michael. We didn't even know you were here.' She shot me a look, one that said how unimpressed she was that I didn't mention he was coming, and that I hadn't yet introduced them.

'I feel so embarrassed that we haven't met before,' she continued. 'But how lovely that you're here. Isn't your daughter beautiful? Doesn't she look like a princess?'

And I did what I always do when Linda realizes she has overstepped the mark and starts lavishing compliments or presents on me to compensate: I melt and instantly forgive her any and all transgressions.

'You know,' Linda said, leaning in conspiratorially, checking that Emma was nowhere near, 'I really shouldn't say this, but I feel so blessed to have your daughter in my family. You hear people say their daughters-in-law are the daughters they always wanted, but in Ellie's case it's true. Oh, not that I don't love Emma,' she said quickly, noticing both Dan and Michael looking at her as if she were completely bonkers, 'but Emma's so difficult and we argue so much, and Ellie is just such a lovely, *easy* girl.' And she looked at me proudly. 'You clearly did a wonderful job in raising her, and I'm so lucky to have her.'

116

'And it seems she's lucky to have you too,' my dad said, won over by Linda's compliments and charm.

'Come on.' Linda linked her arm through his. 'You must introduce me to your beautiful wife, and then you shall come and meet all our friends. Perhaps,' I heard her say just before she was out of earshot, 'you'll come over for dinner when the kids are back from honeymoon?'

I turned to Dan with a groan, because, as wonderful as my dad's words were, and as much as I thought there might be a future for us now after all, I wasn't ready for Linda to step in and become his new best friend, not by a long shot.

And Dan put his arms around me and planted a laughing kiss on my cheek. 'Don't you worry, lovely wife of mine. You know my mother's full of hot air.'

I arched an eyebrow as I turned to look at him. 'How come you're allowed to say that and not me?'

But Dan was still grinning. 'Did you hear what I said? Lovely *wife*?'

And I giggled. 'I know! And you're my *husband*. Oh, my God, that's weird!'

'You know what's even more weird?' Dan gestured at my stomach and dropped his voice to a whisper, 'There's a baby in there! Can you believe that? Our baby!'

'I know. A little us.'

'Yup. A mini Cooper,' Dan said, and we looked at each other and started to laugh.

*   *   *

An hour later Dan finds me talking to Fran and Marcus and pulls me to one side. 'I don't suppose

117

we can sneak out of our own wedding, can we?'

'Not unless you want to be disinherited.'

'Damn. Let's go and find the power switch and turn the bloody thing off. I want to take you upstairs.'

'Calm down, calm down,' I whisper in his ear. 'We've got the rest of our lives for that.' And we stand back and grin maniacally at one another, neither of us quite able to believe that we are now husband and wife.

*   *   *

Two hours later, finally, we manage to leave. The guests form a line and we walk down it, hugging goodbyes to friends and shaking hands with many people I have never seen before in my entire life.

And it's only as we drag our feet up the stairs that I realize how exhausted I am, just how bloody tight and uncomfortable my dress is, how all I want to do right now is just collapse on a bed and sleep for a hundred years.

Luckily for Dan my second wind arrives when we open the door of what I was expecting to be a regular bedroom, only to find the hotel has upgraded us to perhaps the most luxurious suite I've ever seen in my life. And let me tell you, working for Calden I've seen some luxurious suites in my time, but nothing compared to this.

'Oh, my God!' I stand open-mouthed in the doorway. 'This is our room?' I look around at the plush carpets, huge sofas, twinkling crystal lamps, champagne and chocolates waiting for us.

'Our *suite*,' Dan corrects, leading me through a large doorway and into the bedroom, where rose petals have been strewn upon the bed and my silk La Perla nightgown is draped across the pillow.

'Now come here.' Dan pulls me towards him, and, wrapping our arms around one another, we both fall, giggling, on to the bed.

*   *   *

Linda and Michael phone the next morning at eight o'clock. First the hotel phone rings and I refuse to let Dan answer it, knowing it can only be my in-laws and furthermore knowing they will want to come and see us to say goodbye. Then Dan's mobile rings, and then mine.

We ignore them all.

At nine o'clock, as Dan is stepping out of the shower and I'm finishing my make-up, reception rings again to say we have visitors downstairs. Not that I'm surprised. This is a woman who thinks nothing of pulling me out of meetings when she wants to talk to me, so I hardly think she's going to be put off by our not answering the phone. And of course Linda and Michael are downstairs. Where else would they be, for heaven's sake?

Nor am I put out. How could I possibly be, given what she is like, and given what a wonderful wedding she threw for us yesterday?

Because the truth is, that although my wedding had almost nothing to do with me, although I was merely a participant and not a particularly important one at that, even I have to admit that Linda did an amazing job.

And so we talk on the phone to Linda and Michael, and ten minutes later we are on our way downstairs to have the final breakfast with them

119

before going off on our honeymoon.

And over our final cup of coffee and last croissant Linda smiles at me. 'One day,' she says, 'you will have a daughter and she will get married, and then, please God, you will get to have *your* wedding.'

'You mean I was right all along?' I shake my head as I laugh in disbelief, not at what she is saying, because the words don't surprise me in the slightest, but at the very fact that she makes no bones about admitting it. 'This wasn't *my* wedding, it was yours?'

'Of course you were right.' Linda smiles. 'Just as I never had a wedding until now. When I married Michael, whose wedding do you think it was? Mine? No, don't be silly. It was my mother's wedding. But your time will come.' And she puts her arm around my shoulders and gives me a squeeze.

'What if I only have sons?' I muse out loud, trying to catch Dan's eye as I wonder whether now might be the right time to tell them about the baby, now that the wedding is over, now that, as if by magic, the stress and duress of the past few months seem to have completely disappeared.

And, more than that, I want to give Linda a gift, want to thank her for everything she's done, find a way of apologizing for not being as grateful as I could have been. And her first grandchild is the very best gift I can give her.

'If you only have sons,' Linda says, taking a sip of coffee and winking, 'then you'll do as I did and offer to pay for everything.'

'Mum.' Dan shakes his head. 'You're quite the operator, aren't you?'

'See what I have to put up with?' Michael smiles and shrugs, aware that he is only a minor player in his marriage, that he is only allowed the odd comment such as this, that he takes centre stage in the courtroom, and that that must be enough.

'Linda. Michael.' I catch Dan's eye for a second and I know he knows what I'm thinking and he nods, almost imperceptibly, and reaches under the table to take my hand.

'We have something to tell you,' I continue, a smile spreading on both our faces.

And now it really is like watching a movie. Linda appears to freeze, looking first at Dan, then at me, then back to Dan, while Michael merely raises an eyebrow and waits.

Dan grins. 'We're having a baby.'

Linda screams, bursts into ecstatic tears and flings her arms around Dan, then disengages to hug me.

'I don't believe it,' she says through her tears. 'No wonder you put on so much weight!'

'Oh, thanks, Linda.' You could never accuse my mother-in-law of not knowing what to say.

'But I should have known,' Linda says, wiping the tears away, a smile now etched on her face. 'I can't believe I didn't guess, I can't believe you kept this a secret. Oh, my goodness, Michael!' She turns to Michael, who has finished hugging us, and who may not have said anything but is smiling just as hard as Linda. 'Michael! We're going to be grandparents!' And the tears start all over again.

'Er, Mum? Are you sure you're happy about this?' Dan says doubtfully.

'Happy? This is the greatest day of my life!' Linda laughs. 'I just didn't expect it quite this soon.

121

How far gone are you, Ellie?'

'Ten weeks.' I grin.

'And how are you feeling? Any morning sickness?'

'Nope. Nothing. Just starving.'

Linda sits back down and shakes her head. 'I can't believe I didn't guess. Oh, my goodness, a baby! A grandchild! What do you think, Ellie?' She turns to me excitedly. 'Is it a boy or a girl?'

I shrug. 'I think it's definitely far too early to tell.'

'But you *must* have a feeling,' Linda says. 'I knew with all my three. Tell me, what do you think?'

'Honestly, Linda.' I shake my head. 'If I had a feeling, I would tell you, but I don't.'

Linda sits back and studies me, then nods. 'It's a girl. You're definitely carrying a girl.'

'Mum, you couldn't possibly know that,' Dan laughs. 'That's ridiculous.'

'I do know. And trust me. I've never been wrong.'

*　　　*　　　*

Twenty minutes later we all say goodbye just outside the hotel. Dan and I climb into a taxi that will take us to Heathrow, where we're catching a one thirty flight to Antigua.

'Look after my grandchild,' Linda says, waving furiously from the pavement. 'Be careful and keep away from the rum.'

'How about have a wonderful time, Mum?' Dan shouts out the window as he closes the door.

'Don't be silly, of course have a wonderful time,' Linda says, and Linda and Michael stand on the street, clutching each other, still in shock, long after the taxi has turned the corner and disappeared.

*   *   *

Dan and I cuddle up in the taxi and smile at each other, and we talk softly about their reaction, about this new child coming into the world.

And I realize that there are some people who might take a while to adjust to being grandparents, especially when they're as young as Linda and Michael, too young surely to fulfil the roles of grey-haired grandmas and grandpas, but I just know that Linda cannot wait to be a grandmother. By nature maternal and warm, Linda, I know with absolute certainty, cannot wait to hold a tiny baby again, to inhale deeply at their wobbly delicate necks, to smell that unique baby smell. She cannot wait to push a pram proudly into the village, to turn their spare room into a nursery, to fill it with mobiles. After all, it's been decades since her own children were toddling around, bumping into walls and leaving sticky fingermarks all over every window in the house, and yet she still says it feels like yesterday.

As our taxi pulled down the street, I turned round and saw something I'd never seen before: Michael had his arm around Linda. And it was only then that it occurred to me that I so rarely saw any warmth or love between the two of them. I was so used to hearing Linda picking at Michael—because she didn't like the way he ate, or the way he sat, or she wished he was more this, or less that—that it was incredibly odd, and heartwarming, to see them

123

looking happy together.

And perhaps, I thought, as the taxi headed on to the Westway on its way to the airport, perhaps a grandchild is exactly what they need. Perhaps it will be a new start for everyone.

10

Can I just say that I love being pregnant! I completely adore every second of it. Initially, when we first got back from our honeymoon, I was dreading putting on all the pregnancy weight, and I found the beginning, the first trimester, so exhausting and debilitating that I couldn't wait for it to be over.

But as soon as I hit week thirteen I began to feel fantastic. It helped of course that the crocuses and daffodils started sprouting, and the sun made a welcome appearance after such a long, cold winter. And mostly it helped that I was finally able to tell everyone I was pregnant. Thankfully most assumed it was a honeymoon baby, so that became our story. I stopped feeling fat and awkward and started feeling deliciously womanly and voluptuous and feminine.

I feel for the first time that my body is doing exactly what it has been designed to do. I love my ballooning breasts and rounded protruding stomach. There are no tents in this wardrobe, so proud am I of my new body; I'm showing off rather than trying to hide my burgeoning figure, and I feel sexy and gorgeous in my tight sweaters and low-cut hipster maternity trousers.

And my pregnancy glow seems to be catching. Everywhere I go people smile at me, comment on how 'fantastic' I look, and, much to my surprise, I seem to be generating far more male attention than I've ever had before. I've never been one of those women that men have particularly looked at. I've never even had to dread walking past building sites because the worst that's ever been offered is a polite 'good morning'. But all of a sudden I'm getting wolf-whistled left, right and centre. At first I thought it must have been someone else, a blonde beauty who was getting all the attention, but I quickly realized it was me, and I am loving finally being the sort of woman who can attract all these men.

Not that I want any of them, not when I have my wonderful Dan, but it is so strange and so wonderful that pregnancy can do this.

'I swear all these men must have pregnancy fetishes,' I said once to Fran, when Dan and I had gone out to lunch one day with her and Marcus, and the boys had taken off in front of us, leaving us to dawdle in the May sunshine, looking in shop windows and idly chatting.

'Not at all,' Fran had said seriously. 'You look amazing. Really. You just look'—she paused, searching for the word—'lush! That's the word! Lush! Completely fertile, and sexy and delicious. Plus you have the pregnancy glow that everyone talks about. A man would have to be nuts not to fancy you.'

'Hear, hear,' echoed Marcus as we caught up with them and he heard the tail end of Fran's sentence.

Fran had laughed. 'But seriously,' she said,

'you're bloody lucky. I looked disgusting with both my girls. Greasy hair, covered in acne. I threw up for the best part of nine months and felt like shite. You're probably having a boy, looking the way you do. Don't they say that you look fantastic with boys, whereas girls sap your energy?'

I rubbed my 27-week-old bump. 'My mother-in-law swears I'm having a girl and apparently she's *never* been wrong,' I say seriously.

'Well, everyone told me I was having a boy and a girl when I was pregnant with the twins, and funnily enough none of them had ever been wrong either.'

I laughed. 'And what did they say when you had the girls?'

'That next time I would *definitely* have a boy,' and Fran laughed too.

*   *   *

Dan is convinced it's a boy, and I have no idea whatsoever. I've quizzed everyone I know with children on whether they had known, and if so, how, but I have no idea. Some days I wake up and have a very strong feeling that I'm carrying a boy, and other days I am equally convinced it's a girl.

When I'm seven months pregnant, the nesting instinct starts to kick in, and suddenly all I want to do is decorate. I am filled with an extraordinary energy, and spend hours at Homebase choosing paint colours, even more hours in John Lewis mooning over nursery furniture and baby clothes, but not daring to buy anything, superstitious person that I am, waiting to buy baby's first outfit just as soon as I get back from hospital.

But when I've done as much as I can do, when

all the walls are painted and all the furniture has been rearranged and I *still* have energy to expend, Dan suggests a housewarming party.

Admittedly it's rather late, but then again the maisonette took far longer to buy than we had anticipated—two other buyers came in at the last moment and we found ourselves in a bidding war we couldn't afford. Dan eventually sat down with the vendor and told him that he was acting with no integrity, that his behaviour was unacceptable, that he had agreed the price and the sale with us, and that if he was a gentleman he would stick to it. Dan stressed the word *gentleman*. Which is one of the things I love about Dan. He has an incredibly strong sense of right and wrong, and is not the slightest bit scared of confronting people if he feels they have acted immorally, or have somehow done him wrong. And it worked: Dan shamed him into selling to us, at less money than he clearly wanted. But what goes around comes around, and if he had sold the flat to one of the other buyers the karma would eventually come back to bite him, Dan said, or words to that effect.

But the point is that by the time we moved in we were both so exhausted by the cumulative stress of the wedding, the possibility of losing our dream flat and then the actual move itself that we could barely unpack the boxes, let alone think of decorating.

Linda offered to unpack for us every time she came over, looking round the flat in despair at the books stacked in piles against every wall, at the pots and pans that were rarely used still in boxes in a corner of the kitchen. Each time I politely but firmly declined her offer, saying that I had to do it myself or I'd never find anything.

So of course no one could be happier than Linda that the nesting instinct has now kicked in and the flat finally lives up to her oh-so-high standards, and no one could be more excited than me at the prospect of organizing a housewarming party.

We invite friends that have been to our wedding, neighbours we have come to know surprisingly quickly and people who are, as Dan puts it, friends-in-training—the couple we bump into as they walk their dog in the early evening (we've only ever exchanged a smile and a hello with them, but we agree they look like our kind of people); the girl who works in the lingerie shop and always comes out to say hello when I pass and who asks how I'm feeling; the other customers at the Polish café every Saturday morning—people we like despite not really knowing them, people with whom we haven't been able to establish true friendships, because of lack of time and energy. And what better way to initiate something further than to invite them to a party?

I'm in charge of the lights, and, after carefully consulting various books, I decide to line the paths with luminarias—brown paper bags weighted down with sand and containing a small tea light—place large torches all around the garden, string white fairy lights through the two apple trees at the bottom and drape Japanese lanterns above the patio.

Dan downloads dozens of recipes for cocktails, and, once we've picked our favourites, he makes huge pitchers of Mojitos and Caiprinhas, setting up a bar in one corner of the garden, a huge bucket of ice resting underneath.

I wanted to cook. Really I did, but even with the

nesting instinct at full force I know my limitations, and instead hit Sainsbury's and Marks & Sparks, buying ready-made salads, garlic bread that I just have to warm up in the oven and delicious-looking cakes. Then, on the day, artfully laid-out platters of prosciutto, Parma ham, cold chicken, carpaccio; Brie, Camembert, Roquefort and Chèvre; olives, stuffed peppers and bright green cornichons.

Dan has regressed to his music- and club-obsessed early twenties. I knew about his former obsession with music, but I didn't really *know* it, not in the sense that I now know, having seen him spend hours hunched over his CD player, carefully and methodically choosing the music, starting off with mellow Ibiza beats and gradually picking up the tempo to ensure that everyone will dance.

And I'm so excited, *we're* so excited, it's all we can talk about in the weeks leading up to the party itself. Don't get me wrong, both of us spent our respective twenties going to hundreds, if not thousands, of parties like this, but the parties gradually tapered off as we hit our thirties, our friends still entertaining but in a different way.

Those without children seem to have graduated to cosy supper parties. Not as formal as the dinner parties our parents might have thrown, these tend to revolve around the kitchen, all of us standing around chatting, usually helping to cook the meal before sitting at the kitchen table with several bottles of good wine.

The people with children tend to have lunches, or summer barbeques in the afternoons, or else they do nothing at all, the concept of socializing and looking after children at the same time being simply too large a concept for them to handle.

But, either way, people don't drink, dance or have fun in the same quantities or with the same regularity as they once did, and Dan and I are determined to change that. Particularly me.

*   *   *

Oh, bugger. Am I imagining it or is that the doorbell? And who's coming over while I'm lying in the bath like the heavily pregnant whale that I am an hour before the party's due to start? 'Dan!' I yell from the safety of my bathroom. 'Doorbell! Can you get it!'

No response, the only sound being very loud salsa music from the stereo in the garden, which is almost as loud in the bathroom as it is outside.

'Dan!' I scream again as the doorbell sounds, eventually huffing and puffing as I heave my body out of the bathtub, wrap Dan's robe around me (the only one that still fits) and drip my way to the front door. I'm really not expecting anyone for at least another hour—two, if, as I suspect, no one shows up at the appointed time.

'Hello, darling,' Linda gives me an air kiss, then steps past me into the flat, followed closely by Michael. 'Are we early?'

'You could say that. No one will be here for at least another hour.' My voice and expression are grim. All I wanted to do was take a relaxing bath and take my time in getting ready, and now I'll probably have to sit here and entertain Linda and Michael. My mood, to put it mildly, is suddenly not good. And then I notice that Michael is carrying several large carrier bags from Daisy & Tom.

'Oh, good. I wanted to show you what we've

130

bought for the baby.' Linda smiles. 'I'm so excited and Michael wanted it to be a surprise, but I can't wait to see what you think.'

Frankly, I haven't got the time. Everyone I know, and a few people I don't, will be arriving in—I check my watch—less than an hour, and here I stand, dripping water on to the carpet, my hair still soaking, the flat still needing one final tidy before the first guests—family excluded—arrive.

'Why don't you go in the garden and find Dan while I get dressed?' I smile through gritted teeth as I eye the bags warily. Linda knows how superstitious I am, knows I purposefully haven't bought anything yet. So what on earth is in those bags? 'Have a drink.' I try to keep my voice calm. 'I'll be with you just as soon as I'm ready.'

'Righto.' Michael's already heading out there, clearly uncomfortable around his daughter-in-law in her dishabille state.

'Don't be too long,' Linda says, and I strongly resist the urge to hit her, knowing that I will now rush so as not to offend them, and will doubtless end up with frizzy hair and smudged eye shadow, and that already I'm more wound-up than I have been in months.

But somehow, thankfully, I manage not to rush. Lying back in the now-lukewarm water—I quickly add about a gallon more of hot—a calmness comes over me again, and I take my time getting ready, only occasionally peering out the window to admire our handiwork, how lovely the garden looks as the sun sets and all the lanterns and torches come into their own, how festive it all is.

Linda and Michael are chatting animatedly to Dan, both sipping from large Mojitos, Linda obviously delighted to have her son on his own—a rare occurrence these days. And, as a result, my hair doesn't frizz, my eyeshadow is perfectly blended, and the beaded Temperley vest fits beautifully, despite not being maternity. I slip my feet into newly acquired sparkly sandals—a special treat, given that I'm pretty much only able to buy shoes these days—scoop my hair back into a rhinestone clip and, feeling beautiful, walk outside to join the others.

'Oh, good,' Linda says, clapping her hands, 'here she is,' as if she has spent the past forty-five minutes in pained conversation while waiting for me to arrive, instead of happily monopolizing her favoured and favourite son.

Michael passes Linda the plastic bags he was carrying when he walked in, but before I sit down I pour myself a glass of iced tea, looking longingly at the Mojitos but knowing that alcohol and pregnancy do not mix, and that it's not long before I'll be able to drink again.

The minute I sit down off Linda goes. She reaches down into the bags and starts to pull out the contents. Out come vests in a rainbow of colours, as she delightedly points out their cuteness and practicality. And then come muslins, packets and packets of them, followed by hooded towels complete with rubber ducks. There are romper suits and Babygros—yellows and greens, purples and oranges.

'If you don't like them, you can change them,' Linda keeps saying, as the pile of things on the table grows higher and higher. 'I just didn't want to get pink or blue, but once we know—'

'I know,' I say, feeling completely overwhelmed

by the sheer amount they have bought.

After the clothes come toys. 'I know I shouldn't have,' Linda says, 'but look! Isn't this bear gorgeous? I couldn't resist. And this musical thing hangs on the crib and has lights and helps them sleep—isn't it wonderful? I saw an ad on TV, and this mobile helps their developmental skills . . .'

Dan, I can see, is thrilled. He keeps giving me these looks, and I know he's looking for confirmation, reassurance, 'Isn't it fantastic, Ellie?' he says as I grunt. 'Wow, Mum, that's amazing. Isn't it, Ellie?' But I don't say anything, can't say anything, because, as ungrateful as this may sound, with all of this stuff, all of these things in front of me, everything that a newborn baby could possibly want or need, what is left for me to buy?

Do they think I haven't bought anything because I haven't *wanted* to? God knows it's been a fight every time I look at things, and each time I pass a baby store I've been desperate to run in and buy everything in sight—but because I'm superstitious I haven't wanted to tempt fate before six months. And now that I'm past twenty-four weeks, now that I've reached viability, the point where, should the baby be born, it would have a chance of survival, all I've been dreaming about is going on a shopping spree, choosing all the things that are currently piled up high on my garden table in front of me.

So, yes, I know I should be grateful, and yes, I know I should be thrilled that my baby has such loving, generous grandparents, but I feel as if I'm going to burst into tears, and at this moment my overwhelming feeling is one of hatred, and it's all directed at Linda. Hatred that Linda has stolen my thrill and excitement and joy, and is claiming it as

133

her own.

'It's not your child!' I want to spit, 'it's mine! I should be buying these things! Not you!' But I can't. Instead I try bloody hard to fight back the tears, try to swallow the lump in my throat, and force a smile while saying thank you.

None of which works. What happens instead is that as I try to swallow the lump, it somehow escapes me and comes out as a sob, which then turns into full-blown sobbing. I jump up and run inside, not giving a damn that Linda looks horrified—presumably at my ingratitude—while Michael looks angry—God knows why—and Dan, poor Dan, just looks completely confused.

I calm down inside, and, from the safety of my bathroom and the open window, manage to hear exactly what is going on outside. I hold my breath and listen.

'What?' I can imagine Linda opening her eyes wide and shrugging, the picture of innocence.

'Don't "what" me,' Michael says, his voice not the voice I'm used to hearing, but instead the powerful, firm courtroom voice, the one he uses at work, the one that intimidates and scares, that ensures his continuing reputation as one of the best QCs. 'I told you Ellie would be upset. I told you this wasn't your job, that Ellie would want to buy all this herself, but you insisted.'

Linda jumps on the defensive immediately. 'How do you know that's why she's crying? I doubt her tears have anything to do with us. Honestly, Michael, what kind of ungrateful girl would cry just because a grandparent bought some things for the baby.'

Michael shakes his head in a warning. 'Do not

try that with me, Linda. You know that Ellie couldn't wait to buy the baby things, and you know she was waiting until now because she didn't want to tempt fate, but you couldn't wait, could you, you had to steal her thunder.'

'How dare you,' Linda storms. 'I was not trying to steal her thunder, I was trying to help them out, for God's sake, and if you felt so strongly about it, why didn't you say something?'

'I did,' Michael says coldly. 'Repeatedly but as usual you chose not to hear.'

'And what's that supposed to mean?' Linda is happy to turn this row into something bigger because of course she knows that Michael is right, doubtless knew it the minute she picked up the first Babygro and put it in the shopping basket. She is the matriarch in this family, and no matter how many children we end up having, how much this family grows and who else may come into it, Linda is the star around whom everyone, everything else, revolves. This child may be growing in *my* stomach, may be *my* child, but as far as she's concerned this is first and foremost *her* grandchild. Make no mistake about that.

And it is at this point that Dan mutters something about a last-minute music crisis and disappears inside to fiddle with his CDs.

'What *that's* supposed to mean,' Michael continues, and I know he's upset that I'm upset, because I know he has a soft spot for me, and he saw this coming and probably feels he could have tried harder to stop it, and didn't only because he is so used to deferring to Linda, to letting her stronger personality win, 'what *that's* supposed to mean,' he says again, 'is that you hear only what you want to hear, and that every time anyone says anything to you that you might not like you just ignore it.'

Linda snorts. 'You do come out with the most ridiculous things sometimes,' she says dismissively. 'Maybe I don't listen to you because you haven't got a clue.'

'That's right. It's exactly what you're doing now, dismissing what I have to say because it's not what you want to hear. Why do you think I don't bother speaking to you half the time? Hmm? Because there's no point. Because you're so bloody intransigent nothing gets through.'

Linda turns to Michael, fury now in her eyes. 'I. Will. Not. Have. You. Talk. To. Me. Like. This,' she says. 'Do you understand?'

And this is the way it always ends. Linda will fight until she knows she can't win, and when she runs out of steam, or it looks as if Michael may have the final word, she tells him she won't stand for it any more, and on the rare occasion when Michael still has more to say and the will to say it, Linda will walk out and slam the door until Michael apologizes.

Which he invariably does.

But Michael—oh thank God for Michael—won't let her ruin our party, and when he next speaks he is sterner than I have ever heard him, sterner than I ever thought he could be, and it is all I can do not to run outside and kiss him. Instead I just sit in the bathroom and smile quietly through my tears.

'You will go inside and you will apologize to Ellie,' Michael says so coldly and quietly that I have to strain to hear him from my frozen position underneath the window. 'You will offer to return

136

everything and you will keep saying sorry until Ellie forgives you.'

Linda evidently opens her mouth to speak, then closes it again in acquiescence. She stands up in silence and comes inside to find me.

*   *   *

'May I come in?' The door opens gently as Linda walks in, and I grind my teeth together, sure that tonight I will tell her how I feel and exactly why I find her behaviour so despicable. I will tell her that I know exactly what game she is playing, that it is all a power trip, and that I will not have it any more.

My fury is taking me beyond merely accepting her apology. Tonight I have had enough. I will make her take everything back, and I will, for the first time, get it all off my chest. No holds barred. I just don't care any more.

'I'm sorry,' Linda says uncomfortably, unable to look me in the eye. 'I knew you were looking forward to buying the baby things, and I shouldn't have bought them instead, and really, I didn't mean to upset you, I just didn't think, I was just so excited to see all those gorgeous things and I realize now how thoughtless it was and . . .'

I don't believe this. Linda starts to cry.

She sits and she sobs, and she takes in great gulps of air, and it completely throws me off. Because I am ready for a fight. I am ready to shout and scream if need be, to tell Linda exactly how I feel about her, and the very last thing I expected was to see Linda in tears.

I didn't even know Linda had the ability to cry,

137

and it's so alarming, so disarming, it renders me completely speechless, and I find myself placing a soothing arm around her shoulders and comforting her instead, telling her that of course she is forgiven, that I understand she was only trying to be thoughtful, that no, I don't want her to return all those wonderful things and that in fact I was just upset because of my hormones, that I'm thrilled at her generosity and thoughtfulness.

Of course it's all bollocks, but I do feel something I never thought I'd feel for Linda: pity.

I actually feel sorry for her, and even though I know exactly how devious and manipulative she can be, and know exactly what she was trying to do tonight, a part of me truly believes she may have just been thoughtless, that perhaps it wasn't a malicious move, merely a tactless one, and all of my anger dissipates.

Five minutes later we are friends again, as close to a mother and daughter as this mother and daughter-in-law can be, and we rejoin Dan and Michael, who are visibly relieved to see how quickly we seem to have cast aside our differences.

And we join them just in time, it transpires, for barely have we sat down when the doorbell rings announcing Fran and Marcus—the first of our guests—and after that it seems that everyone arrives at once, and soon people are rubbing shoulders and refilling glasses and calling out to friends that they haven't seen in months.

Despite the bad start, we all have a wonderful evening. Even Linda and Michael: Linda is in her element with 'the boys', those friends of Dan she has watched grow up into strong, handsome men; and Michael, quiet, unassuming Michael, is, much to my amusement, taken aback and more than a little flattered to find himself talking with Sally, loquacious, flirtatious Sally, who, with a clever comment and a twinkle in her eye, appears to make him wish he were twenty years younger and still single.

People drink, they chat, they eat, they laugh. At some point during the evening the music is turned up and the lawn is turned into a makeshift dance floor. It is exactly the party that I wished for—a party where everyone remembers who they used to be, before life, children and responsibility got in the way.

I think it fair to say a good time was had by all.

11

. . . the birthday of my life
Is come, my love is come to me
Christina Rossetti

There's a gentle knock on the door and I softly say 'come in', bestowing a beatific smile on Fran and Sally, who walk in and gasp, immediately coming over to the bed, where I'm cradling a tiny Thomas Maxwell Cooper in my arms.

'Oh, my God,' sighs Fran, 'you forget how teeny they are.'

'He's *gorgeous*,' Sally says, both of them jostling to get a closer look.

'Do you want to hold him?' I pass him gently to Fran, who sits down on the hospital bed, holding Tom ever so carefully as she marvels at all his

139

perfect features.

'How do you feel?' Sally puts a large bunch of tulips on the windowsill, not realizing that they'll be dead within the hour, as this bloody hospital is heated to about three hundred degrees, even though it's mid August and boiling outside; none of the radiators (installed, I think, in Victorian times) can be turned off, nor can the windows be opened.

'I feel fine,' I say, beaming. 'Great, in fact, which I'm not sure you're supposed to feel after a Caesarean, but I'm dying to go home.'

'When *are* you going home?'

'Tomorrow.'

It's been a long four days. I thought I might have a chance to catch up on my sleep. Every night I hand Tom—he's already become a Tom rather than Thomas—to the nursery and ask them to bottle feed him so I can get a good night's sleep. And every night at precisely 1.33 a.m. I'm wide awake, and I know I should be trying to get back to sleep, but as soon as I wake up I remember that I have a baby! And he's here! And excitement threatens to burst out of me and before I know it I'm padding down the hallway in my slippers to reclaim him for myself.

It is much like having the greatest birthday present I have ever had—magnified a thousandfold—and I can barely stand to let him out of my arms.

I wasn't the first to hold him. Dan was. Neither of us had expected a Caesarean, but twelve hours of labour led to a diagnosis of 'failure to progress', and frankly I was so bloody exhausted that when they suggested a Caesarean, they could have suggested amputation of all my limbs and I would

140

have happily agreed.

I didn't react well to the anaesthetic, and as soon as they pulled Tom out I was using the little strength I had left to battle the growing nausea, and when they tried to hand me the baby I was frightened I'd throw up all over him. So instead Dan took him, and I closed my eyes as they finally gave me valium, enabling me to stop shaking and drift off to sleep.

When I came to I was in the recovery room, and Dan was slumped in the one chair in the corner.

'Hi.' He scraped the chair over to the bed and took my hand, kissing me softly on the forehead and smiling into my eyes.

'Hi, yourself,' I croaked. 'Where's the baby?'

'He's fine,' he said. 'He's in the nursery. They cleaned him up and dressed him.'

'Is he beautiful?' I said.

'He's *amazing*,' Dan said, as tears welled up in both our eyes. 'He's just amazing.'

'Can you believe it?'

Dan shook his head. 'I can't. I can't believe we made anything that perfect.'

'Can I see him?' I asked. Dan rang for the nurse and within five minutes I had Tom in my arms, and spilled fresh hot tears of joy all over his new John Lewis Babygro, which, though sized for newborns, looked like it was three times too big.

'Who do you think he looks like?' I whispered, barely moving, after Tom had stopped wriggling and squeaking and had fallen asleep in my arms.

'I think he has your hands. Look. Look at his long fingers,' and we both leant down and looked and I kissed each one gently.

'My parents think he looks like me,' Dan said, as

he kissed Tom on the top of his head. 'Apparently I had loads of hair when I was born too. But even if he does look like me now, I'm sure that will change. Apparently biologically all babies look exactly like their fathers when they're born so we don't reject them. As if!' And he laughed.

My heart started to beat rather too hard.

'Your parents think he looks like you? How do they know? They've seen him?'

There was a deathly pause as Dan looked at the floor. 'Yes,' he said uncertainly, and I knew he was looking for a way out, a way to end this conversation now, a way of not telling me something that I so didn't want to hear.

'What do you mean they've seen him?' I knew I was repeating myself, and my voice was calm, but my emotions were churning. How *could* they have seen him? I'd only just seen him myself. And what were they doing here anyway?

Linda and Michael had asked me a few weeks ago if they could be present at the birth, had said how much it would mean to them, that this was a moment they had always been waiting for.

And I had been completely thrown. I have never understood wanting anyone other than your husband present at the birth of your baby. Did Linda really think that I would ever be able to look her in the eye again once she had seen me lying spreadeagled, a baby's head emerging from my vagina? The very thought makes me sweat. I have watched those documentaries about childbirth, seen whole extended families clustered around the mother in the delivery room, and felt nothing other than sheer horror. Isn't this the most private moment of your life? Who wants to be that

142

exposed, that vulnerable, in front of anyone other than a doctor or midwife, a nurse and your husband?

But I hadn't known what to say when Linda asked me, hadn't wanted to be impolite, was still, despite all that's been said and done, trying to be the dutiful daughter-in-law, and so I had said politely that I would think about it and would let her know.

'Is she out of her fucking mind?' I had said, turning to Dan as soon as we were in the car.

He shrugged uncomfortably. 'I told her that she would have to ask you.'

'Oh, great. You mean she already asked you?'

'Yup, and I told her it wasn't up to me, that it was your body and your birth and she'd have to ask you.'

'Hmmph,' I said, gruntingly acknowledging his support.

Two days later—during which time I'd avoided her phone calls, letting the machine pick up and only calling back when Dan said she was out—I phoned and spoke to her, explaining that I wasn't comfortable with anyone being there, but that Dan and I would phone her as soon as we were done and that then, after we had phoned, of course she and Michael were welcome to come to the hospital.

Wasn't that clear? That *Dan and I* would phone her and *then* they could come to the hospital?

So how the fuck has she seen my baby?

'How the *fuck* have they seen my baby?' I spit in a shrill voice, hysteria barely contained. '*I've* barely seen my baby.'

Dan started to shake his head. 'Oh, God, I'm really sorry, Ellie, I don't know what to say, and I

143

swear to you I didn't know they were here.'

'What do you mean?'

'My mother called when they were preparing you for the theatre. She just wanted to know how we were, and I couldn't lie and not tell her we were in the hospital, and the next thing I knew they were here.'

'Here? Where? In the operating theatre?' For one horrible moment I thought I'd been so out of it that they could have been huddled in a corner of the operating theatre watching the Caesarean and I wouldn't even have known.

Oh, God. Which is worse? Your in-laws having a bird's-eye view of your vagina or your entrails?

'No, but they were in the waiting room, and . . .' He stopped, clearly reluctant to carry on. 'After Tom was born they were wheeling him to the nursery and whichever nurse it was said congratulations to them and then apparently . . .' He tailed off again miserably.

'Apparently what?' I screamed.

'Apparently she invited them into the nursery to see him and they held him. Briefly.'

I burst into tears of frustration and rage, and Tom woke up and started to yell, and all I could think at that moment was that it was me and Tom against the rest of the world, and I hated everybody except the tiny little helpless baby kicking and screaming in my arms.

The nurse came in, looking worried, and ushered Dan out, telling him that it was all too much for me and he mustn't upset me, a Caesarean is major surgery after all, and I know that Dan, who should have been feeling on top of the world right then, felt like the biggest idiot that ever lived.

Good. Served him right.

But now, four days after the operation, I have forgiven Dan. I'm not sure, on the other hand, I'll ever manage to forgive Linda.

I know it's ridiculous. I'm happy to let my friends hold my baby. But each time Linda and Michael come to visit, she immediately swoops over me and reaches out to take Tom from my arms, and I turn away and say no, I'm not ready to have anyone else hold him. She then sits miserably in the corner, her face stony, and I know she feels rejected. I lie in bed, cradling and cooing over Tom, and I can't help but feel triumphant. You may have held my baby before me, I think, but you will not win.

He is not your baby, he is mine, and I will make sure you never forget it.

*   *   *

Nothing could have prepared me for Tom, for how my life changes when Tom comes into it, and nothing could have prepared me for the overwhelming love I feel for this creature, whom I've only known for a few weeks.

I can't sleep at night. I'm either up because Tom is hungry and crying—we go together down to the living room where I nurse him, MTV turned on with the volume low—or I'm tiptoeing around his cradle, peering in at his sleeping face, still unable to believe that he's mine and he's here.

I've taken three months' maternity leave from work, and I miss work, miss the buzz, the routine, the being with adults, but when I stop to think about going back and leaving Tom, handing him over to someone else to look after, I start to feel physically sick.

I try not to think about it.

Instead I'm focusing on my new life as a mother, with all the newness that entails, including, much to my surprise, new friends.

Every day at three o'clock, after Tom's afternoon feed, I put him in the pushchair and we walk over to the park, where we wander around for a little bit and then sit in the playground watching the older children. After a while you realize you see the same faces, and the women with children the same age tend to gravitate towards one another. When Tom is six weeks I start chatting with Lisa, who has Amy, a two-month-old girl, and Trish, who has Oscar, five weeks.

We start by sharing our birthing stories, continue with swapping tips on how to get our babies to take a bottle when we've exclusively breast-fed, and graduate on to talking about our husbands and our lives.

In the beginning all subjects, even when we're talking about work, about parts of our lives that were hugely important before children, eventually come back to the babies.

But, after a while, these regular daily meetings—meetings that move from the playground to the coffee shop, and then shortly afterwards to our homes, where we decide to form an impromptu playgroup—become the highlight of my day.

Lisa, Trish and I may have bonded initially because of our children, but it doesn't take long before they start to feel like friends, and shortly after that they start to *become* friends. By the time Tom is about to turn three months and I'm counting down the days with dread before I go back to work, I wonder how I ever got by without Lisa and Trish in my life.

How I ever got by, in fact, without close female friendships. Of course I have Fran, and Sally, and now Emma, although having Tom seems to have distanced me slightly from Emma. I still see her every Sunday at Linda and Michael's, and we still spend the whole time chatting together, but because I'm not working in the West End she can't pop in and steal me away from lunch, and she doesn't seem the slightest bit interested in babies, and frankly that's all I'm really interested in talking about right now.

Really close female friendships have always eluded me, and I know you don't have to be a psychologist to deduce that the only woman I was ever close to was my mother, who died, hence abandoning me, albeit accidentally, and that the likely reason I've never allowed myself to grow close to anyone else is that very same fear of abandonment. But I never realized until now what I was missing.

I love that I can pop Tom in the pushchair, walk around the corner to Trish's house and bang on her door without phoning first to see if she's in. I love that I can kick off my shoes and open her kitchen cupboard doors to help myself to tea while she's upstairs changing Oscar's nappy.

I love that Lisa will pop in sometimes in the afternoon, and if she's made a cake that morning (which bizarrely she frequently does), she'll have made some extra for Trish and me, which she'll bring over, beautifully wrapped in toile.

I love that we all feel as comfortable in one another's houses as we do in our own homes, and

147

that they have brought an element of lightness and laughter that wasn't in my life before I found them.

Part of the comfort factor is, I'm sure, that we all live within a couple of minutes of one another. Life is so much easier when you don't have to plan. We still see Dan's friends on the odd Sunday for lunch (not nearly as frequently since Tom came into the picture), but seeing them for, say, dinner during the week requires a couple of weeks' notice, and even then one or other of us usually phones to cancel because life has got in the way or we are simply too tired to socialize.

For a while, it doesn't occur to Lisa, Trish or me that we can see each other on the weekends or in the evenings. Dan refers to them as my 'girlfriends', as in 'Your girlfriend Trish is on the phone' or 'Are you seeing your girlfriend today?', which makes me laugh.

For a few weeks they are simply names to Dan, but eventually my girlfriends and I plot to get everyone together, and then one Sunday afternoon Lisa—who, despite being single, or perhaps because of being single, is the most domesticated of all of us—has us over for tea.

*   *   *

'This is my husband, Gregory,' Trish says, as a short, smiling man reaches out to shake my hand as we all cluster on the doorstep of Lisa's house.

'And this is mine, Dan,' I say, as the front door opens and I expertly manoeuvre the Maclaren (hooray—we've graduated to a Maclaren) over the threshold.

We walk in to kiss Lisa hello and introduce

ourselves to her boyfriend Andy, and within a few minutes Amy, Oscar and Tom are all lying contentedly on the baby gym in the middle of the living-room floor as Trish and I follow Lisa into the kitchen to help prepare tea.

As often happens when I walk into Lisa's house, the smell is delicious, and I sniff contentedly as I follow the others into the kitchen. 'So what did you make today? Whatever it is it smells incredible.'

'Sometimes I really think I should hate you,' Trish says to Lisa. 'How can you possibly have time to cook the way you do when you have a tiny baby? I barely have time to wash my hair, and you're making bloody cakes every day of the week.'

Lisa shakes her head bashfully, but it's true. She not only manages to cook cakes and biscuits day after day but also meals for her boyfriend whenever he comes over, which seems to be pretty much every night of the week.

Lisa's ex-husband—his name is Paul but he is commonly known as The Deserter—left her three months before Amy was born. It turns out that their marriage was a huge mistake. He was nowhere near ready for commitment (something you think he could have realized during their three years together, and preferably before she fell pregnant) and certainly not ready to deal with a baby. (The Deserter was an Hon. and one of London's Bright Young Things, known for his reputation as a playboy long before he met Lisa.)

So off he went.

Yet I have never met anyone as capable or strong as Lisa in my life, and every time I tell her that she just laughs and says she and Amy are far better off without him. Trish and I have talked

149

when we are on our own, and quite honestly neither of us can believe that anyone would leave a woman like Lisa. Because not only can she cook like a dream, she's also *gorgeous*. Seriously. If she wasn't so nice I'd hate her, and as it is it took me a while to stop being intimidated by her. Sun-streaked blonde hair and legs that go on for ever, accented by the four-inch Manolo Blahnik boots she wears—even to the park!—Lisa turns heads wherever we go. There is a part of me that probably ought to feel threatened, and it has occurred to me that perhaps I should be nervous about introducing her to Dan. Not that I don't trust him, because I absolutely do, but when Linda heard I had a new friend who was beautiful and in the process of getting a divorce she raised an eyebrow and told me to be careful.

Which is completely ridiculous. Not to mention the fact that Lisa has a boyfriend.

I have, however, started making a bit more of an effort lately. I don't consider myself a competitive person, but Lisa's just so immaculate all the time, so perfect at everything, it's forced me to start doing things I haven't done for a while.

Cooking, for example. If Dan is very, very lucky, I'll have remembered to stock up on ready-made meals from Sainsbury's, or occasionally the deli if I have time. Most nights he's running out for takeaways or making do with scrambled eggs on toast.

But last week I managed two Jamie Oliver recipes and a crème brûlée.

As for what I looked like prior to meeting the girls . . . let's just say I was still in maternity clothes for the first six weeks after I had Tom. I might have pulled myself together enough to banish the maternity clothes to the attic until the next baby, if there *is* a next baby, but I am, none the less, a good size larger than when I started, and that's only in large baggy jumpers and Gap stretchy trousers. God knows what would happen if I tried to get into something that didn't have a bit of stretch to it.

So I may not be going shopping just yet, but I have started putting on a touch of lipstick and mascara before I leave the house.

On the other hand Trish is a woman after my own heart. She knows she can't keep up with Lisa and doesn't give a damn. Oh to be that secure! Trish is still happily wearing Mothercare leggings, only just manages to wash her face in the morning, never mind going to the trouble of applying make-up, and has given her husband, Gregory, all of the cooking duties.

In many ways I love that the three of us—Lisa, Trish and me—are so completely different, and when we are out I often imagine how incongruous we must look. Perhaps in different circumstances we might not have been friends. Lisa so glamorous and sophisticated, Trish so laid-back and down-to-earth, and me? Me so ordinary, I suppose.

But we *are* friends, and, as the three of us carry trays of tea and cakes into the living room, it seems that our husbands, or at least Dan and Gregory, may be destined to be friends too.

12

I shouldn't be the slightest bit surprised by this, but Andy, Lisa's boyfriend, is quite fantastically handsome. He's handsome in a way that makes me slightly nervous, and I can't quite manage to look him in the eye.

Together he and Lisa look like the perfect couple, both tall, both gorgeous, and if I didn't know better I'd think they were a match made in heaven, but something about him unsettles me.

I may not manage to look him in the eye, but I settle myself down on the sofa opposite him to try to suss him out, at the same time keeping one eye on Dan, who's making Tom giggle by blowing raspberries on his tummy. I smile as I watch them, watch how lovely they are together, and then turn my attention back to Andy.

It takes only five minutes for me to realize what it is I don't like.

I don't like the way he talks to Lisa, and I don't like his arrogance.

'Babe,' he says, lounging on the sofa and turning his head slightly so his voice carries over to where Lisa is changing Amy, but he doesn't actually make any effort to look at her. 'Did you forget the sugar?'

'Did I?' Lisa says distractedly.

'Uh huh,' he says, still not moving as he helps himself to a cup of tea without offering to pour for anyone else. 'Could you get it?'

Trish and I exchange a look, both of us expressionless but both clearly thinking the same thing, merely waiting for Lisa to say it out loud: could you get it yourbloodyself?

'I'll be there in a sec,' Lisa says, at which point I stand up and plant a quick kiss on the top of Tom's head. 'Don't worry,' I say to Lisa, studiously avoiding Andy. 'I'll get it.'

'I'll help you.' Trish jumps up and we both practically run into the kitchen.

'Do you believe what you just heard?' I turn to Trish in disbelief as soon as the kitchen door is closed.

'Unbelievable!' she echoes. 'Just who does he think he is?'

'How about a major arsehole?'

'Yup. That would just about describe it.'

'God.' I shake my head and lower my voice, in case anyone's outside the door listening. Crazy I know, but my personal paranoia. Which also makes me pick up the phone as soon as I've put it down, just to check I can hear the dial tone, although I do have good reason with that one . . .

Fran was over at my house one day, when Tom was about four weeks old and horribly colicky. Linda phoned and I said I couldn't talk and would speak to her another time.

I put the phone down and Fran asked me how things were going with the mother-in-law. I told her. It wasn't good. I needed to vent and this was the perfect moment. Out came a torrent of rage and frustration.

Later that evening Linda phoned again. This time I let the machine pick up and she proceeded to leave a message, saying that I hadn't put the phone down and she had heard everything.

I sat there feeling sick. Oh, my God. It was one

thing hating her but quite another having her know quite how much I hated her, and trust me, having heard my session that afternoon, I'm surprised she didn't go straight to the police in fear of her life.

So I sat there feeling sick and scared, and far too much of a coward to call her back. I was immobile until Dan got home, at which point I relayed the story to him in a frightened feeble voice, leaving out quite how bad my venting session was, simply saying she may have heard some things that were not too kind.

And Dan called her back. What she had heard, what she had continued listening to for twenty minutes while Fran and I had—thank God—gone into the kitchen to make a bottle—was Tom screaming.

Thank you, God. Thank you. I'll never do a bad thing again.

But meanwhile it's made me completely paranoid about phones being put down and people listening outside doorways, so before I carry on talking to Trish, even though I'm practically whispering, I double-check outside the kitchen door to make sure there's no one standing there.

'So maybe I'm being completely stupid,' I whisper, 'or maybe there's something I'm just not seeing about Lisa, but how come she always manages to pick such bastards?'

'I know!' Trish agrees. 'You would think that after The Deserter she'd deserve someone really lovely, but he's just an arrogant prick.'

'And she's so wonderful,' I muse. 'Is it insecurity?'

'What's going on in here?' The door opens and Lisa strides in, grinning. 'Are you two having a

154

private conversation or can anyone join in?'

'We were just saying how handsome Andy is,' I bluster.

'I know,' Lisa nods. 'He is gorgeous, isn't he? Even though he is a bit of an arse.'

Trish and I breathe an audible sigh of relief. 'Oh, God,' I say. 'Actually we were just saying that we couldn't believe how he talks to you.'

'I know. What did his last slave die of? Overwork?'

It's an old one but hearing it in this context makes us both laugh with relief.

'So why do you put up with it?' I ask. 'Does he treat you like that all the time?'

'Not all the time,' Lisa says, 'and I know he isn't a keeper, but it keeps the loneliness at bay, and, as horrific as I know it sounds, it's better than no one at all.'

'Really?' Trish looks doubtful. 'I always think you're so incredibly self-sufficient. Surely it's better to wait for someone really special than to put up with someone just for the sake of it.'

Lisa shrugs and admits, 'I'm not so good at being on my own, and anyway, he has his plus points.'

'Such as?' I'm still a sceptic.

Lisa grins. 'Such as he treats me well in some respects. Look.' She proffers a new bracelet-clad arm. 'He gave me this the other day. And he takes me to nice places. Plus'—she leans forward conspiratorially—'he's bloody amazing in the sack.'

There's an awkward silence as Trish and I look at one another, not quite sure what to say. Not because of the revelation, but because we can't see how this could possibly be a plus point when you have a tiny baby.

Trish bursts out laughing. 'You've got to be kidding!'

'No. Honestly. It's the best sex I've ever had in my life.'

'How can you even *think* about sex? Aren't you too tired?' My eyes are wide with disbelief. And just a smidgen of respect.

'Too tired? Are you crazy? It's about the only thing I have to look forward to right now.'

I think back to just the other night. As usual I'd climbed into a hot bath at eight o'clock, and was tucked up in bed in my flannel pyjamas by eight forty-five. Bliss. I figured fifteen minutes of reading and then lights out at nine. I knew I'd be asleep within two minutes.

But at eight fifty-four Dan walked in, sat on the bed, on my side, and leaned over to give me a kiss. I was hoping it would be a mere peck on the lips, but when he didn't move his head back more than three inches a familiar feeling of dread came over me.

And, lying in bed, resting against the pillows, with my husband coming in for another kiss, which I suspected would involve tongues, I did a quick calculation.

We had sex last Monday, which means it's been ten days. Once a week is probably a reasonable expectation, not an unreasonable one for me to fulfil, so do I have to do it tonight, and, if so—I glanced at the clock—could I get it over and done with in fifteen minutes?

I'm hoping to match Trish's world record of six.

Or could I do what I often do—but not too often because I don't want Dan to get too upset—and tell him I'm too tired? Because frankly I *am* too

156

bloody tired. I'm permanently exhausted, and still nursing during the day so my boobs feel, and look, like cow udders and I've never felt less desirable, nor less desire, in my entire life.

And so sex has become about going through the motions. Something I have to do to keep my husband happy, but I try to do it as little, and for as little time, as is humanly possible.

'Okay.' I take a deep breath. 'Let me just state for the record that if I never had sex again in my entire life it would be too soon.'

'Hear hear!' cheers Trish. 'Every time Gregory looks at me and raises his eyebrow my heart sinks.'

I burst out laughing, and then compose my features, raising an eyebrow at Trish. 'Coming to bed, darling?' I say, doing my best Dan impression, as Trish splutters.

'Oh, God! That's it! That's the look! It's the same as Gregory's! Either you've been sleeping with Gregory or all men have exactly the same look!' And she falls about laughing.

The kitchen door opens and Andy looms in the doorway. 'Babe?' he says sternly, looking at Lisa. 'The sugar?' and the three of us laugh even more, as he looks confused for a second before shutting the door and going back to the living room.

*   *   *

By the time we get back into the living room Gregory and Dan are getting on like a house on fire. Gregory is exactly the sort of man I would have chosen for Trish. He's short, ever-so-slightly tubby but in a cuddly, attractive way, and incredibly jolly. He seems to have a constant smile on his face,

157

and jolliness just exudes from every pore. I can't imagine anyone disliking this man. Ever.

Nor can I imagine him at work, and yet he's the head of public affairs for a huge television company, and prior to that was the head of public affairs for one of the nation's leading politicians, and before that he was a lawyer.

In other words you don't get much more high-powered than Gregory, and yet you could not hope to meet a more down-to-earth or more humble man, and I am delighted to see that he and Dan have found loads of things in common, and more delighted, in an incredibly puerile way, that Andy is completely left out.

Ha!

But the fact that he is an arse and that even Lisa thinks he's an arse begins to make me immune to his good looks—I'd go as far as to say he's becoming less good-looking by the second—and I start to feel slightly sorry for him, sitting by himself on the sofa. And so I go to sit next to him, figuring I'll at least make a bit of an effort, maybe give him a second chance.

'You seem to be very comfortable with Amy,' I lie, given that I haven't even seen him look at Amy, but it seems like a good place to start. 'You must like children.'

Even as the words come out of my mouth I'm regretting them, because as soon as he looks at me I know what he's seeing, and I hate what he's seeing.

He's seeing a dowdy suburban mother who can talk about nothing but her child, children in general or variations on the theme, such as nursery schools, nannies and the pros and cons of

158

Gymboree.

I had a career! I suddenly have the urge to shout. I *have* a career! I'm a successful professional! I'm not just a mother, I'm a person too!

Although now that I'm supposed to be going back to work in a couple of weeks, I'm starting to rethink the whole thing. I never thought for a second I'd be the kind of woman who would be satisfied with just looking after a baby, but now that I'm home I love it. Seriously. It's the most fulfilling, wonderful thing I've ever done, and I'm not sure I'm ready to go back to work. I just have to figure out a way to broach the subject with Dan.

But meanwhile I still read the newspapers, thank you very much. I still watch the news from time to time. I still know what's going on in the world and I hate that this man is looking at me with the kind of expression that says I couldn't possibly have anything to say that would be of any interest to him whatsoever.

'I'm not that used to children,' he says. Looking bored. 'But luckily Lisa takes care of all that.'

I just bet she does.

'Lisa tells me you're a photographer,' I attempt. 'What kind of work do you do?'

'Editorial mostly,' he says. 'Although I'm looking to branch out into more commercial work, and I've been talking to a resort in the Caribbean about doing their brochure, which looks like it's going to come off.'

'Really? That sounds great. We're always looking for new photographers when we do our campaigns. Maybe you've got a card?'

Go on, I'm thinking. Ask me what I do. Let me

159

tell you how interesting I am, how much more than just a mother I am.

'Sure,' he says. 'I've got some upstairs. I'll give you one before you go.'

And I can't help it. At this point I should have just left it, admitted defeat in the face of such self-absorption, but I was on a roll, and determined to show this arrogant man that I was his equal. Hell, I was even better than him.

'Our last campaign was done by Bruce Weber,' I say. 'You probably saw it. Calden. We won three awards for it. He did a great job.'

Finally his ears pricked up. 'Calden? The hotels?'

'Yes.' Now it's my turn to be nonchalant and bored.

'What do you do there?' His tongue is practically hanging out, so eager is he now to talk, because the campaign was huge, and anyone worth their salt—and even a few who aren't—knows about it, and all the creative people are desperate to get involved with the next one.

'I'm Marketing Director,' I say, and before he has a chance to engage me further I stand up. 'Whoops, I smell a nappy that needs to be changed. Come on, Tom.' I scoop Tom up from his position on the Gymini and walk over to the changing table. 'Let's sort you out.'

When we are finished and Andy is still looking at me in that eager, enthusiastic, networking sort of way, I purposefully sit next to Trish and Lisa and start talking sleep training with them.

And I spend the rest of the afternoon successfully avoiding Andy's attempts to talk further.

160

*   *   *

'So what did you think of them?'

Dan, Tom and I are back home. Tom has been bathed, fed, read to, and is now fast asleep, Dan is reading the *Sunday Times* at the kitchen table, and I am opening fridge, freezer and cupboard doors in search of some inspiration for supper.

Dan puts his paper down. 'I thought they were really nice,' he says. '*Really* nice.'

'What about Gregory? You seemed to hit it off with him.'

'I did. He was at that lunch I went to last week and knows the speaker really well, and he was just so interesting. I liked that Trish as well.'

'What about Andy? Wasn't he awful?'

'I barely spoke to him, but I heard your conversation.' Dan grins at me and I smile back, the picture of innocence.

'He was desperate to get in with you and you wouldn't give him the time of day!' he chuckles. 'That's my girl!' and I shrug and laugh.

'So did he manage to palm a card off on you, then?' Dan says as I nod, taking Andy's card from my pocket and tearing it into pieces over the dustbin.

'As if I'd work with someone as arrogant as that,' I say, snapping the lid of the dustbin shut.

'Quite right too,' Dan says. 'He was arrogant. And far too good-looking.'

'Yes, but less good-looking every second you talked to him. What about Lisa? Didn't you like Lisa? Isn't she lovely?'

'To be honest,' Dan says, shrugging, 'I didn't

161

spend that much time talking to Lisa either. I was just so caught up with Gregory.'

'Oh.' I'm disappointed. I wanted, want, Dan to love my new friends as much as I do, want him to be as enthusiastic about them as I am, want so much for his approval.

'Well, next time you'll get to talk to Lisa, and you'll love her. She's great.'

'Speaking of loving people.' Dan stands up from the table and comes over to me, putting his arms around my shoulders and pulling me close. 'Have I told you recently that I love you?'

'Hmm. I'm not sure I've heard that for a while.' I look up at him and smile. Dan has a raised eyebrow. He has *the look*.

Tonight I let him kiss me. Tonight I do more than let him kiss me—I kiss him back. We move to the bedroom, and forty minutes later—clearly tonight is not the night for world records—Dan is pulling his clothes on and heading out the door to get a curry, and I am lying in bed knowing that I have just won myself another week's grace.

13

Those moments of loving, of caring and kindness, of knowing exactly why we married one another and exactly why we plan to be together until death us do part seem so rare these days.

I didn't expect the first months after having a baby to be so hard, didn't expect a child to come between us instead of pulling us closer together.

I suppose that if anyone had warned me, warned

of the exhaustion, the loneliness, the loss of identity, I would either have thought they were lying or assumed that it may happen to other women, to other couples, but wouldn't happen to us.

But of course it does happen to me, does happen to us. Those first few weeks are terrible, and send me to bed most nights with my back turned to Dan, the result of yet another argument, more unspoken resentments that erupt late at night in a show of fierce words and raised voices.

For I am the one who gets up each night with Tom. Several times a night. I am the one who is unable to leave the flat until lunchtime, unable to even get out of my pyjamas, having to walk my colicky son up and down the stairs to keep him from screaming.

I am the one who deposits him in his father's arms on the weekends so that I can have a break, swiftly reclaiming him when I see, with mounting exasperation, that Dan has no idea how to soothe his own son.

And I am the one who is filled with anger, and resentment, and just plain damned exhaustion. Who has desperately started to miss going to work, but who could not deal with leaving her son for an afternoon, let alone the entire week, and who has made the decision to stay at home with Tom, working as a freelance consultant for Calden, instead of returning as Marketing Director.

Dan doesn't understand. *Couldn't* understand. Not when he leaves the house each morning and spends the rest of the day with grown-ups talking about grown-up things and not having to take responsibility for anyone other than himself. Not

163

when he is still perceived by everyone who knows him as the same old Dan Cooper, Producer Extraordinaire, who just happens to now have a son.

He could never understand what it is to lose your identity, to go from being a professional, successful woman to someone who is screamed at just because she is behind the wheel of a four-wheel drive.

He could never understand what it is like to manoeuvre a tired screaming baby in a buggy through the narrow aisles of a supermarket, trying to avoid people who stare at you and the baby in disgust, who even stop you to tell you that you shouldn't bring a baby to a supermarket.

The crowds rush to help Dan on the rare occasions he will take Tom out for a walk on a Sunday morning, so charmed are they by the sight of a man with a baby.

He could never understand, and I shouldn't blame him, but I do.

I blame him, and I blame his mother.

'How is my darling grandson?' says the message that she leaves every day, numerous times, on the answer machine. 'How's my darling baby?' she croons, as I shake my head wanting to shake her: he's not *your* baby, you silly cow. He's *my* baby.

And a few days ago: 'Hello, my gorgeous boys,' she says, as I fight the fury rising up within me. I may be the mother of her darling grandson, wife of her beloved elder son, but I seem to have become largely irrelevant. It is all about *the boys* for her, and I now know how difficult it is for Emma, the daughter Linda never really wanted.

Because whatever Linda says about her

daughter, however much she professes to adore Emma, I know, everybody knows, that the boys are the true loves of Linda's life, that she lives for Dan and Richard, and that as far as she's concerned Tom is another of her boys.

And I will not let that happen.

Linda phones, and when I don't pick up or return her calls, she drops in unannounced, and it's becoming a daily occurrence. I have tried pretending to be out, but she knows which car to look for on the street, and I have never been much of a liar, so reluctantly I let her in.

'But I phoned,' she'll say innocently, 'and you weren't here, and I just happened to be passing . . .'

She always just happens to be passing, and always just happens to have a package with her. These days her unannounced arrivals bear gifts for Tom: an outfit, a toy, some decoration for the nursery she just happened to see and couldn't resist.

I know how ungrateful I must seem, but she turns up with these ridiculous things that we don't need. Last week it was a winter coat, when we already have a beautiful winter coat that I picked up in the sale at Selfridges, and the week before a Fisher-Price aquarium that Rob and Anna bought him when we first brought him home.

I wish she would just ask me. If she would ask me whether he needs anything, whether *we* need anything, I would at least have the opportunity to say no, or to tell her that yes, actually, we need more towels, or more bibs, or the things we really do need.

Instead I know what she is doing: telling me she does not approve of my taste. Of the things I buy.

165

Of the way I dress my son. Telling me that she can do better. She is telling me that this is a competition—I have absolutely no doubt that in her mind this is a competition—and that she is winning.

She will not win.

I tell Lisa and Trish that I am at war with my mother-in-law, and every time I refuse to accept one of these gifts, send her away, inform her that we already have that toy, or that coat, or that mobile, I am winning a battle, on the way to winning the war.

I tell Dan too, try to explain how I feel, how I know she is in competition with me and that these acts are not bred of generosity but of competitiveness, and that I refuse to let her win.

We argue about it. About her. A lot. Far more than we ever did during the run-up to our wedding, which now feels a million years ago, as if it happened to someone else in another lifetime.

Dan hates being caught in the middle. Tells me repeatedly, as he always has done, that if I have a problem with his mother I should discuss it with his mother. Which of course is something I will never do.

He tells me I am being hormonal, which is guaranteed to send me into a blind rage, and that he refuses to get involved, sometimes just standing up and leaving the room.

And yet, despite my growing hatred of her, there are times when we seem to find a kind of peace. Times when I manage to let go of the hatred, times when I feel guilty, think I am perhaps over-imagining everything, that Linda is just being a doting grandmother. I then try to make it up to her: by inviting her to join Tom and me somewhere, or by phoning her and asking her over for tea, or by simply handing Tom to her when she walks in—something I am usually averse to doing.

Because Linda just *wants* so much. She is so damn needy. She doesn't know when to stop, she has no sense of boundaries. If I am holding Tom when she walks in, she will physically try to wrestle him from my arms, or if he is asleep she will bend over his crib, putting her face millimetres from his, and coo over him and stroke him until he wakes up and cries, at which point she will immediately try to scoop him up.

Although I usually get there first.

I talk to other women about their mothers-in-law, and their problems are always the same: they don't think the women are good enough for their beloved sons.

But I don't have that problem with Linda. My problem is that Linda doesn't know when to back off, to give me, us, space. So, although there are times when we find a kind of peace, it never seems to last. Linda always manages to say or do something that sends me into yet another fury, and I can't tell her, could never let it out, and so I withdraw yet again into a silent rage, praying that she'll just leave us all alone.

'You love Grandma the most, don't you?' Linda coos to Tom on a regular basis and I want to kill her.

'When Mummy and Daddy are horrible you'll come and stay at Grandma's house,' was another choice one that left me shaking with rage.

There are times when I wish I could confront her, just get it all out in the open, but that has never been my style, and I swallow all the feelings, taking them out on Dan instead, which isn't fair and isn't right, but I can't seem to help myself.

Do you think I don't know that Dan has started to dread coming home? Of course I know that. I know exactly how much he hates it when he walks in and I've had a bad day and take it out on him, and by the same token I know how relieved he is, how happy, when I have had a good day, when Linda has managed not to intrude on my serenity, and I am loving and warm to my husband.

My poor husband.

When we manage to discuss it calmly, Dan will admit he knows his mother can be overbearing, knows that sometimes she doesn't know when to stop, but he knows, he truly believes, that her heart is in the right place and that she is only trying to help.

He even admits that she's not good at taking no for an answer, but tells me that all I have to do is stand up for myself. But I have tried to explain that I want *him* to stand up for me.

When Linda swoops down while I'm giving Tom a bottle and tries to lift him out of my arms, what does Dan do? What does Dan say? Absolutely nothing.

'I'll wind him if you like,' Linda says to me, reaching out to lift Tom from my shoulder, and I literally have to turn away, saying, 'No thanks, I've got it,' and again Dan says nothing.

The latest thing, now that Tom is over three months and almost sleeping through the night, is for her to offer to have him overnight at their house to give Dan and me a break.

Dan thought it a brilliant idea, said that she

could see how exhausted we both were and that it was a genuine offer. He was ready to jump at the chance.

'Not that I don't love our weekends with Mr T.,' Dan cooed at Tom, flying him through the air and making whooshing noises, 'but it would be so nice for both of us to have a night off. Think about it. A romantic dinner. A lie-in. Tom thinks it's a great idea, don't you, Mr T. ?' he said, planting soft tickly kisses on Tom's neck.

No way. No bloody way. I don't care how exhausted I am, how blissful a night's unbroken sleep sounds right now, I will not let that woman have my son when I am not around.

*   *   *

As time goes on, it only seems to get worse.

'I just *hate* her,' I say wearily to Fran, having told her the entire story over lunch. Fran—God bless her—has brought her own nanny over to look after Tom while the girls are in nursery school, and has stolen me away for a grown-up lunch on Marylebone High Street.

Fran makes a face. 'Is it really that bad?'

I nod. 'I didn't think it was possible to hate someone this much, but I swear, she's the mother-in-law from hell.'

Fran frowns again. 'Okay, admittedly she's saying some stupid things, but I think she's probably just an incredibly insensitive woman who doesn't know where the boundaries are. Because, let's face it, she has been incredibly good to you.'

'Are you nuts? Only because she's trying to take over my life,' I say vehemently, my voice rising as I look at Fran in disbelief.

'It sounds awful, but she's not going anywhere,' Fran says. 'Listen, God knows I of all people understand what you're going through, but she's your mother-in-law. As long as you're married to Dan you're stuck with her.'

And I take a deep breath and say the thing I haven't yet told anyone. Not Fran, not Sally, not Trish and Lisa. The thing that I've been too scared to admit to, for fear it will make it come true, make it more real.

'You know,' I say slowly, looking at the table, unable to look Fran in the eye, 'I lie in bed at night and think about leaving him. I think about whether Tom and I could make it on our own.' I'm shocked that I've managed to voice my biggest secret, but Fran, instead of looking horrified as I had expected, merely laughs.

'And you think I didn't dream of that every night after I had the girls? I'd lie in bed hating Marcus and dreaming of divorce. So don't worry, it's absolutely normal.'

Relief washes over me. 'It is?'

Fran smiles again. 'Absolutely. But, Ellie, have you ever considered going to see someone?'

'What sort of someone?'

'A therapist.'

'Nope. Not for me. I couldn't sit there and talk about myself to someone for an hour, plus I couldn't find the time, and who'd look after Tom?'

'You could always ask your mother-in-law to babysit,' says Fran with an evil grin.

'Oh ha bloody ha. By the way, I left a message for Sally the other day and she hasn't called back. Is everything okay with her?'

170

Fran rolls her eyes. 'Yes, but she's developed this huge crush on Charlie Dutton, and I don't think it's going anywhere.'

Charlie Dutton. Charlie Dutton. The name's familiar but I can't place it, and I shake my head as I look at Fran and shrug my shoulders.

'The film producer? He was at our house that day you and Sally came over for lunch, remember?'

'Oh, yes.' Now I remember. 'Cute. With a son.'

'Exactly. Well, Sally managed to finagle a date with him and evidently she decided he's The One.'

'You mean she's finally found someone who's good enough for her?'

'Only because she barely knows him. He took her to Isola for dinner, then on to Soho House, where apparently they ended up sitting with Hugh Grant, so of course she's completely starstruck and is now dreaming of marriage.'

'You mean she didn't switch allegiances and develop a crush on Hugh Grant?'

Fran laughs. 'I think even Sally knows her limitations. Plus he was with a rather gorgeous brunette, apparently. But still, Sally's pretty much planning her wedding day.'

'And Charlie Dutton?'

Fran shrugs, looking pained. 'Hasn't called. Sally's begging me to get Marcus to phone him and find out what's going on, but, as Marcus said, we're not sixteen any more, and I don't really want to do that whole "my mate likes you" thing.'

I laugh. 'I know I'm supposed to say I'm so happy I'm not still out there, and obviously I wouldn't change Tom at all, he's just so amazing, but I do miss being single. I miss all the adventures. I miss sitting in Soho House and meeting people like Hugh Grant.'

'Bollocks,' says Fran. 'You're just forgetting what it's really like. The adventures happen maybe five per cent of the time if you're lucky, and the rest of the time you're doing what Sally's doing and sitting by the phone waiting for Prince Charming to ring, and then spending the next few months convincing yourself that it was because you weren't thin enough, or pretty enough, or trendy enough, or just simply anything *enough*. That's what you'd have to deal with if you were single again.

'Plus,' she continues, 'you'd be a single mother if you were to split up with Dan, which would not only be unbelievably hard, but you automatically reduce the number of men who would be interested.'

'Okay, okay,' I mutter. 'I was just saying that sometimes I miss it.' Which I do.

'I know. I'm sorry. And I *do* understand, but the other thing I know is that Dan is a really good man, and I think that whatever you're going through will pass, and that you mustn't act on anything right now, just sit tight and wait. Things will get better, I promise you. How old is Tom now?'

'Seven and a half months.'

'Thank God for that. You'll start getting some energy back and soon you'll be like a new woman again. Trust me.'

'You're sure?'

'I told you. I've been there. As for your mother-in-law, you have to trust me on that as well. She's not evil incarnate, she's just trying to find a way to fit into your life, and you have to find a way of letting her in.'

'I know,' I sigh, and Fran, even though she hates

172

her own mother-in-law, is probably right. 'I will try. I promise.'

* * *

And I do try. When Linda's name flashes up on my phone later that afternoon I put a smile on my face—I once read that if you force a smile when you talk on the telephone you will automatically sound happy—pick up the phone and say a breezy hello.

'Hello,' says Emma.

'Oh! I thought it was your mum.' Relief floods through me, despite my resolution.

'Nope. She's out. I just popped home to pick up a book I left here last weekend and I wondered if you were in. Can I come over?'

'That would be lovely.' I smile, missing Emma. 'The sun looks as if it's coming out so we can sit and play with Tom in the garden. I'll put the kettle on now.'

* * *

'I agree, the woman's a nightmare,' Emma says, cuddling Tom and covering him with noisy kisses, which makes him squeal and laugh. 'But I think she means well.' Emma echoes Fran's words and I wonder whether it is actually a good idea to confide in Emma. Linda is, after all, her mother, and they do say blood is thicker than water.

'She just wants to be involved and this is her first grandson,' Emma continues.

'But she won't bloody leave me alone,' I protest. 'She rings me every day, at least twice, and she keeps bloody popping in unannounced.'

Emma shrugs with a resigned smile. 'I know she's impossible. You should just do what I do and keep her at arm's length.'

'I try,' I say, 'but she doesn't get the message. Every day, for God's sake. Every day! What does she want to talk to me about every day? I don't even pick up the phone any more. If I see her name come up, I let the machine get it, and even then, if she's left a message and I don't call her back, she just keeps ringing and putting the phone down until I answer. I swear, your mother is completely mad.'

'Tell me about it,' Emma laughs. 'And you thought you were marrying into the perfect family.'

'Don't even remind me.' I grimace, knowing that Emma is unaware of quite how close to the truth that is. I watch Emma tickle Tom with her long hair as Tom giggles uncontrollably and reaches out to pat her face. 'You're really good with babies, aren't you?' I smile. 'Yet another hidden side of you.'

'I love babies.' Emma plants a noisy kiss on Tom's neck, making him laugh even more. 'Any time you want me to babysit, just ask.'

'Are you serious?'

'Absolutely.'

'Because we were invited out with these new friends of ours for dinner on Thursday, but we don't have a babysitter so I was going to say no, but if you could do it . . .'

'Oh, God, I'd love to, but this Thursday?'

I nod.

'I'm so sorry, but there's a do I can't get out of. If only you'd asked me earlier. What about my mum? Why don't you ask her? I know, I know,' she laughs, seeing the expression on my face. 'I know you don't want to, but, let's face it, you need a babysitter and she's practically wetting herself to babysit. She'd definitely do it.'

'Maybe.' I shrug, knowing full well I won't ask. Oh well. Maybe Trish and Gregory and Lisa and Andy can come here instead.

14

We don't go out that much any more, and the thought of a holiday is something that's completely beyond me at the moment. Spring was drizzly and miserable, there were two stunning weeks at the end of May where everyone stripped off to their underwear in the park to try to make the most of it, and now we're in June it's back to being warm and drizzly, and I've honestly forgotten what sunshine even feels like.

But today was a good day, and not just because the sun managed to break through the clouds. Today was a day that I wish could be repeated more often. I knew something would happen today, woke up this morning with a feeling of excitement, except I didn't think that anything was planned, that today would be different from any other Saturday.

Dan took Tom to see Linda and Michael this morning. This has started to become something of a routine, and I'll admit it is working out for all of us. I am finally able to let Tom out of my sight, Dan is able to spend time with his parents without worrying about Linda and me having some kind of passive-aggressive confrontation that would doubtless entail both of us bitching to him about the other.

And, just for the record, Dan would never admit that his mother bitches about me, but I'm sure she does. Of course she does. He's just too clever to tell me about it.

This morning Dan got Tom up for breakfast, gave him his bottle, fed him his Weetabix while he read aloud to him from the *Guardian* in a sing-song childlike voice, adding his own commentary when necessary.

'Listen to this, Mr T.,' he'll say, reading him a review of a film. 'Should you and I go to see it? Sounds like a good one.' And Tom will gurgle with pleasure.

So my Saturday mornings are much like my Saturday mornings of old. I have breakfast, a cup of tea, then climb back into bed with all the papers. Once I have finished reading, I usually switch off the telephone and drift back to sleep, and by the time I wake up again, usually late morning, I actually feel human.

Dan brings Tom home around lunchtime. Linda and Michael have already turned Dan's old bedroom into a fully equipped nursery, complete with a beautiful new cot that's just waiting for Tom to sleep in it, but even if I were willing I don't think Tom would sleep anywhere other than in his own bed in his own room.

Today Dan brings Tom home to put him down for his midday nap, and I can see, as soon as he walks in, that he's in a good mood. No, make that a great mood, and once Tom is down Dan grabs me and swings me around in a way that he hasn't done in months, and plants a huge kiss on my lips and

176

asks me how I would fancy a holiday.

How would I fancy a holiday? What a question! I would fancy one very much, thank you, but our Primrose Hill flat has left us house-poor, to put it mildly, and, given that I am no longer working full time, we had agreed that holidays were a luxury and not something we would be able to do in the foreseeable future.

Which is not the end of the world, holidays being something I very rarely think about. The only time I have actually missed them, or even thought about them, or thought that I might like to have one, was a few weeks ago when I went to the doctor.

They kept me waiting for forty minutes, and I idly picked up a copy of *Condé Nast Traveller*—I know, God knows what a magazine like that was doing in the doctor's surgery—and by the time I had finished the magazine all I could think about was white sandy beaches and warm turquoise waters.

Luckily I stepped out of the doctor's surgery on to Finchley Road, where I was almost run over by the 113 bus, which brought me swiftly back to the present, and all thoughts of sun and sand were entirely forgotten.

So how would I fancy a holiday? If I thought there was the remotest chance it was going to happen, I would say almost more than anything else in the world.

'Sit down,' Dan says, grinning like a maniac and pushing me down on to the sofa, where he proceeds to tell me what had happened at his parents' house that morning.

*   *   *

'There's something your father and I would like to talk to you about.'

Dan said he felt his heart sink. Any conversation that started like that immediately made him feel like a guilty teenager. Despite being an adult, and a husband and father at that, those words, an echo from his childhood, still struck fear in his heart, that dreadful, dreaded feeling that they had caught him doing something wrong.

'There's something your father and I would like to talk to you about.' Dan caught stealing the loose change from his father's dresser.

'There's something your father and I would like to talk to you about.' Dan and Emma caught smoking pot on the flat roof you could climb out on to from Emma's bedroom window.

'There's something your father and I would like to talk to you about.' Waving his school report in front of him, the one that always had those dreaded words written upon it, *could try harder.*

But of course they couldn't have found anything out, he told himself. What could he possibly have done that he wouldn't want them to know about? What illicit secrets could they possibly have discovered?

Dan arranged his features into an expression of interest to hide the vague anxiety that must, he assumed, be a leftover from his errant youth.

And his youth was rather errant, considering his privileged background. In line with almost every other middle-class North London privately educated schoolboy, Dan was, he claims, smoking cigarettes at thirteen, pot at fourteen and doing unmentionable things with girls from the

178

neighbouring schools in darkened bedrooms at parties he had gatecrashed. He was driving his parents' spare Mini—supposedly for the au pair girls—at sixteen with no driving licence and celebrated his graduation from Manchester University with a five-day cocaine and champagne binge.

You'd never believe it to look at him now, this fine upstanding figure of the community. But here in the home he grew up in, with his parents sitting opposite him at the kitchen table, Dan said he felt exactly as if he were still sixteen and about to get into serious trouble.

His father cleared his throat ominously. 'We want to talk to you about France.'

'France?' This didn't make sense to him. Why would his parents want to talk to him about France?

'You know we've taken a villa in the South of France this summer,' Linda said. 'And the idea was that your father and I would spend the whole of July and August there. The thing is, we've been invited on a friend's boat for the last two weeks of August, and we thought that, as the house would be empty for that time, maybe you, Ellie and Tom could do with a fortnight away. You both seem so stressed and tired, we thought that a holiday might do you the world of good.'

Michael then added: 'We know financially things are a bit tight, what with the new flat and everything, so we thought this would be a nice break, and obviously you wouldn't have to pay anything other than air fare.'

'You could even invite friends if you want,' Linda said. 'Goodness knows the house is big enough.

There are, what?' She turned to Michael. 'Four bedrooms? Five?'

Michael nodded. 'Four bedrooms on the main floor plus a tiny maid's bedroom behind the kitchen, so theoretically you could have a whole gang.'

'Although I'm not sure they *should* have a whole gang.' Linda gave Michael a warning look. 'Maybe just another couple. I'm sure that would be fine.'

Michael shrugged. 'It really doesn't matter, darling,' he said softly. 'Dan is a grown-up. I hardly think we're going to have a repeat of that incident when he had the party while we were away.'

'Mum, Dad,' Dan swiftly interjected, 'I don't know what to say.' And a smile spread across his face, and stayed there.

The South of France for a whole fortnight in a luxury villa just outside Mougins. And of course we were desperate for a holiday, hadn't planned on going anywhere this year, or indeed in the years to come.

Visions of swimming pools, coconut-smelling sun cream and lazing around under clear blue skies filled Dan's head, but he couldn't say yes without talking to me, even though he had a pretty good idea what I'd say.

'It sounds amazing,' he said calmly. 'I'm sure we'd love to, but let me just check with Ellie first. Let me talk to her about it and then let you know. But thank you, it's incredibly generous of you.'

Michael laughed. 'No, what would be incredibly generous would be if we offered to pay your air fares.'

'Any chance?' Dan said hopefully.

'Now you're pushing your luck,' Michael

laughed, and Dan had left, barely able to contain his excitement on his way home to tell me the good news.

*   *   *

'Yes!' I dance around the living room with Dan, both of us giggling like schoolchildren. 'South of France! Yesss!'

'So I take it you want to go, then?' Dan finally collapses on the sofa, thrilled at seeing me so excited.

'Phone them *now*!' I grab the portable phone and stand over him, dialling their number before handing him the phone as it starts to ring. 'Quick. Say yes before they change their mind.'

*   *   *

Later that night we lie in bed talking about France. Dan shows me the pictures of the house: an old stone *mas* nestling in the hills, a pretty swimming pool overlooking the valley and the hills beyond, a pergola covered with wisteria overlooking the pool, huge terracotta pots overflowing with trailing pelargoniums on the stone terrace.

It looks idyllic. It *is* idyllic. Like something out of a film. Like somewhere I would never have thought I'd be able to visit, let alone stay in.

'Christ!' I whisper, studying each photograph in awe. 'Look at this place! It's a palace!'

Dan just shrugs, much more used to this kind of luxury than me, for, although it is not the lifestyle we lead now, I know that Dan was brought up in the lap of luxury.

181

I know that on the rare occasions we go to the smartest of restaurants or fanciest of hotels, Dan is comfortable in a way that I never will be. He can speak to maître d's and managers with the ease that comes of having been brought up with the best of the best. I know that Dan probably spent most of his childhood staying in places much like this, whereas I have only seen this sort of thing in the pages of magazines like *Condé Nast Traveller*.

'So should we ask anyone?' Dan ventures. 'Or do you just want it to be a romantic getaway for the two of us?'

'As wonderful as that sounds,' I say, turning to Dan and kissing him softly, 'I think we'd have so much more fun with friends.'

'I think you're right. And now that Tom is practically ten months he'd also probably have more fun with other babies there. So . . .' He raises an eyebrow at me. 'Do I really need to ask who you want to come?'

Once upon a time Dan might have suggested the boys—Simon, Rob, Tom and Cheech and their respective partners. But, as much as I liked them, *like* them, our friendships seem to have drifted; we didn't see much of them after the wedding, and we've barely seen them at all since Tom was born.

Over the past few months Trish and Gregory have become our closest friends. We have what we always say is incredibly rare, which is a friendship that is entirely equal, and that, I think, was what was missing in the friendships with the boys. I liked their wives, Anna and Lily, but never felt I could talk to the boys in the same way, knew that if I had a choice, I wouldn't have chosen them.

But in our new friendship, I like Gregory just as

much as I like Trish, and Dan feels the same way.

If Trish phones, and Dan picks up, the two of them will chat for hours, and I do the same thing if Gregory picks up when I phone her.

The four of us have become, in a very short space of time, virtually inseparable, and I often find it hard to think of what we did before they came into our lives.

'Should I ring Trish and Gregory or will you?'

'I'll ring her tomorrow,' I say, suddenly frowning. 'What about Lisa and Andy? We can't invite Trish and Gregory without Lisa and Andy.'

Dan shrugs. 'You're the one with the problem with Andy. He's not a mate of mine, but he doesn't bother me, so if you want them to come, that's fine with me.'

'What about your mum? She did say one other couple. Do you think she'll mind if we ask both of them?'

'No. I think she'll be fine. It's not as if we're teenagers, despite what they may think. We're hardly going to trash their rented villa.'

'I don't know,' I say with a grin. 'I quite fancy the idea of throwing a huge party.'

'Well, hel-lo.' Dan looks at me with a raised eyebrow. 'This isn't the sedate, conservative wife I know and love,' and he rolls over towards me as I giggle.

Now you see why today was such a great day.

*   *   *

Thursday is the night we are supposed to be going out for dinner with Trish, Gregory, Lisa and Andy. I'd fought the impulse to say anything about France because I wanted to ask them face to face, and, as the six of us would be together, I thought Thursday the perfect opportunity.

Needless to say I don't phone Linda to request her babysitting services, and even though I've planned a delicious menu, I still feel terrible phoning everyone to say we have to bail because of babysitter problems and asking if they can come to us instead.

Trish says, 'Thank God.'

'Thank God?' I echo uncertainly.

'Thank God I don't have to go. I've been having clothes crises for the past week, and the only reason I was going was because I thought you lot wanted to go. I hate trendy restaurants. Completely intimidating and they always make me feel inferior.'

I start to laugh. 'Why didn't you just say no when Lisa first suggested it?'

'I thought we'd still have fun, but I'd much rather throw on my leggings and come to you for supper.'

'I know what you mean,' I grudgingly admit. 'I always feel slightly bad that I'm not into going to all the right restaurants and clubs. Half the time I don't even know what Lisa's talking about.'

Trish laughs. 'I know. I'm not bitching but . . .' I smile, because of course these words always preface something bitchy. We three have talked about the danger of threesomes. No, not that kind of threesome, but women's friendship triangles that inevitably leave someone out, or that turn one into the bitchee, the other two into the bitches. Trish and I resisted it for ages, but Lisa—and I do love her—Lisa is astoundingly superficial.

At first I thought it was funny. Lisa obsessed about these super-expensive Chloé jeans, until she got them, when she then became obsessed about a Prada bag, until Andy bought her one from a contact overseas somewhere, when she next became obsessed about a Cartier ring.

I repeat, I love her, but our lifestyles are very different, and I couldn't care less about nights out at Embassy, or wearing the latest Gucci coat, or being featured in a *Tatler* piece about 'hot mamas'—although that last one did make me feel kind of cool by association.

But the fact remains that Trish and Gregory and Dan and I don't care about the same things as Lisa, and inevitably there are times when Trish and I can't help but talk about it, our conversations always punctuated with 'I love her, *but* . . .' to try to ease our guilt.

'I'm not bitching . . . but I bet you anything Lisa doesn't come for supper.'

'What? You think she'll keep the reservation and go with Andy?'

'Yup. I'll bet you anything.'

'I think you're wrong,' I say. 'I know she's superficial, and I mean that in a caring way because I love her, but we're her friends and the point of the evening is to be with friends, not to go to some hot restaurant.'

'I'm telling you, she'll go to the restaurant,' Trish laughs. 'Go on. Phone her now. She's home, I just spoke to her. Call me back.'

'Okay, but I still think you're wrong.'

*   *   *

Five minutes later I call Trish back.

'You're such a bloody clever clogs.'

'No!' There was a sharp intake of breath. 'She's going to the restaurant?'

'Yup. And don't sound so bloody surprised.'

'What did she say?'

'There was a long pause when I said we'd have to change it to our place, and then she asked if I'd mind if they kept the reservation because they'd been dying to go and I knew how impossible it was to get in and blah blah blah.'

'Okay, so it's just the four of us, then. Even better. At least we won't have to put up with Andy.'

'Thank heaven for small mercies.'

'So what can I bring?'

'You do pudding, how does that sound?'

'Perfect. We'll see you Thursday.'

*   *   *

I love my friends, I think, curled up on the sofa next to Dan as Gregory helps himself to a drink and Trish kicks her shoes off to throw herself on the sofa opposite.

I love that I can have them over for dinner and wear jeans and fluffy slippers, and that it's completely comfortable. I may not have grown up with a close family, but I am creating my own and there is surely as much, if not more, love here than with most blood-ties.

'So.' Gregory sits down and sips his drink. 'You said there was something you wanted to talk to us about.'

Dan reaches under the coffee table and brings out the photo album of the house in France. 'Yup.'

186

He slides it over to Trish and Gregory. 'Have a look at this and tell us what you think.'

'What is it?'

'Have a look.'

I grin as they start to flick through.

'Let me guess,' Gregory says, turning over the pages. 'You've suddenly come into a windfall and you've bought this villa in Tuscany and you're going to pay for all of us to have a holiday.'

'Almost,' Dan laughs. 'It's not Tuscany, it's the South of France, and there's no windfall, but if you're interested it's ours for the last two weeks in August.'

'Ours?' Trish looks at me, her eyes lighting up. 'What do you mean?'

And Dan explains about the house, saying how much we'd love them to come.

'Done!' Gregory slaps his knee and reaches out to shake Dan's hand. 'We're there.'

Trish jumps up and hugs me. 'Oh, my God! This is what we've always talked about! Sharing a villa with friends. This is going to be the most amazing holiday! We're going to have a ball!'

'We're going to ask Lisa and Andy too,' I say, when we're all sitting down again. 'What do you think?'

'Absolutely!' Trish says.

'Unless Lisa gets a better invitation,' Dan says uncharacteristically.

'Mi-aow!' Gregory laughs. 'You're getting as bad as our wives.'

'Hey! That's not fair!' Trish interjects. 'We love Lisa.'

'Which is why the two of you are constantly bitching about her.' Dan raises an eyebrow.

187

'It's not bitching,' I say calmly. 'It's just talking, and anyway, we wouldn't say anything about her that we wouldn't say to her face.' This last statement isn't strictly true, but it sounds good and, more importantly, it sounds true and it's a great mitigating circumstance.

'Calm down, calm down. As far as I'm concerned the more the merrier.'

'There are five bedrooms, so if we bring travel cots the kids can sleep together.'

'Or in with us,' Trish says. 'Whatever. But how exciting! A holiday! And the South of France!' She turns the pages of the photo album back to page one and I sit next to her on the sofa as we study each picture intently, trying to memorize every shutter, every stone wall, every old cherry lit en bateau in the bedrooms.

'Isn't it idyllic?' sighs Trish.

'I know. And the best thing about it is it's only eight weeks away.'

'Oh, God.' Trish looks alarmed. 'Eight weeks? I still haven't got rid of the bloody baby weight. How much weight can you lose in eight weeks?'

'A good stone. Easily,' I say. 'But you'll have to start your diet tomorrow. I've slaved over the kitchen stove all afternoon and you have to eat everything tonight.'

'Okay.' Trish smiles. 'I'll try not to think of bikinis.'

'Bikinis?' I look at her in horror. 'Are you kidding? I haven't worn a bikini since I was about sixteen.'

'I know. Me neither. But one can dream.' She looks glum. 'I bet Lisa wears a bikini.'

'Yeah. And I bet she looks amazing.' I slump

next to Trish and we both look down at our protruding stomachs.

'Do you think I could get rid of this in eight weeks?'

I look down at my own. 'I think it would be a lot bloody easier to just go out and buy a Miraclesuit.'

'A Miraclesuit?'

'It's a new thing. Guarantees you lose ten pounds just by putting it on.'

Gregory, who's listening, starts to laugh. 'If it guarantees you lose ten pounds just by putting it on, then it really is a miracle. Do you mean it guarantees you look as if you've lost ten pounds?'

'Oh, don't be so bloody pedantic,' I huff. 'You know what I mean. So. Shall we go Miracle-shopping next week?'

'Count me in,' Trish says as we walk into the kitchen for supper.

15

Why didn't anyone ever warn me about packing when there are children involved, particularly children who have just turned one, and seem to need everything bar the kitchen sink?

Packing used to take me half an hour. I would scribble down a rough list, making sure I never forgot deodorant or underwear, would pull everything out of my wardrobe, lay it in a suitcase and I'd be done.

This time—our first holiday since having a child—packing has taken me about three weeks. I've made lists upon lists on top of lists. I've had to pack for the holiday, then pack for the flight. I've woken up in the middle of the night in a cold sweat, jumped out of bed to retrieve the Calpol from the medicine cupboard to shove it in the bag that's coming on board with us.

I've had to pack toys, and nappies, and wipes, and snacks. I've packed books, and baby sunblock, and antibacterial wipes and changes of clothes.

We've got the travel cot, the car seat, the bouncy chair and the portable highchair. And I've never been so tired in my life.

If I didn't need a holiday before I certainly need a holiday now.

I'm in Tom's room, looking around, for about the fiftieth time today. We're leaving tomorrow and I've been over and over everything, but I can't shake this nagging feeling that there's something I've forgotten, although, as Dan keeps telling me, we're going to the South of France, not outer Mongolia. If there's anything we've forgotten, we'll be able to get it out there.

The phone rings and I hear Dan get it, as I try to guess who he's talking to—I can usually tell just by the tone of his voice.

It's his mother. Definitely. I raise my eyes to the ceiling, even though the only person to see me is Tom, who starts to laugh because he thinks I'm making faces for him, which I then proceed to do as I shut the door. Whatever she's got to say I'm not very interested in hearing it.

Five minutes later Dan opens the nursery door and comes in sighing heavily.

'Go on, then,' I look at him. 'What did she have to say?'

'Do you want the good news or the bad news?'

he says, and my heart plummets. Shit. I can see it's going to be something really bad.

'Oh, God. It's the holiday. They can't be cancelling. We're going tomorrow, for Christ's sake. I don't believe this,' I start muttering, shaking my head. 'I'm going to kill them.'

'No, no. Relax,' Dan says. 'We're still going. That's the good news.'

'So what's the bad news?'

'They're going to be there too.'

*   *   *

It turns out that the yacht they were going on had an accident and somehow ran aground, and so they're now staying on in the house, but we shouldn't worry, they won't get in our way at all and think of it, won't this be fun, having a proper family holiday.

'Are you bloody kidding me?'

Dan shakes his head sadly.

'But that's insane. That's not a holiday, that's a *nightmare*. I don't want to stay with your parents. We've got to find somewhere else. Go somewhere else. Something!'

'I don't know what to say,' Dan says. 'We can't change the flights and honestly we can't afford somewhere else, not to mention that it's highly unlikely we'd even find anywhere for the last two weeks of August in the South of France. The place is probably booked solid.'

And I start to cry, disappointment and frustration simply overwhelming me.

'Oh, darling.' Dan crouches down and puts his arms around me. 'I know it's not what we expected,

191

but we can still have fun. And who knows, maybe they've got loads of things planned and we'll hardly see them.'

'Let me phone the others,' I sniff. 'God only knows what they'll say.'

*   *   *

I leave a message on Trish's mobile, then call Lisa, leaving a message on her home machine, subsequently catching her on her mobile.

'Where are you?'

'Just doing some last-minute shopping in Selfridges. I suddenly realized Amy doesn't have a bathing suit and while I was here I saw the most gorgeous Missoni bikini, which will be perfect.'

I wait for her to finish telling me about her latest acquisitions—oh, to have a wealthy ex-husband—and then hit her with my bombshell. 'Listen, I've got some bad news.'

'More bad news?' Just last week Andy had told her that he wouldn't be able to join us. A last-minute job had come up that coincided with the trip, and he was really sorry but the job was paying so much that he couldn't turn it down, and work would have to come first. There was a possibility, he said, that he might be able to make it out for the last weekend, but he wasn't sure.

I'm not sure who was more relieved. Us or Lisa. Trish and I were thrilled, even though naturally we couldn't tell Lisa that, but even she admitted that things hadn't been going that well between them and she was probably better off having a holiday without him.

Part of the problem, she said, other than his

general arseiness, was Amy. He just wasn't the slightest bit interested in Amy, so he was never a long-term proposition and they were reaching the point where the relationship was probably coming to the end of the line.

Her only disappointment was that she'd be, as she put it, the odd one out.

'You'll probably pick up some millionaire on his yacht in the harbour,' I'd said half jokingly, because Lisa was exactly the sort of woman you see on the arm of those European playboy millionaires.

'Hmm,' she'd said. 'Now there's a thought. Maybe it won't be such a bad thing after all.'

'No, this is really bad news,' I say to her now on the phone. 'Dan's parents are going to be there. Can you believe it?'

'What do you mean, they're going to be there? I thought they were going on a yacht?' And so I explain and Lisa starts to laugh.

'Oh, darling, that's not so terrible. I thought you were going to say the holiday had been cancelled. I'm sure his parents will be fine and I bet you we'll hardly see them. They must feel awful about it— they'll probably be out all the time.'

'That's what Dan said.'

'See? And they're his parents, he knows them better than anyone. Anyway, your mother-in-law won't dare be a battleaxe with Trish and me on your team. If she's horrid to you, I'll punch her. How's that?' I start to laugh. Maybe Lisa's right. Maybe it won't be so bad after all.

'Look on the bright side,' Lisa continues. 'We'll have on-site babysitting every night and we'll all be able to go out for dinner. I promise you, it's going to be great. Don't you worry about a thing.'

193

Heathrow is packed, filled with the hustle and bustle of excited holidaymakers and excitable children. Tom is, thank God, being exceptionally well behaved for a one-year-old, despite the fact that we had to get him up at five o'clock this morning. He dozed off again in the car, but now seems to be quite happy being pushed in his buggy, clutching on to his rabbit—rather unimaginatively called Rabbit—eyes wide at all the noise.

I'm in a Gap sweatsuit, which I swear looks exactly like the much more expensive Juicy Couture version, and new Puma trainers, and I'm feeling pretty good, if I do say so myself, feeling as if I look rather like Victoria Beckham striding through an airport, minus the baseball hat, sunglasses and hair extensions of course.

I can't believe we're actually going on holiday! To the sun! Relaxation! The disappointment of Linda and Michael being there too seems to have disappeared overnight, and now I just feel a bubble of excitement that we're finally going away.

Holidays have never really been part of my vocabulary. I never travelled as a child—my mother's relationship with the bottle made her a dangerous travelling companion—and I've never seen the point of wasting hundreds of pounds to lie around a beach when there are plenty of other more important things that money could be used for.

And although I understand the concept of *needing* a holiday, I've never quite caught on to it myself, and have rarely, if ever, felt that I needed it.

That was all before having children. Now that Tom has arrived and sleepless nights are no longer twice-yearly events as a result of a great all-nighter but weekly, and sometimes nightly, events as a result of simply being a parent, I fully understand the concept of needing a holiday.

But even before this morning, before arriving at the airport and catching the general buzz that fills the air, I hadn't known quite how excited I could be.

So I'm feeling great, and then I catch sight of Lisa, on the opposite side of the departures hall, standing astride a Louis Vuitton holdall, talking animatedly into a mobile phone, wearing tight white trousers, high-heeled mules, a bright swirly Pucci print shirt, huge dark Jackie O sunglasses and gold hoop earrings.

Suddenly I feel all wrong. There I was, admiring myself in a shop window not three minutes ago, and now I feel like a dowdy suburban housewife trying to be trendy. Oh, God, how I wish I looked more like Lisa, who looks very much like Elizabeth Hurley right now, only blonder.

And Amy is the perfect accessory, beautifully dressed in an old-fashioned rose print dress, reclining in a Bugaboo Frog, the very latest designer buggy on the market. The pair of them look as if they've just stepped out of a magazine advert.

Just as we reach them, Trish and Gregory veer in from the left, Trish all a fluster trying to push the buggy, hold an armful of jackets and simultaneously attempting to pick up the trail of Cheerios Oscar is leaving behind him.

She gives me a hug, kisses Dan, then turns to

Lisa, who clicks her phone shut and hugs all of us.

'Lisa!' Trish shakes her head when we disengage. 'How on earth do you manage to look like such a glamourpuss at this godawful hour of the morning? Why can't I look like you? Tell me how you do it!' Lisa laughs and I relax—how silly to be intimidated by such a good friend, and we all check in and go through security to wait in the lounge.

The boys watch the kids as we three hit the bookshop for our beach reads, then duty free for what Lisa calls the obligatory bronzing powder, and we get back just as our flight is being called.

Air France stewards manage to ignore Trish and me, give Gregory and Dan a perfunctory nod, and then practically gush all over Lisa, who, it turns out, speaks more than passable French. I should have known, although once we sit down she swears that she has a crap vocabulary but a great accent, so everyone thinks she speaks the language far better than she actually does.

We're settling into our seats, getting the babies comfortable, as Dan sits next to me eyeing all the passengers filing on to the plane.

'Why are you giving them all the evil eye?' I ask after a while.

'Just trying to figure out if any of them are terrorists,' Dan says seriously as I splutter.

'Oh. Fine. So what are you looking for? Someone with a bomb strapped around his waist? Tell-tale wires hanging out of his t-shirt?'

'Oh ha ha.' Dan breaks his evil-eye assessments to look at me. 'They say these days that you should know who your fellow passengers are.'

'So why aren't you introducing yourself? Finding out their life stories?' I can't help snorting.

'Okay. Great idea. I'll just go and introduce myself to her.' He smiles, gesturing at a gorgeous model-type who's making her way up the aisle, sunglasses perched prettily on top of her head.

'Calm down, calm down.' I rub his arm and lean over to give him a proprietary kiss. 'You ain't seen nothing yet, big boy. If you think she's gorgeous wait till you see all the topless babes on the beach.'

Dan grins. 'Why do you think I'm so excited about this holiday?'

'Not the prospect of me going topless, then?' I raise an eyebrow as Trish leans over from my other side.

'Okay,' she says. 'I admit it. I've been earwigging.' And she looks at me in amazement. 'You're not seriously going to go topless, are you?'

'I very much doubt it. Before Tom I might have done, but now that my boobs are swinging somewhere around my ankles, I need all the support I can get.'

'Oh, good. So I'm not the only one, then. You know Lisa had them done.'

I nod as Dan's eyes light up. 'Done?' he says. 'You mean a boob job?'

'Yup.' I nod. 'She had them lifted and implants. Stop panting, Dan, I'm sure you'll get to see them.'

'I'm surprised she's not topless on the plane,' Trish says, and I laugh, because Lisa's openness never fails to amaze me.

She had the operation a couple of months ago, not that there seemed to be any need for it, and as soon as she was healed she stripped off in her living room and insisted we feel them, which Trish and I both did, rather gingerly. It was hard to be objective when one of your best friends is standing half naked in front of you insisting that you feel her breasts.

But I have to say I did feel rather envious. Her breasts were spectacular, even if they did feel rather hard. I have no doubt that Lisa will be wearing nothing more than bikini bottoms, and that Dan and Gregory will be enjoying every second of it.

'Lisa!' The model-type with the sunglass hairband reaches us, and her eyes widen as they alight upon Lisa.

'Kate!' Lisa passes Amy over the aisle to me and stands up to give her a hug. 'Oh, my God! What are you doing here?'

'We're staying with Jonathan and Caro in Grasse! There's a whole gang! Me and Sarah, and Mark and a couple of others! You'll have to come up and see us. But what are you doing here?'

'We've got a house in Mougins, a stone's throw from you, you'll have to come and see us too!' I overhear these words and feel a flush of anger at my in-laws again. If they weren't here, we could gladly host whomever we want; but they are here, and I think it highly unlikely they'll want hordes of people trooping in.

'Oh,' Lisa says, turning to us, 'these are my friends,' and she introduces us all as we smile and lean over to shake hands, and I wish I was in jeans and a white t-shirt, even though I'd have to be at least a stone lighter to look half as good as this Kate.

'Okay,' I whisper to Trish once Kate has disappeared off down the aisle. 'I know this sounds ridiculous but why do I always feel so inadequate next to Lisa and her friends?'

198

'Why do you care?' Trish shrugs. 'Remember, you mustn't judge books by their covers. I know Lisa looks like a model, but we wouldn't be friends with her if she wasn't genuine and lovely. And that Kate's probably lovely too.'

'How do you always manage to see the good in people?'

Trish shrugs. 'Just the way I am. Although I'm not averse to a little bad. For instance, Lisa, lovely as she is, does sometimes astound me with her love of designer labels.'

'Are you trying to say she's superficial?' I say, grinning.

'Absolutely. Anyway, we're not bitching. Part of the reason why we love her is *because* she's superficial. And anyway, we wouldn't say anything that we wouldn't say to her face,' Trish says earnestly, and we both burst into laughter.

'What are you two laughing about?' Lisa leans over from across the aisle, where Amy is perched delicately on her lap.

'We were just saying we wish we knew as much about clothes as you,' I say, figuring that it's probably as close to the truth as I'm ever going to get.

*   *   *

As soon as we step off the plane the warmth hits us, and I take Dan's hand and squeeze it hard. It feels so long since our honeymoon, so long since we were hit by the blazing warmth of a hot sun, that it is completely transformative, as if warmth and happiness were bound up in one.

Dan smiles at me, reading my mind. 'It looks like

we all really needed this holiday.'

'Doesn't it feel good, though?'

'You're feeling better about my parents being here?'

I nod. Because now that I'm here I'm sure it won't make the slightest bit of difference. I need this break a lot more than they do, and I'm going to have a good time, in-laws be damned.

We swap numbers with Kate at the airport, amidst promises that we will all get together, and I am vaguely disorientated when she insists on giving us all a double air kiss, even though she doesn't know us.

'When in France . . .' Lisa laughs as we walk off towards the car rental. 'At least we're not in Paris,' she continues. 'The last time I was there they were up to about five kisses. It went on for ever. Jesus, saying goodbye to three people would take about an hour.'

Two Renaults are waiting for us, and within fifteen minutes we've left the airport and have started the drive up the coast from Nice Airport, through Cagnes-sur-Mer and up towards Mougins.

'Look! Palm trees!' I keep saying, turning round to Tom to point them out, though he probably hasn't the slightest idea what I'm saying. I read somewhere once that the brightest children are the ones whose parents talk to them a lot, even about the most inconsequential things, and of course Tom is a genius in the making, so I do my best to nurture that by chatting to him all day long, usually about complete rubbish.

Dan once caught me asking Tom's opinion about whether to wear the black trousers or the brown. At the time Tom was propped up on our bed with pillows, chewing mercilessly on a rubber teething ring, although he did look at me as I held the trousers up for him to view.

'Um,' Dan said from the doorway as I jumped, 'I think perhaps you've been spending too much time with Tom. Something tells me you need a little bit of adult company,' and we had both laughed.

But it's a hard habit to break, and not one I'm particularly interested in breaking just yet, and so I point out everything we see to Tom. I even do the odd translation from French, which I strain to remember from school.

On the outskirts of Mougins we veer up a steep hill, as I try to follow the directions Dan's parents faxed us a few days ago, Trish, Gregory and Lisa in the rental car behind us, laughing at us through their open windows as we keep taking wrong turns and having to do three-point-turns in strangers' driveways.

And finally we find Rue des Oiseaux and drive on a pot-holed dirt track that seems to lead to nothing—until at the top the track becomes smooth gravel, and then we pass through stone pillars and into a wisteria-covered car port.

We climb out and rush around the old pathway to the front of the house, where we push open a heavy oak door to find a note lying on the doormat.

Dan, Ellie and the gang
Have gone to village for some food.
Make yourselves at home. Towels at the side of pool. Enjoy!
Love, Mum and Dad

'Right, says Gregory, dumping their bags just inside the front door. 'How about a swim?'

Trish raises an eyebrow and turns to him. 'How about finding our room so we can unpack, put our stuff away and put Oscar down for a much needed nap?'

Oscar, right on cue, starts to wail, which sets off first Tom and then Amy.

'Good idea, Trish,' Dan says. 'Let's get the kids out of the way so the grown-ups can have fun.'

'Charming!' I shake my head. 'If your son and heir could only understand what you were saying.'

'Even if he could understand, he wouldn't be able to hear, not with all that screaming.'

'Well, how about helping us all find our bedrooms so we can get the travel cots unpacked?'

'Okay, okay,' Dan heads up the stairs with some bags. 'I'll go first. Let's try to figure it out.'

16

I might have known that Linda and Michael would keep the master bedroom for themselves. For the last two months I've been flicking through the photo album, looking at the house and romanticizing about lying in the huge king-sized bed with the french doors flung open as sunlight streams in, washing over the breakfast tray perched on the bed, piled with hot, fresh croissants, pain au chocolat and steaming café au lait.

And so I think I'm entitled to feel ever so slightly pissed off, given that the minute we walk into the master bedroom it is immediately clear that Linda and Michael have no intention of moving out to make way for us.

Linda's trashy novels are piled high on the bookstand, her shoes lined up on the floor, and a couple of pashminas draped over the armchair in the corner.

Still, I open the armoire door just to check, and sure enough it is filled to bursting with Linda's and Michael's clothes.

'Fuck!' I hiss, sitting down on the bed as Dan looks concerned.

'I'm sorry,' he sighs, putting an arm around me. 'I know you were looking forward to staying in this room, but it will be fine, we're still going to have a lovely time.'

'I know, I know. I'm being horrible, and particularly because this is their holiday and they are paying for it. I was just so looking forward to staying in this room.'

'Well, let's go and check out the others, bag ourselves the next-best room before one of the others gets to it.' Dan grins, pulling me up, and I reluctantly follow him out.

The bedrooms are called, in turn, the blue room, the green room, the yellow room and the maid's room. Although putting the children together seemed like a good idea at the time, when we actually see the maid's room we realize that there's barely enough room for one travel cot, let alone three.

'Couldn't we put them all in the same cot?' Lisa groans as we laugh.

'No, but we should make a deal. Whoever has the smallest bedroom has the maid's room for their child.'

'Bags have the smallest bedroom,' Lisa says hopefully, but in the end we write the room colours on pieces of paper and draw them from an ashtray, Lisa closing her eyes and muttering 'yellow room, yellow room, yellow room' as she fumbles around for her magic piece of paper.

Lisa has the blue room, Trish and Gregory the green, which is probably the biggest aside from the master, and Dan and I the yellow, which may be the smallest but has the distinct advantage of having a tiny little balcony overlooking a red-tiled roof, with an olive orchard below.

A rickety iron table with two chairs sit on the balcony, and as soon as we've shoved everything away in a huge cherry armoire that's squashed against the corner of the room, we take Tom outside on to the balcony and sit for a while, drinking in the sunshine and the view.

'Come on,' Dan says eventually. 'Why don't we put Tom down and go for a swim?'

*　　　*　　　*

I think my Miraclesuit is pretty damn miraculous. It's just a shame it doesn't reach down to my knees because my cellulite could definitely do with a miracle or two. Still. I cover the offending areas with a huge semi-see-through sarong from Accessorize, and swish down to the pool with my sun cream in hand.

It seems we have all had the same idea. Trish is rubbing cream into Gregory's back, and, as we round the corner, Trish looks up and grins, gesturing at Lisa, and I hear a sharp intake of breath from Dan.

'All right, deep breaths. Relax,' I mutter, patting his arm gently, although I have to admit, oiled up and floating round the swimming pool on a lilo, bare breasts pointing towards the heavens, she does look pretty damn amazing.

'Lisa,' I call, as she lazily floats towards us, 'I think your breasts ought to have a government warning. My husband's about to have a heart attack.'

'What's the point in spending all that money on them if there's no one to see them?' she shouts.

'Point taken,' I say. 'Anyway, you'll certainly make my father-in-law's day, if nothing else.' I then mutter to Dan, in a much softer voice, 'Not sure what your mum will think, though.'

'She'll probably turn green with envy,' Dan says. 'And demand to know who her surgeon is.'

Dan pulls a couple of sun loungers next to Gregory and Trish.

'Okay,' Trish says, standing up and shielding her eyes from the sun. 'Given that we are all seeing one another nearly naked for the first time, I need to get a few things out of the way. These'—she turns around and gestures to her calves—'are my revolting varicose veins, which are hereditary but have been exacerbated massively by that little peach known as Oscar. This'—she grabs a handful of dimpled thigh—'is my orange peel, and this—' she pats her protruding stomach—'is, again, the mark of Oscar the terrible.'

'Darling,' Gregory says, raising himself up on his elbows, 'why on earth are you insisting on pointing out all your imperfections? You don't hear me saying anything about mine.'

'That's because you're perfect.' She winks at me.

'I knew there was a reason I married you.' Gregory reaches over and squeezes her hand affectionately.

'Honestly?' Trish frowns. 'I just want to make sure everything's out in the open. I'll never forget going on holiday with my parents and some friends of theirs, and as soon as we were back at the hotel my mum kept talking about how saggy her friends' boobs were, and how she never had any idea how pear-shaped she was. I couldn't stand to think of you going back to your room and talking about my cellulite and varicose veins, so I figured if I made a big deal of them myself there wouldn't be anything left for you to talk about.'

Dan looks at Trish, shaking his head. 'You're really weird, do you know that?'

Trish shrugs. 'Just practical.'

I look over at Lisa doing her best Hawaiian Tropic ad impersonation.

'Has Lisa had the pleasure of counting your imperfections yet?'

Trish nods. 'Of course.'

'And let me guess, she doesn't have a single imperfection of her own, does she?'

'I do!' Lisa shouts from the pool. 'I have the worst spider veins on my thighs you've ever seen. Look.' She points to her thighs. Acres of taut, golden skin.

'She doesn't, does she?' I grin at Trish.

'Couldn't find a one.' Trish grins back.

'And I've got loads of ingrowing hairs on my bikini line,' Lisa yells. 'Horrible huge purple bumps—'

'Okay!' Dan interrupts her. 'I think that's enough for today.'

'Hear, hear,' echoes Gregory. 'And for the record can I say that all three of you are the most gorgeous women I've ever seen. OW!' He shoots Trish a look as she gives him a sharp nudge. 'Although, and I'm not biased, I do have to say that my wife is the most gorgeous of all.'

'I knew there was a reason I married you,' Trish says to Gregory, and leans down to give him a kiss.

*   *   *

'Isn't this completely blissful?' I put my book down, roll over and plant a kiss on Dan's hot shoulder. 'Mmm. You taste of coconut.'

'This is wonderful.' Dan smiles at me. 'Isn't it funny how you never realize you need a holiday until you're actually there, and then you wonder why on earth you don't do it more often?'

'Until you get home, and then three days later you forget you were ever even away,' I say, smiling. 'I'm going to go and check on Tom.'

'Will you look in on mine?' Lisa shouts. 'Although I think she'll still be sleeping.'

'I'll come with and check on Oscar.' Trish hauls herself up from her lounger and stretches. 'Wouldn't it be lovely if they were so exhausted they just slept all afternoon and we could laze around all day pretending we didn't have children?'

'Not that we'd change anything . . .' I give her a look.

'Absolutely,' she laughs. 'Not that we'd change anything. Except perhaps that we'd all have full-time nannies on holiday.'

*   *   *

Oscar is still sleeping peacefully, arms and legs akimbo, snoring and snuffling quietly.

'Aren't they so gorgeous when they're asleep?' Trish whispers, gently shutting the door as we go to look in on Amy, also fast asleep.

We walk down the corridor towards our room, and Trish turns to me, looking puzzled.

'Sssh,' she says, and we both stop and listen.

'That's weird.' She frowns. 'I could swear there's conversation coming from your room.'

'Is there? I mean, I know my child's a genius but isn't that a bit much, even for him?' I start to laugh, and then I hear it. The unmistakable sound of Linda's voice.

'There's my good boy.' Linda's sitting on the bed, bouncing a giggling Tom as I open the door. 'Who loves his grandma?' she's crooning. 'Who loves his grandma?'

Tom looks over at me and immediately his little face crumples and he holds out his arms for mummy.

Ha!

I rush over and take him, patting his back and kissing him, looking furiously over at Linda.

'Did you wake him?' My voice is murderous.

'No!' she says, eyes wide and innocent. 'We came back and I just wanted to see him, and I didn't know which room he was in, but I swear, when I opened this door his eyes were open and he was looking at me.'

'So how long has he been up?' I look at my watch, still furious.

'I told you,' Michael speaks up for the first time, shaking his head and looking at Linda. 'I told you not to come in.'

'But I didn't wake him,' Linda insists. 'He was already awake.'

'Fine,' I say. 'But how long has he been up?'

'I came in about ten minutes ago.'

Michael snorts and I know she's lying, but I haven't got the strength. 'Fine,' I repeat. 'So he's had about an hour and a half rather than his usual three hours, which means he'll be horrific by five. Thanks a lot, Linda. Will you be the one to look after him when he's completely overtired and screaming later today?'

'Yes,' she says eagerly. 'Of course. It would be my pleasure,' and I just roll my eyes and leave, stomping back out to the pool.

'I don't believe your mother.' I stand in front of Dan's sun lounger, making sure I block all his sun and throw a big shadow over him.

'What?' Dan sighs. 'What's she done now?'

'She's here, and she woke Tom up from his nap and she's been playing with him, and you know what he's like when he hasn't had enough sleep. Now he's going to be horrible later on. I can't believe she did that. I just can't believe it.'

'Okay, okay. Relax. I'm sure she didn't mean to. I didn't even know they were here. Where are they?'

'Inside somewhere. I didn't even know they were here either. I found them playing with Tom in his room.'

'You stay here and calm down. I'll go in and say hello. They should probably come outside and meet everyone. Here, give me Tom, I'll take him in.'

'So your mother can get her hands on him

again?' I practically spit. 'I don't think so. Tom can stay here with me.' I make myself busy rustling around in the beach bag for the Factor 30. 'Go on, off you go. We'll be fine.'

*   *   *

After twenty minutes—during which time I calm down considerably, although it is beginning to get rather tiring, dashing around after Tom, who keeps trying desperately to crawl into the swimming pool—Dan, Linda and Michael all come outside to say hello.

And okay. I have to admit it. I take great pleasure in Linda's face when Lisa climbs out of the pool and glides over to shake her hand, still wearing only a large smile and the skimpiest of bikini bottoms.

Linda, in leopard-print swimming costume with a matching sarong, is clearly mortified, doesn't have a clue where to look.

'How do you do?' she says formally, shaking Lisa's hand and staring intently into her eyes, pretending not to notice or be embarrassed by the fact that Lisa is about as close to naked as you can get.

Michael, on the other hand, grins delightedly.

'Hel-lo!' he says, raising his eyebrows, and looking like the cat that got the cream as Linda turns to no one in particular and rolls her eyes. 'How lovely to meet *you*,' and he shakes Lisa's hand, still grinning, and gives her a very obvious once-over. 'So you're a good friend of Ellie? It's always a pleasure to meet Dan and Ellie's friends.'

I nearly fall over backwards. This is Dan's dad.

His dad! His hen-pecked, greying, unsociable dad. His dad, who doesn't display an ounce of charm or charisma outside the walls of the courtroom, who appears to have suddenly and rather unexpectedly morphed into Leslie Phillips.

'I *say*,' I fully expect him to continue, 'for young mums you gels are *beng* on.'

Of course he doesn't say that. He turns to shake hands with Trish and Gregory ('I felt like apologizing,' Trish says later. 'Sorry I'm not a six-foot blonde with pneumatic tits'), although he excuses himself at the first opportunity and goes for a swim, only, I suspect, to get a better view of Lisa's body, as she positions herself back on the lilo.

Trish raises her eyebrows at me. '*He's* a bit of a boy, your father-in-law!' We watch him doing some lengths, pausing at each end to take a breath and look over at Lisa.

'I know!' I start to laugh. 'Who would have thought! My old grey father-in-law fancying Lisa! I didn't know he had it in him.'

'Oh, come on, he's not so old and grey,' Trish says in surprise. 'In fact I think he's quite attractive. Maybe your mother-in-law should watch out.'

'Oh, yeuch.' I make a face, but find myself looking over at Michael through new eyes. Could he be attractive if he wasn't my father-in-law? I've never found myself attracted to older men, but I suppose if I were, and if he wasn't Dan's father, and if I didn't know he was quite as hen-pecked as he is, I might find him attractive in a Michael Douglasish kind of way.

And although I'm not going to tell Trish that she's right, she is right about looking at people in a

211

new light when you see them with next to nothing on.

I had never given a second thought to what my father-in-law might look like without clothes, but I have to say seeing him here in swimming trunks I'm pretty surprised by how fit he is. Put it like this, for a man who must be in his late fifties, his physique looks like that of a far younger man.

'Do you think he's really flirting?' I say, watching Michael pause again after swimming a length, and look over at an oblivious, still-floating Lisa. 'It's just so weird to think that he might actually be flirting with a friend of mine.'

'Nah,' Trish says. 'I don't think he's really flirting. I think he's just enjoying the scenery. He's probably never seen anything like it before. Not that close, anyhow.'

'Oh, those famous South of France hilltops, you mean.'

'Those would be the ones.' And we both grin.

Dan walks over and sits on the edge of the sun lounger. 'Ellie, will you do my back?' I sit and massage in the cream, planting a kiss on the side of his neck when I've finished.

'Mmm. Thanks. I'm going to take Tom into the pool. Want to come in with me?'

'Let me just go and get the camera. I'll be back in a minute.'

'Good idea.' Trish stands up with me. 'I'll go and see how Oscar's doing, and if he's awake we can take some group shots.'

*   *   *

By early evening I've forgiven Linda. The

212

afternoon was exhausting. Dan and I took turns dashing after Tom, who is now crawling at the speed of light, and even though he's permanently wearing his floaters, I'm terrified every time he gets within about twenty feet of the pool.

'Didn't we say this was supposed to be a relaxing holiday?' I huffed at Trish at one point.

'Ask your mother-in-law to take him,' she muttered, gesturing over to where my mother-in-law was pretending to read her book, looking longingly at Tom every few seconds.

'No,' I said, but as Tom struggled in my arms I couldn't help myself. 'Linda?' I said. 'Do you want to take Tom?'

Linda almost fell over in her eagerness to reach us, as if she had to get to him before I changed my mind. 'I'll take him inside,' she said. 'We'll play some games. Come along, my darling, Grandma will show you what she's got you.' She whisked him away, and for once I didn't protest, just lay back with a lazy smile on my face and let all the cares of the day slip away.

*   *   *

'What do you think the chances are of going out for dinner tonight?' I ask Dan, when we are alone in our room, one looking after Tom while the other one showers.

'Who? You and me?'

'No, silly! Us! All of us. Do you think your parents will mind?'

Dan frowns. 'I think they might, actually. You know, it is our first night here, and they probably want to get to know everyone. Plus you know my mum, she's probably been working overtime making some delicious supper.'

'So that's a no, then?' I harrumph miserably.

'To be honest I don't even want to ask her,' Dan says. 'We've got masses of time. And tomorrow we'll all go out. They won't mind babysitting and we'll go and find somewhere lovely in the village. How's that?'

'Okay,' I grumble, flicking past my new floaty chiffon dresses in the wardrobe and reaching for a pair of shorts instead. 'I guess my glad rags can wait another day.'

*   *   *

By the evening, our first evening here, if today is a sign of what's to come, it looks like all my fears about Linda and Michael were over nothing, and despite them being here we're all going to have a wonderful time.

I would almost go so far as to say Linda has been incredibly hospitable today, not to mention helpful with Tom. Then, while the girls bathe the kids, feed them supper and put them to bed, Linda rounds up the boys and they throw together the kind of delicious supper that we sometimes have at home—but somehow it never tastes as good as when you're eating it on a terrace in the South of France.

We appear in the living room at around seven thirty to find platters of food laid out on the coffee table: hot crusty baguettes, prosciutto, Parma ham, salamis; Bries, Camemberts, Reblochons; cornichons, roasted peppers, pâtés and olives.

And that's merely the hors d'oeuvres.

Lisa lives up to her reputation in a sixties retro print Diane Von Furstenberg wrap dress that flashes her thighs as she sits down, and Trish and I nudge each other and giggle like schoolchildren every time we see Michael's eyes dart down to her legs.

'That's six,' Trish whispers to me, both of us keeping our eyes glued to Michael's, who thankfully is completely unaware of our puerile behaviour.

'Seven,' I whisper as he casts a quick glance down at her cleavage, and the pair of us fall about giggling.

Dan shakes his head, pretending to be stern. 'How old are our wives exactly?' he says to Gregory.

'I think tonight they've regressed to an approximate age of about five,' Gregory says, grinning.

'Five and a half!' Trish shouts petulantly.

'And I'm five and three quarters!' I shout, and it sets us both off again as the others shake their heads.

I think we're slightly drunk.

*   *   *

By the time we sit down at the table outside, the pâtés and baguettes, which Dan had insisted Trish and I eat copious amounts of, seem to have soaked up some of the alcohol.

'Dad,' Dan says, looking over at Michael seated at the head of the table, 'I'll thank you not to get the women completely sloshed every night.'

Michael laughs. 'Oh, relax,' he says. 'You're on

215

holiday. You should try it.'

Dan looks at his mother. 'Is that really my dad or did an alien come and steal him away during the night?'

Linda shakes her head in exasperation. 'It seems the girls aren't the only ones regressing tonight. Your father seems to think he's young, free and single.'

Dan laughs. 'Oh, he's harmless, Mum. And, you've got to admit, Lisa is rather stunning. Don't worry.' He drops his voice so the others can't hear, except of course for me, sitting next to him and tuning in to his conversation. 'The more you get to know her the less attractive she is.'

'Oh, I'm not worried about *him*,' Linda says. 'I'm just not so sure about *her*.' And she looks pointedly at Dan, as I roll my eyes and take another swig of wine.

'A toast!' Michael calls out from the other end of the table. 'To holidays! And new friends!'

'To holidays and new friends!' we all echo, raising our glasses and drinking, and as we sit, talking and laughing and forgetting that there has ever been any discord with anyone at this table, I feel awash with contentment and a quiet sense of calmness.

True to form, Linda has made an authentic French cassoulet, followed by a hot tarte tatin served with cold vanilla ice-cream.

And as we eat outside, sitting under the wisteria, lanterns on the table casting a soft, romantic light, I forget for a couple of hours the history that I have with Linda, and when she makes the odd comment about her grandson, or tells a story in which she implies that she and I are close, I just nod and

216

smile, too contented, and possibly slightly too drunk, to comment.

Or care.

17

Isn't it strange how adding people can bring a whole new dynamic to the equation? When we have Sunday lunch with Michael and Linda, we discuss the events of our week without really discussing anything at all, finish the meal in about half an hour, then leave the table and count the minutes until we can actually go without appearing rude.

And yet tonight, with Trish, Gregory and Lisa here, it feels as if I am having a wonderful evening with a large group of friends.

Instead of making small talk, we tell stories, each one trying to be funnier or more outrageous than the last.

Afterwards, when I am helping Linda wash up, she turns to me in the kitchen, her face flushed with sun and wine. 'I never knew you had such lovely friends,' she says.

I shrug. 'You never asked. You sound surprised ... *are* you surprised they're lovely?'

'Not in the slightest,' she says. 'I'm pleased for you. I always think that being a first-time mother is the hardest job in the world. I always felt so isolated and lonely, and I think the only way you get through it is to have other friends in the same boat. I think it's lovely that you all get on so well and all the babies are the same age.'

'Yes, you're right. It is lovely. I don't know what I would have done without them.'

'And Trish is such a sweetie,' Linda says. 'She's a very good friend to you, I can tell.'

Uh oh. Here we go. I know even before she opens her mouth that she's about to say something about Lisa, even though Lisa has been charm itself throughout the meal, has gone out of her way to let Michael and Linda know how much we all appreciate their hospitality.

'Tell me about Lisa,' Linda says finally. 'What's her story?'

'What do you want to know?'

Linda shrugs, affecting nonchalance. 'I'm surprised that someone like her doesn't have a partner.'

'Oh, she does. Andy. Although he's probably on the way out. But looking like that I'm sure there'll be plenty more where he came from.'

'She is rather stunning,' Linda says. 'She mentioned she's divorced. Did she ever tell you what happened?'

'I'm not sure,' I say, not wanting to betray my friend, not wanting Linda to know any more, even though I'm pretty damn sure Linda thinks that Lisa had an affair—I can just tell.

'However she comes across,' I say defensively, 'she's lovely. Very genuine and down-to-earth. She's not what she looks like.'

'A tart, you mean?' Linda attempts to make a joke.

'Linda!' I'm genuinely pissed off. 'She's one of my best friends. I'd appreciate it if you didn't talk about my friends like that.'

'You're right.' She's contrite. 'I'm sorry, I didn't

mean it, and she does seem charming.' There's a pause while Linda picks up a glass and focuses intently on drying it. 'How does Dan get on with her?'

And now I know where she's going. My voice is stony cold. 'Dan gets on fine with her, Linda. Why? What are you trying to suggest?'

Linda sighs. 'Look, Ellie, don't take this the wrong way. I'm always so careful when I talk to you because I'm so worried about offending you, but I've been around in the world a lot longer than you, and I've met hundreds of girls like Lisa, and I just think you should be careful.'

'What? Careful of what? You think she's interested in stealing Dan?'

Linda shrugs, with a shrug that says that's exactly what she's thinking. 'I just think that it's dangerous to have a beautiful friend who's divorced, particularly when she has a child. A lot of those girls, girls like Lisa, are looking for security, for a wealthy man who can keep them in the manner to which they've become accustomed.'

I let out a short bark of laughter. 'Wealthy man? Well, that rules Dan out, then, doesn't it?'

'You may laugh,' Linda says, not a trace of a smile on her face, 'but I'm telling you, I know her type and I'd be very careful. I'm not saying don't be friends, I'm just saying that you can be friends with her without letting her become too close to your family. This holiday, for instance—you might not want to do it again.'

I take a deep breath, shaking my head at the ridiculousness of this entire conversation, so ridiculous that it's almost impossible for me to take offence. If anything, I just think the whole thing is funny. Of course Lisa's gorgeous, you just have to look at her to see it, but she's also a really good friend.

'Look, Linda, while I appreciate your concern,' the sarcasm heavy in my voice, 'and while I appreciate everything you've done for us with this holiday, I think you really ought to . . .' I stop while thinking of a nice way to say mind your own business, you old bat. '. . . keep your thoughts about my friends to yourself.'

'I'm sorry if I offended you. That wasn't my intention and I'll try not to do it again, okay?'

'Fine.' I put down the tea towel and go off to look for Dan.

'You will never bloody believe your mother,' I whisper, as soon as I find him, sitting on the sofa playing backgammon with Gregory.

'What?'

'Hurry up and finish, then we'll go to bed and I'll tell you.'

*   *   *

I repeat the entire conversation to Dan in the privacy of our bedroom, and he looks at me for a few seconds before bursting out laughing.

'She is ridiculous, isn't she?' My voice comes out hopefully; it emerges as a question rather than as a statement. I trust Dan. I absolutely do. I don't think he's the type of man ever to have an affair, and even if he were I don't believe he fancies Lisa in the slightest. But Linda has planted a seed, and while Dan was playing backgammon with Gregory, I couldn't help but watch him closely to see whether he might have been glancing at Lisa more

220

than would have been normal, whether there was anything going on that I might have missed.

And all that was going through my head was, did Linda spot something that I hadn't? I always thought that if I was ever with a man who was unfaithful I would know instantly. You see those television programmes where the husband phones home and says, 'Sorry, darling, my meeting's running on,' or they go away on business trips and don't leave hotel numbers, and you watch the poor, dim wives and want to scream at them: 'HE'S HAVING AN AFFAIR, YOU SILLY COW! DON'T YOU RECOGNIZE THE SIGNS?'

And of course we all congratulate ourselves on how clever we are for spotting it, but perhaps we wouldn't be quite so clever if it were happening on our own doorsteps; perhaps our instinct for self-preservation would protect us from things that we would rather not know.

I had always thought, always said, that if anyone was ever unfaithful to me, I would leave immediately, with no second thoughts. But Fran once told me that I would change my mind as I got older.

*   *   *

She had told me that before she met Marcus, the great love of her life was her university boyfriend, Tim.

She and Tim were together for five years, and she had known, from the moment she met him, that Tim was the man she was going to marry.

They had talked about it from the beginning. How many children they would have, where they

221

would live, what their children would be called. ('Just so you know I'm consistent—one of my names was Sadie, and this was before Sadie Frost made it fashionable,' she explained. 'Just so you know,' she had laughed.)

They had spent hours planning their future together, in the romantic, idealistic way you are supposed to plan your lives together when you are twenty and in love for the first time, when love sweeps you off your feet and you can't possibly envisage a moment, let alone a lifetime, without the man who is unquestionably your other half, the half you've been looking for your entire life.

'Jesus Christ,' I had laughed. 'Who would have thought you were such a romantic?'

'Not any more.' Fran rolled her eyes as Sadie came up with chocolate-covered fingers and grabbed at her cardigan. 'Young and very, very stupid.'

After graduation Fran and Tim had moved down to London, Fran working as a young PR assistant and Tim doing some kind of sales job that took him travelling all over the country.

She hadn't suspected anything.

'Nothing?' I said in amazement, when she told me about how he was unavailable for days, about women phoning up and saying they'd got the wrong number before putting the phone down, about his sudden need to take his phone calls in the privacy of their bedroom, with the door closed. And finally she told me about finding scraps of paper, love notes in his pockets.

'God, you really must have been naive,' I remember saying.

'I don't know whether it was naivety so much as

not wanting to know. I think deep down of course I knew, I must have known, but I didn't want to believe, and so I blinded myself to it.'

She would confront him, and he would always have an explanation, which sounded reasonable to someone who so wanted to believe. The phone calls were business, the deals were being conducted with the utmost secrecy, hence the closed doors, and finally the love notes were the result of this incredibly annoying, middle-aged secretary called Angela who had a huge crush on him.

'What does she look like?' Fran said she had asked nervously.

'She's revolting.' Tim had laughed. 'A middle-aged spinster with bad breath and greasy hair who thinks I'm the best thing since sliced bread.'

Fran had laughed along with him, until Tim started spending more and more time in Manchester, and less and less in London, and eventually he confessed that he had been having an affair. The only thing that he'd said about Angela that had been true was that she had a huge crush on him. He hadn't been entirely truthful about her being a hot blonde nineteen-year-old.

'I hope you sent him packing,' I said.

'Well, no. That's the amazing thing. Like you, I'd always said that if anyone was ever unfaithful to me, I'd be out of there quicker than you could say Mrs Robinson. I remember saying it over and over to Tim, that if he ever had an affair he'd lose me, as if it were the worst thing imaginable. And yet when it happened, I collapsed in tears, sobbed my heart out in this pathetic little heap on the floor and begged him to stay.'

I looked at her, not knowing what to say. The

prospect of Fran, super-cool, super-successful, super-trendy Fran begging anyone for anything was beyond me. Particularly in a pathetic heap on the floor. The whole image was enough to render me completely speechless.

But that was the point, Fran explained. You never know how you're going to react to something until it happens. Up until that point she had genuinely thought she would just walk away, would have enough dignity to remove herself, head held high, and find someone who would appreciate her.

But in her hysteria she said she would have done anything to keep him, kept insisting that she would forgive him, that they could carry on as if nothing had happened, that it would take time for her to get over the breach of trust, but that she could do it. She believed enough in the two of them to do it, and how could he throw away so many good years together?

'Thank God,' she said, taking a sip of wine, 'he chose to throw it away, and now that I'm'—she paused—'thirty-something, married to Marcus with children, I know I'd have a completely different reaction.'

'Not that Marcus would ever have an affair,' I said quickly. 'But if he did, how would you react?'

'It wouldn't be an issue,' she said, smiling. 'Because I would dismember him.'

I was newly married when we had this discussion, and remember being horrified when she went on to say, with all seriousness, that she wouldn't necessarily leave if Marcus had an affair. She hoped to God she'd never be in a position where she would have to deal with it, but she suspected that she would find a way to carry on.

'I love my life,' she said simply. 'I love my girls, I love my home, I love Marcus, who is, by the way, a wonderful man. Of course it would depend on the nature of the affair—was it a one-night-stand, a few fucks or a full-blown love affair?—but on the whole I'd have to say that I'd have to seriously question whether it would be worth changing everything, uprooting the girls and changing all of our lives, for the sake of what was perhaps just a minor indiscretion. You won't understand,' she said, smiling, 'until you have children of your own.'

*   *   *

I didn't understand, but this evening I try to watch for signs that I might have missed something, that Dan might be more interested in Lisa than I may have thought.

I don't see any signs, but perhaps I don't know what I'm looking for. Gazes that last a split-second too long, a hand resting on a shoulder in a show of intimacy that you're not supposed to see between your husband and your friend? I don't know, and so I watch, but don't see anything that might be misconstrued as something else. Something more.

Maybe they are too clever, maybe they know I'm watching them, maybe there is no smoke without fire, and Linda would never have said anything if she hadn't genuinely spotted something amiss, something that would give the game away to a woman like Linda, a woman far older and wiser than me.

I don't see the signs, but I start to think about what might happen if I did.

Could I have missed something that Linda

hadn't? Did she perhaps bend down to pick up a napkin and notice hands brushing, or fingers linked underneath the table? Even if she didn't, even if it were, just as I thought, mere supposition, what if Dan *were* to have an affair? What if Dan were having an affair now? What would I do?

I don't feel that my life would end without Dan. For the first few months after Tom was born quite frankly I wished he'd piss off altogether. Does that mean he's not the great love of my life? Am I supposed to feel that my life would end if Dan walked out the door?

I've felt that way about men before, but not men with whom I've had healthy relationships. I've felt that way when I've been giddily, crazily in lust, when the entire relationship has felt as if I'm balancing on the edge of a precipice. I never wanted that for my marriage. I never wanted those ups and downs, the feeling of never being in control, of giving yourself over entirely to another person.

And yet the thought of Dan with another woman, specifically with Lisa, does make me feel rather sick. The betrayal. My husband and my best friend. How would you ever get over a betrayal like that, how would you ever be able to trust anyone ever again?

Which is why Dan and I are standing in our bedroom and I am asking him hopefully if his mother is being ridiculous. I am waiting for him to tell me she is, to laugh at her inferences and implications, to tell me that I am the great love of his life.

'She is being completely ridiculous,' Dan laughs, putting his arms around me as I start to relax. 'I can't believe my mother thinks I would be interested in Lisa!' He starts to laugh again, then sits me down on the bed and takes my face in his hands, looking at me very intently as he stops laughing. 'Ellie, I love you. I love Tom. I love being married to you and having a family with you, and I would never have an affair. Not to mention the fact that, although I can recognize that Lisa is a beautiful woman, I have never been attracted to her in the slightest.'

'What if you were single?' I persist. 'Would you have asked her out then?'

Dan sighs and shakes his head. 'The truth is that Lisa is the kind of woman I would have asked out on a date, and by the end of the evening I would have been itching to get away. She's beautiful, and she's funny, but her superficiality drives me up the wall. I would never want to be with anyone that shallow.'

'Oh, thanks, Dan. She is one of my best friends.'

'Stop it,' he says. 'You asked, so I answered.'

*   *   *

'I can't believe what a bitch your mother is,' I say, a few minutes later as we're getting undressed. 'What a total bloody bitch.'

'Ellie!' Dan turns to me with a bark. 'Don't talk about my mother like that.'

'Okay, okay. I'm sorry. But why did she have to say all that stuff? Why would she even think that, let alone say anything to me? I swear she just wanted to upset me.'

'First of all you know that's ridiculous. You're always complaining that my mother wants to be

227

your best friend; the last thing she wants to do is hurt you. And second, she wasn't trying to upset you, she probably just feels threatened by Lisa and was taking it out on you.'

'Great. Why was she taking it out on me?'

'I didn't mean taking it out on you. Look,' he sighs. 'I don't know. I don't know what got into her tonight, or why she put this ridiculous notion into your head that I might fancy Lisa, but I don't, I fancy *you*, and you know I don't want to get in the middle with you and my mother. If you're that upset, why don't you talk to her about it tomorrow?'

I look at Dan in amazement. How can we have been so warm, so loving just a few minutes before, and how can he inspire such fury in me now?

'I don't believe you,' I practically spit at him. 'You never bloody stand up for me, do you? All you ever say is that you don't want to get in the middle. Well, how about you do get in the middle for a change? How about you realize where your priorities lie? I'm your wife, for God's sake. I'm your family now. Not her. She is not the most important woman in your life any more, I am, and if you stopped being such a bloody wimp and made sure she knew that, if you stood up for me for a change, she might stop playing these stupid fucking games.'

Dan just shakes his head at me in silence, and I know I should shut up, I know that we're having the same argument we always have, and that it will end up in the same place it always ends, which is neither of us speaking to one another, sometimes for days at a time, but I can't help it. His silence only serves to increase my rage, and when he turns

228

his back on me to get into bed I have to resist the urge to hit him.

'Don't turn your back on me,' I hiss, walking round to his side of the bed and standing there, hands planted on my hips. 'Don't you dare turn your back on me. Who do you think you are?' Echoes of my mother, my mother in a drunken fury, play around my ears, but I don't care, blinded by my anger at my husband's silence, at his refusal to defend me against his mother's attacks, just as my father had refused to defend me all those years ago against my mother's verbal attacks.

What goes around comes around.

And it ends as it always does. With both of us lying in bed, not talking, barely moving, pretending to sleep, although I can tell from his breathing that he is not sleeping, and I know, from previous experience, that I will probably lie here until the early hours of the morning, heart pounding with anger, wanting everything to revert back to normal but not having the ability to say sorry.

I know exactly what to say to make it all better; I'm just not able to say it.

18

They always say never go to sleep on an argument. If only it were that easy. When we do row, we always go to sleep on it, and when we awake, there are the same silences, the same resentments, the same recriminations.

This morning I pretend to be asleep. I don't want to have to look at Dan, talk to him, be around him, and I lie in bed listening to him getting up and leaving the room. I plan on following him, to give Tom his breakfast, but the next thing I know I wake up again, groggily reach for my watch on the bedside table and see that it's 11.16.

11.16? I stare at the numbers as my brain attempts to click into gear—this is what happens when you don't get to sleep until 5 a.m.—11.16! I leap out of bed and run out of the room to look for everyone, my immediate thoughts being of Tom. Would he have coped without me? Could he still be—irrational as it sounds—in his cot waiting for me to come and get him?

Tom's face breaks into a huge smile, his little chubby arms reaching out for me as soon as I round the corner to the swimming pool. Everyone's there, chatting and laughing, and they cheer as I blearily make my way over to where Tom's sitting on a towel.

'I wish *my* husband let me have a lie-in,' Trish says, looking pointedly at Gregory as I approach her sunbed and sit down on the edge, perching Tom on my lap.

I look over at Dan, but as soon as our eyes meet he looks away. He's still pissed off about the row last night, but so am I, and, while I appreciate his letting me sleep, I can't make everything instantly fine. I don't know how to do that.

'Thanks,' I say coldly to Dan, and it comes out grudgingly, and he merely nods without looking at me and stands up, diving into the pool to swim.

Lisa smiles up at me, her book resting on her stomach, her hands behind her head as Amy sits between her legs playing with some brightly coloured plush blocks. 'Do you remember that girl

230

we bumped into on the plane? Kate?'

I nod.

'She phoned earlier. Wondered whether we'd like to go over there this evening for a drink, and then out for supper. We were waiting for you to see what you thought.'

'Sounds lovely,' I say. 'But what about the kids? Tom goes down at seven sharp.'

'Don't worry,' Linda calls out. 'Michael and I already said we'd babysit.'

'What? All of them? Anyway, I don't think Tom will go down here without our being there. I'm not sure it's such a good idea.'

'Oh, don't be ridiculous,' Dan snorts. 'What do you think's going to happen, for God's sake? Tom will be fine. They'll all be fine.'

He's right. If it were anyone other than my in-laws, I'd happily leave Tom. I'm being childish, I know, so I shrug and nod my assent.

'As long as we don't have to bathe all of them,' Michael says quickly. 'I'm not sure Linda and I could manage that.' He laughs. 'It's been a long time since we had to look after three children and we're not as young as we once were.'

Lisa rolls her eyes, as if he's talking rubbish, a fine specimen of malehood like my father-in-law. 'We thought that we could leave after all the kids go down,' she says. 'That way Tom and Amy probably won't even know we've gone.'

I hesitate. 'What about Oscar?'

*   *   *

I know Trish is more liberal with Oscar than Lisa and I are with our children. While Lisa and I have

231

practically memorized *The Contented Little Baby Book*, while we spend hours expounding our theories of babies needing routine, and structure, and discipline, Trish believes in feeding on demand, letting the baby sleep in the family bed, and generally allowing Oscar to run the household.

Aside from paying the bills, of course.

It is the one aspect of our friendship that I find difficult. I am so sure that I am right, that my way of parenting is the right way—that we, Dan and I, are the parents, the adults, the ones who dictate how and when our children do what they do—that I find it infuriating that Trish can't see the light, as it were.

I had Tom on a routine from the beginning. He is up at seven, has breakfast, then goes down for a short nap at nine. At half eleven, every day, he has lunch, and then is always, always, down for a nap, in a darkened nursery, by noon at the latest. He's up at two, has a bottle at half past, a walk in the afternoon and then supper at five on the dot, bath at six, then his last bottle before bedtime at seven.

Oscar, on the other hand, tends to do pretty much what he feels like. Trish is still breastfeeding, although she's now doing a combination of bottle and breast, and has admitted devastation as Oscar is beginning to choose the bottle over the breast.

I swear, if Trish had anything to do with it, she'd be breastfeeding Oscar until he went to university. Not that I think there's anything wrong with breastfeeding, but I do find it rather disconcerting when you see children who are walking and talking latched on to their mother's breast.

Trish has admitted she's not at her best in the mornings and luckily Oscar wakes up quite happy, so they stay in bed together for a good hour at least, watching breakfast television. He gets bottles throughout the day when he starts getting grizzly, and doesn't usually nap unless he falls asleep in his buggy.

The consequence is that by five o'clock Oscar's impossible. Trust me. I've seen it. The only thing that makes him happy is being held, so Trish holds him from five until he goes to bed, which is basically whatever time he wants. Gregory likes to play with him when he gets home around half seven, so on a good day Oscar's asleep by nine.

Heaven forbid Oscar should cry at any time during the night. He's immediately pacified with Trish's breast, before being rocked to sleep in Trish and Gregory's bed. And she wonders why she's permanently exhausted.

My GP, with whom I've discussed Trish on many an occasion, is adamant that an eleven-month-old baby does not need any night feeds, and I did pass the information on to Trish, who shrugged and laughed, saying she went to bed every night hoping he'd wake up, so much does she love his cuddly warmth.

And her life is so hard. Many's the time she's phoned to cancel something because Oscar's just too difficult, or he's fallen asleep when we were supposed to meet at the park, or he's not tired and won't go to bed.

I know I ought to be supportive of the way she is doing things, ought to accept that all of us do things differently, and there is no right or wrong way to bring up a child, but when you look at our children, at how happy and easy Tom and Amy both are, because both Lisa and I follow routines, and then you look at Oscar, who's fairly unhappy most of the time because I'm convinced he's not getting nearly enough sleep, you do have to ask yourself whether Trish is doing the right thing.

I love being a mother, and now that I am experiencing the joys of female friendship, I love being a woman. I love the way that you can share anything and everything with your girlfriends, that you are not judged but accepted for who you are.

And I count myself incredibly lucky to have found friendships like this at this stage in my life. And yet, despite the support we give one another, it has been a shock to discover that raising a child is the one area in which women are absolutely not supportive of one another, not unless you find kindred spirits who agree wholeheartedly with your philosophy, whatever your philosophy may be.

Trish and I may bond over a shared lack of appreciation of the way Lisa appreciates the finer things in life, but Lisa and I have in turn bonded over our shared way of bringing up our children, and I have found myself, many a time, asking Lisa how Trish can possibly not see that ours is the right way.

We've tried to tell her, but carefully, subtly, for mothers cannot be criticized in the way they treat their children, not even by their best friends. But I don't dare risk losing her, and so I have learnt to keep quiet, to vent my frustrations with Lisa when the two of us are alone together.

*   *   *

So when I ask Trish, 'What about Oscar?' it is because I am quite sure Oscar will throw a tantrum if we attempt to leave him with Linda and Michael. Not that I'd particularly mind. It might be quite funny. Then again it could scupper our chances of having them babysit for us again.

'I know.' Trish frowns. 'I have to say I am worried about leaving Oscar.' She turns to Linda and Michael. 'Not that I think you're not up to it, God, I'm so sorry, that didn't come out the way I meant it to, but Oscar's so sensitive'—Lisa and I look at each other and she almost imperceptibly rolls her eyes—'and he might completely freak out if we're not around.' She turns to Gregory for advice, but he just shrugs—motherhood is very much Trish's domain in their household. She makes the rules, even if there aren't any.

'Would you mind if we brought him with?' Trish looks at the rest of us. 'He'll be fine, I promise you. We've been bringing him out a lot recently and he usually falls asleep in his buggy. I'm just nervous he'll be terribly unhappy without us.'

Nobody says anything, but the look of relief on Linda's face is enormous. She's the first to speak. 'I think that's an excellent idea, Trish,' she says. 'If the baby will get upset without his mummy, then you're far better off keeping him with you.'

Great.

*   *   *

Dan and I barely talk throughout the day. We make a show of everything being all right for the others, but I'm waiting for him to apologize first, and he's clearly waiting for me.

He's going to be waiting a very long time.

We sit and play with Tom, and if you didn't know

we'd had the mother of all arguments the previous night, you'd certainly never guess. We manage to talk to one another, look at one another, ask one another questions, but there's an underlying coldness that I'm sure no one could possibly detect, so good are we at putting on a brave face.

*   *   *

'Everything all right?' Linda says to me when I'm in the kitchen helping myself to a Diet Coke.

'Fine,' I say breezily. 'Why?'

'You and Dan haven't had an argument?'

I look at her incredulously. 'No. Why?'

'Nothing, nothing. None of my business. I just know Dan very well, and I can always tell when he's cross about something; he gets these little frown lines right here.' She points to between her eyebrows. 'Tom's going to have them too. I can see already.'

'Not necessarily.' I try not to snap. 'Everyone says he looks just like me when I was a baby.' Not strictly true. There's no one to actually say that, as my father hasn't seen Tom in months, and there's no one else who would know.

'Really?' Her eyes widen. 'How strange. He looks exactly like Dan did. You really can't see it?'

'No.' I finish putting the ice in the glass and walk out of the kitchen. 'I really can't see it.'

*   *   *

I can't go bitching to Dan, not after last night, but I need to get Linda off my chest, need to talk to someone. When I get back to the pool, I find that

236

Lisa's disappeared, gone for a walk down in the olive orchard, so I slip on my sandals and wander down to join her.

'What are you doing?' She's sitting on the ground, guiltily shoving a hand behind her back as a tell-tale waft of smoke drifts over her head.

'Smoking?' I'm shocked. 'Jesus! You are! You're smoking!'

'Sssh, sssh,' she says guiltily, bringing her hand out to reveal a cigarette. 'I don't want the others to know.'

'But you don't smoke. At least, I never knew you smoked,' I say, still in shock. 'How can you manage to be one of my best friends and not tell me you smoke?'

'First of all I don't consider myself a smoker.' Lisa takes a long drag on the cigarette and exhales as I wave the smoke away. 'And second it's not exactly the sort of thing you talk about. How are you? How are the kids? Yes, we're great and by the way did you know I smoke?'

I frown. 'I know, but still.'

'I don't really smoke,' Lisa says.

'Clearly.' I can't help but grin.

'No, seriously. I gave up for years, and just have the odd one now and again. If I'm out drinking I tend to have a cigarette, and sometimes on holiday.'

'Tell me you don't smoke in front of Amy,' I say sternly.

'Oh, God, no! What do you think I am, some sort of reprobate mother?'

I shake my head. 'No, you're a great mother. Sorry, I shouldn't have said that.'

'That's okay. You had to ask.' She grinds the

cigarette out and buries it under some twigs. 'So, what's going on with you and Dan?'

'What do you mean, what's going on? Nothing.'

'Right. And I wasn't just smoking a cigarette, it was a figment of your imagination.' I can't help it. I laugh.

'Okay,' I say. 'We had a huge row last night and neither of us is willing to admit we're in the wrong, so nobody's apologized and right at this second I pretty much hate him.'

'Was it the usual?'

I sigh. 'Yes. Can you believe it? You'd think we'd be a bit more creative about our arguments instead of rowing about his bloody mother over and over again, but I just can't stand the way he never sticks up for me.'

And I vent. I don't tell her what it was about specifically, obviously, but I vent general stuff about Linda, and how she always tries to take over, and how Dan never sticks up for me. 'What do you think?' I finish. 'Tell me what *you* think about her.'

'I don't know what to say,' she says. 'I mean, I understand how you feel, I really do, and maybe I would feel the same way if I were married, but I've never known what it's like because The Deserter's parents lived in America and I barely knew them.' She looks at me and sees the expression on my face. 'Okay, I think it sounds like Dan probably could, and should, stick up for you more than he does, but Ellie, they're really not that bad.'

'Not they,' I say. 'Her.'

'Yes, okay, then. *Her*. I just don't think she's that bad. God, it could be so much worse. She's just trying to be a good mother-in-law and grandmother. You've got yourself so worked up by

238

your hatred of her that you jump down her throat at everything she says, no matter how innocuous.'

'Thanks for the support,' I grumble, in what even to me sounds like an incredibly puerile way.

'Ellie, you know I support you, but you have to get things into perspective. Have you ever thought that maybe she's the way she is because she isn't happy?'

'Not happy? What does she have to be unhappy about?'

Lisa shrugs. 'Look, I don't know enough about them, but there's definitely tension between her and Michael. For all you know she's a really unhappy woman. I don't know.' Lisa shrugs. 'Maybe she's lonely. Maybe she lived for her children all those years and doesn't know what to do, how to live, now that her children have grown up and moved on.

'Maybe that's why she's interfering so much, she's probably just lonely. Instead of hating her, maybe you should feel sorry for her.'

I frown, thinking about Linda. Could Linda be unhappy? Lonely? Vulnerable? I always think of her as so strong, having built her up in my mind to be this Über-mother-in-law, a giant figure capable of great evil. But in that instant Lisa manages to humanize her for me.

Suddenly I don't see Linda as a monster, as capable of creating only mayhem and destruction wherever she goes. I see her as rather pathetic. Poor woman. She gave up her life for her children and now her children don't want to know. Emma's permanently exasperated by her, Richard only phones when he wants something, and Dan? Dan has me now. And Tom. A family of his own.

'I can't believe it,' I say softly. 'I think you're right. She is unhappy. I should make more of an effort with her. I should try to include her more.'

'I think that she's not nearly as bad as you made out. And he's hysterical.'

'Who?' I look at her in confusion.

'Your father-in-law, Michael.'

'Michael? Hysterical?' I say slowly. Surely some confusion.

'Yes. He was telling us his old law school stories this morning, and we were all rolling about.'

'Michael?' I can't get rid of the frown. The incomprehension. 'My father-in-law? Are you sure?'

'Oh, don't be so ridiculous,' she snorts. 'We were all on the floor. We'd better get back, before Trish comes looking for us and smells the smoke on my breath.'

I laugh. 'Are you seriously frightened of Trish?'

'Put it like this,' Lisa said. 'For Christmas, Andy got me a fur collar.'

'I thought you said he got you a bracelet.'

'Nah. I went out and bought myself the bracelet because I couldn't tell Trish I actually owned real fur. It's been hiding in the attic. Every time I think about wearing it I'm convinced I'll bump into Trish and she'll scream at me.'

'You wimp,' I laugh.

'Would *you* wear fur in front of Trish?'

'Well, no. But it's not exactly an issue for me,' I say, knowing that even if we could afford it, Dan would never buy me a fur collar.

'Look, I love her, but we're very different.'

'I know, I know. And you're right. She probably would give you a horrible time if she knew you

240

smoked'—I give her a look—'even if it is only on holiday. Still.' I stand up, brushing off the grass. 'I can't believe I didn't know that about you.'

Lisa stands up with me, hiding the matches in the knot of her sarong, and she smiles mysteriously. 'There are a lot of things you don't know about me.'

19

I caught the sun today, and, although I may not be feeling that great—rowing with Dan always unsettles me, makes me feel slightly unbalanced, gives me a constant nagging feeling that there is something wrong, no matter how much I pretend to the outside world that everything is fine—I have to say I'm looking pretty good.

Lisa may have bought out every designer store in the West End, but I did pretty well with my cheaper alternatives, and tonight I'm wearing a whispery chiffon dress that sets off the beginning of my sun tan, and floats gently against my knees.

'That's gorgeous,' Lisa says as I walk into the living room. 'Where did you get it?'

I wish I could lie, could tell her it was Diane Von Furstenberg or some such, but Lisa, the perfect picture of Euro-chic in her Allegra Hicks shift and gold hoop earrings, would undoubtedly know.

'It's second-hand.' I say, grinning. 'Isn't it beautiful?'

She smiles, comes over to feel the fabric and agrees that it's lovely. 'Darling, don't say it's second-hand. Nobody says things are second-hand any more. Say it's vintage.'

'Vintage,' I murmur, and she's right, it does sound much better.

'But it's beautiful,' she says. 'You look gorgeous,' and I smile, thankful for the compliment, for any compliment in fact, given that Dan and I still appear to be on non-speakers.

Well, tough on him. I'm determined to have a good time tonight. I may not know these people but I'm on holiday, I can be anyone I want to be. And tonight, Ladies and Gentlemen, I'm not going to be Ellie Cooper, wife, mother, suburbanite-in-the-making, tonight I'm going to be Ellie Black, single girl-about-town, vivacious, funny, sparkling. I plan on drinking champagne (please let them have champagne, surely with names like Jonathan and Caro they're bound to have champagne), and who knows, perhaps we'll even go dancing, I could do with some dancing, and after the day, and night, I've had, I could certainly do with some drinking.

How is it that we've been married less than two years, yet already I feel like a completely different person? Is it marriage per se, or motherhood that changes you so much?

Or perhaps it is my marriage. Those nights when I lie in bed, hating Dan, wanting to leave, I think that I really did make the wrong choice. Usually I wake up in the morning and those feelings have passed, have been left behind with the darkness, and I tend to discredit them, to call them my night sweats. But perhaps they're not. Perhaps I'm not supposed to feel this different, perhaps it means I made the wrong choice. I made the wrong marriage.

But then I think of Lisa. And Trish. And Fran.

242

Think of how we all seem to go through the same things, have the same feelings about our children, our lack of social lives (okay, perhaps it's not quite fair to include Lisa in that particular aspect), how we all constantly complain of a lack of energy, permanent exhaustion, and I think that this must be normal. That it is not that I chose the wrong man, but that my life has changed so much, immeasurably, that surely it takes longer than two years to adjust.

But tonight I'm not willing to adjust. Not willing to make any concessions at all. Tonight I want to forget that I'm married, that I have responsibilities. Tonight I will be on holiday from my life. And I'm going to have a good time if it kills me.

*   *   *

'Come in! Come in! Lisa! How lovely that you're here!' Jonathan is a big, bluff, exuberant man, and as soon as he opens the door I can see I'm going to like him, that I won't need the champagne to feel relaxed.

But I'll drink it anyway.

Jonathan's wife, Caro, is standing just behind him, and I extend my hand to shake hers, but she laughs and gives me a hug. 'Ellie, is it? Lovely to meet you. Come on in and have a drink.'

Everyone in our party gets slaps on the back from Jonathan and hugs from Caro, and we walk through to the living room to meet the others, and I have to admit I do start to feel slightly nervous.

These do seem to be the Beautiful People I so often read about. They're the people that frequent Calden, that believe their looks and charm will get

243

them anything they want.

'Concierge, my good man, will you just phone the Ivy and get us a table for six at eight o'clock this evening.'

'Would you do me a tiny favour and phone BA. Ask them if there's an upgrade available. Tell them it's for me.'

'Darling, just phone Hermès and see if they have any Birkins lying around. Mention my name.'

I encountered these people every day at Calden. Marvelled at their easy confidence, their ability to charm their way through the world, because invariably they would get what they asked for, no matter how unreasonable the request. Their wishes would be granted, and they would never seem surprised, would already have accepted that as they asked, so they would receive.

I would watch them afar, but I had never known them, had never thought of socializing with them, had been far too intimidated to ever think I might have been spending an evening with them, until I met Lisa.

But Lisa on her own is just Lisa. It wasn't until I saw Lisa hugging Kate on the plane that I fully realized how much Lisa is part of that set. Of this set. These people that make me feel so awkward and dowdy.

'We've met before.'

I register the words as I shake this man's hand, knowing that his face is slightly familiar, but then everyone in here is slightly familiar, their photographs cropping up in the pages of the magazines on a regular basis.

I squint slightly, trying to place him. I'm sure he's not just a picture in a magazine. I'm sure his voice is familiar too.

'I know,' I say. 'You're terribly familiar, but I've lost my memory since having a baby. Sorry.' I shrug an apology as he laughs. 'Help me out. Remind me.'

'We met at Fran and Marcus's,' he says. 'You work with Sally, right? Ellie, isn't it? I'm Charlie, Charlie Dutton.'

'Oh, God! Of course. Charlie Dutton!' Charlie and Sally, the Charlie that Sally ended up stalking for months before realizing that he was absolutely not ready for commitment and she should move on, which she very quickly did.

'How on earth do you remember me?' I say, pleased. I am used to being the girl that people can't place, the girl that is constantly reminding people how they know me, or that I'm a friend of Fran, or Dan's wife, or someone's something.

I think I must have one of those faces.

'Yes, you're common,' Trish had laughed one day when I told her, but it's true. I think I remind a lot of people of someone else, and so it is rare for people to actually place me, or remember me.

'You're the film producer, right?'

He nods. 'And you're the Marketing Director for Calden.'

'I can't believe you remembered that too!'

He shrugs. 'I've always had an excellent memory.'

'But I'm not the Marketing Director any more,' I say. 'I do freelance consulting now. It must have been ages ago that we met. God, I'm not even sure I was married.'

'You were engaged, I think, just about to get married. And you mentioned you've had a baby?

245

Congratulations! That must have been quick work.'

'We pretend he's a honeymoon baby, but actually I was pregnant when we got married, so yes, I suppose it was fairly quick work.'

'A shotgun wedding?' He raises an eyebrow.

I laugh. 'No. We were getting married long before I found out I was pregnant.'

'So which is your husband?'

'Dan.' I turn and notice that Dan is sitting next to Kate, talking to her animatedly. So, I think, two can play that game. If you're having such a good time talking to another woman, I can have a bloody good time flirting with another man.

Sorry, I meant *talking* to another man.

'Here.' Caro comes up to us and hands me a glass—hooray! Champagne! 'Have some champagne. Do you two know each other?'

'Ellie used to be the Marketing Director at Calden,' Charlie says. 'We met at a lunch. You know Fran and Marcus, don't you?'

'Of course,' Caro nods. 'I love Fran, and any friend of Fran's is a friend of mine.'

'Thank you.' I smile, knowing that in my vintage dress and high strappy heels, with champage in hand and a connection to both Charlie Dutton and Fran, I truly feel exactly as I wanted to feel tonight: sparkling and sexy.

I love wearing this dress. I love wearing these heels. Normally I wouldn't be seen dead in anything higher than an inch, and a dress? You have to be kidding. Not when trousers are so much more comfortable, not to mention practical.

I'd forgotten how wonderful you can feel in a dress. Especially one as floaty and feminine as this one, that ensures you feel as floaty and feminine as

246

the dress itself.

In with the in crowd. How lovely. What a shame I didn't make more of an effort to socialize with these people, hell, to dress like this, before I was married.

I follow Charlie to a sofa and sit down, proffering my glass for a refill from Jonathan as he walks round the room. My darling husband is still talking to Kate. Fuck him, I decide. I will not let him ruin my night.

I turn to Charlie Dutton, trying to think of something scintillating, funny, clever to ask him. I'm trying to flirt, I realize with a shock. Not because I find Charlie Dutton attractive— although, trust me, he's not exactly painful to look at—but because I am now convinced that Dan is flirting, and he is not the only one who can do this.

Except I can't. I never was any good at flirting, was always taken by surprise when men started flirting with me. I can think of scintillating, funny, clever, flirtatious things to say, but only when the moment has passed, and usually when I am back in my bed. Alone.

'So how is motherhood?' Charlie Dutton asks, thank God, before I can think of anything.

'Lovely. Exhausting, but lovely,' I say.

'Isn't it extraordinary how much your life changes?' he says, smiling. 'I remember when Finn was born. My ex and I used to talk about how he'd just fit into our lives, like a cute little accessory, how we'd take him with us everywhere and he'd have to learn to adapt. Boy, were we in for a shock.'

I laugh, having forgotten that he had a son. 'Exactly, that's exactly what we said. We had no idea it would turn our lives upside down.'

'But you're surviving it,' Charlie Dutton says, taking a sip of his drink. 'We didn't manage to survive it, but then we would never have stayed together if she hadn't been pregnant.'

I want to ask more, suddenly. Want to ask about his ex, how they met, why they decided to keep the baby, how exactly his life was turned upside down.

He is attractive.

The words enter my head with a shock. I look at Dan guiltily, trying to reassure myself by connecting with a husband to whom I'm not speaking. Unsurprisingly it doesn't work.

And I find myself blushing. For no reason at all. Other than that I'm immediately aware that I'm attracted to Charlie Dutton. I haven't been attracted to anyone for such a long time. I'm a married woman—I'm not supposed to feel like this.

Of course I had theorized about attraction. Had spent hours theorizing about infidelity, and affairs, and why we did or didn't commit adultery.

I had confidently proclaimed that of course you didn't stop being attracted to people just because you were married, but that you had a choice: you would weigh up what you had, what you stood to lose, and would realize that nothing would be worth risking your marriage for, and that your crush, for that would be all it was, would pass.

But that's the thing about theories. You can theorize all you want, but at the end of the day when your theories become reality, when the situation you have theorized about is suddenly presented to you, your theories go flying out the window.

Just as Fran said she hadn't known how she

248

would react to infidelity until the fact of it was presented to her, at which point she'd reacted completely differently to the way she'd always thought she would, I am sitting here completely shocked that I am attracted to Charlie Dutton. And with a start I realize I am staring at his arms.

Strong arms. Fair, unlike Dan's dark, hairy arms, Charlie Dutton's arms are tanned with blonde hairs. Nice. Oh, God. Am I completely out of my mind?

I look guiltily at Dan, who doesn't look at me at all. And Charlie Dutton is asking me something, but I can't look at him. I can't look him in the eye or I may go scarlet.

Oh, for God's sake, Ellie! You're a grown woman! Compose yourself! You're a wife and a mother, and a GROWN-UP! Stop behaving like a child.

'I'm sorry?' I say to Charlie Dutton. 'What did you say?'

'I asked where the baby was. I see that your other friends have brought their son.' He gestures to Oscar, sitting peacefully in his buggy at Trish's feet, ignoring the chatter all around him, grinning happily at being with his mother.

'Sorry.' I shake my head to dislodge the thoughts. 'Tom's at home. My in-laws have rented this house for the summer. They were supposed to be on a yacht, but the yacht had an accident so they're there. The only plus is they're available for babysitting duties.'

Okay. I did it. I managed a coherent sentence without blushing. Anyway, I'm clearly being ridiculous. Didn't Fran once say he was this massively eligible bachelor? Why would someone like him even look at someone like me? Not to mention that I'm married.

I start to regain my equilibrium, breathing more easily. Not that I want him to be interested in me of course, although I'd only flirt anyway, would never do anything more, but even that won't happen. He's gorgeous. He'd never look at me. And nor should he.

I relax.

'You've obviously managed to get some sunbathing in as well,' Charlie says. 'You look . . .' He pauses and I look up, manage to look him in the eye. '. . . delicious,' he says slowly, without a hint of a smile, and my heart starts to pound.

And then I turn scarlet, from the tips of my toes to the top of my head. Oh shit.

'Oh, Charlie,' Caro says, from the other side of the room. 'What have you been saying to poor Ellie? Whatever it is, stop it, she's gone completely beetroot. Did he embarrass you, Ellie? Just ignore him, he's a terrible tease.'

'No, no, it's okay,' I mumble, as Dan looks at me quizzically.

'Is he flirting with you?' Jonathan grins, at which point I blush even more.

If that's at all possible.

'Oh, Charlie,' he says. 'You're such an old dog.'

'What a horrible thing to say,' Charlie Dutton says indignantly, as I wish very much I could click my heels together like Dorothy, and be home.

'Don't take offence,' Jonathan says. 'Poor Ellie. She's just trying to be polite and you're embarrassing her horribly. Leave her alone.'

'Okay, okay.' Charlie Dutton puts his hands in the air and grins before turning to me and bowing.

'Sorry for embarrassing you,' he says loudly. 'If you'll excuse me, I'll just go and powder my nose.'

'I told you not to bring any cocaine into this house,' Caro admonishes.

'Not that kind of powdering.' Charlie Dutton grins. 'I'm going to the loo, okay? How's that?'

He turns to leave as I sit there, still blushing, more so because I've just been the centre of attention, and because I think I've just made a horrible fool of myself. Not that, thankfully, I flirted back. I run back to our conversation, to what I said, and I breathe an audible sigh of relief. Nothing I said could have been construed as flirting, nothing would have given away that shock of attraction I felt.

My blush starts to fade and the others start to talk amongst themselves again. I relax. And then I hear a voice in my ear.

'Just for the record,' Charlie Dutton says incredibly softly, 'I meant what I said,' and I sit there, as still as a stone, and pretend I didn't hear. But I cannot help the small smile that plays upon my face.

*   *   *

Later, just as we're leaving for the restaurant, I go to the loo to make sure I'm not shining, and to reapply my lipstick.

I open the door and walk smack bang into Lisa.

'Are you having fun?'

I nod enthusiastically, having spent the last half hour chatting with Jonathan and Caro, trying to ignore Charlie Dutton altogether, finding myself exhausted with the strain of there being two men

I'm having to ignore—albeit for different reasons—and exhilarated by this flirtation, by the knowledge that I'm still attractive! I'm sexy! Someone other than my husband thinks I'm . . . *delicious*!

'They're all so nice!' I say. 'So warm, and charming. And I love Caro and Jonathan, what great people.'

'I know,' she says. 'And what about that . . . Charlie Dutton?'

'Charlie Dutton?' I affect nonchalance, willing myself not to blush, willing myself not to give the game away. 'What about Charlie Dutton?'

Lisa raises an eyebrow. 'What do you think of Charlie Dutton?'

'I think he's also lovely,' I say.

There's a pause. 'Just be careful,' she says. 'I don't know him, but I've heard about him. He's very attractive, with a horrible reputation as someone who is not, how shall I put this, okay, someone who is not discouraged by the fact that people are married. If anything it seems to be something of a turn on for him.'

'Oh, for God's sake,' I say, wanting to ask more, wanting to find out everything about him, everything about the women he's known, what he's attracted to, what his reputation is exactly, but not of course asking any of those questions, not wanting anyone, not even Lisa, to know how I feel. 'So he was flirting with me a bit. I'm married, Lisa, and not the slightest bit interested in being unfaithful to my husband.

'It was flattering,' I continue. 'That's all. God, do you know how nice it is to have a man pay you a compliment when you're still feeling fat and frumpy after having a baby, and men never ever look at you or flirt with you or compliment you because you're now a mother in their eyes, and a dowdy one at that?'

I look at Lisa, and I can see she doesn't know. Of course she doesn't know. How could she possibly know? 'You wouldn't understand,' I say more gently now. 'Look how gorgeous you are, but for the rest of us mere mortals we take it where we can get it.'

Lisa laughs. 'Okay, okay. Forgive me. Just promise me you're not going to have an affair with him, because I've heard he really is a heartbreaker, plus you've got a good one in Dan. Trust me. I know.'

'I absolutely promise I'm not going to have an affair with him. You know how I feel about that. I wouldn't risk losing everything I have with Dan. No way.'

She hugs me and we go back into the living room, where Dan is standing there white as a sheet, holding the telephone receiver, and nobody is talking.

Everybody is looking at me.

And I know. Instantly I know that something terrible has happened, and the world stops moving.

'It's Tom,' Dan whispers. 'There's been an accident.'

20

I'm not aware of much that happens immediately after that.

Dan takes me by the arm and leads me outside to the car, and I'm vaguely conscious of being hugged, of worried faces, of mumblings about who should come to the hospital, who should stay.

I'm aware of what's going on, but aware from afar. It's like being submerged under water—I can see and hear, but everything seems fuzzy, and I am completely calm, as calm as I have ever been in my life, and my heart, rather than pounding with sheer panic, the reaction I would have expected, given that the worst possible thing I could ever imagine happening seems to be happening, my heart feels as if it's slowed to the point of almost stopping.

I am aware that Dan is still as white as a sheet, and that Trish insists on driving, and that Dan and I sit in the back, each looking out our respective windows.

I am aware that Trish asks Dan what happened, and Dan says something about someone carrying Tom and tripping, and dropping Tom down the stairs, but not being able to say any more because he starts to cry.

I am aware that I am completely numb. That I cannot think about anything, say anything, feel anything, until we pull into L'Hôpital des Broussailles in Cannes, park the car and rush to the emergency room.

'Tom Cooper,' Dan says urgently to the nurse behind the desk. 'Mon fils. Nous cherchons notre fils.'

And then we hear 'Dan?' and we turn to see Linda and Michael rushing round a corner, tears streaming down Linda's face.

'We got the neighbour to come in and watch Amy,' Linda explains through her tears. 'We came straight here.'

'Where's Tom?' Dan demands. 'Where is he? What's going on?'

'I'm so sorry,' she says, keeps saying, and my heart turns to stone, and all I keep thinking is please God, no. Please, God. No. No. No.

'Oh, my God.' Dan inhales sharply. 'He's not . . .' He can't say it. The word won't come out.

'No!' Michael says, gently elbowing a now-hysterical Linda out of the way. 'He's still being examined by the doctor.'

And finally the feelings explode out of me in a primal scream, exploding into the worried whisperings of this all-white space.

'Let me see my son! Where's my son? Let me see my son. Now!'

*   *   *

The doctor speaks English. Thank God.

'He has a broken leg and a fractured wrist, but we are more concerned about any head injuries.' He pauses. 'He is an infant, and his bones are still soft, and the orthopaedic surgeon is on his way to . . .'

'What do you mean, you're more concerned about head injuries?' Dan speaks, as the fear those words have induced has rendered me speechless. It's all I can do to carry on breathing.

255

The doctor sighs. 'We have X-rayed his body and established what has happened to his bones, but it is not so easy with the brain. The head trauma that is causing his lack of consciousness has been caused by a contusion to the brain.'

I look at him blankly.

'We need to do a CAT scan to check for bleeding in the brain.'

'When?' Dan says softly. 'When are you going to do that?'

'We are preparing for that now,' he says.

'But what does that mean?' I whisper. 'What do you *mean*, bleeding in the brain? Could he still be fine? What does that *mean*?' My voice is rising, on the verge of hysteria, and the sense of calm, of lack of reality, leaves me in an instant, replaced by an icy-cold clutch of fear around my heart. 'Does that mean brain damage?'

The doctor looks away. 'I think it is too early to speculate. There are a number of outcomes, and the CAT scan will tell us more. The best-case scenario is that the blood is reabsorbed naturally into the body.'

'And then he'd be fine?' Dan has again gone white.

The doctor nods. 'Then he would be fine.'

'And the worst case?' I don't want to know. But I have to ask.

'If the bleeding is causing a swelling of the brain, or increased pressure in the brain, we will begin treatment immediately to relieve that pressure.' The doctor lays a gentle hand on my arm. 'We will know more after the CAT scan,' he says. 'Have faith.'

I look down at Tom's tiny body, his eyes closed,

wires all over him hooked on to various machines, and I start to cry. Huge, gulping sobs that I can't keep in any more, and Dan puts his arms around me and I can't stop sobbing. I just lean into him and cry and cry and cry.

This can't be happening to me, I keep thinking. How can this be happening? I lost my mother when I was a child. Isn't that enough tragedy for one lifetime? What have I done that's so awful that this could be happening to me again? Why me? Why us? Why this tiny helpless baby?

* * *

We don't go home that night. Nor the next. Nor the next week. The doctors and nurses are kind and solicitous in a way I fear they reserve only for the parents of the truly sick, the ones that may not make it through.

Tom is taken in for regular CAT scans, and so far the news is good. There has been some bleeding, but no swelling, and, as we hoped, it appears the bleeding is being reabsorbed back into the body.

Oh, God. *The body*. Not the body. Tom. My baby. Why is this happening to us?

Dan and I sleep, and I say that with a large dose of irony because of course we barely sleep, in makeshift cots next to Tom's bed. We take turns sitting with him, singing to him, holding his tiny hand, and I leave the room only to go to the bathroom or to get some more coffee in the middle of the night.

I am aware that people come to the hospital. I know Linda and Michael are outside in the waiting room a lot. I know Trish and Gregory have been, and Lisa, but I can't see them. Can't see anyone. There's nothing to talk about, nothing to say, and all my energy is going into being there for my son and praying to God that he will be fine.

His leg has been pinned, and he is surrounded by a huge contraption, hooked up to various machines, on various IVs. Sometimes I thank God he is not conscious, unaware, I hope, of the pain it must have caused him, to have these metal pins going through his bones and these needles going through his skin.

Linda tried to talk to me once. I had left Tom's room, desperate for some air, and she came over to me and started to speak, started to say something, but I couldn't deal with it, couldn't even look at her, so I just turned and walked away, left her standing in mid sentence.

I don't care.

This isn't about her. This isn't about what she may or may not have done, did or didn't do. I'm not interested in hearing how terrible she feels about dropping my son. I'm not interested in hearing what she was doing carrying my son in the first place, when I know he was supposed to have been sleeping. I'm not interested in her asking for my forgiveness.

All I'm interested in is Tom. Linda doesn't exist for me right now. I'm not sure she ever will again.

*   *   *

We spend seventeen days in the hospital. Each day we have a little more information. His bones are healing nicely. The brain scan hasn't picked

258

anything up, but now he needs to regain consciousness before we can tell any more.

On day twelve, I'm sleeping in the cot, when a baby cries in my dreams. I'm in my old office at Calden, in a meeting, and all we can hear is a baby crying. Damn, I think in my dream. I'm not allowed to bring a baby into work and now they'll all know. In my dream the baby is in my office, and I excuse myself, rushing frantically back to the office to soothe the baby, who, incidentally (and I'm not sure what this means), isn't Tom, and I can't find the baby, I can just hear the wailing that goes on and on.

I rouse myself out of sleep, leaving the dream behind, except I can still hear the crying, and I suddenly realize it's Tom, and I leap out of bed and Tom is wailing, his mouth wide open as he screams, his eyes squeezed tightly shut, and I attempt to soothe him, to hug his tiny body through the wires and frames, and I start to cry and laugh with relief.

He's awake.

He's alive.

Dan rushes in, a cup of steaming coffee in his hand. He immediately leaves it on the table and comes over to join me, shaking his head in disbelief, then bursting into tears.

'I didn't think he'd ever wake up,' he says, sobbing into the bedclothes as he clutches Tom's hand. 'I didn't think this would ever happen.'

The nurse comes in, and then the doctor, and we are moved out of the way while they examine him.

'What are they saying?' I keep asking Dan, but he doesn't know. His A-level French didn't extend to hospitals and medical terminology.

'Sssh, sssh,' he keeps telling me, attempting to

259

understand, to pick up a word perhaps, or a sentence that might shed some light, but they are all talking so quickly, and with such unfamiliar vocabulary, that he can't understand.

'Well, we know one thing,' the doctor finally says, walking over to us in the corner of the room. 'His lungs are not affected,' and he smiles, and for the first time since this accident I feel relief. Relief that there suddenly appears to be a light at the end of the tunnel, relief that this doctor, who has been so serious and so careful with us all this time, now sees fit to make a joke, which must mean that he is confident, or at least optimistic, about the outcome.

'This is good, though, isn't it?' I say. 'Does this mean he's fine?'

'This is very good news,' he says. 'But we must run a few more tests.'

*　　　*　　　*

On the day we leave, the day after Tom was finally given the all-clear, Linda is sitting in the waiting room by herself. Dan is still inside signing the discharge papers and organizing the insurance. I am cradling Tom in my arms and about to go downstairs, where we will take the rental car straight to the airport to fly home.

I don't see Linda immediately. She comes over to us and reaches out a hand to Tom, and I move my body to shield him from her, won't allow her to touch him, not any more.

Because now I know what happened.

Tom was lying in bed babbling, and Linda decided to bring him downstairs because he clearly wasn't ready for sleep. Just for the record, Tom often lies there babbling, but seven o'clock is his bedtime and so I let him lie there until he babbles himself to sleep.

Linda chose to ignore my instructions—because I did make it very clear before we went out that he would talk and she should ignore him—and picked Tom up. As she started down the stairs, she tripped and (she still can't believe she did this, will never forgive herself for doing this) instinctively put her arms out to catch herself.

She caught herself, and in doing so dropped my son.

If you had asked me, before this happened, what I would do, how I would feel, should Linda ever cause harm to my child, I would have told you that I would scream at her, unleash my rage, my hurt, my fury.

I imagined screaming my hatred for her, venting that poison and enjoying the shocked look on her face, her inability to reply.

But, in the event, I don't feel any of that. I just feel tired. And relieved. But mostly tired.

'Please let me see him,' Linda says softly, tears already running down her face. 'Just let me look at him,' and for the first time I actually stop and look her straight in the eye.

'No,' I say, ever so softly, but my voice has never been firmer, and never have I meant anything in my life as much as I mean these words now. 'You cannot look at him and you cannot hold him. You need to know now that I will never ever forgive you for what you did. Do you understand? I. Will. Never. Forgive. You.'

And with Tom in my arms, I turn and walk away.

I'd like to say that life returns to normal once we are back in London, but I'm not sure what normal is any more. I'm not sure I'll ever feel normal again.

Tom spent six weeks in a frame until his bones healed, and now he is absolutely fine. We have been assured he'll be playing football and rugby with all the others.

And brain damage, or permanent damage of any kind, has been ruled out. As our GP here in London said, Tom's as good as he was before. Hell, with the metal pins in his leg he may even be a little better.

The same cannot be said, however, for Dan and me. Every time I look at him I remember him that evening, before we went out, saying, *'What do you think's going to happen, for God's sake? Tom will be fine. They'll all be fine.'*

Did I know something? Could I have prevented it? Maybe not, but, irrational as it may be, I look at Dan and I hear that conversation. I look at Dan and I see Linda.

Needless to say I blame Linda more than anyone.

But I also blame Dan.

21

Christmas comes, and Tom is fine. Better than fine. Delicious, gorgeous, delectable. We don't spend Christmas Day with Linda and Michael. Bizarrely (and yet it was so nice) we spend it with my father.

My father and Mary phoned and left a message, saying how wonderful it would be if we all spent Christmas together, and instead of phoning back and saying we had plans, I phoned back and said yes. We'd love to come down and spend Christmas Day with them in Potters Bar.

Dan was furious. But it got us out of being with Linda and Michael, and gave my father a chance to be with Tom; and, while he may not have been the greatest father in the world, he was wonderful with Tom, and they bonded instantly.

Dan sulked for most of the day, but I found it strangely relaxing, and infinitely more relaxing being with them than with the Coopers.

So Tom is fine, but Dan and I, on the other hand, are not. How ironic that the holiday in France, the holiday we were so desperate for, went from paradise to hell in such a short space of time, and is continuing to impact on our lives every waking moment.

Dan says, over and over, that it's not his fault. And rationally I know that to be true. Dan says that it's all in the past, that the only thing that matters is that Tom is fine, and as soon as I let go of the anger, we can move on with our lives.

But the problem is I can't let go, don't know how to let go, and at this moment in time can't see myself being able to let go, ever.

I remember how surprised I was when Tom was in the hospital, surprised by my calmness, my lack of emotion, my failure to blame. I didn't have the energy to blame anyone, not then, but now that Tom is fine, now that we are back home and everyone expects us to resume our lives as normal, as if nothing had happened, I find myself filled with a fury that I have never ever known before.

How dare Linda—even the thought of her name makes my blood boil these days—pick Tom up. How dare she deliberately ignore my wishes. If that stupid woman had just left him alone, Tom would have been fine.

I know he's fine now. I know that's all that matters, but all I keep thinking about is Linda dropping my precious boy down the stairs, reaching out her hands to protect herself, putting herself before my son.

I know she'll never forgive herself. Her letters have implored me to forgive her, have said that the fact she will never forgive herself is surely punishment enough, and I should not punish her further by not letting her see Tom.

I read each letter in the beginning. Now I don't even open them, just put them straight in the bin. I used to read them impassively, snorting with derision when she asked to see Tom. As if I would let her near my son ever again.

She's worked on Dan too, I know the days he's been to see her, or spoken to her on the phone. He'll come home and soon thereafter he'll suggest inviting them over, tell me how much she misses Tom, how this is killing her.

We'll both be there, he'll say. Nothing will

happen. Will you stop being so overdramatic and ridiculous? Stop punishing her for what was a terrible accident without, thank God, a terrible outcome.

And finally: Will you stop being such a fucking bitch?

'How dare you?' I scream at him, scream, literally, at the top of my lungs, amazed that I have this ability to let out this rage, amazed that I am able to speak to another person in the way I now speak to Dan. 'How dare you call me that? How dare you suggest they see him after what happened? How dare you call me a bitch? Get out! Just get out!'

It's all I can do not to scream 'I hate you', but each time the words threaten to escape something makes me swallow them. I don't believe there would be any way back if those words came out, even though I think them every day.

I don't know what's happened to us. I don't understand this anger, this hatred, this permanent sense of injustice. But I do know that Tom and I are happy when we are by ourselves. *Happier* by ourselves.

Dan has started to leave the house before I get up. I'm always awake, but I lie there pretending to be asleep, my body filled with tension, my breaths short and tight, counting the minutes until the front door closes and I can finally relax.

I get Tom up and we have breakfast together, most of which usually ends up on the floor or squished all over Tom's face.

'Mama,' he says now. And 'A-ee', which is Harry, the name of his stuffed cat. Amy seems to be talking much more, and at sixteen months I do rather worry that Tom's vocabulary ought to be bigger, but I also know that every child develops at their own pace, and Oscar isn't saying that much more than Tom.

We go to Gymboree, and music class, and meet Trish and Lisa for playdates. Unless it's pouring with rain we're usually in the playground every afternoon, and I love every minute of every day, right up to our giggly bathtime and snuggling a wriggly Tom in my arms as I read him a bedtime story and put him to bed.

My day only ever starts to sour as the front door opens and Dan comes home, bringing all the tension and stress back with him.

We barely talk any more. When we do, we talk about Tom, perfunctory conversations about what Tom did today, and that's about it. We've become one of those couples that I used to dread becoming: the couples that sit in restaurants all night and don't say a word to one another.

Because of course we still go out. I have neither the energy nor the will to cook, and we still have to present a united front to the world.

We'll join Trish and Gregory for dinner at least once a week, usually somewhere local, Lemonia or Manna. I like to think that you wouldn't know there was anything wrong between us, that when we are with other people we do a pretty good job of pretending everything's fine, we are just like every other young couple.

Lisa and Andy broke up soon after France. I still see her during the day, but she's being the single-girl-about-town in the evenings, and it's rare that she's able to join us for dinner.

I haven't really spoken to anyone about what's

going on. I'll make jokes about Dan and me rowing, but haven't told anyone just how unhappy we are, too scared to voice what I already know, too scared to set the wheels in motion.

Because I am living in a kind of inertia. I know something has to change. Know that I cannot go on living, or not living, like this, but I don't know what steps to take next, how to change it.

Part of me keeps waiting for it to pass. Keeps thinking that one morning I will wake up and the anger will have passed and I will look at Dan and feel love again, but then I look at him and the feelings I once had are only a fading memory. I can just about remember how I used to feel, but I don't feel it any more. Nothing. Not a shred.

All I feel is anger, and irritation, and the need to push him even further away.

*   *   *

Lemonia is packed, and Dan and I weave through the tables until we spot Trish and Gregory in the corner. I plaster a bright smile on my face, as does Dan, and we wave as we go over to join them.

'How's the new babysitter?'

'She's wonderful!' Trish says as she reaches up to kiss me hello. 'Oscar's in heaven, didn't even look at me when I tried to say goodbye, he was far too busy playing with Emily.'

'Thank God you've finally found someone.' I sit down next to Trish as Dan sits next to Gregory and starts to talk work. 'I don't know what I'd do without Rachel.'

Rachel is my angel of mercy, my current second-favourite person in the world to see after Tom.

She's a strong, confident, funny Australian who's been here for eight months, lives in a house in Acton with, from what I can make out, one hundred and twenty-four other Australians, and she's been our part-time nanny for the last four months.

I didn't think I'd ever be able to trust Tom with anyone, not after what happened, but Calden gave me a big project, and suddenly I was going to meetings again and actually having to shut myself away from Tom to focus on conference calls and read marketing plans.

I had to have a nanny, for two days a week I decided, and three nights' babysitting too. Rachel works the rest of the time for a friend of Fran, which is how I found her, and as soon as I spoke to Fran's friend, as soon as I heard how wonderful Rachel was, I started to relax.

And then, when she came for the interview, the first thing she did was to scoop Tom up and tickle him with her eyelashes, which made him laugh. She so clearly loved children, was so completely comfortable with them, that I took her on.

Admittedly the first three weeks were tough. I couldn't get the thought of Linda dropping Tom out of my mind, so I made sure they didn't leave the house, and I kept a very close eye on them.

They were fine.

Then Trish suggested that she, Oscar, Tom and Rachel should go to the playground together, and she said she'd keep an eye on them. She reported back that Rachel was amazing, that even Oscar loved her. After that I let Rachel go wherever she wanted.

'Rachel is amazing,' Trish says, 'but then again

you could leave Tom with pretty much anyone and he'd be happy. Oscar's much more sensitive. He loves Rachel but she doesn't have any more nights free for us, so Emily's the first one we've found who he's been happy with. God!' She rolls her eyes before continuing affectionately, 'Oscar can be such a troublemaker. Why do I end up with the sensitive one?'

Sensitive. What a perfect simile for nightmarish. I feel horribly guilty even thinking it, but Oscar is turning out to be something of a horror. I love Trish, really, she's become my closest friend, but Oscar I could very definitely live without.

Oscar has no rules in his own house, so naturally he believes the same lack of rules applies in our house too. He'll grab a crayon and scribble all over the wall as Trish vaguely attempts to stop him while telling me admiringly how artistic he is. He'll climb up on the sofa wearing his boots, thickly plastered with mud, and Trish will tell him softly to get down and just shrug when he ignores her and carry on chatting as I have minor heart failure. I mean, those sofas cost a *fortune*.

He'll point to food and scream if he can't have it, so Trish always ends up giving him exactly what he wants just to keep him quiet. 'I know I shouldn't,' she'll say, 'but I just can't bear the screaming.'

And poor Trish has been through babysitter hell. Oscar has clearly hated his mother leaving him with anyone, so thank goodness she's finally found someone of whom Oscar approves.

'I hope you're paying her well,' I say.

'If Oscar likes her I'll pay her pretty much whatever she wants,' Trish laughs. 'Anything to keep the little devil happy.'

269

I laugh too. Oh, if only she knew.

*　　*　　*

We have a lovely evening. Lovely because it feels normal. Because it's loud, and noisy, and barely noticeable that Dan and I don't really talk to one another.

Sometimes I watch Gregory and Trish, watch how he will squeeze her arm affectionately, or lean over and give her a kiss; watch how Trish includes him in so much of her conversation. 'Isn't it, Gregory?' 'Don't we, Gregory?' 'What do you think, Gregory?' And I wonder whether they notice the lack of affection between us.

Every couple is different, I think. They would only notice the difference if they knew us in the beginning, before we had Tom. We did use to be affectionate. We used to talk kindly to one another, kiss one another for no reason at all, rest a head on a shoulder or stroke a cheek softly.

That feels like a lifetime ago now. A different Dan. A different Ellie. I wonder what would happen if I did that now? If I reached out and kissed Dan's cheek? I look at Dan's face, thinking about his reaction and he senses me looking at him and stops speaking to Gregory, to look at me.

And for a second, as our eyes meet, I remember how he used to look at me with love. I remember he would turn and his eyes would be warm and sparkling, and I would feel safe, and warm, and loved.

Tonight, as with every other night now, there is only coldness. And possibly a hint of irritation.

'What?' Dan asks.

'Nothing,' I say lightly, and he turns back to Gregory as if I didn't exist at all.

We pay the bill and stand up, pulling our coats off the backs of our chairs and putting them on. Gregory stretches and lets his hands rest on Trish's shoulders.

'Oh, good,' he says, glancing at his watch. 'An early night,' and he winks at Trish, who smiles and rolls her eyes.

'Oh, God,' she moans. 'Do we have to? We had *an early night* last night.'

'You can't ever have too many early nights as far as I'm concerned,' Gregory says. 'Isn't that right, Dan?'

Dan shrugs. 'Frankly I wouldn't know. We haven't slept together for six months.'

There's a deathly silence as Gregory looks first at Dan, then at me, waiting for one of us to say we're joking.

'Dan, shut up,' I say softly, aghast that he's announced this fact to our closest friends. Aghast that it's finally out there.

'What? You don't want your best friend to know that you refuse to have sex with me? Why ever not? Because she might think you're abnormal?'

My face is scarlet. I can't believe this conversation. Can't believe what Dan is saying. 'Dan, stop it,' I warn. 'I will not talk about this now.'

Dan looks at me and just shakes his head, a disgusted look on his face. 'I'll see you at home,' he says, walking off through the restaurant.

'Um, um.' Poor Gregory. He doesn't have a clue what to say. 'Ellie, I feel awful for saying anything. I didn't mean to start . . .'

'My husband is such an oaf.' Trish nudges him. 'Go outside and talk to Dan.'

Trish holds me back just inside the door, and when Gregory has left she turns to me. 'I know that I keep asking you if everything's okay and you keep saying that everything is, and if you really don't want to talk about it of course I understand, but I want you to know that you can talk to me about anything, and that I won't judge you, and that I will do my best to understand.'

I nod. I think I'm going to cry. I would say something, but there's a sob just queuing up in my throat, and all I can do is try to swallow it away as tears well up in my eyes.

*   *   *

By the time I get home Rachel has been paid and has left, and Dan is sitting on the sofa, staring into space. I walk in and shrug my coat off, then sit on the sofa opposite him. I can't carry on any more. *We* can't carry on any more. Something has to change, and before I even think about the words they're out there, ominously quiet, almost a whisper in the silence.

'I can't do this any more.'

Dan doesn't say anything, doesn't even look up, just continues to stare at his hands clasped between his legs, elbows resting on his knees as he looks down.

'Dan, we have to talk.' I take a deep breath. 'All we seem to do these days is make one another unhappy. I think we can't carry on like this, something has to change.'

Still, nothing.

272

'Dan, will you look at me?' Slowly Dan raises his eyes until they meet mine, and I'm shocked to see how much pain is in them. He looks away again and then speaks. 'So what do you want to do?'

'I don't know.' And I didn't think that I knew, but then, almost unconsciously, I say, 'I think we ought to separate for a while.' And I take a deep breath. Shocked. Dan looks at me, and I can see he's shocked too.

It feels surreal. And clichéd. And rubbish. I wish I could come up with something more original, something better than these lines that sound like a bad made-for-television movie. But there isn't any other way to say it.

'Dan? Aren't you going to say anything?'

'What do you want me to say?' His voice is flat. Emotionless.

'Tell me how you feel. Tell me what you want? What do *you* think?'

He shrugs. 'I think you've made up your mind.'

I keep pushing. This may be the end of the marriage, but I can't let it go quite this easily. I can't let the marriage end on this note of silence, on this lack of communication. Suddenly I want to *know*, all the things I haven't asked him for the last six months, I now want to know.

'But do you *agree*? Is this what you want?'

'What difference would it make what I want?'

'You're not happy either.'

'No. But I wouldn't necessarily throw in the towel just yet.'

'Look,' I sigh. 'It's not permanent. Maybe we just need some space to reassess. I don't think we should talk about . . . divorce . . . or anything.' Oh, God. *Divorce*. The very mention of the word sends

273

shivers down my spine. 'Hopefully this is just a phase.'

He doesn't agree. Or disagree. Doesn't say anything at all until he looks up and says softly, 'And what about Tom?'

Oh, God. What about Tom?

'What do you mean?'

'I mean what happens with Tom? I suppose you'll want to stay in the flat with Tom.'

I hadn't thought about it, but now that he has brought it up, yes, of course I want to stay in the flat with Tom. I may only work part time, I may bring very little money to the table, but our flat couldn't have been bought without the money from the sale of my old flat, not to mention the fact that this is Tom's home, and the less his life is disrupted the better.

'Well, yes,' I say, 'I mean, you'll obviously see him whenever you want. You can come over any time. Or maybe on weekends. Or . . . I don't know. Whatever. I haven't done this before either. We'll work something out.' And I think finally the shock starts to sink in, even though I can hardly believe that this conversation has so quickly become a reality. We've spent months screaming at one another, sleeping with our backs to one another, barely speaking to one another, and now that we're actually managing to have a calm conversation, our marriage is ending.

Just like that. In a few minutes everything has gone. Poof. Another lump in my throat, and again I swallow it away. I don't know what I expected. Maybe more arguments, more discussions. Maybe just to talk about things and go to bed, then wake up with everything exactly the same.

But suddenly everything is completely different. Suddenly my marriage is over. Because I might have said we're just separating, it's only temporary, but who am I kidding? My marriage is a failure and I'm on my own.

'Do you think we should talk about this more in the morning?' I say, stalling for time, unable to believe how final this has become so quickly.

'No.' Dan sighs and stands up, running his fingers through his hair, and for a second I want to run to him and cling to him. No, I want to cry. Make this okay, make it better. Stay and fight. But of course I don't. I just bite my lip and look at the floor.

'I'll go and pack a few things,' Dan says. 'I'll go and stay at my parents' until things are a bit more sorted out.' He leaves and I hear him go into the bedroom, then the sound of drawers and cupboard doors being opened, the sound of clothes being shoved into a sports bag.

I can't move for a while. I just sit on the sofa, unable to believe this is real, that we have actually had this conversation, that my husband is leaving me. That it's really over.

I get up and stand in the doorway of the bedroom, watching him, wanting to say more, wanting us to talk more, wanting one of us to fight for this marriage, to turn everything back to normal, even if normal means those long silences of the past six months, not speaking, not touching, not talking. Anything rather than this.

Dan doesn't look at me. Just finishes packing some things. When he goes into the bathroom, I turn and walk back to the living room, hearing my own heart pounding in my ears.

After a while I hear footsteps in the hall, and then I hear Tom's door being opened, and finally, very quietly, I hear Dan start to cry.

And I start crying too.

22

I don't move for a long time after Dan leaves. I just sit, crying intermittently, unable to believe that this has actually happened, he has actually gone. Part of me thought we would just carry on in exactly the same way, that living together unhappily was better than change.

You got what you wanted, a voice in my head keeps saying, but now that this has happened, now that the flat seems to echo with the stillness, with the absence of Dan, I'm not sure.

But no. Of course this is better. And, as I said to Dan, it isn't necessarily permanent. Hopefully it's just a temporary separation, an absence that will enable us to find our way back to one another.

My eye catches our wedding photograph, mocking me from its prime position on the mantelpiece. God. Look how happy we were. How I thought I was marrying the perfect man, marrying into the perfect family. And how ironic that I expected Linda, Linda without whom none of this would have happened, to step into the role of mother, to be the mother I'd always dreamt of.

Filled with sadness, I take the photograph and place it gently in a drawer. I don't need to be reminded of what once was, what will probably never be again, because I don't honestly believe

Dan and I will ever find that happiness again. The hurt has been too great, the distance we've moved away from one another too far.

In the early hours I go into Tom's room and watch him sleeping. He's on his tummy now, something I worried about in the beginning—cot death and all that—but they say once they can turn over by themselves it's fine, and he's been turning over for months now, edging up into the far right corner of the cot, scrunching up into a tight little ball, bottom sticking high up in the air.

The love I feel for him is so often, as now, completely overwhelming. I want to pick him up and squeeze him, find a way of merging my body with his again, but I leave him, just stroke his back gently, careful not to wake him, and eventually I leave his bedroom and fall, exhausted, on to my own bed.

I do sleep. I lie facing Dan's side, something I haven't done for months, unable to look at him, unwilling to be anywhere near him, and I empty my head of thoughts until finally, finally, I fall into a deep, dreamless sleep.

*   *   *

Trish wakes me up the next morning, the phone jolting me awake, and for a few seconds, even as I fumble for the phone, I'm not sure who, where or what I am.

'Hello?' I mumble, squinting as I focus on the clock. Oh, God, 8.11. Tom must be starving. I can't believe I overslept this much.

'Hi. It's me. Did I wake you?' She's amazed.

'Yes. I overslept.'

'I'm so sorry. I just wanted to call and see if everything was okay. You seemed pretty . . . tense last night. I was worried about you.'

'I'm fine,' I say. 'But . . .' How do you tell people? How do you admit your husband has gone, you've failed at your marriage? In the course of a mere twelve hours your life has changed irrevocably. 'Dan's left.'

There's no other way to say it.

Trish gasps. 'What do you mean, he's left? You mean, he's *left*?'

'Yes.'

'But where? Where's he gone? Why? I don't understand.'

I take a deep breath. 'Oh, Trish. We've been so unhappy for so long. I suppose it just came to a head last night. We came home and finally admitted that it's not working, that we can't carry on as we are.'

'And what about Tom?' I can hear the shock in her voice.

'He'll still see Tom. I don't know how we're going to work out the finer details, but I wouldn't do anything to jeopardize his relationship with his son.'

'Oh, God, Ellie,' Trish says, sounding dangerously close to tears. 'I don't know what to say. I mean, I can't believe it, I just . . . I knew you were unhappy, but isn't it just a phase? I thought it would take a bit of time and then you'd be fine.'

'I know.' I shrug sadly. 'I think I thought the same thing. Look, who knows? Maybe it isn't permanent, maybe we just need some space.'

'I can't believe it,' Trish keeps saying. 'It's awful. I can't believe it.' She pulls herself together. 'What are you doing now?'

'Now? I'm sitting in bed and I've got to feed poor Tom. He must be starving.'

'No, after that. This morning.'

'I don't know. Adjusting to my new status as a single mother, I suppose.'

'I'll come over. I'll bring Oscar and we can really talk about things.'

'I'm fine, Trish. You don't have to do that.'

'Of course I do,' she says. 'That's what friends are for.'

*   *   *

Lisa and Trish sit next to one another, hunched up on the sofa, infinite sadness on their faces.

Lisa had phoned at nine to see what we were doing today, and how could I not tell her, how could I withhold something so big? And so I told her, and her reaction was much like Trish's, only more subdued.

For a minute I thought back to the conversation I had had with my mother-in-law, back in the days when we had conversations. How Linda had warned me about Lisa, implied that Lisa was the kind of woman who would have an affair with Dan. Dan could have had an affair, God knows he left the house early enough and came home late enough, at least since the accident, but Lisa wouldn't do that to me, no matter what Linda thought. And that wasn't the issue between us anyway.

'Oh, for heaven's sake,' I say. 'It's not the end of the world. It's probably a good thing. Honestly, Dan and I have barely spoken for months, unless

279

we're screaming at one another. I've been so tired of pretending that everything's okay, and it had to come to a head somehow. This is a good thing, honestly.'

'I just feel so sad,' Trish says. 'And Gregory will be devastated. I mean, we see so much of you two.'

'You'll still see me. And Gregory will probably still see Dan,' I say, but I know what she means. It won't ever be the same. Not that I'm asking them to make a choice, I wouldn't do that, but I know the dynamic will be different, that it won't ever be as comfortable, going out for dinner with me as the third wheel, pretending that Gregory hasn't spoken to Dan, or that our friendship is exactly the same.

I hadn't thought of that. Of how friendships change when a couple splits up. Of course I'd heard about it, heard various—and I thought bitter—divorcees say they really learnt who their friends were when they split up from their husbands, how they were no longer invited anywhere, how all their 'happily' married friends suddenly perceived them as a threat, thought that being newly single would automatically mean they had set their sights on their middle-aged, boring, unattractive husbands.

The newly single women said they had to start afresh. That even if their friends stuck by them, they were always far more comfortable when another man was added, making up a cosy foursome instead of an awkward threesome.

I never thought I'd be in that position, but now that I am, are my friendships going to change? Trish, Gregory, Dan and I had grown so familiar with one another, that it's probably naive of me to think it will all stay the same without Dan. I don't expect my friendship with Trish to change a great deal. I imagine we'll still see just as much of one another during the day, and I know she'd never be threatened by me, would never worry about me flirting with Gregory. But sadly I realize it won't be the same now that I'm on my own, that we won't be sharing dinners with quite the same regularity or ease.

And what about Lisa? She's single, and God knows sociable. For a while, when we first met, the three of us seemed about equal, but lately we've been seeing Lisa less and less, lately she's seemed so busy, and Trish and I have grown closer still while Lisa has seemed further apart.

But now will Lisa become my partner in crime? Will Lisa replace Trish as my best friend? Replace Dan as my evening date?

A huge sigh escapes me and I shake my head. 'I know it's for the best,' I say, 'but I can't quite believe it either. A part of me thinks that Dan's going to come home this evening, just walk in the door as if nothing ever happened.'

'How would you feel if he did?' Trish asks.

'The same. What's terrifying is change, and doing everything on my own, but even if Dan were to come here this evening, it wouldn't make anything different. The fact is we've just been hating each other for months.' Trish and Lisa both look shocked. 'I know, I'm sorry, but it's true. We've been horrible to one another, and we needed something to happen, we really couldn't carry on.'

'Is he staying with Linda and Michael?' Lisa asks, and I nod. 'Have you spoken to them?'

'God, no!' I snort. 'I haven't got anything to say

281

to them. I'll let Dan explain. Anyway, they hate me already. I'm sure Linda will be delighted I'm out of the picture.'

'I don't think so.' Lisa shakes her head. 'I don't think they hate you. I think they just didn't understand how to be in-laws, and then of course, after the accident, they had all that guilt to deal with, and you wouldn't let them near.'

'Jesus.' I look at Lisa in horror. 'Whose side are you on?' I notice that even Trish gives her a warning look, a look that says, shut the hell up, now is neither the time nor the place.

'I'm sorry, Ellie.' Lisa is contrite. 'I didn't mean to upset you. I'm just trying to help.'

'That's okay,' I say. 'I understand. Anyway, the last people I need to think about now are my in-laws. Or ex-in-laws.'

'*Out-laws*, you mean,' says Trish. And I smile.

'Out-laws, then. But what matters most is Tom. He needs to know that he's still loved and safe.'

'Do you think he'll realize what's going on?' Trish looks concerned.

I nod, sadly. 'I'm sure he will, but frankly Dan's hardly been around. It's not like he's suddenly losing this amazing father who was with him all the time. He only really saw Tom on the weekends, and as I said, he'll probably still see him then anyway.'

'I have to tell you,' Lisa says, 'as a single mother, it's bloody difficult but not impossible. There will be times when you'll be completely exhausted, when you'll want to scream with frustration, cry with the loneliness and responsibility of it all, but those moments always pass, and you're strong, you'll be absolutely fine. At the end of the day those little monkeys'—she stops and leans down to

282

kiss Amy—'are worth it. You're absolutely right, they need to feel loved, and safe, and secure, and I think far better to have one happy parent who makes them feel that way than to grow up in a household with two parents who are always arguing, who clearly should never have stayed together.'

She's right. I look at her in amazement, suddenly realizing that the uncomfortable feeling I haven't been able to shake since Dan left last night is guilt. Guilt about Tom. What gave me the right to deprive Tom of growing up with two parents, a mother and a father? What gave me the right to deprive Tom of a happy family?

Lisa has just given me a huge sense of clarity, because of course we *weren't* a happy family. Tom was never going to grow up in the family that I had always dreamt of providing for my child, not when our house was always filled with rows, and accusations, and silences.

Far better for us to be on our own, to be able to fill the house with nothing but friends, and love, and laughter.

For the first time since last night I start to see that there might be a light at the end of the tunnel after all. This may be a terrible thing to happen, but it's not the worst thing ever to happen to me, and, as I learnt when I was thirteen years old, it may feel like the end of the world when it's happening, but everything passes, and everything gets better.

'Thank you, Lisa.' I get up and spontaneously hug her. 'Thank you for saying that. You have no idea how much better you've made me feel.'

'It's okay,' she says, hugging me tightly and

smiling. 'That's what friends are for.'

* * *

Dan phones on Friday morning. It's a shock to hear his voice. So familiar and so distant at the same time. My heart pounds as soon as I hear it's him. Nerves. Anxiety. Loss. And hope.

Because, while I know it's over, while I'm relieved there's finally an end to the rows, the hatred, the horrible atmosphere in the flat, hearing his voice makes me think of the early days, of the days when we were happy, when I just loved him so much, and for a few seconds I find myself hoping he's phoning for a reconciliation.

Oh, God, Ellie. Could you be any more fickle?

I wait to hear what he's going to say, knowing he'll want to talk, expecting him to break down, but there's almost no emotion when he speaks. Short. Succinct. To the point.

'How's Tom?'

'He's doing fine. Lovely.'

'Good. I miss him.'

'I know. I'm sure.'

'Ellie. We need to talk.' There, he said it. I knew it. He wants to find a way of working this out. I steel myself to tell him it's too soon, I'm not ready to try again, still need some more space, but before I can speak he continues. 'There's still a load of stuff I need from the flat, and we need to talk about Tom, find a way of working this out between us. I know we talked about my seeing him on weekends, but I was thinking about maybe taking an afternoon off during the week as well, seeing him during the week too.'

'Oh.' My voice is flat. This, I didn't expect.

'I thought perhaps I could come over this afternoon to pick up some of my stuff and we could talk.'

'Sure,' I say, looking at my watch. 'About four?'

'Fine,' he says, his voice still cool, detached. 'See you then. Bye.'

I'm surprised that I'm shaking slightly as I put down the phone.

*   *   *

It doesn't get easier. I am as nervous today as I was on our first date. Actually, that's a lie. I wasn't nervous on our first date at all. I fell in love with Dan precisely because I wasn't nervous, because I'd never felt so relaxed with anyone, that it felt more like being with my best friend than with a date. I fell in love with him because when I was with him I felt as if I'd come home.

Today I am more than making up for my lack of nerves on our first date. I take Tom out for a walk and pause outside one of Primrose Hill's trendiest and most expensive clothes shops. In the window is an amazing beaded cardigan. It's soft, and cashmere, and clingy, and quite the most beautiful, and probably expensive, thing I've ever seen.

What am I doing?

On auto-pilot I find myself going in, pointing to the cardigan and standing, a few minutes later, looking completely unlike myself. I smile at my reflection and the shop assistant smiles back. 'It looks fantastic,' she says.

'I don't look like me,' I say, turning to examine myself from the side, from behind. 'It's so

285

beautiful. I'm just a mother.' I gesture to Tom, happily gurgling in his pushchair. 'I don't get to wear things like this, not unless I want sick all down the sleeve within about five minutes.'

'You'll wear it in the evenings,' she says, smiling, 'after the baby's gone to bed. And anyway, with a little one that's all the more reason to treat yourself.'

I twirl, hum and ha and then gasp as I look at the price tag.

'Oh, treat yourself,' she says. 'It's very sexy. Your husband should come in and thank me.'

I don't say anything. But a few minutes later I'm outside, carrying the treasured cardigan in a large shopping bag.

And a few shops down I find some beautiful high-heeled shoes, strappy mules, ridiculously impractical, I won't ever wear them, can hardly even walk in them, and yet a few minutes later they're added to my collection.

What am I doing?

Some new make-up, a pair of earrings and finally Tom and I are home. I look at the clock: 3.15. Forty-five minutes in which to make myself more beautiful than I have ever looked.

At 3.55 I'm finished. My new crystal earrings sparkle in the lamplight, my cardigan feels as soft as butter against my skin, giving me a waist I haven't seen in months, and a cleavage that is rather spectacular, if I do say so myself. My heels give me a height and an elegance I haven't felt since my wedding day, and I smile as I look at this new improved me smiling back.

What the hell am I doing?

I tear everything off, shove my old grey sweater

286

back over my head and run into the bathroom to wash off all the make-up. I'm being ridiculous. He'll know I'm being ridiculous. And it's not that I want to win him back, to make him change his mind, I just want him to know what he's missing. I want him to feel some regret, because the Dan I spoke to earlier today sounded far too together for my liking.

I may not want him, but I want him to want me.

But how unfair, I realize, as I wipe the last of the lipstick off my lips. How childish, and silly, and selfish.

I look like me again, and it's better this way. It's better that I'm not trying to prove anything, not trying to play games, and now that it's time, now that my watch says four o'clock, I start to feel horribly nervous.

It's just Dan. It's just my husband. How can my husband, the man who knows me better than anyone else on earth, make me feel so nervous?

The doorbell rings, and I start to feel slightly sick. He has a key. He's always had a key. And I know he still has it and that he's telling me this is real. This is not a game. Not something that's going to be made better in a few hours, or a few days. He has a key but he's not using it because this is no longer *our* house.

He has a key but he's not using it because we are no longer a couple.

He has a key but he's not using it because he no longer has any rights.

Oh, my God.

Like a sledgehammer it hits me and finally becomes real. My marriage is over. I am a single mother. I am a failure.

287

23

'Um. Hi.'

'Hi.' Shit. And now I wish I hadn't changed, hadn't washed off the make-up, had at least looked a little better than I know I look right now.

'I thought I should give you this.' He reaches into his pocket and brings out an envelope. 'It's the front-door key.'

'Oh,' I say, reaching out for it and jumping slightly as our fingers touch. 'Yes. Thanks. You could have used it, you know.'

Dan shrugs. 'It didn't feel right.'

I nod. 'Yes. I understand.' I turn to place the envelope on the table, and when I look again at Dan I can't help but think how odd this is. How can it be that just a few days ago we were sleeping in the same bed, and now we are talking to one another as if we were strangers?

'Where's Tom?' Dan cranes his neck, looking around the room.

'He's having a nap. It was a bad night last night and then he wouldn't go down today until two. He might be awake. I'll go and look.'

'Would you mind if I went and got him up?'

'No, not at all. Fine. Go ahead.' I sit down on the sofa and examine my fingernails. God. How did we get to be so polite with one another? Any second now I'll be offering him tea.

After a while I walk softly to Tom's bedroom. The door is ajar and Tom is standing in his crib, giggling, and holding Dan's face in his little, chubby hands.

'Daddy misses you so much,' I hear Dan whisper as he turns his head to kiss Tom's fingers. 'Daddy thinks about you every minute of every day.'

'Dada,' Tom says delightedly, pulling Dan's hair as Dan squeals in mock pain and lifts Tom out of his crib, swinging him high up in the air, then holding him tightly. 'I love you, Mr T., do you know that?' he says, burying his face in Tom's hair. 'No matter what happens I love you more than anything.'

I turn and go back to the living room. They didn't see me. It's right that they didn't see me. It's not my place to intrude upon their moment of privacy. I feel like a stranger in my own home, uncomfortable, with heightened awareness of every noise, every sound.

Relax, Ellie. Relax. Deep breaths. Loosen up. I attempt some deep breaths, then pick up a magazine lying on the table. *Homes and Gardens*. I flick through, pausing every now and then as if I'm genuinely interested, but I barely register what I'm looking at, one eye staying constantly on the clock, waiting for Dan to come back in. Waiting for us to at least talk a little more about this, to try to sort it out, because surely this separation has occurred too quickly and too easily, surely there need to be more tears, more talking, more trying perhaps.

Five minutes go by. Fifteen. Twenty. I walk back to the nursery and see Dan lying on the floor, flying Tom high in the air above his head. Thirty-five. Dan is sitting in the rocker, reading *Guess How Much I Love You* to Tom. Forty minutes.

'Would you like some tea? Or anything?' I can't believe I'm offering my husband some tea. Not least because I've never been known to make him tea, nor has he ever been known to drink it.

'No, thanks,' he says. 'I'm fine.'

'Right.'

I close the door and sit on the bed in our room for a while, feeling completely blank. But then I realize I don't want him to see me sitting staring into space, so I get up and attempt to look busy in the kitchen by making myself some coffee.

The phone rings. Trish.

'I'm just ringing to see how you are,' she says.

'I'm okay. Dan's here.'

'He is? How's it going?'

'Fine.' I drop my voice to a whisper. 'Weird. It's like he's a stranger.'

'So what has he said?'

'Nothing. We haven't spoken. He's been in Tom's room for an hour.'

'Oh. So what are you doing?'

'Trying to pretend I have a life.'

'Shall I call you later?'

'Yes. Hopefully I'll have more to report.'

*   *   *

At 5.20 Dan comes into the kitchen with Tom.

'Do you have any plans now?' he asks.

'No,' I say eagerly. A little too eagerly. I want to talk more. Need to talk more. Can't believe the dissolution of a marriage can happen so painlessly. I need tears. Heartache. Grief. It can't just happen as it seems to be happening now—fading quietly into nothingness.

'I thought maybe we could have supper out.'

'Sure.' I smile with genuine delight. 'Sounds great.'

'I'll have him back by 6.30,' Dan says.

I look at Dan in confusion.

'For bathtime?' Dan says. 'I thought I'd take him to one of the cafés in Belsize Park for supper. If that's okay, I mean. If not, that's fine.'

'Oh, no, no.' I attempt a smile, but I'm embarrassed. Humiliated. Thank God I wasn't more obvious, thank God I didn't grab my coat or anything. 'It's fine.'

'I know this is more rushed than I'd like, but can I have him on weekends? Say, Friday night to Sunday night? Would that be okay? And then, maybe an afternoon a week?'

'Um, sure.' I'm still trying to get over the humiliation, praying he didn't think I wanted to have dinner with him, not wanting him to have that kind of power over me, or to know that's what I wanted. 'The weekends sound fine. I'll look at my diary and let you know about the day during the week.'

'Thanks, Ellie,' he says, my name suddenly sounding strange on his lips. 'We'll see you later. Say bye bye to Mummy,' he tells Tom, and I give Tom a huge kiss, resisting the urge to squeeze him tight, tighter, as tightly as I can.

'I love you,' I tell Tom and my eyes meet Dan's over his head. It's too strange. Too painful. Too familiar. And we both quickly avert our eyes as Dan busies himself putting on Tom's coat, and I pretend to be fascinated with washing up the negligible contents of the sink.

Is this how it's going to be for the rest of our lives?

*   *   *

291

Dan brings Tom back and I resolve to sit him down, to continue the process of the other night, for surely this is a process, surely we both need to work through it somehow, first together and then apart. I may not have been happy, and I may have made a mistake marrying him, but it doesn't feel normal that it should be this easy.

'Can I get you anything?' I say, after Dan has bathed Tom and put him to bed. 'Coffee? A glass of wine?'

'I'd love to,' he says, 'but I have plans.'

'Oh.' I feel like an idiot. Second time this evening.

'I'm sorry, Ellie,' he says, placing a hand on my arm.

'It's fine,' I say. 'I just thought there were more things left to talk about.'

'Okay,' he nods. 'What kind of things?'

I shake my head. They are far too many, far too complex. 'It doesn't matter,' I say. 'Another time. Anyway'—I look at my watch—'God, it's already 7.15. Rachel's coming here in a little while. I've got to get ready.' A lie, but a plausible one. If Dan has plans, then I'll bloody well have some too.

'Oh. Off anywhere nice?'

I shrug. 'Just out for a drink.'

'With anyone I know?'

The power is back in my hands. Finally. Thank you God. 'Just Lisa and a couple of her friends,' I lie. 'Anyway, must rush. Thanks for coming,' and I hustle him over to the door.

I slump in the doorway as I watch him start to walk up the steps. Don't go, I want to scream. Come back. Stay. But I don't. He hesitates as he takes the top step, and my heart skips. He's coming back, I think. He's going to turn around and come back. Talk about things. Resolve them?

And he does turn around. He turns around and looks at me sadly, then attempts a smile. 'G'night, Ellie,' he says, and then he's in his car and gone, and neither of us has mentioned the fact that our two-year anniversary is in two days' time.

I go back inside and spend the rest of the evening sitting on the sofa by myself, gazing blankly into space and wondering when in the hell it all went wrong.

*   *   *

It's been eight weeks since Dan left, and I can't believe how upside down my life has become. Did we always get this amount of paperwork when we were together, or do the powers that be somehow know that I am far from equipped to deal with all these official, officious letters?

Is this some sort of cosmic joke?

Council tax, residents' parking renewals, utility bills, letters from the Inland Revenue—in the eight weeks since Dan left my kitchen has disappeared under piles of papers and I don't know what on earth I'm supposed to do with them.

I used to be organized. Used to do everything myself, never needed—heaven forbid—a man to help me sort out my life. But somehow, since having Tom, those responsibilities became Dan's. And now all these envelopes, these awful printed envelopes that seem to arrive in a flood every single day, which I am supposed to deal with all by myself even though I barely understand what any of them are saying, are completely overwhelming.

My new strategy is this: open anything that is hand-addressed, or might be an invitation, a card, a letter or something fun that I might enjoy reading.

Open anything official, glance at it, and unless it is a red bill (I seem to be getting an awful lot of those lately) that can be paid quickly and easily by making a phone call or scribbling out a quick cheque and stuffing it into a return envelope, balance it on the top of the already precarious pile on the kitchen worktop, to be dealt with at a later date.

When the pile becomes too big, and topples over more than three times in the space of two days, said pile should be carefully placed in cupboard below desk. Again, to be dealt with at a later date.

Said pile should be immediately and effectively forgotten about until one of three things happens: I move house and discover an enormous stack of unpaid bills, subsequently shedding light on why the bailiffs turned up; or I get hugely organized personal secretary who will deal with all the stuff I cannot get my head round; or, failing that, Dan comes home.

None of the above looks likely to happen right now, and my piles are mounting, so I do the most logical thing possible, bar dealing with them of course, which isn't going to happen. I phone Lisa.

'How the hell do you deal with everything?'

'With what?' she asks, bemused.

'With life! With all the crap that people keep sending. With bills. And tax. And demands. And just bloody paperwork.'

'I know, isn't it a bastard?' I can hear her grin over the phone. 'Welcome to the real world.'

'I just can't believe that I have to do everything myself,' I moan. 'I never realized quite how much Dan used to do.'

'It gets easier,' Lisa says. 'It's just habit. I set aside one week every month when I go through everything and deal with it. And look on the bright side, you'll get far better deals from plumbers and electricians than your husband ever would. A bit of feminine charm goes a long way, particularly when people know you're a single mum.'

'Oh, God. Don't say that.'

'What, single mum?'

I shudder. 'I'm just not ready to hear that yet.'

'So what are you doing later? Dan has Tom tonight, doesn't he?'

'Yup. Every Saturday.'

'And you're coping with Tom staying with the murderous in-laws?'

I sigh. Because this has been one of the hardest things about the separation. Every weekend Tom stays at Linda's house. I hate it, worry every second he's away, but I have no choice but to put up with it, even though I made Dan swear never to leave Tom alone with them, to which he agreed.

'It's not ideal,' I say, 'but at this point I really have no choice. Anyway, Dan picked Tom up last night. Why?'

'I just fancied going out somewhere local for a drink and a quiet supper. Do you fancy the Queens?'

'I'd love to,' I say with enthusiasm, having had few girls' nights out since my wedding day. 'Shall we ask Trish?'

'She and Gregory are going out with some friends for dinner,' Lisa says. 'I spoke to her earlier.'

'Oh.' I shouldn't feel aggrieved. How childish to feel aggrieved. And yet for months now I have spoken to Trish first, have known of her plans first. And have, more frequently than not, been involved in those plans. For a moment I wonder if my fears have come true, if our friendship is suffering now that I am no longer part of a couple. It's true that I don't see Trish and Gregory as a couple so much any more. It may only have been a couple of months since Dan left, but the dynamic has already altered. The few times they invited me out I sat and talked to Trish mostly, while Gregory pretended to be interested, but I could tell he felt out of place with Dan absent.

And I know Gregory still talks to Dan. A lot. Trish has told me that she refuses to get involved. That she and Gregory don't talk about Dan and me. That my conversations with Trish are private and not to be repeated to Gregory, and the same goes for Gregory's discussions with Dan.

I wish she'd be a bit more bloody loyal to me. But her discretion is part of the reason I value her friendship so much. And our friendship, at least between the hours of nine and seven, hasn't changed very much at all. Admittedly I see Lisa perhaps more often than I did before, but Lisa and I have so much in common now, both being single mothers, and Trish, however much she loves me and wants to help, couldn't possibly understand how different, how difficult, it is to be a single mother.

Yet it irks me slightly that I didn't know Trish had plans this evening. That I wasn't the first person she called this morning. That I don't even know where they are going or with whom.

And the thought pops into my head that perhaps they are seeing Dan. Oh, God. Perhaps Dan and another woman? To be honest it hadn't occurred to me that Dan might be seeing anyone, but, as paranoia begins to set in, I wonder whether perhaps that was why Trish didn't say anything.

Maybe Dan has fallen in love. Could that have happened in such a short space of time? Could he have met someone? Someone so special that he wants to introduce her to his closest friends?

Would she have met Linda? A picture of this imaginary woman appears: beautiful, sophisticated, the kind of woman who does not do as I do and sleep in men's pyjamas and thick woolly socks, but who sleeps in silken negligees and wakes with sun-kissed skin and perfect hair.

I picture her as a younger version of Linda and resist a snigger—Freud would have a thing or two to say about that. But as the paranoia starts to take hold, I begin to feel slightly sick. The separation I can handle. I did, after all, instigate it. But the thought of my husband with another woman? Absolutely not.

'He's seeing someone, isn't he?' The words come out before I even know what I'm saying.

'What? Who? Gregory?'

'No. Dan. There's something you're not telling me, isn't there? Trish and Gregory are seeing Dan tonight, aren't they? And he has a girlfriend. You can tell me. I can take it. I just want to know the truth.'

There's a long pause, during which my heart starts to hammer. 'Are you completely off your rocker?' Lisa says. 'What on earth are you talking about?'

'Trish didn't say anything about dinner, and I think she's seeing Dan.'

'Okay, you crazy woman. Trish rarely tells me anything about her life, so I don't know who they're seeing, but I do know that they've been seeing loads of different friends lately, and you're jumping to ridiculous conclusions.'

I start to calm down. Maybe I have been jumping to conclusions slightly.

'And I very much doubt Dan has a girlfriend. I promise you that if I knew something I would definitely tell you, but he's going through as difficult a time as you are, and let's face it, you're not exactly interested in other men right now, are you?'

'No,' I grudgingly admit.

'So what makes you think Dan's the slightest bit interested in another woman?'

I start to feel a lot calmer. 'So you think I'm being silly?'

'More than silly. Absurd. I guarantee you Dan's sitting at home every night watching television and counting off each day until he can spend the weekend with Tom. The only thing he cares about right now is getting through the days, not shagging around! Ellie, darling, thank God I called, because you definitely need to get out more and have some fun. I'll meet you downstairs at the Queens at 7.30. How does that sound?'

'Okay,' I laugh. 'Sounds great.'

'Oh, and Ellie? Make a bit of an effort, okay?'

*　　　*　　　*

I should be pissed off, but I'm not. I look at myself in the mirror, at my hair that hasn't been washed for almost a week, that's scraped back in a ponytail to hide the greasiness, at my skin that's blotchy and tired-looking, at my shapeless sweater, and I realize Lisa's right.

I'm tired of feeling like crap, and I'm tired of looking like crap. And while I can't do much about the way I feel, I can at least start with the way I look, and who knows, if I change the way I look perhaps I'll start feeling differently too.

In the back of the bathroom cabinet I find an old Body Shop clay face mask that promises to draw out all impurities. Next to it a tube of apricot scrub, and an ancient Darphin cream that claims to refresh and revitalize.

I draw a hot bath—what are child-free weekends for if not for pampering yourself a little, I think— and lie in the bubbles, savouring the feel of the face pack, and the luxury of indulging in a way I haven't been able to since having Tom.

A couple of hours later I barely recognize myself. In the new cashmere cardigan that was supposed to have been my way of showing Dan what he was missing, with glossy, swinging hair and soft, fresh make-up, I look pretty damn good. In fact I'd say I looked better than pretty damn good, I look great.

How ironic that on a night when I feel like I could pull anyone I want, I'm not the slightest bit interested in pulling anyone at all. Although I'm glad I made the effort, I think, as I shut the front door behind me and double lock it just to be on the safe side, a part of me can't help but feel I'd rather be in my pyjamas watching television in bed.

24

'Wow!' Lisa's eyes widen as I walk over to where she's sitting in the corner of the Queens. 'Can this be the Ellie we know and love?'

'You like?' I do a mock twirl, and show off the new cardigan, flicking my hair and pouting as I do so.

'You look great.' She nods approvingly. 'Who'd have thought you'd scrub up so well?'

'Oh, thanks.' I grimace. 'With friends like you—'

'Sit down,' she says, gesturing to the empty chair opposite her. 'Let me get you a drink.'

'Don't worry, I'll get them. Vodka and cranberry?' I point to her bright red drink.

'Vodka, tonic and cranberry. Thanks.' She smiles as I turn and make my way over to the bar.

It feels so odd to be in a pub on a Saturday night. I haven't done anything like this for months, haven't had the energy to do anything on a Saturday night other than have a hot bath and go to bed. But I can no longer afford the luxury of doing that, now that I'm no longer living with my husband, now that my marriage may very well be over.

I may not want to meet anyone, not yet, but I know already that I have to make more of an effort, have to put myself out there, have to pretend to want more of a life than I already have.

Most of the time I can't believe I'm single. I can't believe that at some point I'll have to go through the dating process again, with somebody other than Dan.

I never enjoyed it, never found it exhilarating in the way that my girlfriends seemed to, still seem to, if you ask Lisa. Lisa adores nothing more than the excitement of meeting someone new, of waiting to see when he phones (it's never a *whether* with Lisa, always a *when*), of planning her outfit for a first date.

She loves setting aside the afternoon to get ready, booking a babysitter for Amy, booking the hairdresser for herself, laying out her clothes, soaking in a bath and spending hours making herself look beautiful.

She loves discovering who someone is, the thrill of the flirtation, the discovery of whether there is chemistry, whether this is something they may want to take further.

Lisa claims not to be a one-night-stand sort of girl, not since having Amy, but she also says there's nothing quite like a strong chemistry ending with a fumble on the sofa, or a passionate kiss on the doorstep at the end of the night.

I've never understood that, was so grateful when I met Dan that there wasn't any of that awkwardness, that he felt like my best friend from the very start, that I'd never felt so comfortable, so myself, with anyone. I can't bear the thought that I have to find someone new, that there's a very strong possibility no one will ever make me feel quite so comfortable again.

I am so not ready for this, yet at the same time I can't shut myself away in a closet, waiting for a life to come and find me. I'm not looking for a man, but I do have to start looking for a life, a life outside of Tom, outside of discussions about playgroups, and nursery schools, and nannies.

301

So here I am, placing a vodka, tonic and cranberry on the table in front of Lisa, trying to look as if I wouldn't rather be watching a bloody good video.

'I see you're still wearing it, then,' Lisa says.

'What?'

'Your wedding band.'

We both look down at my ring finger, at the plain gold band that once felt so alien and so wrong, and now feels like a part of me.

'I'm still married,' I say softly, feeling the band with my thumb, feeling how familiar it is, knowing I'm nowhere near ready to take it off.

'Separated,' Lisa reminds me.

'I know. But not divorced.'

'Have you talked about anything yet? Are you going to resolve anything yet?' she says.

'It's only been eight weeks, but we don't seem to talk about anything other than Tom. It's just . . .' I sigh. '. . . so weird between us. I know how unhappy I was, how much I hated Dan, and for so long, but now I can't believe how quickly and easily it seems to be over. There still seems to be unspoken stuff, but neither of us is able to start, to find the right words.'

There's a silence, a pause. 'Do you want to get back together again?'

And another pause.

'I don't know. I just know that we seemed to be making one another so unhappy, and I thought I'd made this terrible mistake.'

'And now? Do you still think that?'

'I think I do. But then there are times when I remember all that was good about our marriage, and why we got married, and I can't believe it's over.'

'Do you not think you and Dan really ought to sit down and talk?'

'I've tried—we can't. Maybe we'll be able to in time, but right now we can't.'

'It seems so sad that you're both letting pride get in the way of perhaps getting back together.'

'It's not pride. It's . . . I don't know. Anyway, let's not talk about it, I thought you wanted to cheer me up, not send me into a depression. What about you, what's going on in your life? How come we've hardly seen you?'

'Oh nothing much,' Lisa says. And blushes.

'You're blushing!' I'm shocked. 'Oh, my God. You've met someone haven't you, you've met a guy!'

'No, no, I haven't,' she says, as her cheeks turn redder and redder, giving the game away.

'I do not believe you!' I sit back in my chair and cross my arms, watching her discomfort with a grin on my face. 'I can't believe you've met someone and you haven't given us all the gory details. No wonder you haven't let Trish and me come over to your house! Oh, God, I can't believe how stupid we've been! Trish even said she was convinced you were seeing someone, and I told her she was being ridiculous, and you'd definitely tell us if you were, and you are and you haven't bloody said anything.'

'Oh, God,' Lisa groans as the flush starts to fade. 'It's meant to be a secret. I can't believe I've given the game away.'

'Why so secret?' I'm immediately intrigued and lean forward across the table in a conspiratorial manner. 'Go on, you can tell me. Is he famous? He's famous, isn't he! That's why you're so

303

secretive.' Without giving Lisa a chance to speak, I start to think of local celebrities she might be seeing. 'Is it Jude Law? I bet it's Jude Law! God, he's gorgeous, I'd be deeply jealous if it was Jude Law, but I thought he was seeing that girl—'

'No.' Lisa shakes her head, looking uncomfortable. 'It's not Jude Law.'

'No? What about Les Dennis? Oh, God, tell me it's not Les Dennis—'

Lisa starts to laugh. 'No, it's no one famous.'

'So go on, tell me, then, who is it?'

'You don't know him,' she says eventually. Awkwardly. 'And it's not serious anyway. I mean, he's really nice, but I think it's just a casual thing.'

'So you're blushing like your face is on fire, and it's just a casual thing? You're full of bollocks. Oh, come on Lisa, tell me more, give me something, anything, just a little detail.'

'Okay, okay, but please don't say anything to Trish.'

'Why?' I take a sharp breath. 'Does she know him?'

'No, no. I just didn't want anyone to know. To be honest it's incredibly early days, and it's complicated.'

'Complicated.' I look at her and she looks away. 'You mean he's married, don't you?'

Lisa shrugs. She still can't look me in the eye. She knows only too well what I think of that. 'He's sort of married,' she says. Reluctantly.

'Oh, Christ, Lisa. Surely you know better than that.'

And this time she does look me in the eye. 'He's waiting for a divorce,' she says firmly. 'He's just waiting for the right time, but his marriage is over, and I swear, I believe him.'

My blood runs cold. My heart starts pounding and I think I'm going to be sick.

My voice comes out in a whisper. 'It's Dan,' I say, almost choking on the words. 'That's why you didn't want anyone to know. It's Dan, isn't it?' and I don't know whether to scream, walk out or slap her round the face extremely hard.

But I do still think I'm going to be sick.

Lisa's eyes widen. 'Oh, my God!' she says. 'No! No! God, no! I can't believe you'd think I'd do that to you.' And my heart starts to beat normally again. She's not lying. Nobody could lie this well. Not even about something like this.

'Oh, Ellie.' She starts to laugh. 'I can't believe you thought I'd be having an affair with Dan! Oh, darling! Oh, Ellie!'

'Oh, God.' I sit back in my chair, placing my hand upon my pounding chest. 'I thought I was going to be sick.'

'I thought you were about to slap me,' Lisa says.

'I was thinking about it.' I look up at her, my face serious once more. 'I do believe you, but do you swear, upon your life, that you're not having an affair with Dan?'

'I do,' she nods. 'I swear, upon my life, that I'm not having an affair with him.'

'Okay,' I laugh, relief flooding through me.

'Okay,' she says, laughing too. 'How about another drink? Looks like we both need it.'

*   *   *

An hour later, during which time I've managed to put all those fears aside, Lisa leans over the table

305

and whispers, 'There's a man sitting in the other corner who keeps staring at you.'

'Yeah, right,' I laugh, three vodka, tonics and cranberries having almost got the better of me. 'If he's staring at anyone, he'll be staring at you.'

'No, really he's not,' Lisa says. 'Trust me, I'm the expert at these things. He's staring at *you*.'

'Is he handsome?' I laugh, not really caring.

'As it happens, he is rather cute,' she says. 'And he looks slightly familiar. I wonder if I know him. But he's definitely staring at you.'

'Lisa,' I say, raising an eyebrow, 'why would he be looking at me when (a) you are far more gorgeous and *everyone* stares at you, and (b) all he can see of me is my back?'

'I just say it as I see it.' Lisa sits back in her chair. 'Why don't you turn round and look at him, give him a proper eyeful?'

'Okay.' I turn round and try to see who she's looking at. And I see him. Staring at me. Very obviously.

I turn quickly back to Lisa. 'I know him.'

'You do? Oh.' She's disappointed.

'And you know him too.'

'I do? Who is he, then?'

'Charlie Dutton.'

'Charlie Dutton! The producer! Oh, no wonder he looked slightly familiar. Hang on, wasn't he in the South of France the night that—'

'Yes,' I say, cutting her off. I can still hardly bear to think about that night, let alone talk about it.

'Well, he obviously recognizes you. Aren't you going to say hello?'

'I don't really know him. I met him once at my friend Fran's and he briefly dated another friend of

306

mine, and then that night in France. I'll say hi on our way out if he's still there.'

'Or sooner,' she whispers, leaning forward. 'He's coming over.'

'Ellie?' I hear a male voice behind me.

I turn, affecting a look of surprise. 'Charlie?'

'How are you? I couldn't figure out if it was you or not.'

'Difficult to tell from behind, I imagine.'

'But I was right,' he says, smiling. 'So how are you?'

'Fine. Thanks. You remember my friend Lisa.'

'Hi, Lisa, nice to see you.' He greets her perfunctorily, then turns back to me.

'I heard your son is fine. I can't tell you how worried we all were that night, how much I felt for you.'

'Thank you,' I say. 'That's very kind. And he's fine now, which is all that matters.'

'May I join you?' Charlie says, pulling up a chair before either of us can say no. Lisa just sits back and grins as I awkwardly move over to make room for him.

'What about your friends?'

'They're leaving in a minute,' he says. 'Off to a party, which I'm not in the mood for. I need an early night.'

And as we sit there, the three of us, I wonder why he's come over.

I seem to have forgotten the art of making small talk. I was having such a nice time with Lisa, and I slightly resent his joining us, having to make an effort, having to think of something to say.

'So how's your husband?' Charlie says, taking a long sip of beer and putting it down on the table, then looking directly at me in a way that instantaneously tells me two things. Number one, that he knows. Of course he knows. If he's heard that Tom is fine, he will surely also have heard that Dan and I are not.

And number two, that he remembers something that up until tonight, up until this very moment, I had not. That we were flirting that night. That there was a chemistry between us that I had completely forgotten about, had dismissed or ignored, given all that happened subsequently.

With a jolt, I realize the chemistry is still there. Oh, shit. This I hadn't expected.

'I'm really sorry.' I turn to see Lisa standing next to the table, coat in her hand. 'I hate to have to do this to you both, but I really need an early night. I'll talk to you in the morning, okay?' She leans down, gives me a kiss, trying—and failing—to hide a grin, and says goodbye to Charlie.

You should leave, a voice in my head keeps saying. Stand up now, put on your coat and walk out with her. Leave. Go on. Stand up and leave. But I can't. I turn back to Charlie, and I swear it is like watching a scene from *The Matrix* in which time has stood still and the only two people in the room, the only two people who are moving, are Charlie and me. Me and Charlie.

Oh, God. I'm really not ready for this.

'Dan, isn't it?'

And now it's my turn to blush. 'Um, he's fine,' I say. 'I think he's fine.'

'You think?'

I look up at Charlie. 'You must have heard. We separated.'

Thank God he has the good grace to look

308

embarrassed, and he nods. 'Yes, I had heard, but you know how rumours can spread and I never believe anything unless I hear it from the horse's mouth.'

'Well, this one's true.' I shrug, taking a long sip of my drink for want of something better to do with my hands, all at once self-conscious in a way I don't remember being for years.

I feel like a teenager suddenly. All fingers and thumbs. Acutely aware of everything I say, everything I do, and, despite my three drinks, I am all at once desperate for more.

As if reading my mind, Charlie looks at my empty glass. 'Can I get you another?'

I could still go, I think. I could shake my head and smile, say no, I have to get home, babysitter and all that, but how lovely to see you, what a coincidence, I'm sure I'll run into you again, take care. Bye.

I could still do all of that, I think, those words could come out so easily, but instead I nod. 'Another drink would be lovely,' I say.

*   *   *

Charlie asks me lots of questions. He asks me all about Tom. He wants to know what he's doing now, how I'm coping, what are the hard parts and what are the easy.

He tells me about Finn. About coping as a single father. He tells me that since his film won two Golden Globes he seems to have become quite the catch amongst the single mothers at Finn's school, and he makes me laugh when he describes the daily drop-off as being rather like an assault course in

309

which he has to try to avoid the clutches of socially ambitious single mothers.

And Charlie asks me about me. He asks about my life, about what I do, whether I get lonely, whether I know what is going to happen.

I surprise myself in that I talk to Charlie. I didn't realize he'd be this easy to talk to, but then I suppose it's flattering, someone wanting to know so much about you, particularly when that someone is so, well, yummy.

Because he really is quite yummy. I look at his arms, remember how tanned they were in the summer, and I look back up at his face to see him watching me, and he smiles and I blush.

Oh, God. I'm really not ready for this.

And while Charlie is talking about his divorce, about how he adjusted, what it was like for him, I find my mind wandering off, find myself thinking about whether I really am not ready, thinking about the reality of kissing someone else, sleeping with someone else.

I imagine Charlie's face moving towards mine, his eyes closing, our mouths meeting. I see him, almost feel him licking my neck, can almost feel his shoulder blades under my hands, and I shudder.

Oh, God. Am I really not ready for this?

'Are you okay?'

'What?' I come back to reality with a jolt, the buttons of my shirt having been almost entirely unbuttoned in my fantasy.

'You seem to have gone off somewhere.'

'Sorry.' Damn. Why am I blushing again? 'Just thinking that I probably ought to be getting home soon. Babysitter.' The guilt makes my words come out in a rush.

'Do you live around here?'

I nod and tell him.

'I'm in Gloucester Avenue,' he says. 'Just around the corner. Can I walk you home?'

I nod. What else can I do?'

*   *   *

As we turn into my road, the conversation ceases. I think about Lisa and her tales of passionate kisses on doorsteps. I think about fumblings on sofas. And I think about Dan.

I really am not ready for this.

I turn to Charlie as I put my key in the lock, ready to say something polite and dismissive, knowing that I can't do this, that a fantasy is one thing, but that the reality of kissing another man is something else entirely, and not something I am anywhere near dealing with.

'It was lovely to see you,' Charlie says, shaking my hand. 'Really. I often thought about you after that night, and obviously about Tom. I was so relieved to hear he was okay. I was going to write to you, and I'm sorry that I didn't.'

'Oh, that's okay.'

'But look, we're neighbours. So if you ever feel like getting together for a drink or a movie or something, just call, okay? I know what it's like when you first split up, and friends make all the difference.'

'Okay,' I say, confused. I was ready to fend him off. Ready to push him away, to tell him that no, he couldn't come in for a coffee, and no, thank you for the invitation to dinner but I'm really not ready to date anyone just yet.

'Here's my card,' he says, pressing a card into my hand. 'Take care, Ellie,' and with that he's back up the path and gone.

I walk into my house and close the door, and then I lean back against the wall in the dark hallway for a few seconds, hand on my heart to still it, as I think about what just happened. Or didn't happen. Or could have happened.

It's the right thing, I think. Thank God he didn't make a pass at me, imagine how awkward it would have been, how embarrassing it would have been.

It was definitely the right thing.

25

I groan as I open my eyes and try to focus on the clock: 7.38. Bugger. I lay my head back on the pillow and listen for Tom, but nothing, and then I remember that today is Sunday, and Tom is with Dan.

Oh, why did I have so many vodkas last night? What was I thinking? Nine months of abstinence during pregnancy reduced my alcohol tolerance to approximately zero, and eighteen months later I've clearly yet to get it back.

Stumbling into the bathroom, I look, bleary-eyed, at my reflection and groan again, the glamorous girl of last night now replaced by a puffy-eyed swollen monster. Talk about from the sublime to the ridiculous. I swallow two Nurofen, then shuffle into the kitchen to make some coffee.

*   *   *

At half ten I finally manage to get dressed, and am about to go down to the Polish for a much needed cappuccino and almond croissant when the phone rings and it's Lisa.

'Meet me by the swings in an hour,' she says, as I protest that on a child-free day there's no way in hell I'm going anywhere near a playground.

'Fine,' she laughs. 'So I'll see you at the Polish in fifteen.' And she puts the phone down before I have a chance to argue. I know she wants to do the post-mortem, and I wonder for a minute whether I ought to make something up: hot, passionate sex on Primrose Hill? Not in these temperatures. But she probably wouldn't believe me anyway. She may not know Charlie, but she knows his crowd, certainly knows his type. I'll just have to tell her the truth.

*   *   *

'You look terrible!' she laughs as she pushes Amy's pushchair through the tables to where I'm sitting, already cradling a coffee that's slowly restoring me to a human being.

'I can always rely on you, can't I?' I roll my eyes.

She grins. 'Sorry, it's just I've never seen you hungover before.'

'Is it that obvious?'

'Do you want me to be honest?'

'Oh, forget it,' I snort. 'Anyway, how do you manage to look so bloody perfect? If I recall correctly—'

'Which is unlikely.'

'Not that unlikely, but didn't we drink the same

313

amount last night?'

'We both had three but I'm assuming you carried on drinking with Charlie.'

'Ah, yes. I'd forgotten about that.'

'Well, you'd better start remembering. I want to hear all the juicy details.'

I smile and shake my head. 'There really aren't any juicy details. He walked me home, we shook hands and that was that.'

'That's it?' Lisa looks horrified.

'That's it. What were you expecting? Sex on Primrose Hill?'

'Well, yes, if you really want to know. That's what I was hoping for.'

'I'm still married, you know.' My voice is now serious. 'And the last thing I'm looking for is a romantic involvement.'

'Yes, I know you're still married, but you can't help it if a romantic involvement comes to find you, and let's face it, he is rather delicious, plus the chemistry between you is undeniable.'

'It is?'

'Don't act so innocent! Of course it is. And don't pretend you're not interested. I know you're separated, not divorced, but there's no reason you can't have fun either.'

What did she just say?

I look at Lisa. 'What did you just say?'

'What?'

'What do you mean, "you can't have fun either"? You mean Dan's having fun? How do you know? What sort of fun? Dan has a girlfriend, doesn't he? I knew it. There is something you're not telling me.'

'Oh, Ellie, stop it. I didn't mean that, it just came

out. I doubt Dan has a girlfriend, and no, again, I'm not seeing him. I just meant you don't have to shut yourself away and never go anywhere or see anyone. I understand that being separated is this awful, awkward limbo position, but this could be your last chance, and you have to take each day as it comes.'

'Is that what you do?'

'Take each day as it comes? I try. Whoops! Careful, Amy! Are you all right?' Amy's out of her pushchair and toddling around the café, babbling away to everyone, no one able to understand a word she's saying. She trips over a table leg and falls down as Lisa rushes to pick her up.

When Amy's calmed down, placated by a hot chocolate, Lisa apologizes for the interruption, and I shrug it off, so used to interruptions these days.

'So,' I say, when all is calm again. 'I do think Charlie is nice, and yes, he's attractive, and yes, I feel the chemistry as well, but I really don't think I'm going to do anything about it. And anyway, he was very blasé when he left, I don't think he's interested really.' I tell her how he shook my hand and what he said.

'I think he didn't want to scare you off,' Lisa says. 'So are you going to call him?'

I reach down into the pocket of my coat, which is hanging on the back of the chair behind me, and feel his business card still nestling there. 'Nah.' I shake my head, leaning in to tickle Amy's tummy as she squirms and squeals with joy. 'Probably not.'

*   *   *

On a Thursday afternoon, as I walk up the path to

315

the flat, I see a familiar figure sitting on the doorstep. Familiar and strange because I haven't seen Emma for months, haven't known how to continue our friendship, whether it is in fact possible to continue our friendship. And so instead of talking about it, of exploring the possibility, I have withdrawn.

Oh, not quite so obviously. When she calls I let the machine pick up, and then call her back when I know she's going to be out. I leave upbeat cheerful messages on her machine saying how much I'd love to see her, even though I'm really busy, hoping that message will get back to Dan, hoping Dan will think I'm living the life of Riley now he's no longer here.

I feel so childish at times, Trish tells me how childish I am at times, and yet I couldn't bear for Dan to know just how lonely I really am. I couldn't bear for him to know that I frequently lie in bed and cry, that the only thing that gets me up in the morning and keeps me going all day is Tom.

I couldn't bear for him to know that I am terrified it is going to be like this for the rest of my life. That all the fun, and joy, and happiness has gone, and that this monotonous drudgery is all that is left for me to look forward to.

But I try not to think about that very often or I wouldn't be able to carry on.

And here is Emma, sitting on my doorstep, hugging her knees as she reads a magazine lying open on the ground. I hesitate. She hasn't looked up. Could I leave? Escape without her seeing me because God knows I don't want her to see me looking like this, don't want her to report my horrific appearance back to Dan?

316

Except I have good reason for my appearance. Tom has started crying out for me in the night, and I had less sleep recently than I have had in months. At times I am tempted to let him sleep in my bed, but that's a road I'm not ready to go down just yet.

Emma looks up. Sees me standing there, hesitating, and leaps up and runs over to me, bursting into tears as she throws her arms around me, and I find myself clinging on to her and crying into her shoulder.

'I've missed you so much,' she says, as I rub her back and try to console her, weeping salty tears into her shearling coat.

'Oh, God, I'm sorry. Your coat,' I say, when she eventually lets me go, and we both look down at her wet shoulder and laugh. 'Oh, this old thing,' she says. 'It was free from a photoshoot,' and I realize in that split-second just how much I have missed her, and we both start hugging again.

'You'd better come in before the neighbours start to gossip about my new lesbian affair.' I disengage, wiping away the tears.

'At least they'd be able to say your girlfriend has great taste in coats,' Emma says, helping me down the steps with the pushchair, and when we are inside and the door is closed, she looks at me, suddenly serious, and says, 'You are a nasty old cow, avoiding me all these months. Don't think I didn't know you were screening my calls and ringing me back when you knew I'd be out.'

'Was I that obvious?'

'Yes. You can't beat the master,' she says, unstrapping Tom and making him giggle as she tickles him. 'Come here to Auntie Em,' she says, as he pulls her hair and laughs. 'You little monkey.

Did you tell Mummy I took you to the zoo last weekend?'

'You did?'

'Dan didn't tell you?'

I sigh. 'Dan doesn't seem to tell me very much these days.'

And Emma shakes her head. 'How in hell have the two of you moved so far apart in such a short space of time? I mean, what the fuck is happening? What's going on? This is completely insane.'

'Do you want a cup of tea?'

'Yes. I want a cup of tea and I want to know what on earth is going on, because my brother won't talk to anyone about it, and my mum knows she's the last person in the world you'll want to see, and Dan seems miserable as hell and you look like shite too . . .'

'Actually I only look like shite today because I'm hungover,' I lie, hoping it will reach Dan's ears, hoping he will think I have been out having a good time, and cheered up somewhat by Dan being miserable as hell too. 'You should have seen me last night.'

'I suppose you looked incredible last night?'

'As it happens, I did, rather,' I say nonchalantly, resolving to stop lying right away. This is Emma, and if anyone can see through a lie, Emma can. 'Anyway. Piss off, Emma. I don't see you in months and now you turn up on my doorstep and insult me.'

'I'm only doing it because I love you,' she says. I turn to look at her, but she's sitting at the table, flicking through her magazine.

I stand in shock, holding the kettle. No one's ever told me they loved me before, no one aside

318

from my immediate family and Dan of course. And even my immediate family never really said it. My mother loved me as best she could, I suppose, and my father made reference to loving me at my wedding, but, if actions speak louder than words, the fact that I've hardly seen him since makes me doubt it somehow.

Dan says it. Said it. But how odd to hear it from Emma, who wasn't joking when she said it, but said it completely matter-of-factly, as if it were something I would automatically know, something that couldn't, wouldn't, be questioned.

'Emma.' I put the tea on the table and sit down opposite her. 'I know this sounds stupid, but do you really love me?'

Emma gives me a funny look. 'Not in a neighbours-gossiping lesbian sort of way, no. But if you're asking do I love you in a healthy, non-sexual, sister-in-law sort of way, absolutely. Why do you ask?'

'It's just weird hearing a friend say I love you. Sorry. I know you didn't mean it in a weird way.'

'But I'm not a friend. I mean, I am a friend, but I'm family. I know you're my sister-in-law, but I've always thought of you as my sister, the sister I always wanted. That's not weird, is it? Do you think that's weird?'

'No.' I shake my head. And I start to cry.

Not just tears rolling down my cheeks. Huge, heaving, sobbing tears. I lay my head on my arms and let it all out. Finally.

Emma sweeps Tom up and takes him into the living room, where she manages to get him into a catatonic state by putting on a *Baby Einstein* DVD, before coming back into the kitchen and rubbing

319

my back as I cry.

And I can't stop. All the pent-up feeling of the past few weeks, past few months, seems to come out in one fell swoop. I cry and cry and cry, and when the tears have all dried up and I am doing giant, dry hiccups, Emma sits opposite me and raises an eyebrow.

'Looks like you needed that,' she says. 'Do you feel better now?'

'Yes,' I sniff, pulling out an old tissue from my pocket that releases clouds of lint into the air. 'Sorry,' I sniff, as Emma waves the lint away.

'Don't be silly,' Emma says. 'Not my house.'

'You know that's the most amazing thing anyone's ever said to me?' I say.

'What?'

'That you think of me as your sister.'

'Oh, God, please don't start crying again. The *Baby Einstein* disc's nearly over.'

I laugh. 'No, I'm not going to start crying again,' and I busy myself clearing the table, while I try to process my thoughts.

Because what Emma's just given me is this: I always wanted to marry into a huge, loving family, I thought we would all instantly be wrapped in this warm web of love, acceptance and understanding, but that isn't how it was, how it is, at all.

And yet, despite the differences, despite the lack of understanding, the pain and the heartbreak, Emma still thinks of me as family. She loves me. She accepts me even though I'm separated from Dan, even though I've avoided her calls for weeks, even though I've acted as if I wanted nothing more to do with her.

Up until today, up until I saw her sitting on my

320

doorstep, I thought, I genuinely thought I didn't want anything more to do with any of the Cooper family. I thought that if my marriage to Dan was over, my relationship with his family would be over, but I suppose it isn't quite as clear-cut or precise as that.

Emma still loves me, even though she doesn't have to, even though I didn't consider myself part of her family any more. Maybe that means that they are my family, that despite everything that's happened, and even if Dan and I do eventually get divorced, maybe they will remain my family, and not just because of Tom.

'Are you okay?' Emma says to me, as I stand in a daze, looking out the window.

'I'm fine,' I say. 'So how is everyone? How's your mum?'

Let me just make things quite clear before I go on. I have no wish to see Linda. Or Michael, although he doesn't tend to enter my thoughts so much.

But seeing Emma here brings so many memories flooding back. Good memories. Happy memories. Memories from before the accident, which for so long has seemed to obliterate all that happened before it.

Suddenly I remember Linda hugging me. I remember her squeezing me tight at my wedding and telling me I was another daughter in her family. I remember the earrings she gave me, her excitement when I had Tom, her desire to be involved in everything, her genuine happiness for me.

I still don't want to see her. But I'd quite like to hear how she is.

'Mum's fine,' Emma says. 'Same old irritating self, although I think Dan being at home is beginning to get on her nerves slightly.'

'But I thought he was the perfect son. Dan who can do no wrong.'

'He was.' She grimaces. 'But now he seems to be Dan the sullen son who expects her to do all his laundry and cook and clean for him. All I keep hearing is how messy his bedroom is.'

'Oh, great. Now I suppose she thinks I spoilt him.'

'I think she realizes she did a perfectly good job all by herself before you even came on the scene. We miss you, you know. I mean, not just me, but all of us. Maybe you're not ready to hear this, I don't want to upset you.'

'Set off another crying fit, you mean?'

'Well, yes. Exactly, but my mum really was devastated about what happened with Tom.'

'So was I.' I try not to grit my teeth.

'But she was also devastated about what happened with you, that you wouldn't see her, wouldn't talk to her, and now she thinks that you and Dan separating is all her fault.'

I look down at the table.

'Which I told her was ridiculous,' Emma continues. I don't say anything. 'Isn't it?'

'I don't know.' And I don't. For months I have blamed Linda, have managed to blame her for every bad thing that has happened in my life, have built her into this huge demonic figure, the matriarch of this awful, dysfunctional family, and yet now that Emma, lovely familiar Emma, is sitting here in my kitchen, I don't know what to think any more.

I won't admit this, not to Emma, but a part of me wants to see Linda. A part of me wants to swallow my pride and talk to her, really talk to her about what happened. I want to see just how much she has suffered, see whether she does truly feel what everyone tells me she feels.

But I don't think I have it in me to do it. I don't think my throat is big enough to swallow that amount of pride.

'She'd love to see you, you know,' Emma says quietly.

'Is that why you're here?' There's fury suddenly in my voice, fury at the possibility of there being a hidden agenda behind Emma's sudden visit.

'God, no, calm down, calm down. Absolutely not. She doesn't know I'm here. Nor does Dan. But she talks about you a lot.'

'She does? What kind of stuff?'

'Well, not in front of Dan, obviously. He'd just walk out of the room. But she talks about you like you're one of the family. I heard her, just the other day, telling someone her daughter-in-law does marketing for Calden. She never boasts about me like that.'

'Oh. She did?'

'Yes. She did. So what do you think? Do you think maybe you could phone her or something? Maybe get together and talk?'

'I don't know,' I say. 'I think probably not yet. It's all still too fresh and too painful.'

There's an awkward silence. 'Do you think,' Emma says after a while, 'that you and Dan are going to get back together? Because even though it's none of my business, nobody seems to understand why you're apart, and you know all marriages go through their bad patches, but to make something lasting you have to work at it.'

I look up at Emma in amazement. 'Since when did you take a course in marriage guidance?'

'Oh, you know. Marriage counsellor. Stylist. Dermatologist. There really is no end to my talents.' She laughs before continuing. 'So? Will you get back together?'

'I hope so,' I say before I've had a chance to think about it, and the picture of shock on Emma's face perfectly matches my own.

After she leaves I put Tom to bed, take off my make-up, pull on my pyjamas, climb into bed and switch off the light. I lie there for a while, thinking first about Emma, but then after a while my thoughts go back to where they've gone back to every night since last Saturday.

To Charlie Dutton. And again, as I always do, I go over the events of the evening, replaying every look, every word. Thinking again about all the things that didn't happen but could have. It's the right thing, I think.

But why do I feel just the slightest hint of disappointment?

26

We do have to talk.

Eleven weeks later Dan and I still haven't spoken, and now I realize that we have to figure out what is going on in our lives, whether indeed we do have a life together, or whether this separation is going to lead to something more permanent.

I still can't quite believe what I said to Emma. That my subconscious took over and said those words, when I wasn't even aware of feeling them, hadn't thought for a moment that I wanted to get back with Dan.

Even now, I'm not sure. But I do know that I miss him. I miss being part of a couple. I miss having him around. I miss having someone to do things with.

Trish asked me whether I missed someone or whether I actually missed Dan, and I suppose I'm still trying to figure that one out.

I had thought for a while that I was missing being part of a couple, but I *do* miss Dan. I miss the Dan I married, not the Dan of recent months. I miss the Dan that made me laugh, that looked after me, that made me feel there was no greater feeling in the world than being able to wake up and look over at your best friend lying beside you.

I honestly don't know if there's a way for us to find our way back to one another again. If Dan could be the man I married, I'd get back with him tomorrow. But I am not pretending to be the innocent party here. I think back to when we were married, to how young I was, how naive, and how happy, and I know that I need to rediscover that person as well, need to find that joy within myself before we have a hope in hell.

But one thing remains clear. We do have to talk.

Eleven weeks after I reveal to Emma that I hope we get back together, 19 May, to be precise, I call Dan on his mobile—I can't call him at Linda and Michael's, am not ready to talk to them. My heart beats wildly as the phone rings. I know he'll see it's

325

my number, will have the ability to decide whether or not to answer, but the phone rings and rings, and eventually switches over to voicemail.

In some ways I am relieved. Easier to leave a message than to actually have to speak. And this doesn't have to mean Dan is avoiding me: his phone is probably, as it usually is, snuggled deep in a pocket, or at the bottom of a bag, somewhere where he won't hear it.

'Hi, Dan. It's me. Um, Ellie. Look, I'm really just phoning because it's been nearly three months since we've spoken and I think we need to talk. There's so much that hasn't been said, and I'd really like . . .' Oh, God. Do I do it? Do I put my cards on the table? I take a deep breath. '. . . I'd really like to see whether we can make things work. I mean, Tom misses you so much, and this all seems so pointless somehow. So anyway . . .' Shit. Was I wrong? Should I not have said it? Too late now. 'So maybe you can call me when you get back? Maybe we can talk this weekend?' I have said too much. Way way too much. I put down the phone and feel utterly miserable.

* * *

'How *are* you?' Fran's on the phone, and I can tell from the way she's asking that she knows about Dan and me.

Not that I didn't want her to know, but I'm just so tired of talking about it. Of trying to explain *why*, when I'm not even sure of the reasons myself. And everyone wants to help. Everyone wants to invite me over, take me out for dinner, gaze at me with sad puppy-dog eyes as they tell me they're there for

326

me, if I ever want to talk.

'I'm fine,' I say curtly, softening as I realize that this isn't just anyone, this is Fran. Lovely Fran whom I probably should have phoned. 'You know, don't you?'

'I did hear something,' she says sheepishly. 'And I didn't believe it. You know how rumours are, so I thought I'd better phone and see first, if it's true, and second, if it is, if there's anything I can do.'

'Well, yes. First, it is true, and second, no, there's nothing you can do, although I would love to see you.'

'So he was beating you up, then?' Fran says as I gasp in horror.

'God, no! That's terrible. Is that what people are saying?'

She snorts with laughter. 'No. Sorry. I couldn't resist. I just heard you were separated. I couldn't believe it, Ellie. I mean, I thought you and Dan were so happy together.'

'Not really,' I sigh. 'We hadn't been for a long time, but I'm sure it's not permanent. Actually, I probably shouldn't say that. Who knows what's going to happen, but hopefully we'll find a way through it. Who told you anyway? Sally?'

'No. I don't even think Sally knows. It was Charlie Dutton actually. He was here for supper last week. I have to say it was a bit embarrassing. He was asking all about you and I didn't want to tell him that you'd dropped off the scene and hadn't returned any of my calls. I had to pretend I knew all about it.'

'I'm sorry, Fran,' I say. 'Really. I've been crap at keeping in touch with people. After the accident life became so confusing, and I just hid away from

327

everyone. But I've missed you.'

'We miss you too. We'd love to see you. Charlie Dutton would love to see you too,' she adds, and I can practically picture the mischievous grin on her face.

'What do you mean?' I feign innocence in a bid to find out more.

'Nothing,' she says lightly, all innocence herself.

'Oh, come on,' I plead, not that I'm interested, but if he were interested it would be a lovely boost for my ego, which may sound selfish but God knows my ego could do with a boost right now.

'He said he bumped into you the other night and you ended up spending the evening together. He also said he thinks you're incredibly sexy.'

'He didn't!'

'He did!'

'But I'm not sexy!' I'm grinning like the Cheshire cat. No one's called me sexy in years. I'm not sexy. I'm a mother. A dowdy mum who spends most of her time make-up-free in Gap sweatpants and trainers, apart from when I made the effort to meet Lisa, and ended up bumping into Charlie Dutton.

'I know!' she laughs. 'I tried to tell him you're not sexy, but he wouldn't hear any of it.'

'Oh, thanks a lot!'

'I'm just joking. But seriously, he seemed to really like you. He was bombarding me with questions about you.'

'Such as?'

'He wanted to know everything.'

'God, how flattering.'

'I know. That's why I'm telling you. Are you interested in him?'

I pause, trying to lay the flattery aside for an

instant, trying to figure out the true answer. 'You know, if I were still single, I'm sure I'd be interested, and yes, I do think he's very attractive, and in different circumstances I could definitely fancy him, but I'm really not ready for anything. I'm only separated, and if Dan and I got back together I'd never forgive myself if anything had happened.'

'So you don't fancy him even a little bit?'

'Oh, okay,' I grumble, remembering the surge of desire I felt when I was with him. 'I do fancy him a little bit. But I'm not going to do anything about it, okay?'

'Okay,' she says, happy that she finally got it out of me. 'So if Marcus and I insist you come out for dinner with us on Thursday, should we bring Charlie or not?'

'Not!' I practically yell. 'Definitely not. I'm not going to see him again. Honestly. I'm not interested.'

'Okay, okay, calm down. I only asked. But does that mean you'll come out for dinner with Marcus and me, then?'

'You don't mind me being the spare wheel?'

'I don't mind if you don't mind.'

'Okay. Let me see if I can sort out babysitting, and, providing I can, I'd love to. But no single-man surprises, okay? Charlie Dutton or otherwise.'

'Okay, okay,' she grumbles. 'No single-man surprises. It will just be me, you and Marcus.'

*   *   *

I tiptoe quietly into Tom's room to check on him before I go to bed. His nightlight casts a soft glow,

329

just enough to illuminate his toys. I walk over to where he lies, smiling as I look down.

The smell of vomit is undeniable, and I see Tom, fast asleep, lying in a pool of dried-up vomit.

'Shit!' I whisper, panicking slightly as I turn on the light and Tom stirs, opening his eyes and starting to cry.

I feel his forehead, but there's no fever, and kissing him softly I soothe him as I take him into the bathroom to sponge him down.

'It's all right, darling,' I croon, unsnapping his sodden sleepsuit and peeling it off, lifting his vest over his head, trying hard not to make more of a mess than there is already. 'Mummy's here,' I say, and I try not to let his cries pierce my heart as I wash the vomit out of his hair.

I bring him back into the bedroom and lay him on the changing table, getting him quickly dressed again. He's wide awake now, chattering away, and I sit him in his bouncy chair on the floor to change the sheets.

'Bleeuurgh.' I turn around and Tom is throwing up again—one huge projectile vomit, covering his new clean pyjamas, covering the bouncy chair, covering the carpet.

'Oh shit.'

He starts to wail again, and I pick him up, take him back to the bathroom, and start all over again.

By two o'clock in the morning he has thrown up three more times, and I am rocking him to sleep in my arms. I'm exhausted. I can't decide whether to call the doctor, but there's no fever, nothing else apart from the sickness, and I can't bring myself to disturb the doctor in the middle of the night for something that probably isn't serious.

So Tom and I rock together in the chair, and eventually he falls asleep in my arms, both of us too exhausted to move.

I bring him into my bedroom and place him on the bed next to me. I'm frightened he'll throw up in his sleep again, so I turn the television on softly and stay awake until the early hours, when sleep eventually gets the better of me and I drift off, sitting upright against the pillows.

This is so hard, I think, just before I drift off. Doing this all by myself is just so damn hard.

*   *   *

Fran hugs me very tightly. She doesn't say anything else, doesn't need to—her hug reassures me more than words ever could.

And then Marcus hugs me, and we three pull apart and grin at one another.

'Good to see you, Ellie,' Marcus says. 'We were beginning to think there was something wrong with us.'

'Nope. I'm just a rubbish friend. Sorry,' I offer.

'Don't worry,' Fran says, elbowing Marcus. 'God knows you've had enough on your plate to deal with.'

'So. We thought local, yes? The Chinese in Belsize Park? Is that okay?'

'Fine,' I say, grabbing my jacket from the hallway. 'Perfect. As long as I can be in bed by nine, I'm happy.'

'I'm glad our company is that good.' Marcus raises an eyebrow as we walk out to his car.

'Don't take it personally,' I laugh. 'I'd feel that way even if I were having dinner with . . .' I struggle to think of someone.

'Charlie Dutton?' Marcus offers with a sardonic grin.

'Oh, shut up.' Now it's my turn to shove him. *'Especially* with Charlie Dutton,' I say in a bid to defend myself. I turn to Fran. 'Will you please stop bringing up Charlie Dutton? And, by the way, if he should by some huge coincidence just happen to stop by the restaurant tonight and find us sitting there, I will leave. Okay? Just for the record.'

'Bugger.' Marcus laughs. 'You foiled my evil plan.'

'Don't worry.' Fran links her arm through mine. 'We have no evil plans. It's just that you're our friend and Charlie's our friend, and it would be so nice, that's all. If you were ready,' she adds hurriedly. 'Which of course we both know you're not.'

'So no more teasing about Charlie Dutton?' I ask.

'Fine.' Marcus shrugs. 'I'll stop if Fran stops.'

'Fine,' Fran says. 'My four-year-old husband and I now promise to stop teasing you about Charlie Dutton.'

I am so used to being the third wheel with Fran and Marcus, knew them for so long before Dan ever came on the scene, that we fall straight back into the easy friendship we always had, and for a moment I forget that I am no longer the woman I was when I last had dinner with the two of them, that I now have a child, a husband, a different life.

We talk, and laugh, and I know that I will not let such a long time pass before I see them again; that they are unquestionably within the category of closest friends, and that I was wrong to let our friendship slip because the four of us—Marcus, Fran, Dan and I—never seemed to gel in quite the same way that the three of us do.

Not that Dan disliked them. He always said how nice they were, but the dynamic was always different, somehow more formal, and it's something of a relief to see them without him.

Halfway through our second bottle of wine—which I have to say Fran and I are polishing off almost single-handedly—I get up to go to the loo, and as I weave my way through the busy restaurant, I glance around at all the people, everyone talking animatedly, everyone having a good time, and I think how good it feels to be back in the world again.

Because that is how it feels: as if I have been removed from real life. And now the clouds that kept me separate, that distanced me from everything for all those months, have finally lifted and I'm able to take my place in the land of the living, to feel happiness again.

I know it's not because I'm on my own. I know that I am not happier because Dan is not with me, but that somehow his leaving acted as a form of catalyst, jolted me back into life, forced me back to reality.

I smile as I enjoy the feeling, and then I see them. Tucked into a corner I notice a girl, and I only notice her because she's so pretty. Long glossy brunette hair, big green eyes, and she's gazing adoringly at her date.

And of course my eyes wander over to see her date, knowing he will probably be a tall, handsome, model type, and I freeze. It's Dan.

I stand in the middle of this busy restaurant as

333

time stands still, and I watch the brunette laugh and lean forward to say something. I can't move. I just stand there staring at them, and she clearly feels me looking and raises her eyes to meet mine, questioningly.

And Dan turns around, a smile still on his face from some private joke they shared, and he searches for what she is looking at, and he sees me, and I swear all the colour drains from his face, exactly the way it did in the South of France.

So we stare, Dan and I.

I can't move, and he doesn't seem to know what to do. Eventually the girl places her hand on his, and he turns to her and says something—I'm guessing 'it's my wife', unless of course she doesn't even know he's married—and then starts to rise, and I know he's going to come over but I can't deal with it. Not now. Not here. Not when I'm liable to throw up any minute.

I walk quickly back to Fran and Marcus. 'I have to go,' I say, barely pausing by the table to say the words. 'I'll see you outside.'

'Ellie? Is everything okay?' Fran gets up as I walk out, but I don't stop to say anything, I just walk out into the night air.

*   *   *

The phone is ringing as I walk in the door. It's 9.45 p.m. Far too late for any of my friends to phone, given that all of us have children and know that it is incredibly bad manners to call parents of young children after 8 p.m., 8.30 at a push.

I ignore the phone as I thank Rachel for babysitting yet again, and at such short notice, and

334

I pay her off, noting that whoever is phoning doesn't leave a message but phones again a couple of minutes later.

Whoever is phoning. Of course I know it's Dan. Who else could it be? I pick up the phone wearily, not sure I want to hear what he has to say, just feeling numb, and sick, and tired. So very tired.

And embarrassed. After the message I left on his voicemail. The message to which he never responded. I could kick myself for doing that. I knew at the time it was wrong, knew I shouldn't have let him know how much I cared, how vulnerable I was. He didn't return my call, but I figured he might be away, and I'd see him on Saturday morning when he came to pick up Tom, that he'd bring it up then.

Although part of me hoped that he wouldn't.

'I can explain,' Dan says as I pick up the phone and hold it to my ear.

'There's nothing to explain,' I say dully. 'You don't owe me an explanation. You don't owe me anything. We're separated.'

'Ellie, it wasn't what you think,' he says. 'That was Lola Smith, she's presenting the new series I'm doing. It was a work thing.'

That was no work thing. 'It doesn't matter,' I say. 'She clearly didn't think it was a work thing, and anyway, you're entitled to have a date, or a girlfriend.' I almost choke on the word, but continue nevertheless.

'She's not a girlfriend. She's not even a date.' Dan sounds miserable.

'So where are you now? Outside on your mobile while *Lola*'—even the mention of her name makes me feel ill—'waits in your car?'

335

'No. She's gone home. She has her own car.'

I don't say anything but I'm pleased. Perhaps it wasn't a date. The Dan I know, the Dan I dated, always insisted on picking me up.

There's a silence. Then: 'I got your message.'

Oh shit. The very words I have spent days waiting for. The very words I am now dreading since seeing Dan with her. *Lola. L-l-l-l-lola*.

'Sorry about that,' I say curtly. Oh shit. What can I say? How can I get out of it? How can I excuse it? 'I think I was slightly drunk. To be honest I can't even remember what I said. Whatever it was, just ignore it.'

'You were drunk? At four o'clock in the afternoon?' I can hear the smile in Dan's voice and I want to hit him.

'What is it, Dan?' I'm humiliated beyond belief, and I just want to get him off the phone and curl up in a corner somewhere and cry.

'I thought perhaps you were right. That we should talk. Maybe we can talk this weekend?'

I pause. But then I think about *Lola*. About Lola and Dan laughing. About Dan kissing Lola. I wonder if he makes the same moves with her as he does with me? I wonder if she's better in bed than me? Oh, God. Please let me stop thinking about this.

'I can't,' I say, my voice cold again. 'I just can't do this now, Dan. I'm sorry,' and as my voice starts to break, I gently put down the phone.

*　　*　　*

The tears last an hour, and when they are done I fish Charlie Dutton's card out of my coat pocket.

Fuck it. If Dan can have his little fling, or his big love, or whatever the hell he's having with Lola, I can have mine with Charlie Dutton.

10.45 p.m. Is it too late to call? I'd never call anyone else, but this is a single man, on a Friday night. I doubt very much he's even home. And anyway, tonight has given me courage, false or not, and if I don't phone now I may never call again.

It truly is now or never.

I phone and I was right. He's out. His machine picks up and, trying to make my voice as normal as possible, I leave a message.

'Hi, Charlie. It's Ellie. Ellie . . . Cooper.' For a second I was about to use my maiden name, and as I say my married name I think how duplicitous it makes me feel. 'Ellie Black,' I say firmly, for if I'm going to be unfaithful, as I know I'm going to be, I'm going to do it under the guise of a single girl.

Surely that way I'll feel less guilt?

'I just found your card, and wondered whether you'd like to get together some time. Give me a call.' I leave my number and put down the phone, congratulating myself on what a cool message I left.

And now it's just a matter of time.

27

I can't get the image of Dan and Lola out of my head. I see them at the restaurant, her hand reaching out to his, or my imagination works overtime and I picture them in every compromising position my tired mind can conjure up.

It fuels me. Fills me with rage. Fuels a puerile

desire for revenge in the only way I know how, by sleeping with Charlie Dutton.

Poor Charlie Dutton. I wonder if he knows I have everything planned? I wonder if he knows I am planning to seduce him in the best way I know how: by sensual candlelight, seductive clothing, delicious food.

I'm halfway there, given that he already admitted he thinks I'm sexy. Surely all it needs is a little push. I think of Lola laying her lips on Dan and I know there is no way I will let Charlie Dutton out of my clutches.

He didn't sound surprised to hear from me. Delighted, in fact. He said he'd been meaning to phone me, and only seemed slightly surprised when I invited him over for dinner. On Saturday. A night when Tom's away and the mice can play.

But it feels so long since I've played the seduction game, if indeed I ever really played it at all. This is surely Lisa's field, not mine, and although I could ask her advice, probably *should* ask her advice, I can't admit what I'm doing, can't tell anyone about it until after the fact.

Not that I'm looking for a one-night-stand, absolutely not. But I don't know where it will lead, and I'm not thinking of the future, just of tonight.

The salmon is wrapped and in the fridge, waiting for its coat of tapenade and puff pastry, the salad is sitting crisply in its bag, and the lemon drizzle cake awaits the sighs of pleasure that always greet it, my *pièce de résistance* and, ironically, although naturally it never occurred to me at the time, Dan's favourite.

I may not be wearing new clothes, not tonight, but I'm sure as hell wearing new underwear. My

338

greying, fraying cotton bikini bottoms, unsightly flesh-coloured bras, deeply unsexy but formidably practical, may be good enough for a husband but could never be good enough for a lover.

For that, I did take Lisa's advice. I forgo Marks & Sparks for perhaps the first time in my life and head instead to Agent Provocateur. How embarrassing. How sexy. How completely unlike me. I walk out swinging my guilt on my wrist: delicate and delicious, wisps of chiffon and lace. Underwear for the vampiest of vamps, the sluttiest of sluts.

And it is true that tonight I am role-playing. Tonight I am not Ellie Cooper, or even Ellie Black. Ellie Black, single girl, would never have acted the way I am planning to act tonight. Ellie Black, single girl, would have thought Agent Provocateur was a bad guy from a Bond film. Ellie Black didn't seduce, she allowed herself to *be* seduced, and even then only occasionally, and only if she'd been out with them for at least a month, and only if she was absolutely sure they really, really, *really* liked her.

Tonight I'm planning on being far more like Lisa than myself. I'm planning on lighting candles, playing Norah Jones softly on the stereo, sitting on the sofa with Charlie Dutton and gazing at him soulfully over the rim of my glass of red wine.

If Charlie Dutton doesn't make a move on me, which I have to say I'm sure he will—could ever a situation be more perfect?—I fully intend to make a move on him, fuelled by my desire for revenge— just think about *Lola*—and copious amounts of alcohol.

At eight o'clock I'm ready. Eight o'clock. A throwback in itself to my old life. Charlie's coming at 8.15, and I walk around the flat nervously lighting candles before blowing them out again. Too obvious. Not yet. They will be lit but not until later in the evening.

But the fire is going—the nights are still chilly in late May—and I sit by it as I wait for him to arrive, refilling my glass as I quickly down the wine to build my confidence.

The doorbell rings. My heart starts to pound. Oh, God. What am I doing? Is it too late? Can I pretend I'm not here? But of course I can't. Ellie Black, or Ellie Cooper, or even Ellie Vamp, is still far too polite, far too much of a nice girl to ever do something that rude, far too afraid of anyone disliking her to behave like that.

I walk down the hallway, every footstep sealing my fate. A quick glance in the mirror confirms what I already know. I do look good. Perhaps it's because underneath my clothes I'm wearing the sexiest underwear I've ever seen, perhaps it's because I'm slightly drunk, but there's a twinkle in my eye and a flush to my cheek, and if I were Charlie Dutton I'd definitely want to sleep with me.

'Hello.' I stand and smile at him, and he leans forward and places a chaste kiss on my cheek, handing over a huge and beautiful bunch of calla lilies.

'These are for you,' he says, following me inside.

'Thank you. They're lovely.'

I tell Charlie to sit and wait in the living room while I busy myself in the kitchen, finding a vase for the flowers. Suddenly I'm very nervous. This isn't a dream. This isn't a fantasy. There is a man in my flat who I'm planning on sleeping with and it's not my husband. This is suddenly feeling very strange.

And very wrong.

'Would you like some wine?' I call, wishing now that I could spend the rest of the night in the kitchen, find a way of avoiding the unavoidable.

'A glass of red would be lovely,' he calls back. 'Can I do anything to help?'

'No, I'm fine. I'll be in in a minute. Just make yourself comfortable.' I cringe at my words. How clichéd they sound. How clichéd this situation is. This . . . date. I was so sure my dating days were over, so happy I wouldn't ever have to do this again, and yet here I am.

I take a deep breath and carry our two glasses of wine back into the living room, where I find Charlie standing in front of the bookshelves, examining the books. He turns and smiles at me, and I start to relax. This is only a man, for God's sake. You don't have to do anything, Ellie. Just have a nice dinner and a nice chat. You can get out of this alive. Honestly.

'I always think you can tell so much about people from thcir bookshelves.'

'Oh?' I stand next to him and look where he's been looking: Dan's non-fiction interspersed with my design books, my fiction hardbacks, various wedding gifts dotted here and there—crystal bowls we've never had any use for, Limoges boxes that would look more at home in Dan's grandmother's house than in mine, and lots and lots of photographs of Tom. Tom when he was first born, his scrunched-up face red and angry as he's held up for the camera. Tom being cuddled by Dan, Tom with me, Tom crawling, Tom sleeping . . .

'I suppose you've deduced that we . . . that *I* . . .' I say, correcting myself hastily, 'love my son.' I wish

341

I had thought to remove the pictures of Tom with Dan, remove any evidence of Dan entirely.

Charlie laughs. 'I should hope you do. He's gorgeous.'

'He is, isn't he?' I relax, comfortable in familiar territory at last. 'I'm ever so slightly biased, but I do think he's the most divine baby in the world.'

'When will he be two?'

'August.'

'Just wait till he turns two,' he grins. 'That's when the fun really starts.'

'How old is yours again?'

'Five. But the twos were the worst. You'll have your hands full. Is he here? Sleeping?'

I shake my head. 'No. He's with Dan on the weekends. What about Finn? Don't you have him on weekends?'

'Usually, but my ex and her boyfriend have taken him away to the country for the weekend.'

My ex. I wonder when Dan will stop being Dan and will become my ex, or if indeed he will ever become my ex. When do they stop being part of your life? When are you able to refer to them dispassionately, with no connection, no feeling, no sign of pain? I can't imagine ever referring to Dan as my ex. Not yet. But I will not think about this tonight. I take a large sip of wine.

'So, you still haven't told me what you've deduced from my bookshelves.'

Charlie smiles and turns to the bookshelves, before turning back to me.

'Hmm. Let's see. I'm going to assume that the non-fiction books on history and various film things don't belong to you, which leaves someone who has a passion for design, who reads all the latest bestsellers but who has a secret penchant for crap beach reads, although they try not to display them, and I definitely see that when you got married there were far too many old relatives at the wedding and not nearly enough friends.'

I laugh. 'How on earth could you tell that?'

'Because I got all that crystal and those small painted box things too. They were the only things I was happy to let my ex have when we split up.'

'When did you split up?'

'Four years ago. Why do you ask?'

I move towards the sofa and sit down. 'You seem to talk about her so easily, with no emotion whatsoever. I just wondered when I'd get there.'

'Honestly I think it takes different people different amounts of time. It took me a long time, but we're friends now, of a fashion. Not that I'd invite her over, but we've always tried to be civil, for Finn's sake. This is still very new to you, and'— he pauses, a slight smile on his face—'probably far too early for you to be inviting strange men over to your flat for dinner.' He grins, holding my gaze as he takes a sip of wine, and two things happen to me simultaneously: I blush—God, how I hate my cheeks constantly giving me away—and I feel that rush of desire. I hold his gaze for a second more than I'm comfortable with, then say, with as sweet and innocent a smile as I can muster: 'But you're not strange.'

'Touché.' He smiles, and raises his glass.

'Let me just go and start getting the supper ready.'

I stand up and he follows me into the kitchen.

'I'm a kitchen wizard,' he says, 'let me help.'

We chat, laugh and drink some more as I put the

343

salmon in the oven and Charlie chops the salad. There is something so familiar and yet so unfamiliar about this whole scene. Once again I realize how much I miss being part of a couple, for cooking with someone else, something so prosaic, so everyday, suddenly becomes so special when you're not doing it any more.

It feels so normal to hand Charlie a knife, the chopping board, the vegetables. And yet, as he chops the salad, finely chopping the cucumber and the tomato, I want to stop him, to tell him that Dan doesn't do it like that, that we don't like it chopped, that the tomatoes and cucumbers should be sliced, that he is doing it wrong.

But of course I don't say that. I just enjoy how the kitchen comes to life when there is more than just Tom and me in it. How Norah Jones manages to create a feeling of warmth and relaxation, how I am suddenly enjoying this evening far more than I had anticipated, especially because it is not as I expected.

I do fancy Charlie. *Did* fancy Charlie. There is no denying that. But now that he's here, now that the fantasy has become a reality, it isn't the smouldering, sensual evening I had imagined. I am having fun. We're not flirting, we're talking. And we're not kissing, we're laughing. It feels as if I am making dinner with a friend, and suddenly I realize that I am having a good time, and that actually I don't want to sleep with Charlie, and, more than that, I don't *have* to sleep with Charlie. This is about making a new friend, and that thought relaxes me and makes me smile.

'What are you smiling to yourself about?'

'I was just thinking that I'm having a good time,'

I say. 'Come on. Let's eat,' and together we take the food into the living room and sit down at the dining table.

Charlie goes into raptures about the food.

'You're behaving like someone who hasn't eaten a decent meal in months,' I laugh, as he polishes off his salmon, asks for seconds, then eats three huge slices of lemon drizzle cake.

'Being a bachelor and cooking don't really go together.'

'I thought the way to a woman's heart was through her stomach?'

'No, that's the way to a man's heart.'

'I know, I was joking, although don't all single women say that there's nothing sexier than a man who can cook?'

'I don't know, do they? You're a single woman, you tell me.'

'Okay, there's nothing sexier than a man who can cook.' Now it's my turn to tease.

Charlie holds my gaze with a smile. 'Does that mean you don't find me sexy because I can't cook?'

Jesus Christ. Talk about getting straight to the point. He's looking at me, waiting for an answer, and I don't know what to say. My intentions of seduction are long gone, my plans to behave like Lisa now firmly out the window. I stammer like a teenager, then quickly mumble something about clearing up. I stand, grab the plates and take them into the kitchen, where I attempt to steady myself against the kitchen sink, eyes closed as I take deep breaths to regain my equilibrium.

I don't hear him come in. Don't know he's there until I feel his warm breath on my neck. He's standing behind me, so close I can almost feel his heartbeat, can feel the whisper of his skin against mine.

My heart stops. I can't breathe.

'You didn't answer my question,' he whispers into my ear, his lips brushing my earlobe and my knees feel weak. I start to turn to say something, anything, and his face is there, centimetres from mine, and my eyes close and we're kissing, and I think that I ought to push him away, ought not to be doing this, but it feels so good.

So very, very good.

His arms wrap around me. Arms so different from Dan's. Mouth so different from Dan's. He tastes sweet. Musky. Strong. His hands caress the back of my head and I raise my hands to feel his back, not swept away on the wave of passion I had expected, but curious, wanting to know how he feels, this new body crushed up against me in my kitchen.

His shoulder blades are sharper than Dan's, his waist larger, a small comfortable cushion of spare flesh I hadn't noticed before.

We move without speaking into the living room, where we lie on the sofa, exploring one another's contours, kissing and murmuring, smiling at one another.

I know he is turned on. I can feel he is turned on. And I know I ought to be turned on, especially given the feelings he has roused in me prior to this night, and yet I still feel like a spectator, am continuing with the moment despite not being *in* the moment. It is as close as I will probably ever come to having an out-of-body experience, for every time he touches me, every time I touch him, I am so aware of how it feels, how different it feels to

346

when I am with Dan.

It brings all the memories of Dan flooding back. We hadn't had sex in such a long time when he left that I hadn't thought about it, hadn't remembered how lovely it was, how much we had both enjoyed it, and how wonderful it was to have reached that point with someone where you didn't have to try, you weren't putting on a performance, you were just loving someone in the best way you knew, and they were loving you in return.

Charlie murmurs something about getting even more comfortable, moving to the bedroom, and I nod, because suddenly I can't trust myself to speak, for there is a lump in my throat, and when he moves towards me to kiss me again I shake my head and sit up, pushing him gently away.

Charlie sits back and looks at me, his hair tousled, his shirt half undone.

'I knew this wasn't a good idea,' he says quietly, almost to himself. 'I knew it was too soon.'

'I'm sorry,' I whisper, guilt all over my face. 'I'm so sorry, Charlie. I think you're lovely, really. If it weren't so soon, if I were ready . . .'

'You don't have to explain.' He takes my hand and holds it in his, stroking my palm gently as we both look down at my small hand in his. 'Fran told me it was too soon, which is why I didn't call you. But then, when you called me, I thought maybe you were ready. You know, I think you're a fantastic woman.'

'Thank you.' I smile and squeeze his hand.

'My pleasure,' he says, and we sit there in silence for a while. 'Do you think you're going to get back with your husband?' he says eventually.

'I think the future's still uncertain, but I suppose

the only thing I do know, after tonight, is that I'm not ready for anyone else.'

'I know.'

'Do you think we can still be friends?' I say hopefully, as Charlie lets go of my hand and stands up, and I know he's getting ready to leave. He has no reason to stay. Not any more. I should be feeling guilty, but all I feel is relieved. He smiles and shrugs, and I smile sadly at him, knowing the answer is no.

Another time, another place, another lifetime, perhaps. But not now, not here. Not with me.

28

I get a phone call from Calden first thing Monday morning. They urgently need the marketing proposal to be faxed over by the end of the day.

It's not finished. Nearly, but not quite, and thank God for Trish, who picks Tom up and takes him over to her house so I can finish it off.

I spend the afternoon glued to my computer, making phone calls, fuelled by strong black coffee, until at 4 p.m. I sit back in my chair and punch my arms in the air with a grin. Finished.

Disorganized as it may seem, I have no fax, and Trish has taken the kids to the zoo, so I can't get into her house.

Lisa's away for a long weekend—as usual she became coy when I pushed for more information—and she has a fax, and I have a spare key. Of course I could go down to the local copier shop, but how ridiculous to have to queue and pay when one of my best friends lives around the corner and I know she wouldn't mind in the slightest.

Even more ridiculous, I think, as I pull my coat on, to not have a fax. It was one of the essentials Dan took with him when he left, and it seems I'll now have to put it at the top of my shopping list.

I ring Trish and tell her I'm off to send a fax and that I'll meet her at the café in Regent's Park for tea.

'Your son is an angel,' she tells me, and no matter how many times I hear it from other people, it never fails to warm my heart. 'He's just so good! How do you do it? Why does my son throw tantrums all the time while your son is as good as gold? How do you do it?'

It's a conversation we have over and over again. I've tried explaining my theories, gently urging her to try to introduce more routine, but she's a lost cause, and there's only so far I can push. And so today I say what I always say, which is that every child is different and I'm just blessed.

We say goodbye and I grab Lisa's spare key, then hesitate. I'd better phone her and let her know. After all, I wouldn't want someone coming into my flat without permission, even if they did have a key.

I call her mobile, which is switched off, so I leave a message. 'Lisa, it's me. Look, I need to borrow your fax machine, I hope you don't mind. I promise I won't disturb anything in your house, and I'll only be a few minutes. Hope you're having a lovely time wherever you are and whoever you're with. Call me when you get back. Bye.'

And out I go.

*   *   *

I love days like today. When the sun is shining in London there is no place in the world I'd rather be. You can keep your South of France, your Caribbean island, your Majorcan getaway— Primrose Hill in the sunshine is the place that I love.

Everyone looks happy in the sun, everyone seems to be smiling, everyone is walking with a spring in their step. I feel a burst of energy and happiness that I haven't experienced for a while, and for the first time in a long time it's not the result of someone else. I'm not happy because of Dan, or because of Dan's absence, or because I'm thinking of anyone else.

Walking down Regent's Park Road, waving at the shopkeepers I've come to know as friends since I've lived here, I suddenly feel that life is pretty good. I don't know what's going to happen with my marriage, but all of a sudden I have a sense that everything's going to work out, that everything happens for a reason, and that this is all meant to be.

*   *   *

Lisa's flat is the one I'd love to have if I ever had the money. She's in one of the tall stucco houses overlooking the park. The houses with the huge floor-to-ceiling windows, original mouldings on the ceilings, light flooding into every room.

I love Lisa's flat, even though her decorating tastes are completely different from mine. I love my flat because it's cosy, comfortable, eclectic. Lisa's flat looks as if it's been cut from the pages of

Elle Decor, so incredibly chic, and minimal, and smart.

The only give-aways are Amy's accoutrements which have a tendency to litter the floors of the living room and the tiny kitchen, but, Lisa being Lisa, she manages to sweep them up into smart wicker boxes, and once the boxes are stacked up neatly against the wall you would have no idea that a child had ever set foot in this house, let alone lived here.

For whereas I have the Mamas and Papas brightly coloured huge plastic highchair that takes up half the kitchen, Lisa has the minimalist Tripp Trapp chair, a wooden highchair that wouldn't look out of place in the Conran Shop, may in fact even have come from the Conran Shop.

Whereas I have a nursery that is blue and yellow and green, stuffed with mobiles, and teddy bears, and paintings, Amy's room is coffee-coloured, with chocolate-brown linen blinds and a sisal rug, the only hint of childhood being the cot, and even that is a hand-made cherry sleigh bed that can, Lisa tells me, be converted into a smart daybed once Amy grows out of it.

I have a mishmash of photographs of Tom all over the flat. Lisa has one wall of photographs along the corridor. They are all black and white, beautiful professional shots of Amy, and Amy with Lisa, and some of just Lisa, blown up to larger than life and artfully framed in sleek black.

Everything about Lisa's flat screams taste, style, chic. In the beginning I found it intimidating, found Lisa intimidating for that matter, but I know there is so much more to her than that, and since Dan left, it is true that I have found myself growing closer to Lisa, that I know she understands what I'm going through in a way that Trish couldn't possibly know.

Of course Trish supports me, of course she wants to help, but if she hasn't been through it, she couldn't possibly know. To look at us you would automatically put Trish and me together, know that we were friends, would think that glamorous perfect Lisa was the odd one out, and yet Lisa and I are growing closer and closer, with Trish being, if not the odd one out, then certainly the one who doesn't quite understand.

I'm not comfortable being in Lisa's flat without her permission, but I'm not going to take long. I head straight to her desk, which is in an alcove next to the kitchen, pull the document out of my bag and feed it into the machine.

I try not to look at anything. Just stand and gaze out the window as the fax goes through. Then, just as page three goes through, I swear I hear a noise.

I stand still, straining to hear, and yes, I'm sure I can hear footsteps in Lisa's flat. My heart starts to pound. This I wasn't prepared for. Intruders. My worst nightmare. I look around quickly for something heavy to grab, and I unplug the desk lamp—nice and heavy. And now, feeling fully armed, I tiptoe through the kitchen to investigate.

Most burglars are opportunistic, I think. Most are terrified of being confronted by someone. I'll scare them away. They'll turn and leave. Oh shit. Why does this have to happen while I'm here?

I creep down the hallway and hear the unmistakable sounds of someone in the flat. A door shutting. Footsteps. Banging into furniture. Oh shit. My heart is hammering in my chest and, as

352

I stand outside the bedroom door, I realize I'm not equipped to deal with this, I should just run away, run outside and call the police.

And as I stand, about to run, the bedroom door opens suddenly, and I gasp and drop the lamp, for there in front of me, wrapped in only a towel, holding a bedside lamp in his right hand, and looking just as scared as me, is Michael.

My father-in-law.

* * *

Neither of us says anything, and I imagine the look on his face is similar to the look on mine. Shock. Confusion. More shock.

'What are you doing here?' He's the first to speak, and behind him I see Lisa, in a towelling robe, and she looks horrified, and I am horrified, and why didn't this occur to me, why didn't I realize?

Lisa and my father-in-law.

Remember how smitten he was with her in France? Remember how we all laughed at how he practically salivated every time he looked at her?

It all comes flooding back to me.

And then our conversation of just the other night. Hadn't she said it was complicated, that he was married, but unhappily? Oh, God. My father-in-law.

I start to feel very, very angry. How *dare* she. How *could* she. He isn't hers. He's Linda's husband. Dan's father. How *dare* she.

I look at Michael, then at Lisa, and I can't find the words. I want to slap him. And as he looks at me, the expression on his face goes from shock, to

353

guilt, and finally, I am sure, to just a hint of remorse.

'I'm sorry,' he says quietly, as I stare, unable to quite believe that my friend has betrayed me in this way. The only worse betrayal would have been for her to have had an affair with Dan, but this is not much better. Trust me, this is really not much better.

I resist the urge to slap him around the face. I look at Lisa, and there is defiance on her face as she stands next to Michael.

'I'm sorry you had to find out like this, but why are you here? What are you doing in my flat?' she says, and all I feel is disgust.

'I was borrowing your fax,' I say coldly. 'If you check your mobile, you'll find a message from me. I thought you were away, but clearly I didn't realize quite what a good liar you've become.'

I am glad to see that Michael can no longer meet my eye, but Lisa is looking straight at me, is about to say something in her defence, in *their* defence, and I will not let her speak, am not interested in anything she might have to say.

'You disgust me,' I say quietly, as Michael looks at the floor and seems to shrink in size by the second. 'Both of you disgust me. If Linda knew . . .' I don't finish, don't have to. Michael looks as if he wants to cry, and, as Lisa moves him out of the way and stands in front of him, I know that our friendship has disappeared in an instant, that there will never be a way back for us.

'You don't understand. Michael and Linda have been unhappy for years. We love each other. This isn't just some cheap affair.'

'So does Linda know you're leaving her for

354

another woman?' I look at Michael and snort with fake laughter, because of course she doesn't. Because he's not going to. He may be under Lisa's spell, but even I know that Lisa is quite seriously deluded in thinking he's going to leave Linda.

I don't want to be here any more, don't want to stand here and be dirtied by this association, don't want to have anything more to do with them. I turn and collect my fax, then walk out the front door, rather childishly slamming it behind me.

*   *   *

Linda said not to trust her, I think, as I walk quickly over to the zoo. She knew, she knew what sort of woman Lisa was, although even Linda would never have guessed that Lisa would target her husband.

Linda. Poor, poor Linda. Whatever remaining animosity I have carried for Linda has gone, and suddenly I see Linda as someone who is unwittingly a victim, a victim of betrayal when she has done nothing wrong. I'll admit I'm the first to say she can be overbearing, and stubborn, and difficult, and probably impossible to live with at times, but really, does she deserve this? Does *anyone* deserve this?

What could possibly be worse for a woman in her late fifties than to discover her husband has been sleeping with a woman in her early thirties, and not just any woman, but someone as perfect as Lisa?

Poor Linda.

Even if you managed to keep your marriage together, how could you ever look in the mirror and like what you saw? How could you resist

355

constantly comparing yourself to the younger, better model, and how could you ever be able to accept, or be happy with, your image again?

Poor Linda.

Where does she think her husband was last weekend? Has she had to contend with late nights, mysterious whispered phone conversations that end the minute she comes in the room, unexplained credit card bills?

For Linda may be many things, but stupid she is not. Could she really not know? Or is she one of those women who do know, but figures she is better off not knowing? Is she one of those strong Mary Archer types—someone who probably thinks that she has too much to lose, that she can ignore the indiscretions as long as her life can continue in much the same way as it always has?

And as I reach the zoo I feel something I never thought I would feel for Linda. It is not that I feel sorry for her, but that I want to protect her. I feel— how bizarre is this—almost maternally towards her. I suddenly want to know how she is, want to make sure she's okay, want to help her get through this, and at the very least be there for her, help her deal with this, be her friend.

And I have the same realization that I had with Emma the other day. For better or worse, Linda is family. Whatever happens with Dan, I am the mother of her grandson, and, like it or not, she will always be part of my life. Until death do us part.

I had never understood about blood being thicker than water, but I'm beginning to see what that means. I may not like it, may not, at times, like her, but Linda, and all the Cooper clan, and all that comes with them, are part of me.

Part of my family.

*   *   *

'You look terrible. What's the matter?'

I wind my way through the mass of mothers feeding their small children in the café, and lean down to give Tom a big kiss.

'You wouldn't believe me if I told you,' I say, knowing that of course I will tell her, that I have to share this with someone, have to get rid of the burden of carrying such news all by myself. And as I look at Trish I am so grateful for her friendship, and realize that, despite what I recently thought about having so much in common with Lisa, it is Trish who is the better person, Trish who would never do something like that. Trish is still, and will always be, the better friend.

'What?'

And I tell her.

She exhales loudly when I finish speaking, and then puts her arm around my shoulders and pulls me in for a hug.

'How do you feel?' she says with concern. 'Are you okay?'

'I just feel slightly numb. Can you believe it? Don't you think that's horrible? That's my father-in-law, for God's sake, not to mention that he's a married man.'

'Do you want to know the truth?' Trish says, and I nod. 'Well, I can believe it, and I'm not that surprised. Look, I think Lisa is in many ways a remarkable woman, but she's very tough, and she knows what she wants, and I think women like that are always a bit ruthless. They always put men

357

before friendships with other women.'

'But why didn't you ever say anything before?' I say. 'I've never heard you say a bad word about Lisa ever. How is it you never told me that?'

Trish shrugs. 'A number of reasons. It's not my style to bitch about friends and I'm always very nervous of triangles. I think that even as adults when there are friendships between three women there is usually one that is left out, and I didn't want to be the one to instigate that.'

I don't say anything, because of course Trish is right, and I realize that Lisa and I, in our single-mother-bonding sessions, have left Trish out, and I am so, so, sorry now.

'I've left you out, haven't I?' I say sadly, and she smiles and shakes her head.

'It's okay,' she says. 'I could see that you needed Lisa's help to get through this, and I understood. I've never had to do it on my own, I didn't know what it was like, and I knew that Lisa could, in some ways, support you in a way that I never could. But Ellie'—and she leans forward and puts a hand on my arm—'I knew that our friendship was never in doubt, okay?'

I nod and gulp. If only I could say the same thing. What a bitch I've been.

'And, if you must know,' she continues, 'I figured she was having an affair, because she's been so secretive lately, and I was terrified it was with Dan. If anything, as awful as this sounds, I'm relieved it's with Michael.'

'Did you really think that?' I'm shocked. 'Why didn't you say anything?'

'What could I have said?' Trish asks sadly. 'You would have hated me for even thinking it, and I

358

didn't want to lose you by being the messenger.'

'Thank God you were wrong.'

'I know,' she says. 'Thank God there is at least one silver lining to this cloud. So now what? What are you going to do? Do you think it really is serious?'

I sit and think, but I don't believe this is it, I can't believe this is it. I can't believe that Michael would actually leave Linda for Lisa. They may have their problems, but I am sure that deep down Michael loves Linda, that this is, if you like, a middle-aged crisis, something that will pass.

'I don't think so. I really don't. Maybe I'm just being naive, but I can't see him giving up everything for Lisa. God.' I shake my head in admiration. 'I can't believe that Linda knew.'

'What do you mean?'

'Put it this way. You weren't the only one who thought Lisa was having an affair with Dan. Linda warned me about women like Lisa when she first met her in France.'

'She didn't!'

'She did! She's clearly a much wiser woman than either of us.'

'Poor Linda.'

'I know. That's exactly what I've been thinking.'

'What are you going to do? You're not going to tell her, are you?' Trish looks horrified.

'God no!' I reach over and steal a chip from Tom's paper plate. 'But I think I might call her. Just to see how she is. I know this sounds bizarre, but I suddenly feel protective towards her.'

Trish smiles. 'I don't think it's bizarre at all. I think it's really nice. And God knows she'd love to hear from you. Wasn't that the whole problem, that she wanted you to be another daughter?'

I nod. Why does that suddenly feel not so strange after all?

*   *   *

'Linda? It's Ellie.'

A gasp. Then silence as she recovers her composure. 'Hello, Ellie,' she says, in as cold a voice as I have ever heard. 'What can I do for you?'

Well, what did I expect? That she'd burst into tears and tell me how much she's missed me? How grateful she is that I've finally extended the branch of peace? Well, yes, actually. I had expected something like that, and it's a shock to hear how cold and unresponsive she is.

Although this is the woman I've refused to speak to for months. *Months*.

I take a deep breath. 'I'm sorry.' I say it quietly, and, as I say it, I feel tears well up in my throat.

'Sorry for what?' Linda says, her voice still icy.

'I'm sorry for everything,' I say, and manage to break down completely. I sit sobbing into the phone, and keep trying to speak but every time I start to cry again, and when I finally manage to regain my composure I don't even know if she's still there.

'Linda? Are you still there?'

'Yes, Ellie,' she says, and her voice is soft now. 'I'm still here.'

'Can we talk?' I say, even though I hadn't planned for that. 'Can we meet? Maybe for lunch?'

There's a long silence. I pray that she says yes, that she doesn't just put the phone down on me, although I don't deserve any more than that, and

360

she'd be absolutely within her rights to refuse.

'Yes,' she says eventually. 'I think that's an excellent idea.'

29

'I don't know what to do about Lisa,' admits Trish as we wheel the pushchairs around the park.

'What about her?' I growl.

'We can't just cut her off,' Trish says. 'You can't just cut her off. I'm also appalled by her behaviour, but she's a good friend, and you can't judge her because of this mistake.'

'Mistake?' I stop and look at Trish, aghast. 'Mistake? Is that what you call it?'

'Okay, it's bigger than a mistake, but think of all the good things about Lisa. Think about how good a friend she is to both of us, how amazing you always say she's been since Dan left. It just feels wrong to blame her. She isn't that bad a person.'

'Well she's not that *good* a person,' I interject sourly.

'I know,' Trish sighs. 'I'm just trying not to get too involved, trying not to make a choice.'

'Look.' I stop and turn to face her. 'Seriously, I'm not asking you to make a choice. As far as I'm concerned I don't want anything more to do with her, and yes, I'd be lying if I said I wouldn't mind if you carried on being friends with her, but I also know how childish that would be, so don't stop talking to her for my sake. The only thing I'd ask is that you don't tell me about her, because right now I don't want to hear anything.'

Trish muses for a while as we keep walking. 'I'm probably worrying over nothing,' she says finally. 'She hasn't returned my calls anyway. Are you really done with her?'

'Done and dusted,' I say with finality. 'As far as I'm concerned, my mother-in-law was right.'

'And what about your father-in-law?' Trish asks. 'What do you think will happen there?'

*   *   *

As it happens, I do know what will happen there. I know what will happen because three days after I walked in on Lisa and Michael, he rang. Naturally he rang from the safety of his chambers, clearly uncomfortable, and my voice was cold as I listened to what he had to say.

Even though I said I wasn't interested, that was a lie.

'I wanted to explain,' he started, clearing his throat.

'You don't have to explain anything to me,' I said. 'I think it was all perfectly clear.'

'Ellie, please. I know you're having lunch with Linda, and I have to explain, have to ask you not to say anything to Linda. Please.' I could hear the fear in his voice. 'Please don't tell Linda about Lisa.'

'I suppose you're now going to say something ridiculously clichéd like Lisa doesn't mean anything to you, or that you've been unhappy.'

Michael sighed deeply at the sarcasm in my voice. 'Ellie, life doesn't always go in the direction you expect it to, and sometimes we make mistakes, and sometimes we do things that we're not proud of, but the only way to learn is to make those

362

mistakes . . .'

I interrupted him, irritated by his piousness. 'Michael, I'm really not interested. I'm happy that you've found a way to justify your affair to yourself, but I don't—'

'I haven't', he said firmly.

'You haven't what?'

'I haven't found a way to justify it to myself. I just . . .' He sighed. 'I just couldn't resist her. Oh, God, I really am sorry, Ellie. I'm sorry because I didn't mean to upset you, or hurt Linda, or get involved. I swear to you I had no intention of having an affair, I was just flattered by her attention, she's so young, and . . .'

For a fraction of a second I felt sorry for him.

No. I would not feel sorry for him. But my curiosity was now piqued. I had imagined Michael to be the seducer, the instigator, the one who led the betrayal. Could I have been that wrong?

'Flattered by her attention? What do you mean?'

Michael, clever man that he is, detected the chink in my armour and leapt in with the whole, sorry story.

Lisa was, it seems, the one to initiate the flirting. He wasn't *unhappy* with Linda, but hadn't really been happy either, not for many years. He had been disbelieving at first, when Lisa had made a suggestive comment and held his gaze longer than was necessary, longer than a young, beautiful woman had held his gaze in years.

It had happened in the South of France. Before the accident, clearly. A series of suggestive comments from Lisa, comments that Michael tried to ignore, but he couldn't help being flattered. My God, how could we have missed all of this? How

363

could Linda have missed all of this—for, as suspicious as she was of Lisa, she never thought Michael would be the target.

He was used to his intellect being flattered, he explained. His skills in the courtroom, his knowledge, his quick mind. But he had not been praised for his looks, or his prowess, *himself*, for years.

'Was she the first?' I asked at one point. Not that it was any of my business. Not that I was even expecting him to answer.

There was a long pause. 'You have to understand,' Michael sighed. 'I've been married for thirty-five years. It's a long time.' He didn't say anything else. Didn't have to.

Poor Linda.

Lisa had phoned Michael after the accident. Had found his number in chambers from the internet. Had phoned to say how sorry she was, and was there anything she could do to help, and if he ever wanted to talk she'd be happy to meet him.

That *bitch*. Using my son as the means to start an affair with my father-in-law.

For I have no doubt in my mind that this was entirely premeditated. That she had decided Michael was exactly what she was looking for. That she would move mountains, if that was what it would take, to ensure he would somehow have an affair and presumably leave his wife for her.

So. Lunch. An innocent lunch, Michael said, for he did need to talk, Linda being a mess of tears and emotion. I kept quiet at that point, didn't need to add anything about how I felt.

And lunch, he said, led to the inevitable.

'Do you love her?' I asked. I thought I didn't

want to know, claimed I wasn't interested, but now that I knew, I needed to know more.

'I love the way she makes me feel,' he said softly. 'I love that I feel like a young man when I'm with her. But conversely I hate the guilt. For every wonderful moment there's an equally terrible one. I hate the guilt and I hate myself for having succumbed to such obvious ploys.'

I was silent. There was nothing left to say.

'It's over with Lisa,' he added. 'I love my family. I don't want to hurt them. This was a terrible mistake, and again, Ellie, I'm sorry.'

'Does Lisa know?'

'I think so. We had a long talk after you left. I'm not sure she believes it, though. But it is. It's over.'

'I'm not going to say anything to Linda,' I said. 'I mean, I wasn't, even before you phoned.'

'Thank you.' I can hear the relief in his voice. 'Thank you, Ellie.'

'That's okay,' I said, because to have said it was a pleasure would have been a lie.

*   *   *

Trish and I reach the playground, and as we clear the trees I see Lisa, sitting on her own on a bench, talking into her mobile as Amy toddles around the sandpit.

'Shit,' I mutter, grabbing Trish's arm and pulling her back behind the safety of the trees.

'What?' Trish, as always, is oblivious.

'It's Lisa. She didn't see us. I can't. I just can't handle it.'

Trish nods. 'Come on,' she says, 'let's go back to my place.'

'Oh, God,' I groan, as we scurry away like teenagers. 'Do you think we'll have to move?'

'I hear Muswell Hill's very nice,' Trish says, and for the first time that day I laugh out loud.

Then I stop laughing abruptly, because not only has Lisa clearly seen us, she's on her way over.

And there's nowhere to hide.

'Hi,' she says, walking over and looking at me.

'Hi, Lisa.' Trish smiles brightly, trying to sound as normal as possible. 'How are you?'

'Okay,' Lisa shrugs. 'Hi, Ellie.'

'Hi, Lisa,' I mutter, managing to meet her eye for a second, then looking away.

'Ellie,' Lisa says, 'could we go somewhere and talk?'

'I'll stay here with the kids,' Trish offers quickly. 'Why don't you two go off for a walk?' I flash her a furious glance, but Trish pretends not to see, and Lisa leads me off down the path.

We walk silently for a while, and then Lisa says quietly, 'It's over, you know.'

'Yes,' I say. 'I did know.'

'And there I was, thinking this was different.' She sighs heavily. 'Thinking he'd leave his wife for me. Thinking I'd finally found real happiness.'

'Lisa . . .' I start, about to say that I don't want to hear about it, or talk about it any more, but then I see there's a tear rolling down her cheek. I stop, amazed at seeing Lisa this vulnerable, and suddenly realize that this wasn't about betraying me. That this was about Lisa falling in love, and now being hurt.

This is not about me at all.

And I find myself reaching out and hugging Lisa, and, as I hold her and she cries, she apologizes for

366

hurting me, says she never meant to cause me any pain, and she tells me I'm her best friend, and she'd do anything to make things okay between us again.

She can just about deal with losing Michael, she says, smiling through her tears, but she can't deal with losing her best friend as well.

I didn't think I had it in me to forgive her. I thought I would never speak to her again, but I realize she is only human; that we all make mistakes; that I have been judgemental enough with Linda, and that it is not fair to do the same thing to Lisa.

'It's okay.' I rub her back. 'I understand. I'm sorry too. I'm sorry for judging you, for not giving you a chance. I'm sorry.' And I really am. 'Of course we're still friends.'

As we pull apart and Lisa smiles at me, I understand there's only one thing left to do. Now I have to apologize to Linda.

*   *   *

I'll admit I'm nervous. As nervous, and possibly slightly more nervous, than the first time I ever met Linda—that day Dan brought me over for Sunday lunch, when I thought I had found the perfect man, the perfect family.

I feel like I'm on a first date, desperate for her approval, which is such a strange feeling, particularly with Linda. I never had to fight for her approval before, not since that first meeting. The fighting came in trying to push her away, trying to keep her at arm's length, finding a way to incorporate us into her family and her family into ours, without letting her consume us.

And I couldn't do it. Not then. I didn't know how to let her in, a little at a time, and she didn't know how to build our relationship slowly but surely. So she came running towards me with arms open wide, and I leapt out of the way and erected a barrier she didn't have a hope of crossing.

I often wonder whether things would have been different if we hadn't had the accident. Whether we would have reached this point regardless, whether the tension between Dan's family and me was so strong that something else would have blown up, something else would have come between us, would have sent me running away.

The last few days I've wondered whether I would have softened this much if I hadn't discovered what I know now, whether I would be sitting here at all if I didn't now see Linda as a victim, feel sorry for her, want to help her.

And want to be friends with her.

I may not be ready to be her daughter. I may not ever be her daughter, particularly as Dan and I are now separated, and right now the situation doesn't look as if it's going to change at any point in the foreseeable future. But I'm willing to be her friend.

Or at any rate, I'm willing to try.

I look at my watch. She's late. Unlike her. Linda is always early for everything. I look over to the doorway and then I see her. I stand and half wave, and my heart pounds nervously.

Oh relax, for God's sake. It's only your mother-in-law.

She looks old. Older than I remembered. She's wearing just as much make-up as she always did, but I don't remember those lines being there, or perhaps being quite so pronounced.

368

She bumps into a chair on her way through to reach our table, and apologizes, and in that instant I know I'll never see Linda as the omnipotent matriarch of the family again. She's human, and frail, and vulnerable.

Why didn't I ever see this side of her before?

She stands in front of me and smiles, and—oh God, when did I turn into such a bloody crybaby?—I feel the lump in my throat and my eyes well up, and then she puts her arms around me and hugs me, and I think that although she may not be my mother, she's not a bad second, and I am so, so sorry for everything.

And we sit down.

*   *   *

It is the first time I have sensed any coldness from Linda. After the initial hug I had assumed we would fall back into our roles, but she is polite while maintaining her reserve, and it throws me. It is a side of her I have never seen, and I realize that the hug did not mean she had forgiven me, that all was fine and I was once again part of her family.

That hug was only meant to comfort, a Pavlovian response to tears, I realize, and sitting here in this restaurant, toying with a bowl of salad and making small talk, I would do anything, *anything* to take this cool Linda away and bring back the Linda I used to know, the Linda I thought I hated. The Linda I now understand I have missed.

So I talk about Tom. A sure-fire way to soften her up. I tell her everything I possibly can about Tom. I know she sees him on weekends, but she doesn't see him at his Gymboree classes, or with his

369

friends, or hear about all the funny things he comes out with, and so I bombard her with stories about Tom, and I can see it starts to work.

She gradually starts to soften, and, as we sit nursing cappuccinos, I tell her again how sorry I am, and start to explain why I couldn't talk to her, why I blamed her, but I stop. There is nothing left to say. I don't even know myself why I felt so strongly. The anger has disappeared so completely and so thoroughly that it hasn't even left a shadow, and I know that nothing in the world could justify to her why I refused to see her, or stopped her from being part of our family for so long.

'So how's Dan?' I say instead, breaking the awkward silence, trying to sound as nonchalant as I can. I wonder whether she might offer anything I don't know, whether she knows about *Lola*, knows what Dan is thinking, or feeling, or planning to do about us.

Whether in fact there's any *us* to speak of any more.

Linda stirs sugar into her coffee and we watch as the surface swirls around, and then eventually Linda looks at me.

'He's as well as can be expected,' she says, looking at me pointedly.

'I miss him,' I say quietly, and I realize that this is the magic key. Not the beloved grandson, but the beloved son.

And she seems to visibly relax before my eyes. An hour and a half after walking into the restaurant, her face finally softens, and I see the real Linda. The Linda I used to know.

'You do?' she says, and I see the hope in her eyes.

I nod. 'I really, really miss him. And Tom misses him. And we want him to come home. But I don't think he wants us any more.'

'Oh, Ellie. Of course he wants you. He adores you both. I don't understand any of it. I can't understand why you're *separated*.' She makes a face as she utters the word and I see how much she dislikes this situation, whatever she may have thought of me.

'But I've tried to talk to him and he doesn't say anything, and if he wanted to come home why doesn't he say so?'

Linda rolls her eyes, and she is truly now the Linda I know, except today it doesn't irritate me. If anything, I find it endearing. 'Oh, Ellie, don't be so naive,' she clucks. 'He may be my son and the most precious thing in the world to me, but he's also a man. Dan's never been the best at communication when he's hurt. He's always done exactly what he's doing now. He withdraws, curls up into a ball and hides away until the pain disappears.'

Oh, thank you, God. Thank you, thank you, thank you. So he hasn't come out of this unscathed; it's not as painless as it appears. For the first time since seeing him that night in Belsize Park, I begin to feel a glimmer of hope.

'You do think he's hurting, then?' I need to hear it from his mother, particularly after my recent imaginings.

'Of course he's hurting,' she snorts. 'He doesn't know what to do with himself, but his pride has been hurt too, which is why he won't come to you first, even though he wants to. You'll have to go to him. Trust me, I know you know him well, but I've known him a lot longer.'

371

'He hasn't been out partying every night? I assumed he'd fall straight back into the life he had before he met me.'

'Good Lord, no!' Linda says. 'Whatever gave you that idea?'

'What about *Lola*? Isn't he seeing her?'

'Lola? You mean the girl who presents his new show?' Linda looks at me as if that's the most ridiculous thing in the whole world.

'But I saw them together,' I protest. 'And she was all over him.'

Linda shakes her head. 'You can't have seen what you thought you saw. I promise you. She just got married and is pregnant with their first child, and deliriously happy, from what Dan says. He took her out for dinner to talk about work while the husband was working in Leicester, but I can promise you there's nothing going on there. First of all she isn't the type, and second, Dan isn't interested in anyone other than you.'

She isn't the type? I remember Linda talking about another type, the type that would sweep away with a man who belonged to someone else, and I shift uncomfortably on my chair as Linda appears to read my mind.

She signals the waitress for the bill, then turns back to me. 'So how are your friends?' she says. 'Trish and . . . Lisa?'

Is it my imagination or did she pause, did she say her name with more meaning, does she know? Does she know? What do I do if she asks me? Can I deny it? Can I lie?

'They're fine,' I say, unable to quite meet her eye. 'I still see a lot of them.'

There's an awkward silence that I try to fill by

sipping my Perrier, although once the glass reaches my lips I realize it's all gone.

'I was right about Lisa, you know,' Linda says quietly, and I gasp and look at her. Oh, God. She does know. How does she know?

'How do you know?' My eyes are wide with horror, my voice almost a whisper.

'I'm not stupid.' She smiles sadly. 'I could see what was happening in France.'

I sit staring at her like a dumb mute. I don't know what to say. What does this mean? Is she leaving Michael? Is she able to forgive him?

'What are you going to do?' I say finally.

'Do?' She looks at me and laughs. 'Nothing! I could see she was coming on to Michael, flirting with him when she thought we were all engrossed in other conversations, giving him long, meaningful looks. Happily my husband isn't the type to have an affair,' she laughs lightly, 'otherwise I would have been seriously worried.'

She doesn't know. How could she *not* know? How could she have put two and two together and come up with three and a half?

'So nothing happened between them?' I can't help it—I can't believe she doesn't know. I want to hear just what he told her.

'Not for lack of her trying,' Linda snorts. 'Do you know she even had the audacity to invite him out for lunch?'

I attempt an innocent look. 'Really?'

Linda laughs. 'I know. What a young girl like her is thinking of, going after a middle-aged married man, I just can't think.'

There's nothing I can say.

'I never thought she was your type,' Linda sniffs.

373

'And I certainly never trusted her. Anyway, Michael and I are happier than we've ever been. Last night he came home with tickets to Florence for the weekend! As a surprise!' She giggles girlishly. 'So your friend definitely picked the wrong couple!'

I nod and look away. Enough has been said. The fact that she was right about Lisa doesn't mean she ever has to know any more than she already does. God knows how she knows about Lisa's lunch invitation—maybe Michael really didn't mean for it to go as far as it did back then—but she looks happy, and I believed Michael on the phone. It is over, and hopefully Linda will never know.

I change the subject deftly, and we chit-chat as we prepare to leave. I think how much I have enjoyed this lunch, now that Linda has relaxed, now that we seem to have found a way forward.

I had thought that we might get everything out in the open. I thought the lunch might be full of recriminations, talking about who has been hurt, and how we've been hurt, and how we felt, and how we feel now.

I was ready for an emotional onslaught, and I am so grateful that we didn't have to do that, that Linda doesn't want me to bare my soul. Nor does she want to list every grievance she has ever had against me.

We have found a way forward, without having to go back over all of the pain, and this time I really can see how we can forge a relationship, how we can be part of one another's lives.

'So you really think I should go to Dan first?' I say, as we put on our coats and get ready to leave, Linda having treated me to lunch as she always did, too immersed in her role as mother supreme to do

374

anything different.

'I really do,' she says with a smile, and she hesitates before putting her arm around my shoulder and squeezing me, just like the loving, affectionate Linda of old.

'Call him tonight, and tell him you want to talk.'

Epilogue

'Oh, my God! You have to be kidding!' Dan and I let out whoops of delight as we put our hand luggage down on the marble floor and walk quickly over to the huge glass window to see the ocean views.

'This is amazing!' I turn to Dan and grin as he puts his arm around me and kisses me on the lips.

'And who didn't want to come on a family holiday?' he says, shoving me gently.

'Yes, well. This isn't exactly a family holiday. It's your mother's sixtieth birthday, not to mention the fact that your father's paying for everything. Trust me, if it was up to us, we'd never be here.'

'Trust me,' Dan laughs, 'if it was up to us we'd never be able to *afford* to be here.'

'True.' I nod in acquiescence.

Sandy Lane. The hotel of hotels. The destination of choice for the rich and famous. A place I never thought I would be able to go to in my wildest dreams.

Michael announced two months ago that he was bringing the whole family here as a surprise for Linda's sixtieth. They arrived yesterday, and she has no idea that the rest of us will be turning up tonight for her birthday dinner at The Cliff.

Tom gazes in awe at the giant plasma TV screen that faces the sofa in our suite, then he runs into the bedroom.

'Mum!' he calls excitedly. 'Dad! There's another *ginormous* TV screen in here too. Can we watch it now? Can we, Dad? Please?'

'No, darling,' Dan says, following him into the bedroom. 'No TV today.' He turns to me and rolls his eyes. 'He's not even four years old and already he's obsessed with television. What's he going to be like as a teenager?'

I grin. 'Distract him with a giant sand castle. They sell buckets and spades in the gift shop.'

'For about a hundred quid.' Dan shakes his head.

'But it's for your darling son,' I say. 'Go on. Buy a bucket and spade and take him down to the beach.'

Dan picks up Tom and puts him on his shoulders. 'Come on, Mr T. How about we go down to the beach and build a sand castle?'

'Yeah!' Tom shouts. 'Great idea, Dad!' And he drags his suitcase into his bedroom to dig out his swimming trunks and get changed.

*   *   *

The boys go off to the beach as I place a sleepy Millie in the cot they've brought up for us.

She missed her nap, and even though she was wonderful on the plane, her thumb is in her mouth and she's leaning her head on my chest, a sure sign she's ready for bed.

I sneak back into her darkened bedroom after five minutes, and she's already asleep, her eyelashes curling softly above the curve of her cheek, still sucking gently on her thumb, and I resist the urge to lean down and cover her with kisses, knowing it will wake her up, knowing she's not yet in a deep-enough sleep.

It is so very different having a daughter. I was so scared, for so long, that I would somehow repeat the patterns of my own mother, that I wasn't ready for a daughter, that I may never be ready for a daughter.

And yet the minute she was born I fell completely in love with her. Even now, at nine months old, she is so very different from Tom. Softer, quieter, happier. Where Tom was serious, Millie never stops smiling. Where Tom, being a boy, was always slightly alien to me, I know exactly who Millie is, what she's thinking, what she's about.

I leave her in her room—oh the joys of having a two-bedroom suite—and unpack our clothes before grabbing an apple from the fruit basket and going to sit on the terrace outside.

I can't stop smiling at how luxurious this place is. Even on the terrace there's a sofa. A sofa! Outside! It must be costing Michael a fortune, but if this is the price he has to pay for that long-ago indiscretion, then this is the price he has to pay.

I try not to think about those days very often. Two years after Dan and I got back together, we have come so far, all of us, and I feel like a completely different person. When I do think back to those dark days when Tom had the accident, when Dan and I were separated and Michael was having an affair with Lisa, I think how extraordinary it is that I can be so happy now, when I was so unbelievably, excruciatingly unhappy then.

I see Dan holding Tom's hand, scanning the rows of balconies on the Orchid Wing until he sees me, and then they both wave and blow me kisses, and I blow kisses back until they disappear.

We have become the family I always dreamt of

having. Not that it was instant, or easy. Those first few weeks when Dan and I got back together it was often awkward at times, but we worked through it, with the help of a marriage counsellor, knowing that we were together for the right reasons and that we both wanted it to succeed—not just for Tom's sake but also for our own.

Looking back, I remember it as happening overnight, although I'm sure that's just a trick of memory, that nothing was ever that simple. But I remember it being slightly awkward between us for a while, and then one day it was suddenly fine. No, better than fine. One day it was suddenly wonderful.

Then, I quickly fell pregnant with Millie, and somehow I knew that it would be impossible for me to repeat the mistakes of my parents. Tom was never going to be the awkward, lonely single child that I was; Tom would have a sibling, maybe two, maybe more.

We would be a proper family.

And my happiness and sense of contentment grow with every new day. Dan truly is my best friend now. My husband, my lover, my confidant. He is, as Sally put it—poor Sally, who is still single and desperately looking—the perfect husband.

Who would have thought?

And while Linda and Michael may not be the perfect in-laws, we've come a long way since those dark days of old.

It took me a long time to forgive Michael. Actually, it took me a long time even to be able to look him in the eye. Not that he seemed to find it any easier. But as time went on I saw how much warmer he and Linda were to one another. It was as if his affair, or perhaps the ending of it, served to remind him of better days. Whether that made him more loving, or whether Linda started to appreciate him more, either way they too are far happier than they were a few years ago.

In those early days I never saw any affection between them. Michael barely spoke, and Linda spoke to him mostly to put him down. But now they talk, and smile at one another, and I have even seen Linda spontaneously kiss Michael. Oh, sure, it doesn't happen all that often, but even Dan has commented that his parents are happier than he has ever seen them.

Perhaps our happiness is contagious.

Linda is certainly softer than she used to be. She is more cautious with me, more careful than in the days before Tom had the accident, but, as I have said to Dan, that is no bad thing. I would rather she is careful with me than overwhelm me as she used to do, trying to turn me into her daughter, then resenting and occasionally hating me for not playing along.

We have found a way to make it work.

She is not, nor ever will be, the mother I never had, and I have no intention of being her daughter. What we are is mother and daughter-in-law, and as such we have become friends. I do not confide in her, or turn to her for advice, much as I know she would like to give it.

But we meet for lunch, usually once a week, and talk about inconsequential things—like books, and news, and people we know. We chat, and we laugh. We never talk about the important things, like Michael, or Dan, or the children, other than to relay stories of how adorable they are, or of funny things they have said.

I always used to feel that Linda disapproved of me, that she thought she knew better, was better at everything, including motherhood. Now she tells me I am a wonderful mother, and, instead of thinking she has an agenda, I choose to believe her. And we get along just fine.

*   *   *

There's a knock on the door and I look through the spyhole to see Emma standing there. I open the door and she throws her arms around me and gives me a huge hug.

'Can you believe this place?' she says, walking into the suite and grabbing a pear before collapsing on the sofa. 'Isn't this the most incredible place you've ever seen? Makes Calden look like a cheap motel,' she laughs, taking a big bite.

'Oh, thanks!' But she's not wrong.

'And, guess what? I swear I just saw one of the Gallaghers downstairs at the bar. And apparently last week Beyoncé was here. I'm dying to get down there and do some serious celeb-spotting, although my bloody luck I'll only see Michael Winner.'

I splutter with laughter. 'So you've been warned to stay away from the beach too?' I remember Michael's typed instructions of what to do on arrival to ensure Linda doesn't spot any of us. 'You know we're allowed this end. Michael said as long as we stay up by the boats we'll be okay. He and your mum are apparently up by the restaurant.'

'I know, but Jake isn't exactly inconspicuous.'

'Ah, yes. Good point.'

Jake Motrin. The latest celebrity chef that

London has fallen in love with, not to mention Emma, who is, for the first time, saying this is finally it. Jake is *The One*. He is conspicuous for his fame (his last TV series had huge ratings and firmly established him as one of the top five, with his restaurant in Notting Hill currently the hottest and hippest in West London) and for his height (at six foot five he's definitely a person you look at), so I take Emma's point about not parading him on the beach, even if it is on the end that is away from Linda.

I am not surprised that Emma is with someone like Jake. His fame, quite apart from his looks, is an obvious attraction for a girl like her, a girl who likes to see and be seen by all the right people. What does surprise me is that it truly does seem to be a good match. That Emma took it slowly, which she has never done before. That she moved into his bachelor flat in Marylebone and transformed it into a home. That she is now as happy staying in watching television as she is going out to a party.

Richard is the only one who doesn't seem to have moved on that much. Still Linda's baby, still searching for the next hare-brained scheme, still as irresponsible as ever. I do often wonder whether he will ever be able to grow up, whether Linda has babied him just that little bit too much, whether his inability to settle down will stop him from ever finding happiness.

But talk to Richard and he will say he is happy. He will tell you about his new idea for a series of videos with Jake—poor Jake getting roped into this barmy family—he will tell you that this idea is great, that he's already had approaches from several production companies, that this is going to make him a fortune.

And then he may or may not try to hit you up for money, depending on whether he sees you as a potential investor, but I would still say the same thing about him as I said all those years ago when I first met him. Lovely, but be very, very careful. If you're single, and you quite like the look of him, like hearing him talk the talk, I would advise you to walk away now, before you get your heart broken like all of the others.

But still. Emma is happy, and Dan is happy, and, as I always say, two out of three ain't bad, and if you factor Linda and Michael into the equation, that surely cancels out Richard.

*   *   *

You're probably wondering about Lisa at this point. Unsurprisingly we are no longer best friends. The affair with Michael was just too hard a knock for us, and it hasn't ever really been the same since.

I have forgiven her. Absolutely and unequivocally, but we have both moved on. I think it was incredibly hard for her when Dan came back to me, and once Millie came along and cemented our family, Lisa's life—still clubbing and partying and mixing with the beautiful people—seemed a world away from mine.

We still see each other. Still have lunch from time to time, still meet up in the playground, but it's not the same; we both just try to pretend that it is.

Trish, on the other hand, is as great a friend as she always was. Greater perhaps, and undoubtedly my best friend, the best friend, in fact, I've ever had.

I think we've all come a long way.

The last time I saw Lisa she said she had met someone new. In the old days I would have wanted to hear all the details. Who he was, where they met, what their relationship was like, but now I don't feel close enough to ask these things, or interested enough to know.

I'm glad she's happy, I wish her well, and I think that's enough.

Charlie Dutton is very famous now. He married one of his leading ladies, an English girl who managed that rare feat of making it big in Hollywood, joining the ranks of Catherine Zeta Jones and Minnie Driver, although frankly I'll bet she's not nearly as beautiful first thing in the morning without any make-up on.

In fact I opened the *Daily Mail* three weeks ago and there was a huge colour picture of Charlie and his wife frolicking in the waves at—you guessed it—Sandy Lane.

'Why don't you get Jake up here and we'll order some drinks?' I say, stretching out my legs and admiring my bright red toes, especially painted for the holiday. 'I think a Piña Colada's just the thing to wake us all up.'

'Shame on you,' Emma says, as she picks up the phone to call Jake in his room. 'Drinking while your child sleeps.' But she's grinning.

'Oh, shut up!' I laugh. 'I'm on holiday and what's more, your dad's paying for it!'

'Good point,' she says, just before Jake picks up the phone. 'Better make it a double.'

*   *   *

385

By seven thirty when the van comes to pick us up to take us to the restaurant, we're all very giggly. Not so much from the alcohol—although the Piña Coladas were delicious—but because we've all felt like espionage agents, sneaking through the hotel, hiding behind corners and checking out areas before emerging, just in case Linda should be there.

Jake said that on his way to our room he walked past the library and, glancing through the french doors, saw Linda, sitting at a computer checking her email, luckily with her back to the door. Michael was standing gazing out, and apparently he went white when he saw Jake, but Jake managed to skulk away without Linda seeing him.

'Evening, Mrs Cooper,' says the doorman. 'Have a nice time.'

'Wow,' I whisper to Dan. 'How does he remember my name?'

'That's what they're paid for. It's pretty impressive, though, isn't it?'

'Bloody right.' Jake hunches over and squeezes in behind us. 'He remembered my name too.'

'Well, you are famous,' Richard says, as he climbs in. 'Not bloody surprising, really.'

'I'm not famous in Barbados,' Jake protests. 'He doesn't know who I am.'

'You do realize,' I say, turning to Emma, 'that in next week's *Daily Mail* there'll be pictures of you and Jake frolicking in the waves.'

'Of course,' Emma grins. 'Why do you think I've spent the last month working out at the gym, not to mention my new super-duper Missoni bikinis?'

'I have to admit they are rather sexy,' Jake says,

386

smiling.

'Oh, *yuck*,' Dan and Richard say at exactly the same time. 'That's my sister!' and we all laugh as the van takes us off to the restaurant.

*   *   *

I'm not sure how Michael has managed to get the best table in the restaurant, but it is quite spectacular. We are on the deck overlooking a turquoise sea, and the weather, the scenery, the whole ambience could not be more perfect.

Whatever strings he had to pull, however much money this evening, this whole trip, may be costing him, it is surely worth every penny, for never have I been anywhere more like paradise in my whole life.

Champagne is waiting for us at the table, and we toast one another and sip the champagne as we all watch the clock. On the dot of 7.50, just as Michael had stated in his instructions, we see Michael and Linda walk into the restaurant.

Michael has his arm around her and is steering her gently past the tables, and Linda is looking out at the view and gasping at the beauty. She has no idea we are here.

We are all grinning, and I am so excited about this surprise, so excited to see her face, that I am practically wriggling in my chair, and then I look around the table and realize we are all feeling the same way, each of us has a huge grin, most of us with tears welling in our eyes.

Michael stops at our table and Linda looks at him, confused, thinking she was heading to the table for two behind us, and then she looks from him to us, and, as she realizes that her whole, entire family is here, she puts her hands to her face and bursts into tears.

Emma and I start crying too.

And we all stand up and there is much hugging, and crying, and laughing, and Linda looks at each of us and tells us she loves us, and this is the happiest day of her life.

Dan squeezes my hand as we sit down and puts his arm around me once we're seated, pulling me close and kissing the top of my head as we all tell Linda the trouble we've been to, keeping this secret, and make her laugh by telling her of this afternoon's skulking, then watch her burst with joy when she realizes her grandchildren are also here, fast asleep in the hotel.

'This is what it's all about,' Linda says simply, smiling through her tears as she raises her glass and toasts each and every one of us. 'Family.' And we all raise our glasses before wishing her happy birthday and taking long, cool sips.

'To Family,' we toast again, and, as we raise our glasses again, I smile, knowing I've come home.

And this is, after all, what I've been waiting for my entire life.